No movement was visible, but now Wolf could hear something. The low hum of voices, he thought. A scratching of footsteps.

"Radok!" Wolf yelled, his weapon up in firing position to find the bastards scampering away in the shadows of dusk.

"Radok!" Wolf yelled again.

He saw them scrambling up the steep incline and pulled off ten quick rounds just as the hot blast of air from the explosion knocked him over. The sound of it was deafening, a roaring in his ears that blacked everything else out.

No one could have survived that, he thought. They were gone. Fragmented. Dead.

Wolf found his pistol, looking around again for movement, and then he heard them. Radok and Frieda. Unmistakable. Making for the old road. He began running, racing over the rocks to cut them off. . . .

TIME OF THE WOLF

TIME OF
THE WOLF

J. Sydney Jones

A SIGNET BOOK

SIGNET
Published by the Penguin Group
Penguin Books USA Inc., 375 Hudson Street,
New York, New York 10014, U.S.A.
Penguin Books Ltd, 27 Wrights Lane,
London W8 5TZ, England
Penguin Books Australia Ltd, Ringwood,
Victoria, Australia
Penguin Books Canada Ltd, 2801 John Street,
Markham, Ontario, Canada L3R 1B4
Penguin Books (N.Z.) Ltd, 182–190 Wairau Road,
Auckland 10, New Zealand

Penguin Books Ltd, Registered Offices:
Harmondsworth, Middlesex, England

First published by Signet, an imprint of New American Library,
a division of Penguin Books USA Inc.

First Printing, October, 1990
10 9 8 7 6 5 4 3 2 1

 REGISTERED TRADEMARK—MARCA REGISTRADA

PRINTED IN THE UNITED STATES OF AMERICA

PUBLISHER'S NOTE
This is a work of fiction. Names, characters, places, and incidents
either are the product of the author's imagination or are used
fictitiously, and any resemblance to actual persons, living or dead,
events, or locales is entirely coincidental.

BOOKS ARE AVAILABLE AT QUANTITY DISCOUNTS WHEN USED TO PROMOTE
PRODUCTS OR SERVICES. FOR INFORMATION PLEASE WRITE TO PREMIUM
MARKETING DIVISION, PENGUIN BOOKS USA INC., 375 HUDSON STREET,
NEW YORK, NEW YORK 10014.

For Helen

Prelude

"A death in Death's time": that's what he wanted for his epitaph. A bit late now, however. No one to tell it to. Write it in blood, then, on the cobbles. Just one among millions of others dying in a time when man played the wolf to his fellow man.

It wasn't a bad wound, really. The old man could still move his legs. No pain yet—shock was taking care of that. The bullet hadn't hit any organs, going in a bit below the left rib cage. Not fatal. He was being very lucid about it all. Mind clear. Rather messy, though, with blood all over his camel hair overcoat, staining his gray worsted slacks. It was pooling on the damp cobbles where he sat, lodged against the side of a building. Propped up like a doll, sitting where the bullet had thrown him on impact. Not a bad wound. Once *they* stopped the bleeding. . . .

The other man was clearly dead. The old man knew this instinctively. The bullet that had hit him must have been a hollow-point, for the young Czech's stomach was drooping onto the cobbles, piles and piles of pink viscera bulging out with the blood. The dead man's eyes had a terribly lifelike look to them still: a mixture of wonderment and anger. There had been no time for the pain to register. The two of them had barely had time even to introduce themselves before the Gestapo arrived. And now the older man, General von Tratten, would never know if the Czech could have been trusted or not. No papers for the Czech courier ever again.

So it was up to Paganini now, the General thought. Up to Paganini to get the papers out. The boy would know his duty; see it through. Just as the General had known

7

his when first confronted with those heinous documents and photos. Paganini . . . The last hope.

The General looked down at his wound, then heard heels clicking on the cobbles. They were coming for him now. Coming up the mouth of the blind alleyway. He could see their black coats. Blacker even than the darkness waiting for him in back of his eyes.

No. The wound was not fatal. He'd dressed worse on the Western Front during the first go-round more than twenty years ago.

Time slowed and the General thought of his wife and his yet unfinished projects. Up to three years ago this was a world the General enjoyed . . . *and they would staunch the bleeding* . . . and he thought of his villa and its park in back. Raking leaves in the autumn . . . *and after they had him in hospital, the questioning would begin, the drugs, the threats to his wife.* . . .

The Steyr 7.65 mm he held in his right hand was a beautiful weapon. He had thought it so many times, yet never quite so deeply as now. He'd carried it with him throughout the First World War: a blunt-nosed pistol with delicate tracery engraved on its barrel and a hand-fitted mahogany grip. He'd always loved the feel of it in his hand.

The first steps were urgent now, running, running toward him, and the agents were clearly visible, as the General was to them. One of those running was a bulky chap wearing a damned silly fedora along with his long, ungainly black leather overcoat. He yelled out to the General: "Don't! Stop!" Then he slipped on the wet cobbles and went down hard on his ass.

It was the last sight the General had, and he chuckled at it. The sighting chevron of the pistol nudged against his front teeth, feeling cold and pure.

Chapter One

The hell with her then, Radok thought. She could have it all. Even the Schiele. Christ, Helga didn't even like Schiele's paintings. Decadent, she called them. His women were too skinny, too young, too immoral. But Schiele would fetch high prices after the war, and Helga knew it . . . or her lawyer did. He'd said as much in the letter Radok had received from him this morning. So, Schiele, too. Give it all to her. Anything, just to have it over; to shut the door on that part of his life.

Inspektor Gunther Radok shivered, not at the thought of the lost Schiele, but because it was cold tonight. Too cold for a stakeout, but then you could hardly plan police actions around the weather reports. Even such ridiculous ones as this bust of a black marketeer.

His partner, Hinkle, was stomping up and down the sidewalk, clapping his arms around his massive chest, looking every inch a cop on stakeout, while Radok tried to look inconspicuous inside the old forest-green Mercedes the department supplied for undercover work. The leather upholstery was cold against his back and ass; his right toe—the one frostbitten ascending the Dachstein in '36—was numb already. He wiggled it: not even a tingle of sensation. And there was Hinkle on the street trying to make Radok feel guilty about being tucked away from the cold night air.

Over the month that Radok had been on this case, he had managed to convince himself that it was important. Managed to tell himself often enough that black marketeers could lose the war for the Reich; that they were, in fact, major war criminals.

But the tiny, ironic voice inside himself would not quite believe it. A scalper, a small-time crook, that's what this Czech with the unlikely name of Cezak was, but it brought the death penalty in the Reich. Cezak was

bound for the guillotine at the Justice Palace, rather than
a simple five count at the Liesl, the criminals' nickname
for the Central Prison, and Radok was putting his head
on the block. Radok, who'd traced every trip to the
lavatory the bugger had made for the past month; who
knew the Czech's movements better than he had Helga's
hips. Maybe with a little more hip knowledge he wouldn't
be losing the Schiele.

Let it go, Radok. . . .

And so Radok had set up this little trap for the Czech,
Cezak, from Pilsen. Indications were right. Radok was
sure that tonight something major was coming down.
Cezak had been running around all day hitting on the
smaller people in his network, setting the stage for some
big transfer of goods and Reichsmarks. Three Gestapo
goons were trailing him. Radok, a member of the Kripo,
the Criminal Police, was forced to liaison with those boys
from Morzin Platz, while Hinkle and he sat at the Graben intersection waiting for the trap to shut. Waiting for
Cezak to lead them to the big boy in Vienna's black
market network.

Cezak had been regular as clockwork the last month:
always the same alley for his transactions. Radok was
sure he was leading the Gestapo there now. And neither
Cezak nor the big man he was meeting was going anywhere. No problem; everything was taken care of. He
and Hinkle were backup, covering the rear exit.

Now nothing could keep Radok from thinking of something much worse than the black marketeer Cezak, or his
estranged wife Helga. Nothing between him and the sor-
rowful memory of his brother Helmut, and the wife and
baby he'd left behind. Helmut, only twenty, and not
going to get any older. Helmut, dead, killed at Leningrad
last summer, while Radok was safe in Vienna rounding
up black marketeers.

Radok wondered how Helmut had looked dead; if the
bullet took him fast and clean, or if it was slow and
agonizing. Death playing games. Death making you wish
for its peace. Helmut, his kid brother, shot to hell. And
the widow, Irene, and little nephew Helmut. The six-
month-old who would never see the father he was named
after.

When the shots sounded from the alley, Radok was

happy. They tore all thought of Helmut from his mind.
Hinkle jumped at the sound. Tubby little bugger, Radok
thought. It was a laugh to see him move like that. And
then it was overdrive for both of them: the drill took
over. They'd been cops long enough to make this reaction automatic. Radok out the left side of the car, the
metal between him and anyone fleet-footing it out of the
warren of cobbled lanes where the shots had come from.
Hinkle doorwaying down to where the heat was. Duck
and dive; scamper across the street and hug another
doorway. Radok watched his partner until he turned the
first corner out of sight. No more shots; a pounding in his
chest; his fingers rubbing themselves anxiously for the
friendly feel of metal, but he hadn't unsnapped the
shoulder-holstered Walther yet. No need to send the
pedestrians into a blinding squeal-off with a show of
armor. Enough of them panicking already at the sound of
shots. Total war in Europe, Radok thought, and they're
messing their pants over a couple of shots in the night;
running for cover, filling up the coffee houses.

Friendly fire, he told himself. The pistol shots sounded
like the high pierce of the policeman's Walther or the
Luger which the Gestapo carried as standard issue in
Vienna. The jazzy boys and their jazzy weaponry.

Now another shot. Only one. Solitary. Low and faint.
Dull-sounding, as though it had been silenced or had
gone off in a great, empty concert hall.

Radok half crouched behind the driver's side of the
door, not really expecting anyone to come scampering
out of the alley. Too many of us for that. But—and it was
a thought that presented itself to him only now, him
who'd set the damned trap, who'd laid on the extra
Gestapo armory—what if the plucky little shit Cezak
hooked his way out of there, came out into the wide-
open spaces of Graben blazing away on his piece of metal
like a Hollywood cowboy? The goddamn pedestrians. It'd
be like kewpie-doll time at the amusement park in the
Prater. A stupid oversight. He should have blocked off
the street; should have waited until after curfew; should
have taken the Czech in his warm bed in the middle of
the night. A good, clean, terrifying Gestapo action. But
Radok had been greedy. A month of tracking, tailing the
son of a bitch; a month of his big toe acting up and of

eating greasy *Buerenwurst* for dinner at sidewalk stands, hugging the counters, trying to keep rain from dripping down his neck as he gobbled wurst. A month of damp clothing and late nights. So Radok wanted more out of it than the tiny man. Christ, he could have taken Cezak the first day of surveillance with the eggs he'd been dealing in the frigging Prater. Flogging them like they were fat pearls and not range eggs brought it from some pig shit-smelling farm in the Burgenland.

Take it at the worst, Radok, he told himself. Worst case is one of them slips out of the net. Then you don't take him here, friend: not out on the busy avenue. He'll be coming out Braeuner Strasse, if he's coming. Out the same way Hinkle dodged in. And that's where you take him. From a doorway or whatever cover you can find between the music shop on the corner and the snooty men's tailor up the block. Because you were the one laid this on; because you were the one missing such silly contingencies as, what if he gets away? So you leave your Mercedes with its nice thick steel doors and get your ass up Braeuner Strasse and stop him before he can get out to kewpie-doll land.

Radok had just moved away from the car when he heard footsteps running, flying. Dark. Dark as coal with the blackout, and all he could see now was a shape moving fast toward him. The snap came off easily from the holster, the gun butt nestled in his palm. Arms out straight, forming a triangle with the top of his body. Gun held steadily now. Nothing cute. Just take the bastard square in the middle. The biggest target. No shit about leg wounds here. Not in the dark. Not with flying feet. Not with the taste of fear in his mouth and the twist of it in his guts. A trickle of sweat running down his cheek in the cold night.

Radok cocked the Walther. Sweat down his spine now, too, rolling into the waistband of his pants. Take him dead in the middle, he told himself. Now.

"It's been a real balls-up, Radok."

Hinkle's voice. Radok lowered the pistol, slowly letting the hammer back down.

"What the shit?" Hinkle said, seeing the weapon. "You going to take my head off?"

Hinkle was breathing hard. The damned tubby. Tubbies shouldn't move that fast, Radok thought.

"I figured you were somebody else."

"Ex-wife, huh?" But it wasn't funny. Hinkle hurried on: "Blasted the crap out of them. Nothing there. . . ." A hesitation. Hinkle never hesitated.

"What else?" Radok said.

"You better come. Before forensic gets here. A major balls-up."

Too right it was, Radok could see quickly enough after hotfooting it to the dead-end alley. Flashlights played on the scene. Evil, yellow antennae of light sneaking obscenely over twisted bodies. Cezak lay faceup with fingers digging into the cobble grouting. The other man was thrown back against a building, a pulpy mess with half his head gone. And it was this one who wasn't right. Not right at all. Hardly the black marketeer type.

Even in the gloom and the oozing puddles of blood, Radok could put a make on him: class. Tailored slacks, the camel-hair coat, a manicured hand still holding a gun. He didn't want to look at what was left of the head. The man wore a pinkie ring on the left hand. A gold-monogrammed ring, and Radok knew those always meant trouble. Money. Money was trouble. Power. And power was more trouble. He'd learned something during his boyhood when his family had been in service to these types. If they had money, power, they wore the pinkies. And made it look masculine. Held a teacup between pinched thumb and forefinger and made it seem like a benediction. Talked with that nasal Schoenbrunn upper-class accent; except this one wasn't talking anymore to anybody. There was an angle of repose to the body, like he was just taking an afternoon lie-down with the turf book; maybe it was that angle that first triggered Radok's recognition.

"My Christ!"

"Bad indeed," Hinkle agreed.

"I know him."

Hinkle shook his head. "Major balls-up."

"The fuck happened here? I said we take them alive," Radok said, directing it at one of the flashlight-holders, a bulky man in godawful fedora and black leather overcoat.

"Pull it in, friend. They had off at us first." The Gestapo agent came up close to Radok, smelling vilely of gulyasch soup and beer. The leather overcoat was wet and stained, as if the guy had been rolling around on the ground.

"And you returned fire?" Radok said.

"Yeah. Got a problem with that? *You* stand there, let them shoot your balls off you got so many of them."

He was right: Radok remembered the own decision to take Hinkle in the chest when he'd thought he was Cezak on the run. But he needed to shift blame. He could feel it welling up inside, the guilt, the sorrow, like a cancer in his stomach.

"Besides," the goon said, "the old bastard shot his own head off. So you just move on, shithead, or you'll join him. You called us in on this, got your dirty work done for you. So go on and write your report. You're the fucking hero, winning the war single-handed, you are."

Radok eyed the man, taking in the features, measuring them as if for a pine coffin. In a perfect world he'd tear the man's eyes out and stop up his gob with them. But Hitler's Reich was a far from perfect world. He contented himself with words:

"Cobbles are slick after rain. A guy's got to watch out carrying a loaded gun around. He could slip. Bang, bang. No more winning the war for you, either."

"Fuck off." A growl.

Death had made the three Gestapo goons lose interest in the scene. Stick around now and they might even have to give evidence. They holstered their Lugers, pocketed their flashlights, and humped away. One of them was wearing jackboots, Radok saw now. God save us, he thought: jackboots and a business suit. Who the hell were their tailors?

But this was all avoidance. Alone with Hinkle and the bodies now, there was no more avoiding this one. The dream was real. He looked back down to where the General's head should have been, at the black ooze in the deeper blackness of night, and forced the memories down. No nostalgia. Not now.

"Major balls-up."

"Would you mind playing a new tune, Hinkle?"

"Just a couple of stiffs. Lift their ID's and home to schnapps."

"Not now, Hinkle. Okay? No bantering. No joking. Just let me get through this."

"Right."

And they went through the pockets. Radok allowed himself no luxuries with this. The General was his; Hinkle took the Czech. The wallet was where he'd expected it: inside left pocket of the double-breasted suit jacket. No ephemera such as ration cards or petrol coupons. Not even the *Meldezettl* everyone was supposed to carry as proof of police registration. None of this for the General. It wasn't his style. The positive ID came from a Jockey Club membership card and a picture of his wife: the golden hair done up in a soft bun in back, the face clear, proud, unafraid. Radok wondered if it was a recent picture. If so, she hadn't changed much in twenty years.

"Not much here," Hinkle said. "Bit of spare change. Thirteen Reichsmarks, to be exact."

The looping, two-toned siren of the superfluous ambulance suddenly sounded close by.

"No ID. Cautious boy, your Cezak," Hinkle said. "No goods, either. Comical. What the fuck were they swapping?"

Radok said nothing. But that question had already played through his mind, too. There was a strong smell now. The cordite burn was gone and the heavy, sweet odor of the slaughterhouse filled the alley. Radok stepped cautiously: blood was everywhere.

"This was obviously who Cezak was meeting," Hinkle said, looking down at what was left of General von Tratten. "Or was it? Maybe this was just a bad coincidence? But if so, why'd the old guy shoot himself? What did he have to cover up?"

More silence from Radok, but again, that thought had also gone through his own mind. The swap; the suicide: something damned important in this meeting. If it really was a meeting, as Hinkle said, and not just an unlucky coincidence.

Headlights now, ripping down the dark alleyway; a blue flashing light bouncing off the buildings; the siren still bleating. Doors opened, slammed shut. Familiar shape of Lieberman, the head of the lab boys. But Radok wasn't going to hang around. He looked at Hinkle, who nodded at him. They'd been a team long enough to know each other without words.

"It's all right," Hinkle said. "I'll shepherd it here. You see his wife . . . I mean, widow."

A nodded thanks from Radok.

"Hey . . . take this, too. The Czech had it in his coat pocket. May be interesting. May not be. All the same, a damned curious thing for a guy like this to be carrying around."

Radok took the folded paper Hinkle held out to him, and stuffed it in his overcoat pocket without looking at it. He'd wait until later for that. Much later.

"Thanks." Radok gave voice to it this time.

Hinkle was dealing with business as Radok left: "Lieberman, old boy. Hope you brought a shovel for this one. . . ."

Chapter Two

It was the E-flat below middle C. She knew for sure now. Halfway through the first movement of the Beethoven "Emperor" Concerto and the key had just gone out on her. The discord hit like a closed fist; there was a moment of stunned silence in the concert hall. Even the fitful cougher that had been interrupting her performance from somewhere up in the stalls had ceased. There was always at least one of them per performance, laid on by the competing performers. This would be Constantine's man; a paid cougher. Just as her agent had her paid claque down on the main floor to lead the applause, to bring the bouquets of fresh flowers.

But the E-flat was more dangerous than the paid asthmatic. Frieda Lassen muted it when possible, hid behind the orchestra, skipped over one difficult passage so artfully that only the keenest ear could have been aware of the circumlocution. There were plenty of keen ears in the audience tonight. But somehow, by luck and great skill, she got through the first movement and sat staring at her reflection in the highly polished surface of the Bechstein grand piano. She couldn't go on like this, not into the second movement, the Adagio. That was her signature piece, the interpretation of which had first won her international fame. She had never played safe with that bit of music, but had always fallen in a swoon into its sensual coil of sound.

She had taken the notes as written, the terse verbal instructions—*Adagio un poco mosso*—as noted, and put into it all her passion. Much technique, but far more passion. Like a young village skier taking down a few poles with him as he ran the slalom course, racing not so much against the clock as for the very joy of it.

There could be no more hiding or game-playing in the second movement. Perhaps she should take a break and have the piano tuned or exchanged? And how had it gone out of tune so quickly? Surely Constantine wouldn't stoop to something so low? The paid disruption in the audience was one thing; sabotage such as this quite another. But now the paranoid part of her brain took over: she had heard of sopranos doped before a performance from a well-wisher's bottle of homemade peppermint liqueur. Why not a frayed piano string for a concert pianist? Anything was possible in the world of professional performance, a fact she was sadly discovering.

Suddenly Frieda knew that it was not a matter of paranoia to imagine that Constantine was responsible for the sabotage. It was only common sense. After all, a pianist position with the Philharmonic would be open next year. Old Gespeier was finally retiring. A plum position: fourth-level bureaucratic post with a lifetime sinecure. Everyone knew that the position would go to either Constantine or Frieda, the most active pianists on the Vienna music scene. Constantine, a native Viennese, would surely have the inside track over Frieda, who, though born in Vienna, had spent her youth in the United States. Another strike against her: the part-Jew racial rating the Nazis had given her for her Jewish father. A pet Jew, in fact. Goebbels' shining example for the foreign press, which had saved her thus far in anti-Semitic Austria, but a Jew nonetheless. Still, with all this against her, Frieda's successes on the concert stage made her a strong contender for the position.

What no one but Frieda knew, however, was that she would not be in Vienna next year or even next week to provide competition for the loutish Constantine. This was her last public performance in Vienna. She would finish this performance tonight and once more, also for the last time, go to work for the resistance. One more job for the underground, carrying some papers into Switzerland on her concert tour that began this week.

What an irony, she thought. No need for Constantine to sabotage my career. I'm doing that all by myself by working for the resistance.

There was no more time for the luxury of analysis now, however. This E-flat problem had to be dealt with immediately, no matter whether it were sabotage or accident.

Her last concert in Vienna was not going to end in humiliation.

There was a cough from the audience, but not the paid one this time. This was followed by squeaking sounds as people shifted in their seats. She was taking too long, making the audience nervous for her. A bad policy. It sets you up for failure, not for communication, she knew. Felix, the conductor, was looking at her questioningly now. It was up to her to continue or not, for surely he had noted the E-flat. And she was the one naked here; it would not harm his reputation if Frieda Lassen could not perform her piece, despite the valiant efforts of Felix Mieckstein and his orchestra.

She made the decision. No sense in breaking to have the piano tuned or changed. The magic would be broken. She would lose the audience. It left her only one option. She had no score in front of her; needed none. The music was in her head and heart. She sat erect on the piano bench now, her blond hair falling back from her face as she held her head high and closed her eyes, preparing for the start of the second movement. Her fingers, tapered but not overly long or elegant, hung over the keyboard, suspended as if from invisible strings. There was absolute quiet now in the house. She wondered if Constantine was in the audience.

The mental part of her readjustments was accomplished quickly: she would transpose the score an octave upward, thereby losing the out-of-tune E-flat in all but a few key passages. There was no problem with the mental part. But her hands would be difficult: they would have to find a new path over the keys. Her heart would be a stumbling block as well, for it would have to find a new way to love, in a new key. But she felt no fear now, only the exhilaration of wanting to get on with it, to go, just as the village skier paces in his skis before the final run.

She nodded at Felix. He looked surprised but moved his baton with authority, and it began: the lovely, sad, slow melody of the Adagio. Frieda sat erect through the opening in winds and strings, felt the music seep into her, and at the perfect instant she joined the others with her opening chord, an octave above the orchestra, almost dissonant, on edge. There was a startled intake of breath— Frieda would never know if it had been from the audience or the conductor. But there was no going back now. She hoped the breath had come from Constantine having a coronary, the old toad. Playing Solieri to her bad imitation of Mozart.

Then the opening chord came back to her, faintly echoing through the auditorium, and she had no more room left in her consciousness for enemies. Only for love. Her hands instinctively found the right keys for her transposition; she was falling in love all over again with this new and sensuous music, finding new harmonies, new couplings and partings with her octave-higher rendering. The orchestra, timid at first from fear of possible discord, became emboldened by the new sound, meeting her at highs that stretched harmony as far as possible. A mournful, fearful beauty was being created, and the audience, realizing that they were present at the creation of something new and lovely, sat in silence.

The Adagio section ended before she wanted it to. Frieda was trembling. But she did not hesitate before racing into the rondo, and there was no longer any mistrust between piano and orchestra, but a melding, a blending, and a joyful, swirling dance. An infectious dance that all but set the staid audience to tapping their feet to the music.

When it was over, Frieda could not move for an instant. There was a terrifying, absolute stillness in the grand concert hall. The audience was as quiet as the gilded caryatids between tiers of plush, crimson-felted seats. She came out of her stupor to recognize that no one had put palm to palm. Had she miscalculated? Was it so bad? Well, the hell with them, she thought. Viennese were always the last to recognize talent. She was satisfied with what she had done. That was all that mattered. She had put all of herself into the piece. What more could she give?

As she pushed herself back from the piano to rise, the spell was broken. Felix led the applause. The audience had been as drugged by the music as Frieda, but now rose to their feet, clapping with their arms outstretched. Bravos were shouted from the standing room at the back of the parterre seating. Frieda stood; tall, blond, lovely; dressed in a simple black evening gown. She bowed three times to the various sections of the house. Then moved backstage, as if floating. The applause continued for ten minutes, but she made no curtain calls, no encores. Part of her philosophy: leave them wanting more. Save a few pages of a good book for the next night.

Backstage, the well-wishers were thronging her. Felix hugged her, gave her a wink. Words were not needed.

A squat, dark little man made his way through the crowd.

"Purissima," he said. "Absolutely refreshing! Delightful!"

He took her hand to kiss it. She winced, as if violated by the near touch of his lips hovering a discreet millimeter away from her skin, as all books of etiquette advise. She took a lesson from the same books as she spoke.

"How lovely of you to come, Constantine."

She could not take her eyes off the wart on the top of his bald head as he lowered it over her hand. Purissima, indeed! Simply because she'd refused to climb between the sheets with him.

"A most courageous endeavor," he said, looking up into her face now from his vantage point at breast level. "To continue without the E-flat in a concerto written in that very key! Who would have thought it possible?"

She smiled sweetly, but could not help thinking of Constantine between the sheets, naked. A thought horrid enough to put her off her supper.

The applause from some very ardent fans still echoed in the hall as she went to her dressing room. She leaned against the closed door, breathed deeply, and tried to calm herself. For only now, after the performance, did the nerves start. After one performance . . . and before another. If only she just had to play a piano without the E-flat key for this coming performance—that would be heaven. But what she faced now was much worse.

They'd practiced it before, got it down carefully; the program handed over for autographing; the quick hand-off of papers to be stuffed into her oversized theater bag. It had gone smoothly last time, but then the envelope had been empty. A dress rehearsal. Tonight would be for real. Cezak, whom she would meet tonight, was afraid he was being watched; he'd warned her of the risks. But they had to take those risks. These papers were worth it, he'd told their resistance cell.

She sat in front of the mirror and continued to breathe deeply. She had no heavy makeup to take off. Frieda neither liked nor needed it. Just keep your nerves together, she told herself. Another two minutes.

She looked at herself in the mirror and shook her head. Mata Hari I'm not. I don't even like the thrill of danger.

For Frieda Lassen, danger meant facing a hostile audience, not a Gestapo interrogation. Another shake of the head, a slight chuckle. And so how did I get involved in all of this? At times it seemed so childish: risking one's life for a few scraps of paper that the resistance pasted on walls, or owning a forbidden transmitter—with nobody to transmit to.

But Frieda knew why; the question was merely rhetorical. There were enough reasons for her involvement in the resistance to motivate a starlet in a Hollywood B-movie—a role she sometimes felt she was playing. There was her Jewishness, for one. *Mischling Ersten Grades*—Mixed Breed of the First Degree, as the Nazis put it, for the Jewish father and Aryan mother she had left behind in the U.S. Or rather, the mother she'd left behind, for her father had killed himself some years before. Gone for a fly out the window of the insurance firm he worked for in Connecticut. When life got unbearably heavy . . . The Jew in her hated the Nazis for their racism, for what they were doing to the Jews: their systematic expulsion of the people from German society. This while Frieda, Goebbels' pet Jew, pet American citizen, was free to come and go as she wanted, unwatched, unmonitored. Without her resistance activity she would never have been able to live with herself, even though she had done nothing to win such protection—the tiny, crippled propaganda czar had simply seen her perform one night in Berlin, had taken a fancy to her and had found out her history. No sexual advances, although Goebbels was purported to be continuously on the make. No. Frieda was merely grist for his propaganda mill. She allowed herself to be used, but it suited her underground objectives as well.

And there was Emil, gentle, kind, naive Emil, a violinist friend from the Music Conservatory. She would never forget the night that he'd escorted her home from a recital. It was spring, and the air was alive with lilac and promises of a great career for both of them. It had been each of their first public performances, and they had been received well by critics from all the papers. Then came the SS rowdies, drunk from some beer hall where they'd been meeting. They took Emil—the Catholic intellectual from Salzburg—for a Jew, and her—the actual Jew—for some blond goddess he was defiling. They first broke his glasses. Then, when he fought back, they broke his violin and his fingers, and finally they kicked and kicked his inert body until he was senseless. Emil, who still lingered in a penumbral world between vegetation and consciousness in a West Country sanitarium.

Enough reasons to hate the Nazis; to want to do all in her power to bring them down.

But added to these was Wolf, her Wolf. Her lover Wolf. Saying the name to herself brought on the old, familiar pain of loss. It wasn't so bad, normally. After nearly four years, she could now pass entire days without crying for him; without, sometimes, even thinking of him. Her fiery young revolutionary lover, who had introduced her to political theory as well as to passion—of a sort. Her lover and fellow conspirator whom the Nazis had arrested four years ago and shipped off to Dachau to rot. You only have one first love. She had remained true to him for four years.

Thus the nickname "Purissima" from Constantine. Other of her friends and acquaintances in music had harsher ones for her—all alluding to her celibate life since Wolf had been arrested after the Anschluss.

Purissima, indeed. She was not the nun they all took her for, but had, simply, not met any man in the years since his arrest to match her Wolf. In her deepest heart of hearts, Frieda knew that her mourning period must come to an end. She was becoming all stopped-up inside because of it. Jan Cezak had told her as much. Making love to the keyboard was no longer enough for her.

It's been long enough now, she thought. Fans will be out at the stage door. She could imagine them: mostly young, pimply girls who studied piano and fancied that someday they would make a career as Frieda had. She was their polestar, their guiding light. Bundling up in the

Persian lamb coat she so loved, she made sure to clutch her big, open theater bag.

Out the door, and the stage people were wheeling the Bechstein backstage. Her music career seemed already a thing of the past. No way of knowing what would be on the other side of the street door. Cezak's warnings of the goon following him went through Frieda's mind:

"He's a tall guy and dresses like a burnt-out professor. You'll recognize him by the squeaky shoes. Kripo stamped all over him."

She opened the stage door slowly. A crowd had gathered outside. Her young admirers. There was a smattering of applause as she nodded to them. But what she saw, or more importantly didn't see, sent terror through her. Cezak was not among the gathered fans.

"Mingle," he'd always instructed her. "And don't be late. You want no grand entrances. Blend. Melt into the scene. That's the secret of being a good courier. And the difference between being a good courier and a mediocre one is that the mediocre ones die fast."

If he'd followed his own caveat Cezak would already be here, she thought. Something was wrong. But she signed the proffered programs and leather-bound autograph books as if fear and panic were not ripping at her insides.

"To a loyal fan. Regards, Frieda Lassen."

Over and over again she inscribed the same and similar messages. And all the while, out of the corner of her eye, she expected to see Cezak come along with his program and envelope.

By the tenth autograph, she knew it was hopeless. Berndt, the old, stooped stage door man was at the front of the theater now, scouting a taxi for her. She signed the last autograph and still there was no sign of Cezak. Now she felt not only fear, but also deep sadness; she knew something must have happened for him to have missed this meeting. The fallback contingency was for her to get to her apartment fast and wait for a call that rang three times, broke off, and rang three more times. That was the all-clear. No direct contact, Cezak had warned. Not except for the handoff. Not while he was being tailed.

Berndt hobbled back to her; a taxi followed. She slipped a few Reichsmarks in the old man's hand and he blessed her like an aging retainer in a Schnitzler play. The taxi's interior was warm and snug, but it could not offset the chill which Cezak's missed meeting had cast over her.

She gave the driver a First District address and hunched in a corner of the backseat. The driver was of the old school, trying to make conversation, but she remained silent with her thoughts. Two possibilities: either Cezak had broken off the rendezvous because of the Kripo tail, or he'd been taken. And if taken, would he talk? Name names?

Cezak had names upon names. His contacts went all the way up to the Abwehr, Military Intelligence, in Berlin, he'd hinted. That was where these most valuable papers had supposedly originated.

Would the Gestapo be coming for her tonight? Be waiting for her at the apartment?

And what of the important papers? My God, the way Cezak had described them to her and the leader of their resistance cell, the Padre, these papers were the biggest coup yet for the resistance, documents that supposedly would show up the Nazis for the sadistic, insane brutes they in truth were.

Cezak had been secretive, keeping things on a need-to-know basis, but he had let on that his papers were proof of a major atrocity that the Nazis were currently preparing for. It would be Frieda's job to get the papers to Berne on her next Swiss tour; to the Allies.

And now? Did Cezak's absence mean the papers had been lost? That all those lives Cezak had mentioned also would be lost?

The driver soon pulled up in front of the baroque apartment house where she lived. It was on a narrow cul de sac, cobbled, dark, quiet, and lined with other such small buildings, each containing five or six apartments. She looked along the street before getting out of the taxi. Nobody waiting here anyway, she thought. She paid the man, took out the massive house key from her purse, let herself into the building, and climbed the courtyard steps to the open terraced landing where her apartment was located: the first floor above street level. No lights were on inside. She had to risk going in, even if she didn't know who might be waiting for her there already. Cezak still might call. A light went on across the way, startling her, all but hurtling her into the dark womb of her own apartment. Opening the door, she knew immediately that no one was inside. Nothing to do now but wait. She turned a lamp on: the room was long and low-ceilinged, with the correct appointments for a well-known pianist like herself: a bit of *Empir*, a bit of sturdy Biedermeier. The mix was perfect. Normally Frieda loved the space; the Turkish and Persian carpets on the parquet; the oils on the walls; the crystal chandelier reflecting and refracting the light. But tonight the flat felt lonely and empty. She poured herself a large cognac and sat down by the telephone. The minutes dragged by as she sipped her liqueur. Finally the phone rang. Once; twice; three times . . . and then continued ringing and ringing until she picked it up. Not the coded ring, but she was impatient tonight.

"Frieda?"

It was the Padre's voice, and immediately she knew something was very wrong.

"What's happened?" she said.

"The news seems bad. We believe grandmother is dead."

She felt the fear of helpless rage build in her eyes and abdomen. And grief, as well. The double-talk to tell her that Cezak was dead. She was silent for what seemed minutes; only the electric crackling of white noise down the line.

"Are you there?" Padre said.

"Yes." A near whisper.

"From what I gather, she had no parting words."

So at least the organization was not blown, she thought. And then the rush of guilt set in: worrying about her own skin when Cezak was dead. But their resistance cell was not compromised. That *was* important.

"Was anyone with her when she died?" Frieda asked.

"No word as yet."

Another uncomfortable silence. They were both ill at ease using this silly code. Then:

"A period of bereavement is in order," Padre said.

Frieda did not reply. She listened to the sounds in her flat for a time: the tock of a clock, the creak of expanding floor boards.

"Do you understand?"

"Yes." She was not to make contact until things settled

down. She was to go on with her life as a professional pianist as if all were in order.

"I'll get word to you where flowers can be sent."

"That would be nice," she said.

"You're all right, then?" he asked.

She nodded at the phone. "Good-bye," she said. It was as if she were drugged; in a stupor.

Sleep would come hard tonight, if at all. Wolf, where are you now when I need you?

Chapter Three

Radok had left the car door open, the keys in the ignition. He turned the key, rattled the engine to life, and put the car into gear. Keep the mind on mechanics, he told himself as he drove along Kaerntnerstrasse, deserted now with ten minutes until curfew. A right turn onto the Ring to Mariahilferstrasse, and a left there and up the hill out of town.

Keep the mind busy with details; shut down the emotions.

A 52 tram passed him with three passengers and a one-armed conductor, all very sullen and hard-lit by the inside bulbs of the streetcar.

It's time now, Radok decided. I got through it with the Gestapo, did the perfunctory. So let it go now, son.

No need to tell himself twice. The tears had built up at the back of his eyes, a palpable force, a pressure like trapped gas. Now they broke through, pouring down his cheeks, blurring his vision. He had to pull over, and after a time he suddenly found himself white-knuckled, shaking the steering wheel, sounds coming from far away—animal sounds that he finally placed as his own uncontrollable sobs.

Radok finally put the car in gear again and moved out onto the roadway, tears still coming, but slower now.

The General. Dead. The man was an institution. Institutions don't die. Radok hadn't cried like this for his own father, his own mother. For Helmut, maybe.

So long ago . . . Twenty years. Ancient history, but it all felt like yesterday: fresh as bakery rolls were his memories of his life at the von Trattens'. . . .

The Radoks had been in service to the von Trattens: his father was the gardener and chauffeur while his mother was upstairs maid. But young Gunther's position was

something close to that of adopted child to the von
Trattens.

Childless himself, General von Tratten had taken the
young Radok boy under his wing. They gathered leaves
together in the fall, raking them into huge brown-and-
gold piles. And in the spring they set out the early
flowers together. There were treats in the city, as well:
Radok would never forget his first hot chocolate at Demel's
with the General, the *schlag obers* forming an alpine
peak atop the creamy brew. Or walking along what was
left of the old parapet of the city wall at Moelker Bastei—
walls which von Tratten timber had helped to build cen-
turies before during the great Turkish sieges. The von
Trattens were, quite literally, rooted in the soil of Vienna, though much of their money came from the tim-
berlands in Tyrol. There were numerous sailing adventures
on the Wienerwald See, and one summer there had even
been an expedition with the General to his hunting lodge
in Tyrol, Radok acting as gun-bearer and companion. All
a million years ago, but as fresh in Radok's mind as the
scene he'd just witnessed in the First District.

Radok had adopted the General, as well, for his own
father never truly assumed that role. He'd been a profoundly bitter man, Radok's father: a failed musician, a
village fiddler in his native Moravia who came to the
capital to find his place in an orchestra. But an early
marriage, a child, and lack of diligence all conspired
against him, and he slipped into the safety net of domes-
tic service instead. Rather than love, there was resentment from this unwilling natural father. So the General
was as much of a godsend to Radok as Radok was to the
General. Both orphans of a sort. They had been made
for each other.

An idyll, then, Radok thought, rounding now past the
summer palace of Schoenbrunn and down the last straight
stretch to the village-like suburb of Hietzing. Until Radok
was fourteen it was like that: a father-and-son team. The
unbeatable, unstoppable duo. Radok always took his grade
card to the General first; asked this older man about
those strange urges he'd begun to have, and about how
the sight of a girl suddenly made him go hot all over,
quivering in the knees. And suddenly it had all ended,
that life, that intimacy. The Radoks were packed off

overnight like gypsies with severance money enough to start the long-planned tobacco shop. Radok hadn't seen the General since then.

He drove past the parish church now, through the square, into the tree-lined, villa-lined streets of the upper-class suburbs. All ages ago. Radok had all but forgotten the old bastard. What was the General to him, anyway? Two could play at the game of betrayal. Forgetfulness. It amounted to the same thing, really. Put a person out of your life, forget about him: it was a form of betrayal.

So why are your hands still shaking? Radok asked himself. Why have you got a cramp in your side from sobbing over this old bastard whom you completely forgot about donkeys years ago?

Radok had never before grieved over the loss of the General's comradeship. It had all been too abrupt, too final. He'd buried it, locked it away with the other bogeymen of his emotional life. But it was never too late for the pain of grief. There was no statute of limitations there.

Radok had no problem finding the villa. It was the largest on the street, and even though it was nighttime he could see they had kept the building the same colors: the delicate shade of ocher called Schoenbrunn yellow that was trimmed with forest-green at windows and doors. Unchanging. He parked in front, then got slowly out of the car and went up to the massive double doors. Time enough to lose the shakes. Breathe deeply to get rid of the cramp, he told himself. Inspektor Radok, Kripo, ready for presentation.

He pushed the doorbell but couldn't hear it in the distance, and so wasn't sure it worked. He began hammering away at the lion's-head door-knocker. There were sounds of life inside; steps clattering on the oak cobbles of the garage. Radok knew they were oak, for he'd broomed and oiled them often enough in the early days. A maid answered the door, opening it only a few centimeters. She was short and dark, with a moustache and a hairy mole on her right cheek. Eagle face; eyes of purest suspicion. He knew the type: proprietary lady's maid; sort who wouldn't sit in the parks near cooks, nannies, and other such riffraff on her afternoons off. Radok's mind was working fine now, double-time. He flashed his

ID in lieu of introductions. The door opened enough for his foot to be inserted.

"It's quite all right," he said, gripping the door and opening it wider, brushing past her into the entrance. "I know my way here."

The oak cobbles were still in place, just as he'd expected. A Daimler was there, too, using the old carriageway as a garage. Its hood is cold, he noted as he put a palm to it in passing. Some of the cop instincts are coming back into operation, and thank God for that, he told himself. I'll need them for this interview.

Through the garage he could see shadows of barren fruit trees up the splendid lawn. Turn left to the main stairs, he reminded himself. The maid gained on him at the top step.

"I'll just let the Frau know you're here," she said.

"Yes. Do that." He said this to her back as she hurried into the sitting room.

It was all the same here: the pendulum clock over the mahogany chest—sheets kept in that chest; the rustic wardrobe against the opposite wall for winter coats and wraps. As a boy he used to love looking at the gaily colored peasant paintings of dancing couples on that wardrobe. To the right, the kitchen; left to the bedrooms.

The maid came back out.

"The Frau will see you now."

She showed him into another room that had not changed: there were four neat little Biedermeier seating arrangements, and Frau von Tratten sat at a far one, dressed in sensible tweeds, bent over a book, unaware apparently that Radok existed. He squeaked over to her on a shoe that needed mending.

"Good evening, Frau von Tratten," he said when halfway across the room to her.

She looked up, exasperation at first registering on her face. She's still as beautiful as ever, he thought, with that sort of fragile beauty which is really hard as nails. Golden hair was piled above her head elegantly, but at the same time carelessly, for wisps of it spiraled around her ears.

Her exasperated expression was soon followed by one of shock when she recognized him.

"Paganini! Dear Paganini!"

He blushed at the old nickname; another thing he'd

forgotten about his life at the Villa von Tratten: his ambition to become a concert violinist.

She was on her feet and moving quickly to him. He thought she would embrace him, but instead she held her hand out to be nuzzled a discreet distance from his lips.

"Gnaedige," he said. "Dear Frau."

"But I thought Mathilde said there was a policeman. . . ."

"Yes."

Interest showed in her eyes and she stood back from him now, looking surprised.

"No. Not you, Paganini. With our glorious police force? Life does surprise one. I thought you'd still be fiddling."

The adolescent dream of Radok: succeed where his father had failed. The General had fancied the notion and dubbed him Paganini because of it. Nobody but a few colleagues at headquarters had called him by that name in over twenty years, and the violin—his father's—had been gathering dust at the back of a wardrobe for as long.

"But the General's not here." She clapped her hands in dismay. "He'll be so sorry to have missed you. . . ."

She seemed as uncomfortable as Radok felt; happy for the chance to be rid of him quickly. There was too much history between them and far too little understanding. Explanations were needed for the missing years, but she did not want to supply them.

"Frau von Tratten . . ."

"You know, just the other day he mentioned you. This *is* a coincidence."

She was not going to make it easy for Radok.

"I've come—"

"He thought so highly of you and your charming family. I know he'll never forgive himself for missing you. But you must have a cup of coffee before leaving."

"He's dead." Radok felt better now it was out. "That's why I'm here."

She looked at him as one would at a boy who was making rude noises inside church.

"Pardon me?"

"Tonight. He was . . . killed. In the city."

"But he's no longer a soldier. He's an old man." She peered at Radok. "I must say, Paganini, this is a rather crude form of entertainment you're having with me. I'm not amused, I assure you."

"It's the truth."

And he knew, by the simple way he said these words, that now she would have to believe him.

She felt in back of her and found the arm of a chair, then collapsed into it. The pendulum clock in the hall struck nine, the only sound in the house. But the maid was sure to be on the other side of the door, ear to the keyhole.

Frau von Tratten looked up at him again, flexing a muscle in her jaw.

"How?"

"Shot. It was concerning a black marketeer."

"But what does that have to do with my Augustus? He was hardly involved in the black market. What happened? Tell me."

"I honestly don't know," Radok said. "I was hoping you could tell me."

Part of Radok told him not to hurry with this. That to press her on the subject would be brutal and cruel. And part of him didn't care; had to know.

"Tell you what?" she said. No tears yet, but her mouth quivered and dimpled her chin.

"Did the General ever speak to you of a man named Cezak? Jan Cezak?"

She shook her head at this question, looked down to the diamond wedding ring she was twisting on her finger.

"Where did he say he was going tonight?" Radok asked.

A pause, then a deep sigh from her.

"Out on some business." She looked up at Radok again. "I wasn't his jailor. And he never talked of business matters with me. He just said out. That was enough. Be back before bedtime, he told me. And he kissed me here." She patted her left cheek.

"Maybe we should continue this tomorrow?"

"There's nothing to continue," she whispered. "Augustus was a good man. He'd have nothing to do with the black market. This Cezak you mentioned. Did he kill Augustus?"

Radok shook his head.

"No. He's . . . He died, as well."

"Then who?" she said. "Who killed Augustus? Did you?"

"No."

"I'm sorry I asked that," she said. "It's such a shock."

"He killed himself," Radok said. "We laid a trap for this Cezak, were ready to pick him up, and we mistook the General for one of the gang. The General killed himself rather than be arrested. That's what I'm trying to learn about. That's the crazy part."

But she was no longer listening. Her gaze was off somewhere in memories.

"Look, Frau von Tratten. I wanted to be the one to tell you, not some stranger. And now I'm acting worse than any stranger would. This isn't easy for me, either. Can't you help me at all? Has the General been ill? Acting strangely? Any suspicious visitors?"

She shook her head limply.

"Quite a reunion, Paganini. Quite a reunion."

It was obvious there was nothing he would learn from her tonight.

"Is there someone I can call for you?"

She waved the idea aside.

"Your maid?"

"Yes. Send her in. . . . Please . . . I never got that coffee for you."

"It's all right. . . . Don't worry."

She looked up at him again, a whimsical smile on her lips, trying to demonstrate her old bravado.

"You've changed, Paganini. The name no longer fits you."

"It was twenty years ago."

"More than age," she said. "Deeper than that."

He nodded. "The war."

"Yes. That must be it."

But they both knew it wasn't. It was the gentleness that was gone from him; the kindness that was missing. Frau von Tratten could sense the lack of it, even in her grief.

"I'll send her in, then," Radok said, looking one last time at Frau von Tratten.

She seemed so small now, so frail. He had once thought that he should like to see Frau von Tratten brought down a peg or two, for the betrayal, for being party to the destruction of his love and life. To see her punished for reminding him that he was a grubby little lower-middle-class immigrant child whose proper station was on the other side of the counter from people like the von Trattens, when for fourteen years Radok had mistakenly thought he was *one* of them. But seeing her like this now brought no joy to him. He felt the trembling again in his hands and left quietly. The maid was out in the hall, dusting the immaculate surface of the mahogany chest.

"You heard. She needs someone now. Perhaps a close friend?"

Mathilde made to protest her innocence, as if she had not been eavesdropping, but Radok shook his head impatiently.

"Just go to her, girl. Help her. I'll show myself out."

He went down the stairs—his shoes still squeaking—out past the Daimler and then onto the sidewalk, the heavy door slamming to behind him: a hollow thud in the empty night.

The cold bit deep into him now. He was defenseless, naked despite his heavy overcoat. Alone. Very alone. The last man on earth. He thought he heard sobs from the upstairs window.

Digging his hands into the overcoat pockets to warm himself, he felt the paper Hinkle had given him. He pulled it out. Unfolded, it proved to be a program for a concert. Great find, Hinkle. Terrific work. Commend you on this one. Promotion time at the Inspektorat.

But Radok's cop curiosity made him look closer at the program once he was in the car with the green dash light on. It was for a piano recital at the Mozart Saal in the Konzerthaus. Last Friday. Cute. So that's where the son of a bitch Cezak had gone while Radok was tailing him, shivering in the cold outside.

Radok had thought it somewhat strange at the time; he hardly took Cezak for the musical type. He'd put it down to a quick urinal stop, making use of the free facilities at the Konzerthaus. Quick duck in, quick back out. Radok had picked him up ten minutes later near the stage entrance.

So he took a program with him. So great. Never know when a scrap of paper will come in handy. Maybe friend Cezak was a natural klepto—see anything loose lying

around and he'd nick it. Radok looked through the pages
of the program. Mozart. The Twenty-First Concerto. And
Schubert. A few mazurkas from Chopin. Daring, that, he
thought. Polish and all. Not the hearty German from the
Reich which concert houses had had to lay on since
Hitler.

Radok saw the name of the performer: the Lassen girl.
Everybody's favorite export. The tall blond ice-goddess
of the concert hall. Half-American, so they said. Half-
Jewish, as well. Protected by Goebbels himself. Radok
had seen the order from Berlin with the man's signature,
providing freedom of movement for her. The Reich was
getting enough propaganda mileage out of her to make
such special treatment worthwhile. Aryanization and honorary citizenship in the Reich were in store for her if she
played her cards right.

Radok had been to one of her recitals. And yes, she
was not only damn good-looking, but damn good on the
piano, as well. Incredible subtlety and interpretation.
And something you saw all too seldom in the concert
halls these days: real and honest passion.

Radok turned the program over. Hey-ho, he thought.
This does get more interesting. On the back, written in a
lavishly swirling feminine hand was the inscription: "To a
loyal fan. Regards, Frieda Lassen"

What was it Hinkle had said? Damned curious thing
for a black marketeer to be carrying about on him.
Damned curious, indeed.

Chapter Four

SS-Obersturmbannfuehrer Arthur Krahl was born in Vienna in 1910. That was about all he ever wanted to fill in on the forms requesting personal history. Place of birth: Vienna. There was no reason to be more specific; no reason to offer up the information that he had been born in a pauper's ward in the tenth district; no reason to record that he was illegitimate at time of birth. Vienna, 1910; parents' names in neat cursive followed by the deceased box checked for both.

It was *his* past, after all. He could improvise it if need be.

SS-Obersturmbannfuehrer Arthur Krahl's world was a simple one, made up of three elements: his black uniform, which Krahl accepted as the metaphor of monastic duty to the SD (the SS Security Service); his bedridden mother who, contrary to the reports of her deceased state which he dutifully filed on personal history forms, was very much alive and quite chipper, in a bed which he provided her in a suite of rooms adjacent to his own— and much too comfortable in said bed to ever think of stirring from beneath the massive eiderdown cloud covering her; and finally there was his collection of erotica, which he kept in a converted *Dienerzimmer* or servant's room at the top of the house he'd requisitioned for himself in 1940. The walls of this "library" were lined with mahogany shelves and drawers; brass pulls gleamed richly in the low light thrown by the green-globed lamps. In the bookshelves were first editions, secondhand and new copies of all the great erotica from around the world.

A quick perusal of the contents of the library would show that Arthur Krahl's preference in written and graphic art tended toward the eulogizing of love for young boys with firm buttocks and eager mouths. Krahl was, however, no homosexual; rather he was largely asexual. Well, at least not homosexual here in the Reich, he told himself. Earlier, in the twenties, on his fact-finding mission to the Middle East, probing the Zionist question and Jewish resettlement . . . well, his adventures there could hardly be called homosexual. A way of life only. Ahmed and his legion of youthful playmates.

But none of that here in the Reich. No. Too risky by half. Playing with fire, that was. Especially so, now that he was so close to his dream: a full colonelcy and the new villa in Penzing which that rank brought with it. Goodbye to stuffy old Vienna; hello suburbs and country air and a raft of servants to attend his every whim, not to mention Maman.

Krahl sat in his bed now, just beginning a new day. As Section Chief of the Foreign Desk of Vienna SD Station, Krahl was one of the most powerful men in Vienna. Each new day was an adventure for him, another step on his way to Penzing and out of this draughty mausoleum where he was now living. Krahl started work early. Fritz, his servant, brought him the Vienna Activity Reports along with his cup of mocha on the silver breakfast tray. Propped up by several firm pillows, wearing his silk dressing gown against the morning chill, Krahl picked his way through reports of sabotage, suspected illegal radio transmitters, and more of that blasted resistance graffiti: this time it was scrawled in white paint on the rear porch of St. Stephen's Cathedral.

Pathetic. These people had nothing better to do than think up such games and heckle the legitimate officials in the country with their posters and broadcasts. They were not an enemy even worth bothering one's head about. Krahl longed for a resistance such as they had in France. Now the maquis was something one could really grapple with; something one could take seriously. Here in the Ostmark there was a bunch of old ladies and impotent intellectuals firing off at the officials letters of protest rather than guns.

Krahl continued reading the Activity Reports and suddenly there it was, all but buried amidst such prosaic matters: the report of the deaths of one Jan Cezak, suspected black marketeer, and of General Augustus von Tratten at a stakeout the night before in the Inner City. The General was dead by his own hand. And no one at

Morzin Platz, Gestapo Headquarters, seemed to be taking much notice of the two deaths.

Von Tratten's death was, the report wanted to make very clear, a case of mistaken identity. No one had even bothered to ask what the old fool was doing at the scene or in the company of a known small-time crook, let alone why he had taken his own life rather than face capture. The idiots! Must he always make up for the deficiencies in his subordinates and colleagues? This was not just an insignificant footnote to the other operations of last night and yesterday; this was of major importance. Krahl could feel it in his bones. Couldn't anyone else see that? Fools and incompetents were all he had to work with.

Half an hour later, showered and standing in front of his mirror, knotting his gray tie with finicky care, SS-Obersturmbannfuehrer Arthur Krahl was still fuming at the incompetency of his fellow officers. Krahl could smell scandal, or worse. Perhaps none of the others cared if the famous old general was a petty thief on the black market; or perhaps the word had come down from above that such a thing be hushed up. After all, von Tratten was a World War One hero. His name was inscribed in military history books for his actions at the Somme.

But the von Tratten legend meant nothing to Krahl, and if word for a cover-up of the death had been sent from Berlin, he surely had not received it. As head of the Foreign Desk of Vienna SD, Krahl had a duty to investigate this matter further. And a personal grudge to settle, as well. He smiled at the thin-lipped, blue-eyed reflection in the mirror image, and ran a brush over the blond hair that never wanted to lie flat.

First the duty visit to Maman, however.

She really was an old dear, but her habits were most vexing; habits of speech, of dress, of eating, and of reading. At least now that she was married to her bed, Krahl no longer had to worry about her causing him public embarrassment. There had been that one incident on the tram when she'd struck a conductor several times for requesting her ticket. She had told the man that her son was very important and that she no longer needed to pay. An argument had ensued, one ending in physical violence initiated by Maman. Well, the secret that his far from *au fait* mother still lived had almost come out then, and he'd had to pull the most delicate of strings in the Interior Ministry to have the matter dropped. Maman had almost blinded the poor tram conductor with her umbrella.

The old dear.

Out into the chilly hall. Cavernous group of rooms for a bachelor's apartments. Faded elegance; hardly the sort of respectable lodging needed for a young man on the rise in Hitler's Reich.

The crusty old Maman down the hall hardly fit that image, and sometimes Krahl felt a twinge of guilt at hiding her from the world, but there it was. Duty. He had to hide the old dear in order to win advancement. Soon he might even have to take a wife—horrid thought! —to gain further promotion, to win the oak clusters of a full colonelcy on his collar and to merit the Penzing villa.

SS-Obersturmbannfuehrer Krahl stopped at a Meissen vase on a hall table to rearrange the branches of a blooming horse chestnut jutting too far out into the passageway. Did he forever have to correct the mistakes of others?

Maman's suite was at the end of the hall, at one time the nursery and school room but since converted to a frilly, silky, female precinct. He knocked at the door and entered before bidden to do so. She was propped up in bed against a cascade of lace-trimmed pillows, the radio already on, playing "Morning Melodies." Cigarettes littered a cut-glass ashtray at bedside, and a cigarette was dangling from her mouth, as well, its ash drooping threateningly over her coverlet. A cup of coffee steamed on the bedside table.

"Dearest Maman. Did you sleep well?"

She winced as if hit at the sound of "Maman," for she found it too frenchified, but Krahl plunged on. It was ritual by now.

"Doctor says you're looking much better. Perhaps a ride in the Prater this afternoon?"

"I like it here!" she barked. "How many times do I have to tell you, it's nice in here! Warm! An old lady, she wants it warm! *Verstehst*?"

He hated her argot; hated the way she insisted on calling him Arthur with the hard German "t" instead of the soft English "th" he affected with new acquaintances. He

looked at her fleshy, bloated face, the pinched eyes and
fold of fat at the chin; the unkempt hair and dangling
cigarette . . . and he hated her. Then he felt the usual
remorse and shame for such strong aversion to one of his
own blood.

All a ritual.

"Of course, Maman." He forced himself to pat the fat,
pallid hand that lay on the counterpane. "You know best.
Just take it easy. You've earned the right. Get well."

Now was the difficult part, but he forced himself to
give her the perfunctory kiss on her cheek as a parting
sign of affection.

"Au revoir, Maman. . . ."

"I don't know why we're fighting the war. For you to
go around aping the goddamn French and British . . . ?"

He closed the door on this parting criticism. More
ritual.

The old dear.

The six-wheeled Mercedes was waiting for him at the
door, its leather seats cold as Krahl slid in the back. He'd
continually reminded the oafish driver to warm the car
before picking him up. Useless. Louts like his driver had
nothing between their ears but hair.

"The morgue, Sergeant."

The driver grunted, looking at him in the mirror.

"Crypt it is then, sir." Using the stupid Viennese slang
for the place; refusing to speak high German. Infuriating.

It was a fast ride to Alserstrasse, to the General Hospital. Krahl had the driver wait for him.

"And keep the heater going," he said. "I want it warm
in here when I return."

He followed the signs to the morgue. Mankowicz was
on duty, a man of such tiny proportions that he seemed a
midget. Thick rimless glasses magnified his eyes into
those of a frog. He always wore the same lab coat—or
could it actually be another one similarly soiled? This
thought depressed Krahl for some vague reason.

"Cold." It was a typical Mankowicz greeting.

"Yes," Krahl said. "I'd like to see a body."

"I didn't think you were here for tea, sir." Mankowicz
also thought he was a bit of a wag, and spit upon Krahl's
overcoat sleeve while laughing at his own joke.

"Von Tratten. Please take me to him."

"Ahh. The old guy. Not much there to see. The 7.65 takes a big chunk of brain with it."

"Just take me to the body."

"Especially when a guy sticks it in his mouth. Got to be some kind of nut to do that."

"The body, Mankowicz."

"Yes, sir."

Krahl followed him into Forensic 2B. They've just finished with von Tratten, then, Krahl thought.

Mankowicz looked at the marble slabs first; Krahl followed his glance. One of the dissection tables had yet to be washed down from a recent autopsy. Pink, indecipherable bits of tissue flecked the pearly-white surface.

Mankowicz then indicated several four-tier rows of drawers built into the west wall.

"He'll be in one of those. New arrivals."

After examining three name tags dangling from the pulls, he sighed and heaved on one of the drawers. It opened; the body inside was covered in washable oilcloth.

"That's him," Mankowicz said, but made no attempt to remove the cloth.

"Good. You may leave me now."

"Whatever you say."

When the door to the lab had closed, Krahl pulled back the protective oilcloth. Mankowicz was right: not much left to see. The gaping wounds in the head and stomach did not bother Krahl; he'd seen enough of them in his line of work to become calloused to such sights. In fact, at these particular wounds on this particular corpse, Krahl found himself smiling. It had taken a long time, perhaps too long, but he was finally getting his back on the glorious General von Tratten.

Five years. Yes, that long, Krahl remembered. They had never met. Never even addressed one another, yet for some reason the General had committed an outrageous act of cruelty toward him. A vindictive, spiteful, spoiled old man. It had come about over Krahl's nomination to the prestigious Jockey Club. It was a membership Krahl wanted very badly: all the best people gathered there and such memberships looked awfully good on one's record. Krahl had yearned for it; he desired it and had earned it, dammit, with his unflagging commitment

to duty. His rank also qualified him for such membership, even at that time, for five years ago he was already
a major. But though nominated, he was never elected to
membership.

It had been a harsh blow, an ugly slap in the face. He
could have shut the club down, but Krahl did not play
that way. Instead, he set about finding out why he had
been disallowed membership, and what he found out
explained his hatred for von Tratten. Krahl's informant
and supporter at the Jockey Club described the single-
handed campaign that von Tratten had undertaken to
blackball this SD candidate. A regular smear campaign it
was: nouveau riche was not an evil-enough epithet for
the General to bandy about; von Tratten had even
unearthed the unmentionable—Krahl's illegitimacy. By
God, he wouldn't tolerate such impudence! Von Tratten
would pay for that, Krahl decided. And now was the
moment of atonement.

The corpse was naked except for another brown-paper
identity tag tied to the left big toe. The man's penis and
scrotum looked pitiful and deflated; his legs, tiny, blue-
veined match sticks. One side of the face remained:
stubble appeared there. Krahl approached the head end
of the drawer, opened his great coat, unzipped his pants,
took out his penis, and splattered an arching, hot stream
of urine onto the remaining section of the head. He
pissed for a long time, as he had saved up his morning
urination after reading of the General's death. It was
perhaps the most satisfactory urination in SS-Obersturmbannfuehrer Arthur Krahl's entire life.

He finished, zipped his pants, shoved the drawer in,
and walked off, feeling lighter by pounds and years.

The driver was waiting, red-nosed, in the Mercedes
when Krahl reached the gate.

"Headquarters now, sir?"

Krahl did not answer for a moment, so pleased was he
with himself. The driver repeated the question and Krahl
nodded.

Back at the office, the rest of the Activity Reports
from SD and Gestapo stations throughout the Reich lay
on his rosewood desk. He would go over them first as
usual. But a short, transcribed telephone conversation
caught his eye: "Code name Hammer".

Good. Hartmann was finally reporting. The laconic bastard. Let him out in the field and you never heard from him again. Thinks he knows better than the station. But Krahl kept him because, quite frankly, Lieutenant Hartmann was the best damned operative he had. Anybody could follow orders; Hartmann's strength was that he believed in them.

This communication was logged in at 0200 hours, on the private, scrambled line:

"Operative identified himself as Hammer," the decoding clerk had written. "Requested Katze."

Krahl stiffened every time he heard or read the damnable code name Hartmann had given to him. Another of his infuriating peculiarities, refusing to use Krahl's real code name: Koenig, king.

"Message transmitted once only: 'Construction well under way. Hammer to nail imminent.' Receptor on duty is a fresh recruit and was unsure of the copied message. Requested a repeat," read the report, compiled by a senior signals officer. "Code name Hammer's reply: 'Tell Katze to find new worker mice.' Whereupon subject immediately rang off. Length of transmission, twenty-seven seconds."

Krahl snapped the thin sheet of yellow paper between thumb and middle finger like a bank teller testing for counterfeits. A wary fellow, was Hartmann. You'd think he was broadcasting from London rather than from Klagenfurt, in the south of Austria where he was doing infiltration work. This time it was a saboteur ring in an assembly plant. A long, difficult case. Enough problems with Messerschmidts had been traced to one carburetor factory in Klagenfurt to warrant an investigation. It had been Krahl's idea to put Hartmann into the plant to sniff things out. Could it be faulty parts, or the result of sabotage? Three pilots had died already from the faulty carburetors, and more importantly, three aircraft lost. From Hartmann's communiqué, it was clear that the infiltration operation was nearing a successful conclusion. Good. Krahl might well need Hartmann's services soon. Very soon, if the feeling he had about von Tratten proved true.

Krahl was not accustomed to acting on instinct. If questioned as to his methods, he would ascribe any success he had to thoroughness and deductive reasoning. The concept of intuition was as foreign to him as Swahili. Nonetheless, at this very moment, Krahl was overcome with a flash of intuition that seemed to grab him and shake him until he acknowledged its truth: the von Tratten case was going to develop into something big. Something big and scandalous. Something that might make a man's career. Something that could win him that villa in Penzing in a matter of weeks rather than years. For something this big, Hartmann would come in handy. For this, Hartmann's presence was more important in Vienna as backup than in Klagenfurt taking care of airplane saboteurs. No matter how many blasted aircraft went down. That was Goering's lookout, anyway. Let that pompous fat-ass take care of himself for once.

Krahl took out a telegram pad, scribbled out a hurried message to Hartmann, and rang the bell for the adjutant. Fine. All taken care of. He would have a cup of coffee now, strong and black. It was only 10:17 on a cloudy March morning. It had been a good morning's work thus far.

He had no way of knowing then how much better it would get.

Chapter Five

Radok awoke in the strange apartment feeling more disoriented than ever. He had lived there over a year and it was still strange to him. All apartments would be strange to him now. Helga had kept their big one on Ungargasse; the one he'd loved so and had worked hard to restore.

There was a sourness in his mouth and stomach from the brandy he'd had last night to anesthetize himself, and his mind was racing with the dream he'd just had. He'd been sailing on the Wienerwald See with the General when an electric storm caught them unprepared on the lake; the boom had snapped back suddenly, knocking the General unconscious. He, young Gunther Radok, alias Paganini, had saved the day, grabbing onto the mahogany tiller for all he was worth, keeping the boat from capsizing. Getting them to shore safely with all the clientele of the *Gasthaus zum See* there on the beach to welcome the hero to land. He dreamed of how the General, after regaining consciousness, stood aboard his fifteen-meter sailing sloop named the *Principia* and carried out a mock knighting ceremony:

"I dub thee Saint Paganini," he said, just a little tipsy after the knock on the head and some restorative rum and tea. "Patron of fiddlers and sailors. May you sail always as first mate on my boat."

There was a throbbing at Radok's temples when he awoke—a major hangover from the brandy. He tripped over the empty bottle getting out of bed and made his way to the kitchen, putting the sentimental memories out of his mind. Then he forced himself to drink a cup of ersatz coffee and gobble down a stale breakfast roll.

Ten minutes later, his face washed in cold water, his hair hastily brushed, and wearing a baggy tweed suit,

Radok left the old apartment building, heading for the Inspektorat on Schottenring.

Pick up from where you left off, he told himself. Trace Cezak, find out why he and the General should end up together dead in an alley.

A thought was lurking in the back of his mind. Some duty call. Christ, yes. Irene. Note left on the door when he'd returned to the flat last night. Wanted him to call her this morning. Very important.

He was having some trouble negotiating the cobbles this morning, but after a few blocks the blood had begun to flow again, pounding in his head. Wind from the Canal chilled him and he dug his hands into the pockets of the overcoat, coming up again with the program Cezak had been carrying.

Wrong: his sister-in-law had not been the duty call bothering him. It was the call on the Lassen woman, the pianist, that he'd been trying to remember this morning. His synapses were a little slow today, but the connection was ultimately made.

There was a post office in the next block and a phone booth and book there. He was in luck: Lassen's name and address were listed. The address he found was close enough to walk to.

So what are you going to ask her, son? Question her about all her fans; see if she remembered one medium-sized, brown-haired, inconsequential Czech? Long shot. Shit. He hated long shots. They meant he had no other leads. Which he didn't. Just a couple of dead bodies on his hands, one of which was that of a man he'd loved more than his own father. A man who shot away his head rather than be arrested. And it was time to find out why.

Walking felt good suddenly. He had a purpose again. He was going in a positive direction. The dream still played on him; there was still a tremor of fear in his guts from remembering that first time at the tiller of a sailboat. A great way to lose the cherry. It would soon be time to take a look at the sailboat he kept moored at the Alte Donau across the Canal. *Principia II*. A tiny little one-man rig, but he enjoyed the hell out of her. The boat reminded him of the palmier days out in Hietzing, when he had still thought he was on a par with people like the von Trattens and not just their lackey.

Five minutes later Radok entered a narrow, cobbled cul de sac, where a rabbit warren of low baroque apartment buildings greeted him. These were coming back into style now with the gentry and nouveau riche. No traffic, foot or otherwise. He rang the outside bell marked FRIEDA LASSEN; static came from the intercom. He pushed the door but it was still locked, and he rang her bell again. This time a raspy bell sounded downstairs, unlocking the outer door. Radok went up the open stairway and quickly found her apartment. He felt anticipation as he lifted his hand to knock on her door. Just then the door opened from inside.

It was the blond pianist herself. No maids here. She looked exactly as she had on stage, and she was the most beautiful woman Gunther Radok had ever seen. Behind her a scene unfolded before Radok's eyes: room upon room of low-ceilinged, baroque spaces with parquet floors and doors leading off to unknown quarters.

"Yes?"

Her voice was low, and as cool as her blond hair.

He rallied, pulling himself together.

"Sorry. Just admiring your lovely flat."

Moisture at the back of his neck band. Sweating on a cold March day. She eyed him with something between suspicion and fear on her face.

"Name's Radok. Inspektor Radok."

He showed her his identity card, but this did not seem to ease her suspicions, her fear. If anything, it made things worse. She was not the sort who wore suspicion well. It made her fidget and go red in the cheeks and throat. But she kept silent. That was a good sign. Too many of them would make a stupid joke about being finally caught for the parking ticket, or betray some other such nervous flutter that showed they, like most of the rest of the world, had a poorly concealed guilty secret.

"May I come in?"

She stepped aside and he noticed her hands as he passed: not as long as one would think for a pianist. Sturdy hands. Good, strong hands. But nothing like long enough for the reach she achieved. Obviously her talent was a result of diligence rather than physiology. It was the kind of observation he prided himself on making. Alcohol poisoning or no, he was happy to see his head was still functioning this morning. She was in a dressing gown; coffee—it smelled real—and rolls were on the dining room table. An open paper. Radok led the way to this room as if he knew the flat, chose a chair, and sat in it without waiting to be invited.

"Don't mind, do you?" he said.

She shook her head, still standing.

"I've seen you perform, Fräulein Lassen. Most impressive. I was honestly moved."

She smiled wanly, nodding at the compliment.

"But," she finally said, "you haven't come about that, have you?"

"No, I haven't come to rave about your piano-playing. I wish I had." He pulled the autographed program out of his coat pocket.

"Recognize this?"

She took the program faceup, opened it, looked at it quickly, then held it out for him to take.

"A program for a concert of mine last week." She shrugged.

Radok made no move to take the paper from her hand.

"Turn it over."

She did. He thought he could see her stiffen. The cool mask disappeared momentarily and what he saw behind it interested him: a terrified child.

"It's my autograph. I do dozens of these after each performance."

Radok pursed his lips. "You know the guy? Perhaps you remember signing this one . . . remember something about the fellow who asked for it?"

"No." Her hair moved like an ocean wave about her face as she shook her head. "No. I can't say that I recall this one. I've no idea, really." A nervous laugh. "What's it all about, anyway?"

He accepted the program this time when she handed it to him.

"A bit of nasty business last night. The man carrying this, Jan Herr Cezak, was shot. Black marketeer."

While Radok was speaking, Frieda Lassen had the opportunity to replace her mask. He could see it in place again now, that half-smile on the sad face. She had not seated herself, and so finally he stood. The coffee smelled wonderful, but she did not offer him any.

"Sorry to trouble you with this, Fräulein. If you remember anything about the guy, anything at all that could help our investigation, please call. Ask for Radok. . . . Anytime."

"It's just a name," she said by way of apology. "They tell you their name and I write a standard sort of note for all of them. Strangers. I never see the same one twice. I probably wouldn't know if I did. After a performance I'm pretty exhausted."

He nodded his head in understanding and he was close enough now for her scent to reach him. It was something sweet and exotic that he'd never smelled before, but it fit her exactly, just like the green satin dressing gown she wore.

"I'll let you get back to your coffee. It smells good."

She did not act on his hint, but instead showed him to the door. He watched her high buttocks move under the shiny smooth material and he had to restrain himself from putting hands on her. He wasn't a cocksman. Not a rounder and bounder at all. Since Helga there had been no one. One year and no sex. Not even self-abuse. Sex he could live without, he'd convinced himself. It got you in a mess of trouble.

And here he was like an old lech drooling over some young woman's ass. Tempting his celibacy and reputation by following too closely behind her. Visually tracing the outline of each cheek, the crease between.

"So sorry I couldn't be of more help."

She turned before he'd expected, held her hand out to him, and there he was still ogling her ass. He left blushing, tripping over his awkward feet like a schoolboy on his first date.

So much for long shots. Yet there had been something there, he told himself once he got back out onto the street. Cops make even the pope nervous, but the way Frieda Lassen had initially reacted was something more. Something deeper. Radok had the feeling that this was a young lady in a pile of trouble.

Or maybe you just hope so, he told himself. Maybe you just pray she's got woes so you can be her white knight. Maybe. That a crime? Get a five-count for that offense, do I?

Some get life, he reminded himself. Some get life.

Radok's conscience always worked overtime when he was hung over. It was always there in the morning at the foot of his bed to snigger at the poor fool with the rheumy eyes and the inside that felt like curdled death.

"Do piss off," he said aloud to his troublesome conscience. Of course there would be an old beggar woman passing by at that very moment to take the remark personally. He made no attempt at an explanation. Just walk away; get away from it, he thought. Give the old woman Helga's attorney's number. Maybe she could sue him, too. Paintings to Helga; silverware to the old woman.

Chapter Six

Hartmann awoke to the tapping on his door and his hand went automatically to the knife he kept under his pillow. His heart was pounding in his chest and there was a sour taste of fear in his mouth.

"Herr Boehm. Telegram for you."

The landlady, Frau Lautendorf. It took him a moment to register his assumed name, then he took a deep breath and regained control. His hand inched away from the knife. Frau Lautendorf opened the door without waiting for a response. A disagreeable woman, Frau Lautendorf. He would be damn happy to see the end of her as soon as this operation was over.

"Telegram," she said brightly. Her housecoat was loosely gathered together in front, exposing bra, panties, and bare flesh underneath that did nothing to enhance Hartmann's opinion of the fair sex. Blue-veined, heavy dugs above; dimpled, mottled thighs below. He squinted at her, playing the sleepyhead. No confrontations with Frau Lautendorf today, thank you very much.

"Come on, Herr Boehm. Telegram. Perhaps it's important."

Of course it's important, you cow, he thought. But he rolled over onto his belly and said instead:

"Just put it on the night table. Thanks."

"You men," she said coyly.

This he did not understand. She had taken to teasing him as if he were a typical malingering member of his sex. The familiarity rankled Hartmann, but he ignored it. As if sleeping eight hours after working the graveyard shift at Bracow Machine Works demonstrated the most cavalier of attitudes.

He waited for her to leave the room before he opened the telegram. The message inside was partially coded and, strangely for that fool Krahl, to the point.

"Koenig to Hammer: nail up operation soonest. Come home immediately."

He cursed himself for having gotten in touch with Vienna Station last night. But it had been three weeks. They expected weekly reports from field men. A duty call. Hartmann bent orders, but never totally broke them.

He turned the telegram over in his hands. It was his habit to doublecheck everything he handled. Then he picked up the envelope. His eyes were keen, trained by the best tricksters in the trade. He immediately saw the telltale signs of puckered paper on the seal. Signs of steaming. The telegram had been opened and re-closed rather clumsily. Frau Lautendorf.

For a time Hartmann continued lying on his back, staring at an amoeba-shaped water stain on the ceiling above him. Now the decision had to be made, that was clear. Before, it had been merely a niggling sort of question about tying up loose ends. Hartmann had an obsession about such things: that when operations were over, they were well and truly over; that no one could trace the work to him.

His cover had not yet been blown through the course of more than a dozen operations and four years of action. He was the unknown man; the resistance and saboteur circles he'd infiltrated had never caught on to him. Those who knew him in action were either dead themselves or thought him dead. A simple formula: leave no traces. Frau Lautendorf was a trace. She knew him and had been attempting to get to know him better for the past three weeks. But horniness was hardly a capital offense, and he'd been having trouble squaring this one with his conscience.

Now, however, things are simple, clear-cut, Hartmann thought. Frau Lautendorf has read the message from Krahl. Her reading it has compromised my mission. My mission is a matter of life and death to the Reich. Ergo . . .

The sums added up in Hartmann's head now and he was happier. At ease. He knew his duty.

Hartmann allowed himself to fondle his prick now. Things were arranged for the day; he would need all the concentration he could muster. No question of misdirected sexual energy today. That was something he'd learned about from Sergeant Markl at the Bernau cadet

training school: Mad Markl, the recruits had called the
drill instructor, because of his absolute and unblinking
fervor. A more humorless man Hartmann had never met,
and when Markl had broached the subject of onanism he'd
scoffed at it at first; the thing was grotesque, unmanly.
Something children did, playing with their pud. But Mad
Markl was right, Hartmann had later discovered. A man
needs daily release. Otherwise the juices build up, creep
into parts of you that should never be tainted with the
urgency of sex.

"There should be none of the hot blood of sex in your
jobs, friends," Mad Markl had lectured. "No heat. No
revenge. None of that crap. Keep it calm. Keep alive."

So, onanism. Mad Markl again: "Release your seed
daily. Have a woman maybe once a month, just to have
something to fantasize about the rest of the time."

Hartmann fantasized about the Vienna woman again.
The one from his first job; his first betrayal. Strong word,
but as he imagined her now, her long, lean, naked body
spread out on a white sheet beneath him, then he had to
admit it was betrayal, what he had done to her. He'd
schooled her, his young music student, in all sorts of
ways, from politics to sex. And she had loved it all; taken
it all in as if no one had ever tried to fill her before. It
was her Hartmann thought about most of the time lately
while touching himself.

Thinking about her, seeing her again like that beneath
him, her blond hair fanned out around her head, it took
only a few strokes of his penis before he came, hot and
sticky onto his belly. Duty. Only glimpses of pleasure in
it. Then he got up, put his robe on, gathered soap and
razor, and went out into the hall. The rest was ritual. It
was bath day today. Twice a week, and the Frau would
complain about that being too frequent. She was in the
living room as usual, cleaning house in her underwear.
Her laboring outfit. She was parsimonious rather than
teasing: if she wore no clothes while working, then there
would be no clothes to sweat in and no clothes to wash.

Hartmann walked past her slowly today; no attempt to
sneak by.

"Not up to the top now, Herr Boehm, do you hear?"
She shook her finger at him and her great flabby breasts

jiggled like clotted cream in a churn. "Save some hot water for others."

He winked at her and continued down the hall to the bath. Once inside he felt the water heater in the corner of the cavernous bathroom: it was half full. Silk stockings, frayed bras and panties hung about the bathroom like moss in a jungle. There was a faint patch of red at the crotch of one of the panties.

Revolting, Hartmann thought. Like an animal. Like his mother who'd left him when he was only twelve. It had been the Hitler Youth that had saved him from the orphanage. From there it was on to the SS. The Black Corps. The only family he'd ever had.

Turning on the hot water tap, he watched the steam billow up out of the water, waft upward toward the ceiling, and condense there in tiny sweat droplets. He took off his robe and shaved at the sink while the enormous old bathtub filled. Long, slow strokes with the open razor. His hand was steady, sure. Calm. Calm. His body, small and deceptively lean, felt all of one piece today. Ready for action. Stay calm. Stay alive.

Like his mother who, before she'd run away, had never been a mother at all to Hartmann. She'd left him alone night after night to go out with her men friends. Sometimes she even brought them back to their tiny apartment so that he had to listen to her obscene gasping and snorting. And then in the mornings, after the man had gone, filled with bile and remorse, she'd take the young Hartmann's pants down and spank him until his buttocks were stinging red; punish him for the supposed crime of crying in the night or for having got up in the middle of the night to go pee, or because he hadn't. Any imagined offense would be enough reason for these spankings, and just as often no reason was offered. Just the smile on her face as she unbuckled his trousers or ripped open his pajama bottoms. It became a game, and over time Hartmann began to play it with her, began even to take pleasure in it, for it was her substitute for love. Once— the memory made him tense even now—he had gotten an erection from the beating and she'd seen it and begun laughing; laughter high and hysterical which he could still hear. . . .

The knock came as he finished shaving. The bath was almost full.

"Herr Boehm!" Frau Lautendorf was outside the door. "Not too much water, now! I still have my washing to do!"

He slipped into the water, stretching out full in the huge tub.

"I can't hear you!" he cried.

She opened the door, standing hesitantly in the doorway at first.

He smiled at her. "What is it, Frau Lautendorf?"

"Oh. You're in the bath already. But it's so full. I still have laundry to do today."

Her eyes were focused on the black patch of hair below his middle. He willed an erection. It popped above the surface like a fishing bob.

"Herr Boehm!"

But the cow continued to stand there, transfixed, while he tried to look flustered, embarrassed.

"I'm . . . I'm sorry, Frau Lautendorf. It's just . . ."

She didn't wait for him to finish, but started over to the bathtub.

"It's all right, son. I know how it must be, away from home and your girlfriend. Lonely, like."

He looked up at her, his dark brown eyes devoid of passion or feeling, and she interpreted the gaze as beckoning. A giggle from her.

"Just this once, then." Forefinger to her mouth girlishly. "But mum's the word." Another giggle.

"I promise," he said as she stepped out of her underpants. "Not a word to a living soul."

The bra unsnapped from behind. She was enormous and white. A fold of fat creased at the stomach. As she lifted one leg over the side of the tub he could see moisture glistening in the blond hairs around her sex.

"I love the old tubs," she said. "There's room for two."

Water splashed out of the tub as she got in. She put a hand on his swollen penis, directing it into her wet, loose recess. A groan from her as she eased down onto him, straddling him and facing him. He closed his eyes. More water splashed up into his face, over the edge of the tub. But nothing more from Frau Lautendorf than a throaty groan. Her hands were on his hands now, directing them to her massive breasts. Pushing them onto her as she moved up and down, back and forth on his cock. He let her climb to her climax, riding atop him.

Calm now. Hartmann heard her breathing: she was nearing the critical point. He pulled her down to him as if to embrace her. The tenderness made her hips spasm even more quickly. Hot breath in his face. The awful woman was actually trying to kiss him!

She was pleading now for him not to stop, to go faster, harder, deeper. A four-letter word he'd never heard a woman say before. A near scream; breath like a hiss in his ear. He braced himself, his feet against the foot of the tub, hands on her fleshy back.

"Oh yes, yes! Fuck me harder."

And then he thrust his arms upward, cracking her head against the top rim of the porcelain tub and she let out a long, low groan as if reaching orgasm.

Stunned though she was, her hips kept twisting on his. Her pubic bone dug into him and he thrust her forward again, smashing her forehead a second time. She slowed now, as he squeezed out from under her, pushing her face down into the water, a knee in her back. Bubbles came out of her mouth under the water; her body thrashed in a last, violent orgasm. She continued moving long after the sixty count he made. Gasping as she had been, she should have filled her lungs with water and died quickly. But Hartmann hung on until the final twitches, then rolled her over onto her back, checking the contusions. Nothing untoward there.

The bruises on her forehead would be commensurate with those suffered in a fall. It was a slippery damn tub, with no mat at the bottom. No other visible marks. No semen left behind in her. His masturbating earlier had seen to that.

There was no phone in the flat; no time for Frau Lautendorf to have talked with anybody else about the telegram, if that indeed had been her game. That would have come after he'd gone to work. So: loose strings taken care of.

He flopped her onto her belly once again. As he was getting out of the tub, Frau Lautendorf's bowels loosened. Sickening.

Calm. Calm. He dried off, gathered his soap and razor, and went to his room. He dressed in his one suit and packed his work clothes in the cardboard suitcase. Before leaving, he checked his room twice to make sure all signs of him were gone. The man without traces. Then he left the flat, left the awful building which smelled of boiling turnips and rotting foundations, and set off for the train station.

All that was left was to nail the operation up. Hammer to nail.

Chapter Seven

The Inspektorat reception area was empty but for a white-coated cleaning lady who gave his squeaky shoe a suspicious glance, as if Radok might be tracking in mud. He smiled at her unforgiving face and went up the stairs quickly to the third floor. Home away from home. Radok nodded at a few of the men who looked up when he entered the office. Hinkle was at Radok's desk delivering mail.

"It's a good morning for it," Hinkle said.

Radok was looking at the pile of junk mail on his desk.

"For what?" he said.

Hinkle winked. "The old in-out. Why else would you be late?"

Forced humor, but okay. Hinkle knew Radok; Radok knew Hinkle. Neither was as damn silly as they made out to be. But Hinkle, in especial, had a thing about words.

"They're consoling, my friend," he'd say about words, about language. "Or a pat on the head, like. Or maybe even cheering. That's what words are for. Very primitive sort of communication. Save the eyes and arms and other pieces of the old anatomy for the really important messages."

This statement was the result of five years of partnering; of several permanent bits of lead in Radok's backside that had been meant for Hinkle's chest; and of a full liter of Vetliner imbibed at their favorite wine cellar one night. For Hinkle, speech was physical rather than mental. It was the sound of the words rather than their meaning which he emphasized.

Today it was cheering; Hinkle knew it was all bullshit, that nothing could cheer Radok out of the General's death, for Hinkle was one of the few men to know of Radok's other life. But being in a word-driven world, Hinkle used the tools at hand. So he hauled out the wink-and-nudge kit.

Radok understand.

"Fine day for it." Radok decided to join in; indulge in a little wish-fulfillment. "Tall, blond. Tight in all the right spots; loose in morality."

Old drill. The letters on his desk were a real grab bag. Most of them were directed to "Pandering and Illegal Sales"—the Kripo longhand for the black market squad that Radok headed. The squad had an anonymous-tips phone number as well, though most preferred to write. They would have to use public phones to squeal on their neighbors, most of them, and there goes the anonymity. Most of the informants were unpaid; duty-bound patriots, they styled themselves. Radok looked at it differently: the jealous, the spiteful, the righteous. These were like an old lady down the street slowly dying, who wanted to see others suffering with her.

"Usual bunch of weirdos here for you," Hinkle said.

He was lingering by Radok's desk: there was something more on his mind.

"What's up?" Radok said.

"Down, in a matter of speaking," Hinkle said. "The von Tratten thing . . . Shut down."

Radok waited for more. It wasn't coming.

"Don't go cryptic on me now, Hinkle. Shut down. How? Who says so?"

Radok's voice rose in anger. Inspektors at nearby desks looked his way.

"Morzin Platz," Hinkle said in a near-whisper. "Gestapo figures enough is enough. The geezer pegged out, hell to pay if the regular army gets wind of the circumstances. They want it under wraps. Killed in the line of duty—that bit. Black marketeer did him. Or they did each other. You know the story. Shootout, and the hero loses. He was big, your General. No one wants tarnished crowns."

"Is this official?"

Hinkle laughed. "Is anything ever official from Morzin Platz? They're gods. A law unto themselves. But if you mean, did we get a piece of paper signed Gestapo Mueller saying lay off on the von Tratten case, no. No we didn't. But we got word of mouth."

"Okay."

Hinkle squinted at him. "You mean 'Okay, I'll lay off'"

or 'Okay, I'll watch my ass as I continue to investigate this'?"

Radok used the perusal of the letters to hide his annoyance.

" 'Cause," Hinkle went on, "if you mean 'Okay, I'll just watch my ass,' then I'd have to tell you that you're fucking with people who could fuck with you worse. You better not only cover your ass, but cover your whole body. You understand me, Gunther?"

He tapped Radok's arm to get the message across. Radok did not look up, keeping his eyes on the letters. But his mind was racing.

"It's taken me ten years to break you in," Hinkle went on. "I don't want anybody new coming into the partnership. This time of the world, the bastard would have to be either one-legged, or the Chief Homo of the Western World not to be in the army. So I want you should stay healthy. Very healthy. Understand?"

"Sure, Hinkle. Anything you say." Radok wanted to be rid of his partner, for the letter he held in his hand now was not like the others. This was no anonymous tip from a disgruntled housewife. The fine, delicate, old-school penmanship on the envelope was unmistakable.

Hinkle snorted. "Sincerity. I feel the distinct lack of it from you, asshole."

Radok looked up. "I mean it. I understand what you're saying. I'll let it lie."

Hinkle squinted more. He was not convinced.

"Honest," Radok said.

Hinkle shrugged. "Good. It'll all come around later. You'll see. Just let it go for now."

Radok nodded.

Hinkle moved off, continuing his mail deliveries with a joke here, a whispered tale there. He kept the sour faces of the other officers a little brighter; not a bad sort to have around in the long, dark days.

Radok opened the letter from the General:

> *Dear Paganini—*
> *Excuse the drama, but if you are reading this note,*
> *it shall mean that I am dead.*

Great, Radok thought. He could tell Hinkle he was

quitting the investigation; maybe he even believed he was for a minute. But the investigation obviously was not going to quit him. He didn't want to read this letter; he had the premonition that it was going to turn his life upside down. Radok's life was bad enough as it was. Still, he knew it. He was familiar with its pain. The devil you know.

But he read on:

> *I will waste no words of explanation, Paganini. Once you see the documents in my possession, all will be clear to you. For now, I simply beg your forgiveness for what happened twenty years ago, and hope that I can renew the trust between us with a show of trust from me. I bestow a legacy upon you, Paganini. A legacy of trust. A mission.*
>
> *But now you know I have died like a soldier. I have done my duty. I hope this legacy allows you to do your duty, as well. Present the enclosed permission slip at the Schottentor branch of the Creditanstalt Bankverein. Do not waste time. This is of the utmost urgency.*
>
> Augustus von Tratten

The very style of the writing had taken Radok back to those years at the Hietzing villa. The General: imperious but never vexing.

"I'll be back for lunch," Radok said to Hinkle as he passed his desk on the way to the door. The look he received in return let him know Hinkle was not fooled.

"Going back for seconds, huh?" Hinkle said. "Have to give me her address."

The Schottentor branch of the Creditanstalt Bankverein was all marble pillars and mahogany. The von Tratten signature shown to a sallow-faced female teller bought Radok safe conduct on the first stage of the journey to the inner sanctums, and to a wiry, bald chap in blue serge seated at a desk as big as Radok's bedroom. Herr Prokop. And Herr Prokop led Radok—who introduced himself as Huber in case Morzin Platz got wind of his continued interest in the case—to yet another and even more secret room. In this room Herr Prokop seated Radok, alias Huber, at a mahogany conference table while he fetched the von Tratten file. Lighting indirect, coming discreetly from wooden recesses just beneath the ceiling. Prokop took his time with the sealed documents, enough time for Radok to work up a case of nerves.

Urgent, the General had written. Urgent enough to die for. A mission. Radok was grateful for the inspiration, or perhaps cowardice, that had made him use a fictitious name with the bank director.

Prokop sneaked back in with the unctuous solicitude of a mortician, depositing a large orange envelope in front of Radok. He took "Huber's" signature as proof of receipt and sneaked out again.

"If you'd like to examine the contents for a moment?" the director said from the door.

"Thanks," Radok said. "I believe I will."

Prokop closed the door silently behind him in leaving.

The red wax seal on the envelope bore the initials "AvT". Radok opened it and shook the contents of the envelope out onto the table. Several glossy black-and-white photos fell out first, sliding across the table. These were followed by several more separate sheets of paper—official-looking, these, with swastika and eagle on the top, covered with red and black rubber stamps which all but obliterated the message. Names had been checked off against the left margin; a routing system that had put these documents before the most powerful eyes in the Reich: Hitler, Himmler, Goering, Goebbels, Ley, von Ribbentrop, and several generals, including Keitl himself.

There was also a stapled group of papers of some twenty pages or so: the minutes of a conference. The date and location was at the top: January, 1942, Wannsee. Radok knew the place: a posh suburb of Berlin, analogous to Hietzing in Vienna. But he knew nothing of any conference that had been held there earlier in the year.

Save the photos for last, he told himself; check the individual sheets first.

Berlin, 21 July, 1941:

To authorize the Fuehrer's long-awaited plan: requisition of 250 SS-Totenkopf troops to Treblinka and Sobibor KZ as of 0500 hours. Fifteenth Division to be sent to Auschwitz, as well. Full cooperation with the

Fuehrer directive number 80029 to be given to all SS personnel.

Heinrich Himmler,
Reichsfuehrer SS

Fuehrer directive 80029. Great, Radok thought. SS-Death's Head meant business. They were stationed primarily at the KZ's, the concentration camps. All the separate sheets of paper appeared to be orders of sorts. Radok picked up another slip of paper at random and saw it was signed by Goering and was along the same line as Himmler's. These papers were not photo-reproductions, but were the originals. Someone had gone to a great deal of trouble and danger to get these documents out of Berlin. Someone with access to top-secret files.

The third slip proved to be the jackpot: it bore Hitler's signature. The message was simple and clear. This in itself was something new for a Fuehrer who loved to hide the real impact of his orders in double-talk.

Berlin, 18 June, 1941:
To all command-level personnel, OKW and SS:
Whereas the Jewish race has brought on this destructive war,
Whereas the Jewish race is the great polluter of the Aryan race,
Whereas the Jewish race only concerns itself with self-advancement at the debasement of others,
Whereas the Jewish race is the greatest single enemy to Naziism in the world,
The Fuehrer therefore declares that this Jewish race shall be absolutely and irrevocably eradicated. Destruction of the Jews shall follow a humane and methodical program to be arranged at a special conference to be held in six months time. This action is of the highest priority and shall be accomplished at camps now being erected in the East. Meanwhile, Jews across Europe, as well as Slavs and Gypsies shall be concentrated in ghettos and holding camps awaiting transportation and resettlement in the East.

Heil Hitler!
Adolf Hilter

Radok read the directive twice more. It chilled him to the bone, and he knew it was not just so much more of Hitler's usual anti-Semitic blustering. This was real, concrete. Final. He knew now why the General would die to protect such documents. A mission. Yes, indeed. But how far along had this plan progressed?

This question was partially answered by the stapled report, which turned out to be minutes of the organizational meeting Hitler had mentioned in his original directive. He skimmed through it and discovered that all the armed services and ministries had been present at this meeting which had drawn up a blueprint for the destruction of the Jews of Europe. The "Final Solution," the plan was called. *Endloesung.* Round up all the Jews of Europe and send them to the East to be eliminated, either by firing squad or an as yet to be determined method of extermination. Gas was highly recommended as the most efficient and humane procedure.

The meeting had been chaired by Heydrich, head of the SD, the SS Security Services, who was to be the man in charge of the entire extermination plan. All of this set down in hideous, depersonalized bureaucratic language. What they were talking about was no less than the slaughter of millions of men, women and children; what was mentioned in the meeting was "special treatment" and "resettlement." Euphemisms and double-talk. Still Radok did not know how far the actual plan had progressed.

The photos began to answer this. At first Radok did not know what he was looking at in the glossy black-and-white photographs: figure/ground obscuration. It took him several moments to realize that what he saw in the pictures was not stacked cord wood, but bodies. Thousands and thousands of bodies. On the back of this first photo was a caption:

Einsatzgruppe *IV in the East, August 1941*

More photos of the same: huge lime pits full of bodies, with arms and legs askew in the agony of death, while more Jews are being machine-gunned on the muddy banks of the pit above. Naked men, women, and children.

Einsatzgruppe: read mobile killing squads working behind the lines in Russia. Radok had heard rumors of these from soldiers home on leave from the Russian front. Wild rumors which no one would or could believe.

Another picture showed a van full of more of these bodies which so resembled stacked wood. The caption:

> *Mobile killing van—use of carbon monoxide from engine of vehicle itself. Utmost economy.*

This caption was accompanied by a detailed sketch of how the exhaust led back into the airtight compartment where the Jews were held. Out for an airing—find death instead.

The final picture: a public bath by the look of it. Caption:

> *Shower at Auschwitz. Zyklon B emitted from overhead faucets. Sixty seconds death time. Capacity—150.*

Zyklon B. It sounded familiar to Radok, familiar from his gardening days out in Hietzing. Of course: a form of pesticide the General and he had used on the roses.

One more order, this the most recent:

> *RSHA*
> *102 Wihelmstrasse*
> *Berlin*
> *14 February, 1942*
> *To all unit commanders of Death's Head SS:*
> *Be it known that the first transport of goods shall arrive at KZ Auschwitz (Oswiecim, Poland) on 26 March, this year. The first load shall comprise 1,000 for resettlement.*
> *Transports shall follow on a daily basis thereafter.*
> *Early arrivals to the camp shall complete construction of same, along with its disinfecting facilities.*
> *The first public bath shall take place in May of this year, according to a prearranged schedule agreed upon by the Fuehrer and Reichsfuehrer Himmler.*
> *All units are urged to work to their utmost to see that this schedule is abided to. Excuses and slow-downs will not be tolerated.*
> *Heil Hitler!*
>
> > *Reinhard Heydrich CSSD*
> > *Chief of Sicherheitzpolizei and SD*

"Public bath." Radok realized with a sinking feeling that this referred to the Zyklon B gas to be emitted from overhead faucets. The Jews were to be led to their slaughter, believing that they were entering showers! A cruel and ugly final joke. Radok had heard of the camp of Auschwitz, just as he knew of those at Dachau and Mauthausen, the latter located in the Danube Valley only a couple of hours from Vienna. But up to now these camps had been used to house political and other criminals. Up to now. But no longer would it be so, he realized. Now Auschwitz was to be turned into a giant inferno, a killing factory. And he knew exactly when all this would begin. The operation would begin in earnest—not hit-or-miss as with the *Einsatzgruppen*—on the twenty-sixth. Only sixteen days from today!

Radok looked in the envelope for further documents, not that he needed further proof. The one slip of paper he was hoping for was there: a final communication from the General.

"So now you know, Paganini," the General had written in his frail hand.

You can no longer close your eyes to this horror as the rest of the Reich seems content to do. You know your way now. It is all too clear. Word of this outrage must be got out to the Allies, to the enemy. I do not say this lightly, for as a soldier I know this means treason. But think, Paganini—if you have any lingering doubts, think of the higher morality. Higher than the state. It would be treasonous to that universal power not to get the documents out to the West. The world needs to know of these barbarities. That is the only way to stop them. And it is imperative that it be done at least a week before the first transport of Jews arrives at Auschwitz KZ. The Allies will need time to process this information, to verify it; time to organize a strategy. They must somehow destroy the installation at Auschwitz without fear of huge numbers of civilian casualties. Once the camp goes into full operation, I fear no one will risk such an action, even if it means saving lives in the long run. And if the Nazis know that the world is aware of their vile deeds, they will back off. As cowards always do.

You are the only one I can turn to now. The only man I know I can trust. My first mate. I know you will do what is right. I do not involve you in this lightly. If you are reading this, then you know I have paid the ultimate price for my beliefs. I hope you will be willing to do so, as well. This is my legacy of trust to you, Paganini, to make amends for my earlier betrayal.

If, however, you feel unable to undertake this mission, then I leave you with a final legacy. A request. Do with the documents what you must. But I am entrusting you with another human life, as well. At the end of this letter I will give you the name of a contact person and the code word to be used when contacting a certain resistance cell which can aid you in getting these papers out of the Reich. If you choose to suppress the documents, you must pledge to my memory that you will not use information supplied here against that man or his organization. And you must also use your own judgment in approaching these people in whom I have found every reason to trust. I shall, in fact, be meeting with one of their representatives soon, a man highly recommended by my friend in Berlin from whom I received these documents. You are my contingency plan, dear Paganini. I have no way of knowing what that meeting shall bring. Again, use your own judgment. I trust in you. I believe in you. Please forgive me any hurt that I may have caused you in the past. Adieu.

Affectionately,
Augustus von Tratten

And, in a postscript at the bottom of the page, was the contact person and code word:

Father Mayer at Klosterneuburg—"Eroica".

A timid knock at the door. Radok gathered the documents and shoved them back into the orange envelope. Prokop opened the door.

"All in order, Herr Huber?"

"Absolutely," Radok answered. "I'll be off now. Thanks for the use of your room."

Prokop half bowed. "At your service."

Outside, the gray day had darkened even further. There was the smell of snow in the air. It fit Radok's mood.

Mood. Much too weak a word. State, perhaps. State of shock. Of gloom. Of foreboding and helplessness.

It's not real. That was Radok's first thought. It's an elaborate hoax. Faked documents; faked signatures.

But how were the photos faked? he asked himself. It would take all of Hollywood's "extras" to stage those still photos.

Okay. So atrocities had occurred. It's total war. No kid-gloves action. Stupid, inhuman things happen in a war. Atrocities, in fact. The individual ugliness of individual sadists. It happens on both sides.

This is not an individual act of barbarity, Paganini.

Radok physically jumped at the internal voice. The General. The calm, collected tone in which he always spoke to him.

This is a well-organized, systematic plan of extermination.

Far gone, I am, Radok thought. Voices. Send me off to Steinhof soon; sipping holy water from the sterilized trough in Wagner's church, along with the other crazies. I'll be chief candidate for the state loony bin if I don't watch out.

But the voice persisted.

The documents are real. You know they are. You know your history well enough to realize that genocide is nothing new. The Turks had the Armenians, the Americans their Indians. And the Nazi canaille have the Jews. Those in power are capable of such an atrocity. You know that, as well.

Pet peeve, General, Radok answered with his own internal voice. You've never liked the Nazis.

Who likes them? Like is not what we're talking about, Paganini. Do not confuse your categories.

No Kantian bullshit, General. Not now, okay?

The straight stuff, then, Paganini? Is that how you want it?

Yes.

Straight stuff, then. Open your eyes. And your heart.

Radok suddenly had the smell of the General's talc in his nostrils; could see the old man's freckled, blue-veined hands as they wove arguments in the air. The way the old gentleman always spoke: with both his body and his mouth.

Straight stuff, the General's voice went on. *Where are all of Vienna's Jews? Almost a quarter million of them before the war. Where are they now? Gone, that's where. Gone east, young man. To die. Resettlement does not mean sending them to an inland Palestine. This is not more of the raped-Belgian-nun stories we had in the first go-round. This is hard, cold fact. You saw the pictures, the documents. Does your heart really doubt those?*

We're not talking about emotions here, General.

By damn, man, we better be. Too much double-talk in this man's Reich. Too many ways to discount morality. Follow your heart, Paganini. Your heart, not your mind. That part of you has been tainted by four years of Nazi rule. The heart does not lie.

Radok thought about that one for a moment, about the heart and its truths. And about Helga whom he thought he had loved.

Ah-ha! the General said. *Thought. That's the operative word there, Paganini. A bad set of goods, that girl. I would have told you so, had I been there at the time.*

Where were you, General? At the time?

No place for individual grudges now, Paganini. Let that one go. I failed you, I admit. But do not hold it against me with this. I turn to you now at the most important juncture of my life. Doesn't that say something?

A fat snowflake fell onto Radok's nose. Another onto his shoulder. Soon the world would be muffled by this unseasonable snowfall.

Well? the General said.

It's a hole in the ground. A great, empty hole, General. And you're an undigested bit of gravy, not Marley's ghost, Radok thought, for he like the General, was a great fan of the Englishman, Dickens. You're a figment; you're not real. I'm creating you. And I don't need this stagecraft to make my decision.

. . .

Well? Radok said, giving the General a chance for an easy comeback at him.

. . .

Radok felt resentment that the voice did not answer him. He wanted more than figments.

And he was given one. Karl Felichsohn. Karl was no figment, no voice in Radok's head. Karl was real flesh and blood, or at least had been up to six months ago. **Karl Felichsohn, with whom Radok had grown up. He** was the son of a piano-tuner down the block from their tobacco shop. Karl and he had been inseparable from Realschule through Gymnasium. They had written poetry together, dated the same girls, hiked in the mountains and woods any chance they got. They were as close as brothers, for Radok's own brother, Helmut, had been so much younger than he.

Karl Felichsohn, the dark-haired, dark-eyed, quick-witted youth who'd grown up to become a columnist for *Die Freie Presse,* Vienna's most prestigious daily paper. Karl, who'd married Sara, a childhood sweetheart of Radok's, as well. Who'd fathered three lovely children: Beatrice, Theresa, and Joseph. Karl Felichsohn, who was so much a friend to Radok that he'd risked that friendship by warning Radok off Helga. And in fact they had not been close since Radok's marriage; and in fact, Karl had been right about Helga. As he was about so many things.

No. Karl Felichsohn was not a figment. He was merely one of those who had vanished.

It had happened in increments. The rights of the Jews had been chipped away in bits and pieces, from the Nuremberg Laws through the Anschluss of Austria to the Reich in 1938, and then Kristallnacht a little over half a year later.

Radok had seen Karl the day after the Anschluss. He was one of the Viennese Jewish intellectuals whom the rabble forced to clean the streets on hands and knees. Radok, on his beat, had seen Karl, stooped over a bucket of cold, filthy water, his hair thinning on top, scrubbing at the cobbles with that same industry with which he attacked most tasks, ignoring the jeers and catcalls of the oafs all about him. Karl had looked up in time to see Radok, smiled serenely at him, and shook his head. Radok solaced himself with the thought that the head shake was meant to keep him from interfering. It would only have made it more difficult if Radok had intervened.

That's what Radok told himself, anyway. It had saved him from having to make a decision that day. It had saved him from his own weakness.

Radok of the Kripo had walked by the surly crowd as if all were right with the world.

Karl lost his journalist position that week, Radok later learned from mutual friends, and was forced to work as a porter at the West Train Station to support his family. His children were thrown out of their schools; his wife took in washing. All these things happened as if from the pages of a melodramatic novel, but this was real. This was happening in Radok's time, within earshot and view.

But Radok neither heard nor saw.

Soon the Felichsohn apartment was requisitioned and the family forced to take communal lodgings in the Second District ghetto. Karl, normally so sagacious about life, had badly misjudged the Nazis, mistaking real threats for mere bluster. By the time he had realized his folly, it was too late to emigrate: the borders were closed and his savings confiscated.

Radok heard of the family's plight on and off through the old-school-chum network. After a time, Radok was able to convince himself that Karl had brought all this down on himself by his arrogance, by the biting satires of his columns.

When the family was taken away one night last fall, Radok had felt relief. At least they'll be cared for now, he'd thought. At least they'll lead some kind of productive life in the work camps to the east that people are beginning to talk about.

Again, these thoughts had made Radok feel better; relieved his guilt by laying it at Karl's door.

But now it was no longer possible to lie to himself about Karl's destiny, nor that of his lovely family. They were all headed for extinction. And he, Radok, along with all the rest of Vienna, had allowed it to happen.

No. Karl was no figment. Karl Felichsohn was flesh and blood.

A quarter-million Viennese Jews like the Felichsohns were gone. Radok knew it, like everyone else in Vienna, but had managed to turn a blind eye to their departure.

But no longer.

Radok walked in the snow for the rest of the afternoon, not noticing his wet feet, or the cold that was biting into him like jagged metal.

When he finally came to himself, he was sitting in the holy stillness of Stephansdom Cathedral in an otherwise unoccupied side pew, listening to the organist practice a

Bach fugue. Radok had no idea how he had got there. He knew only one thing: he had a mission. The General's mission. His mission, now.

Somehow the Allies had to be apprised early enough of this coming atrocity that they would have time to react. From his work in civil defense, Radok knew that the Allies had no bombers that could reach a camp in Poland, but perhaps they could organize a partisan raid or find volunteers for a one-way mission. A suicide mission. These would take time to authorize and organize. A week, the General said in his letter. Which left Radok with only nine days to get the Final Solution documents to the Allies.

No more Inspektorat today. Radok left the cathedral, threading his way through the pedestrians of the First District on his way to Schottentor, where he caught a tram for Nussdorf. First stage of his pilgrimage to the abbey of Klosterneuburg and the mysterious Father Mayer.

Code word: Eroica.

Chapter Eight

A crack of light showed in the gloom of the enormous chapel. The confessional door was partly open. Frieda could see his hand on the small, shelf-like desk under the speaking screen. A white hand with tapering fingers. There was a delicate cobweb of blue veins on its back; the large, gold-domed SJ ring on the third finger. A book lay under the hand: he always read while waiting for confessions. Philosophy usually. Lately he'd begun the *Notebooks* of Wittgenstein; he said he felt an affinity for the man who'd worked here once as a simple gardener.

Frieda entered the confessional side and settled onto the cold wooden bench. A whispered prayer came from the other side; a rustle of pages as Father Mayer closed his book.

"It's me, Padre," Frieda said before he could assume his priestly role.

Silence from his side.

Finally: "I thought I made it clear . . ."

"I had to come," she said. "Kripo paid me a visit this morning."

"Jesus, Mary, and Joseph," he whispered. "And you brought them here!"

"I made sure I wasn't followed," she said.

And she had: a casual stroll down Kaerntnerstrasse; a duck into Ludmueller's Fur Shop and out the back door to the taxi stand on Neuer Markt. Then the damnably expensive taxi ride all the way out to Klosterneuburg, but it was safer than transferring to public transport. And nobody had followed her. She was sure of that. That was the strange thing. Nobody even posted at her apartment.

"You can't be sure you weren't followed. They're professionals. When I give an order, I expect it to be obeyed."

There was fear in his voice. She ignored his remarks.

"They found Jan's program. The one I autographed."

74

"It's no sin to seek autographs. Well, venal perhaps, but in the new liturgy . . ."

"Padre . . ."

"All right. Sorry. Change of hats."

She heard him shift in his seat.

"So they were curious about the program. Quite rightly so. Jan was hardly your average music-lover." His voice sounded calmer now.

Frieda told him about the Inspektor who'd come to visit her; how she was sure he was the very one the Czech had warned was trailing him. Even down to the squeaky shoe.

"A strange man," she said finally. "Not very much like a cop at all." In fact, she'd found the man rather sympathetic. He had the kindest, saddest gray eyes she'd ever seen.

"So," Padre said. "You think he accepted your explanation?"

"I don't know. But I'm certain there was nobody outside my apartment building when I left. Surely they would have left a guard if they suspected. . . ."

"Perhaps." Drumming a finger on the shelf on the other side of the screen from her. "And that's why you came? To warn me of this man who's been following Cezak?"

"I began to think," she said. "If he traced the program to me, why couldn't he have traced Jan to you? Lord knows how long he was trailing Jan before he spotted him."

"Jan Cezak was an expert in such things," the Padre said with the same assurance in his voice that he used in the pulpit on Sundays.

"Yes," she said. "But even experts can get caught off guard. What if the cop followed Jan here on his meetings with you? What if the Inspektor comes snooping around here?"

"Merest coincidence," he said. "To we who know the facts, such coincidences of course seem all too clear. To us, such things must perforce point to a connection, a tie. Because we know there was one. But think of it from the point of view of this Inspektor. He knows very little, yet is brimming over with suspicion. Who is to say that Cezak was not both a music-lover and a good Catholic?"

A pause, such as he used in his sermons. It always worked to bring a bored congregation back to attention.

"No," he said suddenly with real force. "It is *our* connection, Frieda, that must be kept secret from the authorities. Were it known, were they to trace you to me as well . . . that would be stretching coincidence much too far for credulity."

She realized, now that he'd explained the situation, just how irresponsible she'd been in coming here. It hadn't even really been to impart the information of the snooping Kripo Inspektor. His visit had simply panicked her. She'd come to the Padre not to warn him, but for solace, for the peace that a priest can impart. And by so doing, she had jeopardized him and the entire cell. She was struck with the same sad helplessness that had overcome her last night at word of Cezak's death. She began to cry and felt a complete fool for doing so.

"Please," Padre said. "No tears."

But they were beyond controlling.

"I came to see you," she sighed. "I needed to see somebody."

"We'll go to the vestry. Dry your tears first."

The organist was practicing now and filling the church with rich, round tones. Frieda put a linen handkerchief to her eyes. The Padre was already making his way down the side aisle toward the vestry when she got out of the confessional. In his long gown, with his feet hidden, he seemed to be floating over the stone floor. A big man and round as a pear, but he moved with considerable grace. Just seeing Padre gave her heart once again. She breathed in the incense-laden air deeply and followed, her heels clacking loudly on the stone. She tried to tiptoe along to muffle the sound. A crescendo from the organ. Frieda was beginning to feel whole again. The very atmosphere of the church gave her strength. Somehow they would work things out; she could feel again, see possibilities.

The church was virtually empty at midday and the shadowed naves were not gloomy to Frieda, but rather were intimate, beckoning. She had almost reached the vestry door through which the Padre had disappeared when she heard the massive front portal open; footsteps on the flagstones.

Her hand at the door of the vestry, she turned to see

who had entered the church. The newcomer was brightly lit, standing in a pool of light from one of the clear side windows. No mistaking it, but she could hardly believe her eyes for a moment. Then the Inspektor moved again, and along with the clacking of leather on flagstone came the familiar squeak.

She lunged into the vestry before he could spot her, panting with fear.

"He's here! Christ! He couldn't have traced me!"

Padre was suddenly calm, ready for action. He was the sort of vital man for whom inaction is the only sin. In the confessional he had been nervous because the situation demanded second-guessing; a passive approach. Frieda could almost sense a joy in him now that pure, raw action was required.

"There'll be more outside, as well," he said.

From the drawer of a battered, well-used desk, he brought out an ugly little pistol.

"We know their questioning techniques," he said. "Even if there is nothing to tell, they will continue. It is their way."

He checked the gun for bullets. This was happening too quickly for Frieda.

"You're young, that's the worst of it," he went on, hefting the gun for balance. "I'm not much of a shot, unfortunately. This isn't really in my line. I suppose I shall have to try and make them shoot me."

Her heart was pounding wildly in her chest; she felt as if she were going to be sick.

"There's no real choice, you know." He shook his head. His gun arm hung limply at his side. "But I've got to allow that for you. Free will, that is. It's about all that separates us from them, no?"

She did not want to die; that was the only thing she knew for certain.

"Are you asking me if I want you to shoot me?" she said.

Suddenly Padre looked quite sheepish; his bravado was sapped.

"Yes . . . I suppose I am."

"Shoot me rather than have me taken in for questioning?"

He nodded: a guilty little boy.

"But I don't know anything. Jan was my only contact besides you."

"But they don't know that."

Both of them were quiet for a moment. It seemed an eternity. There was hardly the luxury of time for such a decision.

"If I have the choice," she said, "I'll try to escape."

A knock at the vestry door. They exchanged looks: it's too late after all, their looks told one another. Father Mayer raised the gun.

"Father Mayer." Another knock. It was Brother Thomas, the novitiate verger. His high, unmistakable voice, like a girl's.

"Yes." Padre held the gun straight to Frieda's temple now, not taking his eyes off hers.

"You have someone awaiting you in the confessional, Father Mayer. A parishioner."

Padre looked at the door, then to the gun. He smiled beatifically and shrugged.

"So be it," he said.

"It's a trick," Frieda said.

"Perhaps. Perhaps not. But you're right. Life is the only choice."

He laid the gun down on top of the desk.

"I'll be back in a moment." And he was out the door before she could say good-bye.

Frieda picked up the gun now, tucking it into her handbag. Opening the door a crack, she saw no one else in the church. The Inspektor was nowhere in sight, nor were there police or SS storming the door. Nothing to arouse suspicion. Perhaps it was as she had said: that the Inspektor was here simply because he had traced Jan's visits to the abbey and to Father Mayer.

She hoped it was so, and immediately despised herself for looking for such an easy way out. She'd hoped her father really hadn't gone sky-diving that day out of his office window; had hoped that Wolf somehow had eluded the Gestapo roundup four years ago. To hope was something you did if you were either too dumb or too lazy to confront life on its terms.

She could leave now; just walk out of the church and hope for the best. And there it was again: hope. She could walk out of the church with her hand around the butt of Father Mayer's pistol. Or she could wait and see what happened to the Padre . . . with her hand around the butt of the pistol.

This was her doing. No way around it. The cop had caught her with her defenses down. He'd disarmed her with the way he'd walked into her flat and her life as if he knew both instinctively, intimately. He'd sat without waiting to be asked, but it had been strangely non-threatening. It was his eyes: damn his eyes.

Frieda had not allowed a man to get to her since Wolf, but this one had seemed different from the others who had come sniffing around in the past four years. He seemed so out of step with his job, his office. Bumbling. A great bumbling bear. The kind of man a woman wanted to cuddle one moment and mother the next.

She shut the vestry door again, moving back toward the desk, trying to put her thoughts together. Trying to still the confusion in her mind. She knew what Wolf would say about such confusion: her years in the U.S.A. had done this to her; made her soft. The U.S.A., where they'd eradicated evil along with sadness. America the decadent. The place where there was no time for pain, only for happiness. That's what Wolf would say. And he'd go on to tell her that it took the life of Europe to make one recognize the fact of evil in the world; it took the cynicism of the Old World to force one to confront the true nature of man.

The worst of it was, Wolf would be right. As usual. She had sympathized with the Inspektor too much and had therefore underestimated him.

Frieda was still sure there had not been a tail on her as she came to the abbey today. Positive. It was the one thing in this silly espionage game that she was any good at: recognizing and shaking tails. But it was too late now for protests. The Padre was out there, possibly paying for her stupidity.

The door burst open. She had the gun halfway drawn as the Padre rushed in.

"Leave. Quickly."

"What is it?" she said. "Are the police here?"

A shake of his head. "No. It's complicated, most severely so. The man—I assume he is the one you saw, for he will not yet identify himself—this man says that he has some papers he believes were meant for me."

"They know." She thought quickly. "But why not just take us in? Unless . . ."

"Exactly, my dear. Unless perhaps, just perhaps, he is telling the truth. He mentions a General von Tratten. I assume that was Jan's contact?"

"I don't know." Frieda shrugged her shoulders.

Jan had confided the secret to no one. Of course she knew the von Tratten name. Who in Vienna did not? She had even seen the General and his wife at the Opera Ball last year; also at a fund-raiser for war orphans held last spring.

"It's possible," she said. She remembered the General. Ramrod-straight and a long way from frail, in freshly laundered clothes. There had been a conversation at the Ball, something a ministry assistant had said about this being a war for which the damned Jews would pay. The General had walked away without comment. But she thought she knew how he felt about such words.

"What else?" she said.

"Leave, child. I've stalled him. Get out now so that he does not see you. I'll keep him in the confessional. . . ."

"What else?"

"He used the code word, Eroica. That was his introduction. He said the General died last night trying to get some very important papers to Jan Cezak, and he seemed to know all about the organization. Now he has these papers. The General left them to him in his will. He wants to know our plans for the documents before he turns them over to us."

"It's a trap," Frieda said. "He's trying to net as many of us as possible. Don't let him fool you." Like he did me, she thought.

"It may be a trap," Padre said. "Or it may be one last chance."

"But why would General von Tratten give a Kripo Inspektor the papers? It makes no sense."

"Our man says little. I asked the same question. He laughed and said he served the General once."

"A soldier?" She thought about this for a moment. "No, it's impossible that he served with the General. Von Tratten was retired long ago. This Inspektor is too young."

"I'm only repeating what he says. Now leave."

"What are you going to do?"

"Play dumb." He laughed. "An easy act for me. Until we know something more about our friend. His name. What was it again?"

She looked in her purse, found the card he'd given her this morning. Radok. Inspektor Gunther Radok. She handed the Padre the card and he perused it as if it were a daily missal.

"So," he said, looking up from the card. "Good-bye. Give me a minute to settle in again with our Herr Radok, then leave." He began ushering her to the door.

"I shall contact you in the usual manner," he said.

He hugged her, an act of extreme intimacy for the Padre. His round belly felt good against her. It was what she'd needed all along but had been too ashamed to ask for: the simple gift of physical comforting.

"And Frieda . . ." He took the half-concealed pistol from her. "Leave this here. You're an artist, not a heroine. Remember? Go back to your piano for the time being."

He moved along the tiled floor, back toward the confessional, his cassock swinging to and fro about his feet. She counted to two hundred, forcing herself to be patient, to wait until Padre had the Inspektor's attention. Then she left the vestry door along the west aisle, opposite the confessional. Outside, no one was waiting. Snow still fell, silently, muffling the immense cobbled courtyard of the abbey.

She took three different cabs there. The first one from Klosterneuburg took her to the First District at Schottentor. Then another from that point around the Ring to the Konzerthaus, where her afternoon ritual when not on tour was to practice on the Bechstein. There would be no practice today, however, for Frieda went out the back entrance and found a third taxi to take her to Hietzing. Soon I'll have to give piano lessons again just to pay for the taxi fares, she thought. That she had some bit of irony left in her, something other than fear, was a good sign. Irony was her defense.

She had to do something; not just wait for Padre's telephone call. She felt responsible for all of this; it was up to her to try to do something to resolve it. Perhaps it was because of her that this Radok had found his way to

Klosterneuburg, though she still found it hard to believe
he'd trailed her there. It was, however, inconsequential
how he had gotten there, for there he was. The only
thing she could think of doing was to visit the von Tratten
villa and try to find out if Radok was somehow known
there. If his story of receiving the papers from the General as some sort of legacy was true, then he must have
something to do with the family.

She remembered that the von Trattens lived in Hietzing;
a quick look at a telephone directory at the Konzerthaus
was sufficient to give her the address. She had the taxi
drop her off at Trautmannsdorfgasse and walked to
Gloriettegasse. All these were old habits now, partly the
result of Wolf's training, partly that of Jan Cezak. For all
the good it had done either of them . . .

Frieda rang the bell at the imposing villa and a maid
with a trace of moustache answered the door. Was it
suspicion or irritation that registered on the maid's face
when she asked for Frau von Tratten? Whichever, the
woman led her up the stairs to a dark, cold anteroom,
filled with all sorts of chests and wardrobes, most of
which seemed out of place there. She noticed a row of
small framed pictures lining the walls of the hallway; one
toward the end was askew and Frieda was tempted to go
to it and right it. Just then, however, the maid returned
to lead her in to the Frau.

Frau von Tratten wore elegant widow's weeds and sat
at a desk littered with letters and telegrams.

She did not seem surprised to see Frieda, and even
remembered the few times they had met without having
her memory prodded.

"There is so much to do, you know." Gesturing at the
messages she must respond to. "You'll have some coffee?"

Frieda marveled at the woman: playing the polite host-
ess in the midst of personal tragedy.

"No. Please," Frieda said. "I'm sorry to intrude at a
moment such as this. I was . . . was simply so overcome
with shock at the news of your husband's death that I
wanted to personally say . . ."

Frau von Tratten nodded, waiting patiently for Frieda
to continue with her condolences. Frieda felt a moment
of panic, but then plunged ahead.

"I'm just terribly sorry for you. That's all. I realize that we're virtually strangers, but the few times I met you and your husband I was very impressed. You'll have to forgive me. I guess it's my American manners at work again."

"Quite all right, my dear. It seems that most of my close friends are too tactful by far. They're wary of interfering, you know." A dry laugh, almost a cackle.

Frieda felt truly sorry that she had come, but had to push on with the subterfuge. There were no easy transitions, and to linger on with small talk would be unconscionably cruel.

"Strange," Frieda said, "but I had a visit this morning from a friend of yours. Most coincidental. A Herr Radok. Gunther Radok."

The Frau looked at Frieda closely now, taking her mind away from the pile of papers awaiting her attention.

"So you know Paga—I mean, Gunther?"

"A professional call. Something about a program of mine which was in someone else's possession. Quite confusing. But, you do know him, then? Inspektor Radok, I mean?"

"Oh, very well. He and his family served here for years."

So, Frieda thought, that's how he served the General. In the most literal sense.

"Well then." Frieda looked at her wristwatch. "I mustn't be keeping you. I just had to convey my condolences personally. I remember the General so well from our few brief meetings. He seemed a wonderful man."

Frau von Tratten sighed. "Yes. He was. Quite wonderful. And it was very kind of you to pay your respects, Fräulein Lassen. Very kind indeed."

She rose, full of a quiet dignity that Frieda admired and that made her feel doubly squalid for her cheap ruse. Yet she had had to find out about Radok. At least now she knew that part of his story was true.

Frau von Tratten held out her hand. Frieda grasped it and looked the old lady in the eyes.

"May I ask you something?" Frau von Tratten said.

"Of course."

"How was it you came to hear of the General's . . . of Augustus' death? It hasn't been in the papers yet, you know. Was it Paga—I mean, Gunther? Did he mention it to you?"

Frieda felt herself go red. This was something she

hadn't considered. There were too many things she'd never considered.

"Yes," she said. Her voice quavered with the lie. "I believe he did mention it. Sorry. Have I made another faux pas? Is it being kept quiet?"

Frau von Tratten smiled with tight lips and shook Frieda's hand once again.

"No. Not really. It was good of you to come, Fräulein."

The same maid let Frieda out. The snow had stopped now and the ploughs were out. The world was crisp and white for the time being.

She headed toward the center of the village to look for another taxi. At least she had confirmed part of the Inspektor's story. But what to do now with the information? And had she compromised herself even further by this visit? It seemed she could do nothing right. How nice it would be just to go back to her piano, as the Padre had advised. But she knew she couldn't. She knew that now she would have to see this thing through. It had always been so for her. She brought the same determination and stubbornness to all tasks: from learning to ride a bike to learning to play the piano to learning to become a spy. She must be the best in whatever it was she did.

Lost in her thoughts, she did not notice the tall, thin man in the rather too elegantly cut overcoat approaching. She almost walked straight into him, and he had to step off the sidewalk into the snow to avoid her.

"Oh, I am sorry," she said. "I was daydreaming."

"Quite all right, Fräulein." He tipped his fedora at her. "Fine day for winter dreams."

She smiled. "Yes. Well . . . sorry."

She did not look back as she moved quickly down the street; did not see him as he went to the Villa von Tratten and rang the bell; did not consciously notice the six-wheeled Mercedes waiting for him at the curb, the red-nosed driver staring at her rather lasciviously.

Chapter Nine

The sidewalk had not been cleared of snow; Krahl lost his footing just out of the car, almost falling. Glancing down at the treacherous patch of ice beneath the snow as if it were enemy territory, he thought of the damned lazy street workers who had allowed such a thing.

Everything going to hell lately. Not Krahl, however.

He noticed a tall, strikingly attractive blond woman walking on the sidewalk toward him. She seemed to be oblivious to him, walking along the sidewalk as if she owned it all. One of those damn rich snob bitches, he thought. No consideration for others, even when they are dressed in the best that Knieze of Graben can provide in the way of tailoring. The world existed simply to accommodate her. At the last instant he was forced to step into the snow-filled gutter to avoid colliding with her. Only then did she seem to see him. To recognize his existence. A belated apology.

"Oh, I am sorry," the young woman said. "I was daydreaming."

He tipped his hat to her.

"Quite all right, Fräulein. Fine day for winter dreams," he said.

Rather be giving her a discreet investigation at Morzin Platz, he thought. But this was no time to allow rancor to prevail. The young woman passed and Krahl continued to the von Trattens'. This will be quite a visit, he told himself. He'd begin alone, of course. In ten minutes the others would arrive and the serious questioning would begin.

He reached the door, a smile on his face. Instincts. Hunches. By damn, this time he'd made the scoop. . . .

It had started when he came back from the morgue this morning. There had been the message from Hartmann,

85

the cup of coffee, and then to the Activity Reports. There was good reason he never entrusted these to the likes of his adjutant, young Muellhausen. Only he, Krahl, had all the information ready to hand; all the cross-references tucked neatly into his skull. For the others it was a job; for Krahl it was passion. Krahl had a photographic memory and a mind that worked like one of those cybernetic machines they were said to be working on in Stuttgart. Machines as big as a house which stored, cross-referenced, and indexed hundreds of thousands of pieces of information.

Well, Krahl thought, I have my own . . . what was it they called those infernal things? Computers?

Yes, Krahl had his own computer at work right upstairs in his noodle. It was abetted by the cross-referencing system in the file boxes in his office.

This morning, however, it had been more than his genius at work, more than what the file boxes could provide. It had been more than simply his devotion and ambition could have conjured up alone. There had been that magic element, the fifth actor in every good scene: Lady Luck. Oh, she had smiled on him this morning, all right. Everything was coming together, finally, for Arthur Krahl.

It was in the second of the Activity Reports that he received daily from Berlin. On page three of the one dated 12 March, 1942, was General von Tratten's name!

The word "Vienna" had caught his eye earlier in the paragraph. Krahl routinely scanned such reports for information pertinent to his station. So coming upon the word Vienna had slowed his eye down. He went back a few paragraphs to the beginning of this particular report, headed: "Proceedings: Colonel Niedermayer."

A controlled man, Krahl was accustomed to keeping his spirits in check. He would examine this report from the very beginning, even after having seen the General's name. A thing had to be done in its proper sequence or not at all. No jumping to conclusions. Discipline. Without it we were only animals.

Reading the report, Krahl discovered that this Niedermayer under investigation was a mid-level Abwehr officer whom the Berlin Gestapo had long suspected of anti-Hitler sentiments, perhaps even of participating in what was becoming known in SD intelligence circles as the "Black Orchestra," a league of Wehrmacht officers who were plotting against Hitler. Several attempted assassinations had already been foiled, but still Berlin Gestapo was no closer to breaking this group of military terrorists than they had been three years earlier when such a conspiracy was first uncovered.

All this Krahl knew already, and that Abwehr, the military intelligence unit, and its chief, Admiral Canaris, were some of the worst traitors in the Reich. Even the name Niedermayer Krahl knew. Lodged in his mental filing system between Neumann and Niedrich.

Turning back to the report, Krahl now learned that Berlin Station had tired of quietly watching suspected members of the Black Orchestra. They had pulled Niedermayer, thinking that he might be the weak link. What they had come up with was so unexpected as to convince the interrogators it was a red herring. They had persisted in the interview, disregarding Niedermayer's startling revelation. Indeed, so diligent had Berlin Station been that Niedermayer succumbed to "heart attack" some forty-eight hours after arrest.

What this revelation had been—completely overlooked by Berlin Station, of course—was an allusion to the theft of top-secret documents detailing the organization of what Niedermayer had called "the Final Solution" of the Jewish problem. Documents enough to sink the Reich, if disclosed to the Allies. The detailed plan for the destruction of all the Jews of Europe. If made public, it would turn the world against the Reich, weaken the resolve of Germany's allies, and perhaps cause the people of the Reich itself to rise up against their own leaders. Motive: the old-time soldier class again at work trying to "save" Germany from the upstart Nazis.

Krahl stopped reading for a time. He pushed himself back from the desk and went to the window overlooking Johannesgasse. It was dark outside at midday. Dark and damp. No rain, but the sky was low. Perhaps there would be snow. The day fitted Krahl's mood: solemn.

Final Solution. He'd heard rumors of Hitler's plan; knew by the roundup lists that the Jews were being evacuated from at least his section of the Ostmark. Krahl had no opinions one way or another about this: just one more duty to perform; more figures to compile.

Yes, he imagined there really was a—what did Niedermayer call it?—a Final Solution occurring. And quite possibly there were such documents as the Colonel referred to. After all, it would be quite a large operation. Eliminating several millions of people: this could hardly be done with a simple wave of the hand. Transportation would have to be arranged, as well as centers for such special treatment. An awe-inspiring project. But that was the magnificent thing about Hitler's Reich: no project was so immense that it couldn't be encompassed by the German sense of enterprise and ingenuity. Such a project was obviously of a magnitude too large for the dolts at Berlin Station even to fathom.

Krahl returned to the desk and scanned the report, finishing the final paragraph:

"Subject persisted with this fantastic story and when pressed closer about fellow collaborators in the military, or about planned assassination attempts on the Fuehrer, he simply laughed and said all else was unnecessary; that "the mission had already been accomplished." In the event, he had no further information to offer investigators. Questioning continued until 2:03 A.M. of the second day, at which time subject suffered an embolism and expired. [Physical report available on request.]

"Though Berlin Gestapo gives little credence to Niedermayer's tale, it is thought that Colonel Niedermayer was shielding others in the Black Orchestra circle. Therefore, attached please find a detailed list of personages with whom Colonel Niedermayer has lately been in contact."

It was in this section of the report that Krahl had seen the references to both Vienna and General von Tratten. The General had been in Berlin a little over a week earlier and had spent the day with Colonel Niedermayer. It appeared from this surveillance report that von Tratten's only business in Berlin had been this visit to Niedermayer, a former comrade-in-arms from World War One. They lunched at the Berlin Carlton, not two tables away from Goering and company! A walk in the Tiergarten and then the evening sleeper back to Vienna for the General. At one point, von Tratten and Niedermayer had been alone in the Colonel's quarters for an hour or more.

Enough time, Krahl thought. More than enough for the General to secret documents on his person. The damning evidence of the Final Solution. Documents both men had been prepared to die for. By damn, things were developing nicely. . . .

Thus, the visit to Hietzing. Krahl felt almost like whistling, save that no tune came to mind. A singularly unmusical man, his cultural passions were the books and art works that comprised his special collection. Perhaps he'd reward himself with an uninterrupted hour in his private collection this evening. But for now, there was work to do.

He rang the bell of the von Tratten villa just as another staff car pulled up to the curb. Okay. Early, but okay. Five rather burly characters in black tunics, jodhpurs, and jackboots poured out of the car. Sergeant Gerstl, a no-nonsense sort, was in charge. Krahl liked the sergeant. Well, perhaps "like" was too strong a word. But he knew he could count on the sergeant to be thorough and obsequious. He usually used Gerstl on such delicate searches, for he was as competent a man in his field as Hartmann was in his. He'd been an insurance adjuster before the war. Thorough man. He knew all the nooks and crannies where one might tuck the odd document away.

The five men gave Krahl a communal Hitler salute, which he returned rather deferentially, arm bent at the elbow, as he'd seen Hitler himself do in the newsreels. The men with Gerstl brought along the heavy odor of beer. So typical, Krahl thought. Cretins.

The door to the villa opened finally and Krahl turned to see a small dark woman in a blue uniform in the open doorway. She wore a worried expression at the sight of the party awaiting her. Who wouldn't? Krahl thought.

He stated his rank, name, and business and then brushed past the infernal woman, who looked as if she were trying to concoct some silly story to disallow them entrance. He went through the garage to the park in back of the villa. So predictable: a rolling expanse of lawn gloriously white under the fresh snow, stretching back over a hundred meters to a gazebo-like tea house cresting a little hill.

Krahl surveyed the scene: the pruned fruit trees and mounds of pine boughs mulching tied-down roses. These

would be tea roses, of course; long-stemmed and in a
panoply of hues, to keep the inevitable Lobmayr crystal
vases stocked in the summer months. Such people were
sure to have these things: Krahl was an expert on the
accoutrements of wealth and prestige. He'd made a study
of it in every elegant fashion and architecture magazine
he could lay his hands on. Krahl was an armchair traveler
in the realms of the aristocracy; he knew all the whats
and hows of it, but not the why. And as the why continued to elude him, he began to sense that his study was
incomplete; that he was only mimicking this life he wanted
so much to be a part of. And this sense made him mean
and dangerous.

Memories of that fool von Tratten frustrating his attempts to join the Jockey Club were also very close to
the surface for Krahl. And all of this came rushing into
Krahl's consciousness when he was shown in to see Frau
von Tratten. She was the sort of woman he detested:
cool, arrogant, distant. She gave nothing away from behind her studied facade when he introduced himself. He felt
a cold contempt from her as she eyed the men who had
followed him into the sitting room. He vowed that before
this was over he would elicit emotion from this woman.

Of course she showed no surprise when he requested
to see her husband's papers. In fact she was quite helpful, leading him to the rolltop desk where they were
kept, not even bothering to ask what exactly he was
looking for. After showing Krahl and his men to the desk
she quietly left them to their work, but with the sort of
air that let Krahl know what she thought of him, as if one
did not dirty one's lily-white hands with such common
folk as he.

The key was in the desk lock.

"Kick it in," he ordered Gerstl.

The sergeant stared at him for a moment as if he had
not heard him.

"But the key's . . ."

"I don't care if there are ten keys. Kick it in! Are you
hard of hearing, man?"

An hour later the villa had been torn apart: rugs lifted,
floorboards and walls sounded for hollowness, entire book-
cases turned out, and books spreadeagled everywhere.
The kitchen had received a thorough going-over, as well.

Everything from flour canisters to potatoes in the larder had been dumped out and examined. Still Krahl had found nothing. If General von Tratten had ever had the Final Solution papers—if such things existed at all—in his possession, obviously he had already handed them over to some courier. But, Krahl reasoned, wasn't that what the deaths of von Tratten and Cezak were all about? And according to the reports there were no papers on either body. So that meant that the General had secured the papers elsewhere.

Sergeant Gerstl uncoverd the lead to that certain "elsewhere." In a small, leather-covered pocket notebook in the rolltop desk, he came across the name of Herr Prokop of the Schottentor branch of the Creditanstalt Bankverein.

"He's in charge of safe-deposit boxes," Gerstl said matter-of-factly. "We go back to my insurance days. A trustworthy sort of man, Herr Prokop."

"The sort you might entrust with secret documents?" Krahl said.

Gerstl nodded.

Frau von Tratten stood at the door to her bedroom and watched them as they prepared to leave. Krahl could see the debris of linen and chemises scattering the floor in back of her where the sergeant's men had been most diligent in their searches. He searched her face for a trace of emotion, but there was nothing there: a mask of politesse.

"*Auf wiedersehen*, gentlemen," she said as they were leaving. "Perhaps you will shut the front door behind you."

Oh yes, Krahl thought. I'm going to love watching that woman crawl. Before this is over . . .

Prokop's protests did not last long. Krahl had only to mention Dachau and the bank director suddenly regained his memory of the von Tratten safe-deposit box.

Krahl sat at the large mahogany conference table and examined the contents of the box that the director now set in front of him. There were deeds to lands in the western counties, trust certificates, some family heirlooms, the charter ennobling the Tyrolean branch of the family in the late seventeenth century, and a diamond tiara worth enough to buy Krahl two villas and all the Lobmayr crystal vases he could ever wish for. There were also some medals from the first war, among which were the Iron Cross and the Kaiser Star.

Krahl held the diamond tiara in his hand for a moment. It was heavy with the weight of wealth. Krahl liked the feel of it and considered taking it away with him on some pretext. But what pretext? Soon it would be his by right, rather than by desire. Soon, if his judgment proved right in this case, he would be the darling of the Reich. No gifts would be too large for him, no honors too high. He placed the glittering piece of jewelry back in its purple satin bag and then set it back in the deposit box. Thievery was not his way. No need for it. So close now. He could smell the sweetness of success in his very nostrils.

"Is this all?" Krahl said, his thoughts still very much on the diamond tiara.

Prokop fidgeted; Krahl looked up. It was obvious the man was hiding something.

"I can arrange transport for you this afternoon," Krahl said. "You'll be doing the books at Dachau by breakfast tomorrow."

"It wasn't my fault!" Prokop suddenly protested. "He had a slip of paper signed by von Tratten himself."

"Who?" Krahl asked.

"His name was Huber. He took the papers the General stored here last week. I don't know any more about him."

"You're lying." Krahl enjoyed watching the man squirm. "What else?"

Prokop began sweating; his forehead glistened with it.

"Out with it, man!" Krahl ordered.

"I think Huber was an alias. It was like he picked the name out of a hat. You know?"

Krahl nodded. "And . . ." he prompted.

"I think he was a police officer," Prokop said.

"Why?"

"He had the demeanor. You work in my job long enough and you get a sense for these things. Besides . . ." Prokop wiped the sweat from his forehead with a small white hand. "It's logical. A man his age, why isn't he in the service? He had no obvious physical disabilities. It doesn't make sense otherwise."

Krahl kept the director long enough to get a full description of the man who'd taken the von Tratten documents. It rang no bells with Lieutenant Colonel Krahl.

"You may go now," Krahl said finally.

Prokop did not wait for more. He left Krahl alone with the booty.

Krahl again removed the tiara from its bag and looked around the room guiltily. He lifted it slowly and looked at the kaleidoscope of lights the facets made on his hand, then set it atop his blond head. He closed his eyes for a delicious moment and breathed deeply.

Once back at headquarters, Krahl sent for the entire file on the Cezak case. There had to be a clue to the mysterious "Huber" somewhere. Look for the obvious, he told himself. Someone mentioned in the reports, perhaps.

Krahl had the germ of an idea in his head: it was becoming obvious to him that von Tratten had taken the Final Solution papers from his old friend Niedermayer in Berlin. And there could be only one reason to take these damning documents: to get them out of the Reich to the Allies. To embarrass Hitler. But then von Tratten would have run into a problem, Krahl reasoned: he couldn't very well take the documents out of the Reich himself. For that he would have needed help. Perhaps the resistance, then. A resistance courier to Switzerland.

It was obvious once he had thought it. Why else would the General have shot himself rather than be apprehended? What if Herr Jan Cezak had been more than he appeared to be? What if he were not simply a black marketeer, but a courier for the resistance as well?

That had to be it.

Krahl studied the Cezak file for a moment. It was several inches thick. Whoever had prepared this was thorough. Too thorough for Krahl at the moment. He had no desire to wade through the papers now. Instead he decided to call in the officer in charge of the case, to question him personally. He'd find the missing link by talking with this man. Surely there was some movement of Cezak's that would lead Krahl to the person who had taken the documents from the bank this morning; that would help to reveal this shadowy figure Huber.

At first Krahl was disappointed by his call to Kripo headquarters. His adjutant reported that the officer in charge of the Cezak case was not at the Inspektorat. He had not been back since coming in late this morning, it appeared. No one there knew where he was.

Irritating, Krahl thought, after Muellhausen related the news to him. But more than that. Suspicious, as well. What was this Inspektor doing running rogue around Vienna? Herr Prokop's words came back to Krahl: a cop. Prokop thought Huber was a cop. Who else healthy-looking would be out of uniform?

Krahl jabbed a finger onto the intercom button and it crackled to life.

"Muellhausen. I want the file on this Kripo man. The one in charge of the Cezak case."

Twenty minutes later the file lay on Krahl's rosewood desk, the officer's picture looking up at him from amidst forms and letters of recommendation. Two minutes later Krahl had what he was looking for: the connection to von Tratten.

"Family in service to Augustus von Tratten," one of the forms, a curriculum vitae, read.

Krahl made sure: he had Muellhausen pick up Prokop for a photo identification. Another twenty minutes and it was verified.

Inspektor Gunther Radok was Huber. Inspektor Radok presumably had the Final Solution documents in his hands.

Krahl smiled as he surveyed his desk, littered with papers and photos. It's all so simple, he thought; simple when one thinks clearly and logically. Radok was obviously the General's backup in case something went wrong with the Cezak meeting. I'll have this case wrapped up before daybreak tomorrow.

Perhaps there were further clues to be gleaned from the file on his desk, but for now Krahl got on the phone to Morzin Platz. Inspektor Gunther Radok had a lot to answer for; he should be paid a visit immediately. The most logical place to start looking for the man would be at his apartment.

Oak leaves will look rather well on me, he thought.

Chapter Ten

"Yes," Radok said. "Sure, I understand."

The mouthpiece of the phone breathed back at him: a rank, salty taste. Was it his own breath or that of the previous owner? There was a faint whiff of perfume from it, too. Who did he know who wore perfume?

". . . and then I suddenly feel all lost, you know? Alone. Little Helmut is no comfort then. You know those times, Gunther?"

He did, but there was little consolation he could give his sister-in-law Irene. She was waiting silently on the other end of the connection amid the crack and fizzle of white noise.

All Radok could think of was getting the poor woman off the phone so Father Mayer could contact him as promised.

"Gunther? Are you still there?"

"Yes. Still here."

"Talk to me. I need to hear you. You're the only one I can talk to."

The rattle of the outside bell saved him.

"Look, I'll call back, Irene. There's someone at the door."

"Promise."

"Of course. Just be a minute."

He went to the window: nobody to be seen out it. Just a slushy world now that the snow had stopped. Nobody was expected. He glanced over at the orange envelope on the baroque table. A hot flash of fear burned in his guts.

As an insider Radok knew how incompetent the cops were, but the odds were on their side. Radok knew it was only rotten luck that the General had bought it along with Cezak. Radok had mounted the operation himself; he knew better than anyone else that Cezak's file read black marketeer. Period. No one else could know yet that Cezak had been involved with the resistance, that he was acting as a courier when netted, and that the General's presence at the scene had been anything more than damn bad luck.

But paranoia exists in a world constructed by paranoids, he thought as he checked out the street below. What if whoever had given the General the papers in the first place had been blown? What if this mysterious person had been pulled in and blabbed his damn fool head off, and now the leak had been discovered? Traced even to Vienna? It was not much of a leap from von Tratten to Radok. He'd left his trail all over Vienna, not half of it being in the fucking offices of the Creditanstalt Bankverein downtown this morning. Even though he'd used an alias, Radok still knew the bank director could give a physical description of him. What if, what if . . . ?

What if the priest in Klosterneuburg is a double? A Gestapo plant. It had been known to happen before. And suddenly a thought came fully realized into Radok's mind, something that had only been a hazy association before: Cezak *was* connected to Father Mayer. Radok himself had tailed Cezak to the abbey at Klosterneuburg several times during the past month. And it was all in the reports. Anybody reading those might make the connection much faster than Radok had.

Why, indeed, didn't you make the connection before? he asked himself. Slow on the uptake, you are, and this is no game for the slow ones.

Another jangle of the bell. Lights are on up here, he thought. Anybody with sense could figure I'm at home.

He rang the main-door release without going down to see who it was. Rang the release like a happy sinner shouldering his way to the front of the line to hell. There was no hiding place here. No need for it. He retrieved the envelope from off the table and shoved it into the back of his waistband. The Walther came out of its shoulder holster and into his right hand, safety off. There would be no silent departures for him—and he was amazed at how far he was taking this paranoid delusion. SS doesn't ring the bell, he reminded himself; Gestapo doesn't ask "Please may we come in to talk with you?"

Moments of lucidity were short, however. No silent departures for him. They would have to take him blazing away. And he'd take a fair number of the bastards with him, too.

Radok threw open the latch on the door, so it would swing free with a knock. Then he took up position square in the middle of the tiny foyer, gun at the ready.

Footsteps sounded on the stairs now. Climbing up and up. Through their echo, he thought he could discern only the one victim. Hell of a clacking noise he made, as if wearing heavy boots.

Let it be now, damn you. We'll go visit hell together.

The footsteps were on his floor now, approaching his door, but haltingly, as if the visitor did not know his flat and might be referring to a penciled card in the hand.

An amateur, that's what you are, he thought. He'd drop the bastard like a dead and rotted tree. Like the cord-wood bodies he had seen in the pictures from the General. And die laughing.

He felt no fear now, just the pleasant adrenaline rush of going into action. It's the waiting that kills you; imagining the worst. Thinking. Rationalizing. So let it be now and clean and with a reason. A purpose.

There was a timid knocking at the door, not enough to budge it. Radok was silent. He hadn't counted on timid. But wait, he told himself. His move still. Another knock now, louder, harder, but this time on the door jamb. Good manners, blast him.

Or maybe he's not such an amateur as I'd thought. No foot-in-the-door cowboy games for this guy. The caution is contagious: maybe it's just that clown Schwarz with the coal delivery that's already three days late. The contagion of caution, breeding silly hope. Steel it, he told himself. Grab your courage and do it.

"Yes. Come in." His voice sounded a hundred miles away.

"Inspektor Radok?"

A woman. Not Irene. She was on the phone; had been, anyway.

The door inched open, and he quickly holstered the Walther and took a deep breath. He did not think she'd seen the weapon.

"Fräulein Lassen . . ." His voice almost cracked.

"May I come in?"

"You are. Just take a step." Not now. No goddamn wit now.

"I had to see you."

Self-evident. You're here, aren't you? But he didn't say this, mercifully.

She shut the door in back of her, looking at his open coat, the leather of the shoulder holster peeping from under the left lapel.

"Am I disturbing you? I can come back later."

He shrugged an answer. "Come on in."

"My shoes are all wet."

"The carpet'll survive."

They stood in the crowded foyer a few more uncomfortable moments.

Finally: "Take the shoes off." He smiled. "Good way to catch cold standing in wet shoes."

The comment was so mundane that it brought a snort of laughter from her, quite involuntarily. Her face squinched up in a smile so guileless, so without consideration for what it did to her perfect cheekbones, that he wanted to kiss her for it. Never trust a woman who hid laughter behind a hand. This was one of the only things he'd learned from Helga, who'd hid everything from him, even traces of her Wehrmacht officer's sperm after her daytime trysts. Life as betrayal: whoever betrays first or most, wins.

"We have a friend in common," he said.

This stopped her smile.

"I saw you today," he said. "In Klosterneuburg. Leaving the church. Did Father Mayer send you here to check on my story?"

It was a long shot, but one that he'd been sifting through his mind ever since returning from the abbey this afternoon.

She stood stiffly by the door, as if unwilling to compromise herself by so much as entering his domain.

"Please do take off those damn wet shoes," he said. "I'm not a foot fetishist."

"I went to Frau von Tratten," she finally said, not moving from the door.

"So we're both checking up on each other. Fine coincidence, that. And you know my bona fides. The best little gardener in Hietzing."

"It helps to explain things," she said.

"No haiku, okay? We may be on the same side in this

thing. But I'm not prepared for any riddles. Just the straight stuff." Echoes of the General's voice.

"I shouldn't be here," she said. "But I felt responsible."

"Responsible?"

"For leading you to the Father today."

He shook his head. "It wasn't you. I didn't put a tail on you at all. My oversight. The General left me a message about you people. . . . Cards on the table?"

She nodded from her safe perch by the half-opened door.

"I didn't want any part of this, you know? I'm no hero. Not cut out for this sort of thing."

She made as if to speak.

He held his hand up. "No. I don't figure you are, either. I imagine that it's no more comfortable for you than for me. But there it is. We're involved, aren't we? I didn't go to the abbey either following you or looking for you. Seeing you there was just a bonus for me, so to speak."

She blushed. Christ! he thought. She actually blushes. Women paint the semblance of a blush on now with rouge from the local *Parfumerie*. He began to fear that he was well and truly hooked.

"I went there," he hurried on, trying to break the spell she was casting over him, "because the General said that the Mayer group had a way of getting some valuable documents out of the Reich. You're part of that organization, aren't you?"

She said nothing; neither did she move from the doorway.

"You're a rotten spy, by the way. Never try to catch a peek of someone through an open door. Never know when they might be doing the same thing from the other side, like I was in the confessional at Klosterneuburg today."

She did not react to this.

"So, okay," Radok said. "Let's just assume guilt by association. Cezak visits Father Mayer an awful lot; you visit Father Mayer. Cezak has a program autographed by you. What was that about? Are you the bag man on this one? Was he going to transfer the goods under the guise of getting your autograph?"

She sighed. "You seem to have been giving this some thought."

He nodded. "It's been a long afternoon. I've been waiting for Mayer's call."

"You mentioned documents," she said.

"Like I told the Father, I've got them."

"Here?" Wariness in her voice.

"You know, I'm a rotten card player. No bluffs, okay? I said before, cards on the table. Are you people going to help, or not?"

"Not until we know the contents."

"Christ!" he said. "You really *don't* know what the hell they are, do you? You're going into this blind."

"Do you have the papers with you?" she said calmly.

"Damned amateurs." But he couldn't take his eyes off her; their eyes locked for a moment, and he saw behind her veil, her bravado, into the heart of a young and beautiful woman as frightened and mistrustful as he was.

"Okay," he said. "You need to look at these."

He began to reach for the papers when he heard the hollow whoosh of a car door slamming shut on the street below. Then a second and a third slamming. Radok hadn't heard the cars approaching, but the doors sent alarm bells ringing. Then probably she was here so that he wouldn't notice their arrival. Idiot.

He moved to the front room, to the window overlooking the street, and saw three black Mercedes below. A "Green Henry," the Gestapo paddy wagon, was just entering the street. Frieda was at his shoulder now too, looking down at the activity on the street.

He looked at her, smelling her perfume, so close was she to him.

"You bastard!" she said.

He shook his head violently at this. "Not me! I figured *you* laid this one on."

An impatient shake of her head now, too. As honest as the laugh or the blush.

"All right," he said, making a split-second judgment of her. "Then let's get out of here."

He took her unwilling hand, pulling her toward the door. There was the sound of fists pounding on the house door below. A grumbling from the porter echoed up the stairwell as that woman went to answer the door.

"Wait," he said. "We'll need a few things." He dashed back into the flat and was gone for a little more than a minute. When he returned he wore a heavy overcoat, the pockets of which were stuffed with household candles.

It came to him suddenly that this was exactly what he should have done when Frieda had rung his doorbell to begin with. No last stands, but a dash down the back stairs to the cellar. If he'd done it then, however, she wouldn't be with him now—as if her coming had been a dress rehearsal for the real thing. A reminder of other options.

They left the apartment, and Frieda let herself be dragged along the dark hallway to the fire door at the far end. The estate agent had made much of this exit when selling the lease to Radok last year. At that time it hadn't seemed like much: an internal fire escape to the cellar, which in case of fire would most likely be blocked anyway, he'd thought. But now it was a chance, and what was below, in the cellar, provided even more of a chance. All worth trying. The cellar may already be blocked off, he reasoned. But something told him it would be all right. The Gestapo seldom checked house plans before mounting a raid. It was doubtful they'd even know of the fire stairs. There was no time to wonder how the hell they'd tumbled to him; just pretty damn obvious that they had. They weren't here to sell tickets to the fireman's ball. So, it's a skip down the stairs. The woman moved quickly at his side, no longer needing the tug of his hand.

The fire stairs were pitch-bloody-black and Radok did not hit the lights. Light would leak under the doors on the main stairway and tip off the Gestapo that someone was playing hide-and-seek with them. Frieda tripped going down the third flight of stairs. A good thing Radok was in front, for he blocked her fall; otherwise she would have gone tumbling into the blackness. As it was she bruised her knees and wrenched her left hand breaking the fall, but it was not serious and did not slow her. Radok was impressed; she got up without a word and continued their breakneck descent of the stairs. The landings were the hard part: you expected another step down, and the foot jarred all the way to the hip socket when it came to rest on the same level instead.

Finally there were no more stairs. Only a massive steel door. Locked.

"Shit!" He struck out at the solid door, bruising his hand. He hadn't thought of this: that a fire exit would be locked. But this was Vienna. Everything was locked in Vienna.

"Don't you have a key?" Frieda said.

He heard voices above and the clacking of heels on concrete steps. By now, the Gestapo or police or whoever it was must have gotten to his apartment and found it empty, and would be on to the fire stairs very soon.

"I never thought there'd be a key to the damn thing," he said. "It was open the only other time I was down here. The house porter was storing some things and I wandered in."

"We've got to do something." She tried the door handle. Not a budge. "Try your house key."

He hadn't thought of that. Light shone down the fire stairs. A door had opened above, but he could not tell how many flights. Voices came to them, perhaps two or three of them.

"Fucking fire stairs!" a booming voice from above announced. "Get down there, Baumgartner, and check it out. Bastard's gone somewhere."

Radok could see Frieda's face now in the dim light. The pain in the eyes, the lips quivering. But she held herself together. No panic. No tears. He fished the house key out of his pocket quietly, inserted it in the lock and turned. It did not work. No matter how hard he turned, the lock would not give, though the key did fit.

"The other way," she whispered.

He tried it, humoring her—and it worked! The lock had been set counterclockwise. The silly bastards, he thought. You could fry to death before you got your ass into the cellar.

Footsteps were descending rapidly now. Radok opened the door: a rush of damp, stale air hit them. Those above would smell it, too, he realized, but there was nothing to be done about that except to close the self-locking door as quickly and quietly as possible behind them.

Once on the other side of the door he lit the first of the candles, and saw that they were at the top of rickety wooden stairs leading to a cavernous and half-finished cellar some ten steps down. Part of the subterranean space was still a dirt floor. The high, vaulted ceiling was evidence that this particular cellar was far older than the apartment house atop it. A flurry of activity in the far corner. Frieda jumped at the sound.

"Rats," Radok said. "They'll keep their distance as long as we have light."

She gripped his hand, but he had to free it to shield the guttering candle as they moved down the steps. The flame threw immense shadows across the brick-and-mortar vaulting.

"We can't hide down here," she said, and her voice echoed in the deep chamber.

"No," he said.

"But . . . they're coming down here."

"Maybe they won't have a house key." He tried to laugh, though it was not the least bit funny. "Just bear with me. There's a secret way out."

They were at the soil-floor part of the cellar now. Hard-packed earth. It's been so for hundreds of years, by the feel of it, he thought.

As Radok remembered, the subterranean passage began just behind a large discarded wardrobe. The candle illuminated only a small globe around them—the rest of the cellar remained in gloom. They shuffled to the left, where he thought the wardrobe had stood when he was poking around the cellar shortly after moving in, searching for secure storage space with the porter waiting impatiently by the door. It was she who had told him about the entrance to the catacombs behind the wardrobe. Real catacombs in your own apartment house! she had proudly said. Not many in Vienna can say that.

Again, as with the fire stairs, Radok had not been impressed at the time. Only about half of Vienna had access to the old catacombs: rabbit warrens carved out of the bedrock under the city in medieval days. The ultimate protection against siege: let the bastards surround you while you creep out in back of them via the tunnels.

This was not exactly the perfect escape route Radok would have hoped for: Radok knew the catacombs about as well as he did Outer Mongolia, but for one small section of them on the other side of the First District. He had no notion of where these under his house led. Still, it was better than the option: being beaten silly, or to death, in a questioning at Morzin Platz.

He found the wardrobe at about where he remembered it as being. A good omen.

"Here, behind this."

"We can't hide in here."

He carefully propped the candle up in the dirt and then pulled at the wardrobe. It was heavy with lord knows what detritus from the tenants.

"Help me. This is breaking my back."

"But . . ."

"Just help."

Both began tugging at the wooden box. The handle of the iron door to the cellar began rattling, and he and Frieda looked at the door fearfully.

"Locked!" a voice shouted from the other side of the door. "Tell Berthold we need a key, and get the fucking porter down here!"

The wardrobe began to move slowly.

"Harder!" he hissed. "We've got to move it from the wall."

Frieda's cheeks puffed as she pulled, but her grip was high on the wardrobe and she almost tipped it onto him. He moved just in time to stop it.

"Grab lower, dammit."

"Sorry."

"There. Just a little more."

He poked his head around the back and saw what looked like a giant mouse hole in the brick wall behind the wardrobe: arched, about large enough to crawl through. His nostrils were assaulted by foul air, as if out of the devil's asshole. Putrid, turgid, rank. All sorts of creatures alive and dead were waiting for them in there.

"Through here," he said. "Let's go."

"Christ, no!"

"Get going. You'd rather face the Gestapo?"

She moved. The archway was wide enough for only one at a time; he waited for her to go first, picked the candle up, and then had to pull the heavy wardrobe back in place himself. At one point it felt as if his lungs would burst and that he would tear all the muscles in his upper body, but finally he got the wardrobe back into place and followed Frieda into the passageway. They were sealed off. Alone in the catacombs.

The candle went out. Her hand trembled at his arm.

"Light it please," she said. "I panic in the dark."

Now she tells me, he thought. But he scratched a match alive and lit the wick.

"Better?" he said.

She squeezed his arm. "Where to from here?"

He didn't answer, but crawled around her to lead the way along the tiny passage for a few meters, descending very gradually until suddenly the little feeder shaft they were in joined the main course of tunnels and he could stand almost upright. Frieda was close in back of him; he thought he could feel her breath on his neck. Then he knew better. His hand reached up and swatted at a hard and hairy object on his collar. The spider tumbled off him at the touch and scurried away.

"Which way?" Frieda finally said.

Only two choices now that they had reached the main tunnel: right or left. He was disoriented and had no idea which way the tunnels were headed, other than in opposite directions from each other.

"This way." He pointed to the right.

She looked at him closely. "You don't know, do you?"

He hesitated, about to lie.

"The truth, please," she said. "I can live with it."

He shook his head. "Not a clue."

His honesty seemed to bolster her.

"Good," she said. "So let's go to the left. It's headed west, I think. Out of town."

He felt like an altar boy with the candle in his hand.

"Okay. We'll follow your hunch," he said.

"It's not a hunch. That direction is west." She pointed to the left.

"Okay. West. Great. Let's move."

The tunnel was wet now; the hard-packed soil had given way to mud. Water dripped from above them. Maybe a sewer nearby, who knew? Radok tried to avoid getting the moisture on his candle.

He had no sense of time, but two candles later they suddenly heard voices. His stomach dropped. He put a hand on her, stilling her shuffling feet. Yes. Clearly voices. He automatically blew out the candle. They stood very still. The voices got no louder. Radok inched along, feeling the clammy surface of the wall to find his way. The voices grew louder, nearer. So the voices were stationary, he reasoned. A patrol waiting for them? But how would the Gestapo or SS or even the city's sewer engineer know where the hell he and Frieda were in this labyrinth? Impossible. Inching further along, Radok became aware of what kind of voices these were. Not the slow tones of bored or nervous soldiers, but high and raucous voices. Now the peal of a woman's laugh. Radok noticed a new smell in the tunnel and he moved further, Frieda holding on to his overcoat from behind. It was a musty smell, but fruity, as well. A smell that made Radok happy; that made most Viennese happy.

"It's a goddamn wine cellar," he whispered.

The voices grew louder and louder as they moved forward. A glimmer of light shone through chinks in the brick and mortar.

It'd be the Esterhazy, he reckoned. Or the Urbani Kellar. No; definitely the Esterhazy, for the voices went on and on for almost a hundred meters. There were long galleries at the Esterhazy Kellar. He'd sat in them often enough, nibbling sausage and throwing back glasses of rough Vetliner. He thought he could even discern the peculiar fragrance of that tart white wine as they moved past the drinkers on the other side of the brick wall. To those drinkers, they would no doubt sound like rats; a scratching sound in the walls Radok had noticed often enough, as well, while drinking in the wine cellar.

This chance encounter cheered him and also amazed him, for Frieda had been correct: they were going west and would soon be out of the First District. Having gotten orientated by the wine cellar, Radok now had a pretty good idea where they would come up; thanks, once again, to the General. It was back in the days of the good life in Hietzing, and the General had taken young Radok on an outing into the city, showing him the city walls for which the von Trattens had long ago supplied the timber. The General had walked proudly on the parapet, his gray hair ruffled in the autumn breeze, his face tanned as it always seemed to be. And then he had taken Gunther down the steps to street level, a whimsical smile on his face.

"Would you care to see another world?" the General said.

Radok nodded happily. He'd follow the General anywhere.

And so they had gone underground, down a manhole, into the sewers, as Radok had at first thought. But these were really the catacombs, and they entered an enormous subterranean flophouse, where the vagrants of Vienna found rough shelter from the elements.

There were men, women, and children of all ages under the earth; some sleeping on crude wood and corrugated tin bunks, others playing cards or simply sitting, silent and huddled. They all seemed to know the General; to trust him. One of the General's projects was helping the needy of Vienna. The General took Radok for a tour of the catacombs near this flophouse, showing him the secret passages, the ways in and out. He was proud of his knowledge; proud that he could fit into the *Gauner*, or bum's world.

"Remember them," the General had said when they returned to daylight. "When we're eating our roast pork tonight, think of these people here and how they must live."

Radok did think of them now, some twenty years later. And he belatedly thanked them and the General for the experience. For he knew the way now, knew where he and Frieda were headed.

A sharp, metallic scream brought him out of this reverie. A hand gripped tightly at his coat, and something large and terrifying fell on his shoulder; something else equally large scurried about his legs.

Chapter Eleven

It was Krahl's fault, actually. His goddamn telegram with the silly spy language that any first-form student could decipher.

Hartmann was angry. The telegram threw everything off schedule. The meet was not until later this afternoon. Hartmann had planned to spend most of the day in his rented room, preparing himself for the operation. But that option was lost to him now.

From Frau Lautendorf's, he went to the train station and collected the suitcase he'd checked there three weeks earlier. Then he went to the men's room to change into the suit he had packed away. The arsenal was under the false bottom in the suitcase along with fresh identity papers. This hidden compartment he now opened and took out the papers and two hand grenades, which he fixed to specially designed holsters that fit on the middle of his forearms. The holster straps unsnapped when he flexed his forearm muscles: down the grenades would slide into his hands. He'd designed the straps himself: to the uninitiated they felt like sleeve garters and could escape detection in most frisks. The suit coat was wide-sleeved, tailored specifically for special operations, and lined in dark brown, rip-proof parachute silk so that the weapons would not catch on the fabric when released.

It was Hartmann's trademark use of the stick grenades that had earned him the code name of Hammer, for his specially designed grenades resembled hammers.

All was in readiness. He packed his old clothes in the suitcase after strapping on the arsenal and slipping on the suit. The image he looked at in the mirror was that of an ordinary, slightly built figure in a rather worn brown business suit. Beneath his sleeves he carried, unseen, death warrants for several men.

The man in brown; the man with no traces: it was how you stayed alive in Hartmann's business.

He'd be traveling under his own name for the return to
Vienna; his old papers, under the name of Boehm, he
burned and flushed the ashes down the toilet. Just as he
was doing this a fat, bulbous-nosed man entered the
lavatory and sniffed suspiciously at the smell of ash, but
said nothing. Hartmann smiled at him and left, checking
the suitcase in a locker in the main hall. In a month it
would become just one more piece of abandoned luggage. Nothing to draw attention to him. He would be
long gone by then, on another assignment somewhere
else in the Reich. Vanished. The shadow warrior slipping
back into the shadows.

The rest of the day was long and trying for a man like
Hartmann. No hiding place in which to shield himself
from the peering eyes of the pedestrians. All the healthy
men were in uniform, gone to the front. The eyes of
passersby searched for his defect, his white feather. TB
had been the cover in Klagenfurt; an intensive machinist
workshop at the Potsdam spy school had prepared Hartmann for the work at the machine shop. But those in the
streets knew none of this; to them he was a malingerer,
perhaps even a deserter. That was why he'd planned to stay
in his room all day. The damn fool Krahl, he thought.

It was those eyes that Hartmann wanted finally to
escape. He had wanted to escape them all his life. When
this war was over and people knew what a silent hero
he'd been all these years, he'd be a celebrity of sorts. His
picture in the illustrated tabloids. They'd love him; everybody would love him. And he'd find himself a secluded cabin somewhere atop a snowy peak and make
the people beg for autographs and for snippets of his life
story to fill their stupid papers with.

Yes. He would find himself a snowy peak, as white and
pure as his vision of duty. Far away from the peering eyes.

Hartmann finally walked the streets of Klagenfurt defi-
antly like a day-tripper: stopped for coffee in the Café
Rathaus in the old city, had a greasy sausage for lunch at
a sidewalk stand. Then he walked some more in the
parks and on a shopping street, looking in windows bereft of goods, taped with black X's for support in case of
aerial bombardment.

A long day. He was tired by the time he reached the
meeting place: a butcher shop on Villacher Strasse, part

abattoir and part retail shop. Hartmann was fifteen minutes early. Waiting unseen in a darkened doorway across
the street, he watched the others arriving. Frieland, the
hollow-chested mechanic at the works who'd befriended
him, was early too. He was with Dietrich and Kulhavy,
both from the machine shop. Siemrich would be inside
already, for it was his shop. Their master; the planet they
revolved around. Siemrich was the butcher with Marxist
tendencies who'd masterminded the Messerschmidt failures.

A burly, moustached fellow in a cap and work clothes
lingered by the front door. That would be Bobo, the
enforcer, as Frieland had described him to Hartmann.
Three weeks it had taken Hartmann just to score this
initial meeting with the cell. There were five of the con-
spirators altogether. Frieland had confided that much
information to Hartmann after he'd won the mechanic over.
Simplicity, that winning over. Hartmann had set up the
turning machine to corkscrew, to attack the operator as it
were, and then he had jumped in and rectified it immediately to save the poor bastard in danger of losing his arm.
Frieland in this case. He'd won the fool's never-ending
gratitude.

Set them up, save them, win them. A simple formula
taught at Bernau. One of Mad Markl's recipes.

There had been a night of wine-drinking together afterward, shared secrets of past loves and political dogma,
and the bargain was sealed. Frieland, the weak link in
the cell, had bought it; had championed Hartmann, or
Boehm as he was known in Klagenfurt, as a new recruit
to the underground organization.

Bobo walked up and down the sidewalk nervously
looking at his pocket watch. Time now, Hartmann decided. They had no backup; this much he had ascer-
tained. This would be by the book. The only tricky part
was getting past Bobo's frisk. A pleasant adrenaline rush
pulsed through Hartmann. It was always like this before
going into action and he looked forward to it.

Hartmann waited for the strongman to turn his back,
then came out of the doorway and walked hurriedly
toward the shop, as if afraid he were late. He had the
mask on: the expectant, friendly look that he could assume instantly. It had taken hours of practice in front of
the training mirror at Bernau to perfect that mask. This

was his most valuable weapon of all in Austria, where
people never looked beneath the skin for motives.

Bobo turned, saw him coming, and crossed his arms,
standing directly in front of the shop door.

"Pleasant evening," Hartmann said as he approached.
The words Frieland had coached him in.

Bobo answered appropriately: "Could be a storm before morning, though."

Hartmann thought how ironic this saying was. Much
sooner than morning, my friend. Much sooner.

"Storms clear the air," Hartmann replied.

Bobo nodded. He looked like the type who would be
unable to handle any more complicated passwords than
these. The black cap worn tight on his massive skull
looked ready to pop off at any moment. Hartmann kept
smiling, sizing the man up all the while for the weak spot
that must be there; the weak spot that Hartmann would
need to exploit in a few minutes.

"This way," Bobo said.

Hartmann followed him through the door, into the
empty shop, and then through another door to a long
hallway. The smell of the slaughterhouse was overpowering here: the raw copper stench of blood and death. The
man in front of him was flat-footed and moved ponder-
ously. As a fighter, he would not be hard to reach. He
was the kind who thought his size was his protection, the
kind to move in slowly for the kill; overpowering his
opponent, trusting to brute strength rather than to cunning. Long arms dangled loosely at his sides as he walked.
Hartmann figured he'd be a wind-up puncher—no quick
jabs for him. His punches would be thrown with the
length of his arm, with all his weight in back of them.
Taller than he by a good ten centimeters, still Bobo could
be taken, Hartmann knew.

They stopped outside the massive metal door to a meat
locker; it was held to by a diagonal metal brace lodged in
the floor outside. Thick, fur-lined leather jackets hung
from hooks to the right of the door. Bobo took an
enormous one and put it on, handing another to Hartmann.

"That's okay," Hartmann said. "I've got thick blood."

Bobo squinted at him suspiciously. "Suit yourself. Let's
see what you're carrying."

"I'm clean. Just like Frieland said to be."

Bobo shrugged, his hands held out to frisk. Hartmann voluntarily raised his arms. The watcher tapped along the side of his body, down his legs and then up the inside of the legs. His head nodded while he was still bent over. Clean. Hartmann's hands went down. First score to me, Hartmann thought.

Bobo stood, reached for the bar holding the door closed, then had a second thought.

"Sorry," he said.

Bobo's hands went to Hartmann's arms now, along the outside, and stopped momentarily at the outline of the straps holding his grenades. He must have taken them for garters, however, for he did not search the insides of Hartmann's arms. He pushed back Hartmann's cuffs, looking for wrist weapons: the strapped knife or gun.

"Just doing my job. No hard feelings?" he said after finishing the frisk.

Hartmann smiled the Bernau smile.

"We've all got our job to do. Better safe than sorry."

"You sure you don't want a coat? Damned cold in there."

"Maybe next time," Hartmann said. "I've got this thing about wearing other people's clothing."

A grin from the mountain of flesh.

"I know what you mean. You never know about the other guy. I mean, maybe he's got some disease, right? You ask me, I think it's dumb we meet in here. Siemrich says it's the only absolutely safe place to talk. Nothing but carcasses for eavesdroppers."

Bobo laughed, spittle forming at the corners of his mouth. A fleck of the spit landed on Hartmann's cheek and he drew back, flinching at it, bracing himself as if assaulted. The momentary flex of his body registered also in his left arm. It was enough to pop the snaps holding the grenade in position there.

Hartmann was barely able to cup his hand, catch the released grenade, and move it in back of him in time to keep it out of sight from Bobo. No way to restrap it now; he could only pull his sleeve down and hope to keep the grenade out of sight from the others, too. That took one hand out of action.

Smooth, very smooth, Hartmann, he chided himself. Which left only his right hand to deal with the lumbering Bobo.

The door was open now and Bobo stood aside for him to enter first. No simple push in the man's back was possible now. That's what Hartmann had been hoping for: let the oaf lead the way, then kick his ass in. Add one grenade, stir lightly, and bango. But now . . . Call it off? Go for it another time? He might have under ordinary circumstances. He might have just used this first meeting as a trust-builder, then the second time take them out. But Krahl's telegram and Frau Lautendorf's death disallowed ordinary measures. His cover would be blown by morning. It was tonight or never.

He summoned the smile again and entered the bizarre world of the meat locker. One naked light bulb illuminated the white walls; pink halves of cattle and pigs hung from hooks. Standing in a group were the other four men in the saboteur cell, each of them bundled in a leather jacket such as the one Bobo had offered him. Hartmann nodded at Frieland and the others whom he knew from the plant. Bobo closed the door in back of them: a hollow whooshing sound like a door shutting on a tomb.

Siemrich nodded at him. "It's good of you to come, Herr Boehm. Frieland here says you would like to help us. To join us."

Hartmann thought Siemrich was looking at him mistrustfully as hell. He's not taken in by my smile, Hartmann realized. He's a wary bastard who would just as soon have my carcass hanging here as look at me. The thought made everything else fall into place for Hartmann; made what he had to do easier.

"Weren't you offered a jacket?" Siemrich looked condemningly at Bobo.

"He didn't want one, boss," Bobo complained.

"But you're cold, Herr Boehm. You keep your hands up your sleeves. . . ."

The decision was made for Hartmann. It was now, not never. He knew how far Bobo was in back of him and made a quick backward step onto the man's arch, digging the special, leather-covered steel heel into the man's instep. He heard a bellow in his ear as Bobo reached down to the crushed foot, and Hartmann swung his right elbow up into the bridge of the man's nose, never taking his eyes off the others. There was the crunch of cartilage and another yelp from Bobo, this one muffled by blood in the mouth. A gurgling, choking sound as the big man went down.

The others were transfixed for a moment. It was all happening too fast for them, and the moment was all Hartmann needed. Siemrich was the first to move, but it would be too late now, Hartmann knew. He flexed his right arm and both stick grenades were in his hands. Tripping their seven-second fuses, he threw both grenades at Siemrich like twin hammers. They bounced off his chest, stunning him. Hartmann leaped over Bobo's body and found the latch to the door. He was nearly out.

"But what . . . ? Why?" Frieland's voice reached him as he was closing the door behind him. The voice to carry with him as a memory of this operation, along with Siemrich's amazed face. The eyes large, the whites showing like a frightened horse's.

Siemrich made a leap for him, but Hartmann slammed the door shut, fitting the metal rod into position in the floor to brace it. He dashed madly down the corridor, and was almost to the front door of the shop when the grenades went off with a roar. The explosives would, in the confined space of the meat locker, mingle chunks of their bodies with those of the cattle and pigs, Hartmann knew. The firemen would be separating the pieces for the next several days before any positive identifications could be made. And by then he'd be long gone.

Hartmann was across the street and heading south toward the train station by the time any of the residents of the area had even poked their heads out of windows. He turned around for a moment: just one of the curious bystanders. Smoke rose in back of the shop. No fire. The flesh was all there was to burn in the confines of the meat locker. The central section of the building collapsed and suddenly the street was full of shouting and wildly gesticulating people.

Hartmann wore his curious face now, making his way through the groups of people. His heart was racing and a streak of white energy was racing up his spine to his brain, almost like an orgasm.

Hartmann was on the Ring heading for Bahnhofstrasse and the station by the time he heard the first whine of fire engines. A yellow ladder truck raced by him as he walked calmly along.

Chapter Twelve

A high, terrifying scream pounded in her ears and
froze her in her steps. Only instants later did Frieda
realize the scream was coming from her own throat, and
that it had come involuntarily, automatically, when a
large rat had dropped onto her head from somewhere in
the blackness above. Huge and obscene, the rat was
wrapping its naked tail around the back of her neck. Hot
breath in her face; tiny claw-like paws digging into her
scalp. Radok had turned at her scream, dropping the
candle, and now they were in total darkness with many
of the other rodents crawling over both their bodies.

"Scream again, damn you!" he yelled into her face.
And when she did not, when she knew her voice and will
were both gone, he began beating at the creatures with
an open hand. One of the slaps landed on her face and
she screamed again.

"That's it!" he said, delighted. "Scream until I get
another candle lit! It'll scare them off!"

So she stood, stamping her feet at the hairy animals
trying to crawl up her skirt, and she screamed like a
Wagnerian soprano. All the while she dug her fingers
into Radok's heavy coat. He did not move, as if aware
that he was her only landmark. Finally he lighted another
candle and thrust the flame at the rats. They cowered
backward, their eyes red in the light; beady little points
of fire in the surrounding darkness.

"Take it." He thrust the candle at her and she grabbed
it. Then he lifted her, as if knowing instinctively that she
could no longer move of her own will, and began hurrying along the low, tunneled passage. No one had carried
her so since her father had played sack-of-potatoes with
her. She let herself fold into him, feeling strangely secure
for the first time in years.

"All right," he kept mumbling to her, as if she were a baby. "It'll be all right now."

And she believed him. It was the sort of consolation she needed. She felt hot tears at her cheeks. It had been so long since she'd allowed herself the luxury of crying. Not even when Wolf was taken away had she cried. She'd sworn off tears since her father's death. Sorrow was a pitiful emotion; it changed nothing. But now the pent-up tears flowed freely and she felt cleansed, whole again, as if she could really feel once more.

After what seemed a blissful eternity, he put her down.

"Okay now. All gone," he said. "It's all right."

He spoke to her as her own father had done, trying to calm away her tears. Speaking as if to a baby, using language as a soothing caress. An example of the male's profound misunderstanding of the benign effects of emotion, she thought. Trying to plug up the tears rather than allow them; not realizing they were necessary, purgative. Only fearing them. But there was a sweetness to his words, as well. A desire to make everything whole again; to repair the world for the woman, and she understood them on this level as a gift.

"Thanks. I'm better now," she said.

"We're almost there."

"Where?" She hadn't thought of destinations.

"Out of here. I know the way now." A low laugh from him.

She did not ask for explanations, but simply followed him as he pushed forward through the damp gloom. She no longer felt the terror; no longer the lost feeling of doubt. This man she knew she could trust. Perhaps even open to.

He stopped suddenly. The candle flame seemed to grow, to encompass a new world of light around them. They were now no longer in the vaulted passageway, but in a cavernous space littered with wooden slats and corrugated metal sheets.

"This way," he said. "Yes. Just as I remember. Thank Christ, it's not been mortared up."

She couldn't see what he was so joyous about at first, then finally her eyes focused on another rabbit hole to the right, leading out of the cavern.

"I can't go through there," she said.

"We're almost out. Just a bit further now."

"I'm claustrophobic."

"Fine," he said. "You'd rather stay down here, then?"

"You don't understand." She felt the trembling overcome her; the completely irrational but palpable fear.

"I understand only that you have no choice," he replied.

There was a hard edge to his voice, as there had been to Wolf's when he'd grown impatient with these fears of hers, but in Radok it quickly dissolved.

"It'll be all right," he said, cupping her cheek with his hand. "Really all right. Believe me. Please. I wouldn't let anything go wrong now. Please."

She felt herself give in then, and give up. She gave herself to him.

He moved her toward the tiny opening, feeling the acquiescence in her.

"You first," he said. "I'll be right here with you. Don't be afraid."

She went down on her hands and knees and moved into the dark opening. When she hesitated, his hand was there on her ankle; a reassuring tap. No words. Just the hand, the warm touch. She knew it would be all right, now. The tears still flowed in her eyes, but joyous tears now, as if she were crying the other world away, crying all her past life out of her. It was like a rebirth. Now there was only the movement forward through the channel, the secure touch of his hand on her leg. She came out into another large chamber and stood erect. Fresh air reached her from somewhere very near. He scrambled out after her and she folded into him, felt his arms close around her, his breath and then his lips on her hair.

He moved her toward a metal ladder, went up first, and pushed a metal cover aside. Cold air rushed down to her; lovely, cold, fresh air. She climbed up the ladder and they were out now, up in the real world again, and the slushy streets smelled delicious. The odor of diesel and melting snow: late winter in the city. He held her again, tight to him, and then pushed her out at arm's length, looking into her eyes. She opened herself to him, let her eyes be naked to his glance. Naked and open.

"I have an apartment," she said.

"We can't go there. They may be on to you."

"No," she said. "A secret place. It's registered under a

different name. For when I want to get right away from
the world. We'll go there. All right?"

A taxi passed. Luck was with them. Radok hailed it
and it stopped. Luck would always be with them, she
knew.

The taxi stopped in front of the building Frieda indicated and Radok reached for his wallet. Where it should
have been, in the inside coat pocket, was one final candle. The hardware still rested in the shoulder holster nice
and tidy. He'd even grabbed an extra booklet of ration
coupons on his way out. But no wallet. He'd thought of
everything, it seemed, but money. Not a groschen on
him.

Frieda sensed the problem, dug into her purse, and
handed a bill to the cab driver. The tip was neither too
large nor too small to attract attention. Radok wondered
if it had been done purposely.

Once out of the taxi, he realized what a truly dumb
bastard he was: you could trace a cab. There were few
enough of them around these days. He, like every other
rookie on the force, knew the drill. It was the easiest
trace around. Radok was about to have the cabbie drive
them once around the park and drop them elsewhere.
But that would have been sure to raise suspicions, even
from one who looked, as this cabbie did, as though he
were rather more directly descended from Cro-Magnon
than other passersby. Nothing for it now but to hope
the man forgot his late-night fares.

They were out on the street watching the rear lights of
the cab pull away into the night.

"It's a few blocks from here," she said. "You don't
mind the walk?"

He smiled at her, nodding. A pro . . . of sorts. She'd
learned her lessons better than he had. But Radok said
nothing, taking her hand as they walked. Just a couple of
lovers out for an evening stroll. It was a good enough
excuse to hold her hand, anyway.

Another block and they arrived at a large, gloomy-
looking tenement, one of those thrown up hastily in the
mid-nineteenth century to accommodate the influx of
workers into Vienna. There were no trees on this street

as there were in Hietzing; none of the quaint baroque
charm of her other apartment house in the First District.

She put a large key into the house door. "It'll be safe
here. My little haven."

In through one courtyard. Separate stairs led to different wings of the tenement. Stairway six. Radok registered it in his memory as he would an identity number. A
courtyard and stairs right away from the world. They
went up four flights with the sour smell of boiling
cabbage lingering on the stairs, reminiscent of the apartment the Radok family had taken after leaving the von
Tratten nest in Hietzing. Too familiar for Radok. What
he had left behind. What he had bartered by joining the
force. The hall lights were on a short timer; he had to
push the red illuminated button on each landing. Radios
sounded from behind closed doors; a baby cried behind
one; a man's voice, loud and angry, came from behind
another, followed by the consoling soothing tones of a
female. Life.

Number Forty-three. Her door was painted green, as
in some student lodging. Inside, the hallway was filled
with cheap art reproductions: Van Gogh's "Church at
Arles"; Rembrandt's "Night Watch." More posters hung
in the simple living room, but these announced concerts:
the Musikverein; the Konzerthaus; a guest appearance in
Graz; another in Berne last year. The one in Berne was
Frieda's concert, Radok noted.

She pulled the curtain closed on the one window in the
living room while Radok surveyed the place: a small
room crowded with a deal table, two café chairs, and a
cheap, sagging flea-market couch against one wall. He
took in the stale smell of the unused apartment, saw a big
bed through the open door to the bedroom. Where was
the kitchen? Most likely through the closed glass doors in
the entryway, he thought. Bathroom down the hall. Public baths once a week. Just like the Radok family's "manor"
in the Tenth District.

When she turned back to him, looking red-cheeked
and frightened next to the curtained window, Radok
knew he was lost; knew that he was open to the old pain
once again. It was a part of him he thought he'd closed
off for good once Helga was out of his life, part of him
that he distrusted. But there was no going back now. Not

with any of it, least of all with this woman. You can stare
at a thing right in the face for as long as you want, he
thought; walk around it; fidget and squirm. But in the
end, the old emotion takes over. A bargain sealed with a
dead man and his trust. A bargain cemented with a
woman via an evening's stroll in the catacombs.

And so, here you are, he told himself. Here you are
and there is no going back.

"So, here we are," he said.

"Yes." A slight nod of her head. "I'd like a look at
those papers now."

Very cool, he thought. Collected. An ice-goddess. He
knew he had to trust her. There was no choice; no
deliberation. He said nothing as he pulled the envelope
out of the back of his waistband and handed it to her.
She took it, still wearing her overcoat, and sat down on
the couch. The papers spilled out onto her lap as they
had onto the table at the bank earlier today. She took
her time with them, going, as he had done, through all
the written documents first, saving the photos for last.
The apartment was silent but for the cluck of her disap-
proving tongue once, twice. A long sigh, a murmur as of
sorrow from her. Then another deep breath, followed
by the rustling of sheets of paper.

Finally: "It's worse than we thought."

"Bad," Radok agreed.

"They start transporting the Jews on the twenty-sixth
of this month," she said. "That doesn't give us very long.
Sixteen days."

"Nine," Radok corrected, "if we follow the General's
advice in his letter. And I think we must."

A nod from her as she gathered the documents, put
them back in the envelope, and handed it to him. She
shook her head sadly. He wished they could have left this
until morning; could have prolonged the moment of intimacy created by their escape.

It was as if she felt the same. "So here we are," she
said, echoing his words, and looking hard at him with a
face both serious and expectant.

Yes, here we both are, he thought, and there's no
running away from it. No hiding in the safe half-life of
shut-down emotions any longer.

"Nine days," he said, trying to keep things pragmatic, trying for one last time to avoid the tumult of emotions he was feeling for her.

She shivered at his words.

"You're cold." He took off his coat, wrapping her in it as he leaned over the old couch.

"No. It's not that kind of cold," she said, still shaking under the two layers of coats.

She began to cry then, her chin puckering like a child's. He could see she was making an effort to contain the tears, but it was no good. They needed to come out, a healthy response to the combined effect of the chase and the shock of the heinous documents. Radok understood this, but he could only sit by her woodenly, patting one of her exposed hands. Radok could handle all sorts of dangerous situations: he could lead them blindly through the catacombs one step ahead of the Gestapo; he could save his partner's life by taking a load of buckshot meant for Hinkle; he could even face his own past. But a woman or child crying reduced Radok to a state of absolute helplessness. He sat stiffly by her and she leaned into him finally, sobbing against his shoulder. He put a cautious arm around her and held her quietly for a time.

"Come on," he finally said, rising from the couch, helping her up. "Get some sleep now. Things will look better in the morning."

She let herself be led into the bedroom. Radok felt the walls for a moment and finally found the light switch. It was a small bedroom filled by a large double bed, a nightstand, and a pine wardrobe. He sat her on the bed, took her shoes off, lifted her legs onto the bed, and put the eiderdown over her. She was bundled like a mummy in the overcoats and feather blanket. She had stopped crying now, but her shoulders still shook with sobs as she lay back. Her eyes were closed against the light.

He wanted to say something reassuring, that it would all be okay—but he wasn't so sure. Instead he remained silent as he smoothed the hair out of her face. This seemed to soothe her better than words could, and he sat on the edge of the bed, his right hand on her hair.

He looked at a photo on the bedside table. It showed

two fresh young kids in lederhosen and checkered shirts squinting into a harsh alpine sun; mountain peaks were in the background, jagged and snow-capped. Two healthy young people, obviously in love and daring the world to do something about it. And of course the world had, and did, and would again. Frieda was the girl, all sunburned and milkmaid braids. The young man was slighter, darker, and with that kind of absorbed, dedicated expression on his face that told you he would make others pay for his idealism.

Frieda opened her eyes and saw him looking at the photo.

"Another life," she said, turning the photo facedown on the table.

He nodded, feeling jealousy rising. Right. He was well and truly in it now. Jealousy!

"He's gone," she continued. "Rounded up in thirty-eight. We think he's in Dachau."

Relief was all he felt. What kind of a man are you? he asked himself. Happy the poor bastard bought it in the concentration camp. It leaves the track clear for Radok and Company. Cuts down on the competition. He knew now that he had learned nothing from the pain of Helga; knew that he was still the same old Radok, out to claim the queen as his and his alone. Part of the shit he wished to avoid.

"What do they call you?" she said, breaking the silence between them. "I can't keep calling you Inspektor Radok."

He shrugged. "Radok. Just Radok."

This made her laugh. "Okay, Just Radok. Thank you."

"Thank the house porter. She's the one who showed me the entrance to the catacombs."

She shook her head on the pillow.

"Not for that," she said. "Thank you for not telling me to stop crying."

He looked into her blue eyes now, saw the little flecks of gold around the irises and felt a twinge of passion in his stomach.

"Sleep now." He patted her hand.

She held his, looking at him. Her eyes had an intensity that almost scared him.

"You're a good man, Just Radok."

She said it with a hint of teasing, and it reminded him suddenly of the first girl he'd ever been with, up in a mountain hut so many years before. She'd teased him afterward about his ardor.

"What would you do if I ran away from you?" she'd said. "If I *versteckt* myself, hid right away from you?"

He'd loved her so, that first young girl; so much so, that he'd had no sense of humor about it at all.

"I'd find you," he had replied. "Wherever you went, I'd find you and I'd tie you up and never let you run away again."

It was the sort of obsessive first love that knew no bounds between self and other. A kind of love Radok had thought you could experience only once. But now he was no longer sure. No longer sure of anything.

He got up, the bed springs sounding as he moved.

"I'll take the couch," he said. "Tomorrow we'll figure out what to do."

Her hand trailed away from his. As he moved to the door, he thought she was already asleep.

"Radok?"

He turned.

"Stay in here. Please."

She placed pillows down the middle of the bed, creating separate sleep spaces for them.

"Just be near, okay?"

She was smiling at him, warmly and openly.

"Sure," he said. "Okay."

He got into the bed fully clothed, as she was, and they lay face to face in the darkness, separated by the pillows, looking into the glistening whiteness of each other's eyes. Neither spoke as they lay there innocently, happily. Frieda sighed once deeply, nodding her head.

"A good man, Radok," she whispered.

He wanted to be, for her sake.

After a time, Radok stretched an arm over Frieda and she sighed again, moving closer to him. He moved the pillows aside and held her, rocking her, loving the feeling of her hair on his face, her breath on his mouth.

They slept like that for several hours, like children. Radok awoke in the middle of the night and she was looking at him.

He moved his mouth instinctively toward hers; they

bumped noses and laughed. Her lips were soft and a little dry. She moved her tongue over them, moistening her lips, and met him again. Lightly. A caress.

He felt her cool fingers on the buttons of his shirt. They squirmed out of their layers of clothing while still in bed, giggling at the absurdity of it, but neither wanted to leave the bed to disrobe, neither wanted to break the magic spell. After a long and clumsy moment, they met each other again, skin against skin under the eiderdown. He wrapped his arms around her, feeling her smooth and supple skin as he moved his hand to her shoulder and down her back, touching each of the tiny knobs of her vertebrae and down to her buttocks. There was a sigh as he cupped her there, and he was amazed that this time the sound came from him, from deep in his throat.

They stayed wrapped together like that for a very long time, silently, he stroking her body and she feeling out his lips with hers; little nibbling kisses that drew him deeper and deeper into her. If this could go on forever I'd be happy, Radok thought. Just the warmth between us, the blood pounding and her lips on mine.

"Is something wrong?" she finally said, mistaking his reverie for lack of ardor.

"No." Moving on top of her, spreading her legs. "Something's right."

She was moist as he nudged against her and whimpered when he partly entered her. There was no thinking now, just the deep and holy warmth of it. Bodies moving together, clinging to each other.

Frieda breathed in sharply as he fully entered, pushing past the last barrier, pushing and going into her as if he himself were going back to the womb. He was still now as he felt her contracting around his penis, tiny flutterings of strong muscles on him. No need to move; the interior touch was enough for him and her now.

Her hips began to move first, involuntarily, and the movement was contagious. She was breathing in his ear, long, slow breaths that picked up tempo with the movement of their hips. Faster and faster. He felt himself building and building, about to burst inside her and she felt it, too. He was about to pull out of her, but she held him to her instinctively, her hand on the small of his back. Opening and opening to him. Deeper and deeper.

When he came it was new and strong, as if it were his first time. Her orgasm followed quickly then, the deep muscles gripping and releasing, over and over.

They stayed together, sweat bonding them at the hips, even after his penis finally slid out of her. Sleep came quickly for her, but before Radok drifted off he looked down at their bodies together, at the convex and concave of them that fitted so well.

Then he fell into a deep and dreamless sleep.

Chapter Thirteen

It had been a pleasantly relaxing evening thus far. Maman was tucked in bed with a fresh box of chocolates from Demel's and a new romance novel by that Scheider woman to keep her happy. She had looked better tonight, and had not even reprimanded him for calling her "Maman" as he kissed her florid cheek good night.

Now, ensconced in the mahogany-wainscoted library, with green shaded lamps giving the room a warm glow, Krahl was truly relaxing. A portfolio of photos he'd purchased in Damascus was spread out on his desk: familiar photos of familiar youths, though they never failed to amuse. An unopened package, delivered today from Herr Frankl's specialty art shop on the Neuer Markt, awaited his inspection. Perhaps he would wait on opening it until he got word from the Gestapo agent, Berthold, that the Kripo chap was in custody. He would want to interrogate Radok straight away; the package could remain here unopened as a reward for work well done. It was necessary that a man organize his life so: that he not drink too deeply from each cup. Moderation was Krahl's motto.

A knock at the door. He hurriedly gathered the photos into their folders, thrust it into a drawer, and opened a biography of Frederick the Great he kept on his desk.

"Enter!" he commanded.

The serving girl opened the door, a terrified expression on her face—for the household knew Krahl did not like being disturbed when at work in the library.

"Sir?"

"Yes, yes. Come in."

She was tiny and flat-chested, with the consumptive look, Krahl thought, of the Viennese working class. She stayed half hidden behind the door.

"An officer to see you, sir. He says it's urgent."

"I'll see him in the drawing room."

"Sir . . ." A man's voice.

Krahl saw Lieutenant Hartmann lurking behind the girl. Impudent bastard.

Krahl now turned his gaze upon the anemic serving girl, turning it into a glare.

"I thought I told you . . ."

Hartmann edged past her, gently moved her out of the doorway, and closed the door behind him.

"Sorry, sir."

An elfish grin on his lips. This bastard needs to be brought down, Krahl thought.

"I took your orders literally, sir. You weren't at HQ, so I came here. Not the girl's fault. I told her I was a courier from Treuer Heinrich."

The use of this derisive name for Himmler, Loyal Heinrich, irritated Krahl.

When the war is over, Krahl thought, we'll be able to get rid of cowboys like this one. The glory boys we need now for our dirty work. It would be a pleasure to ship Hartmann and others like him off to the East.

The Lieutenant was dressed in a drab brown suit, but even this could not hide a certain glowing self-satisfaction and pride the man wore eternally like a private uniform.

"I assume you bring good news?" Krahl said.

Hartmann sat in a chair without waiting to be asked, looking about the room, checking the titles of the books in the cases.

"Yes, sir," he finally said.

Hartmann was the only man Krahl knew who could invest the word "sir" with enough irony to make it sound like an insult.

"Shall we say that I blew their operation . . . ?" Hartmann said it very deadpan.

Krahl could not help laughing, low and tight in his throat. He'd been notified by Klagenfurt Station about a disruption in the Villacher Strasse this afternoon. So it *was* Hammer's doing, after all.

"I see," he said.

"Nice library," Hartmann grinned. "Man needs a hobby."

Krahl's turn now for the ironic sneer. "Lieutenant, I'm not really interested in your opinions on hobbies. I summoned you back to Vienna as backup for a very delicate operation." He folded his hands together in front of his face, forming a steeple.

"Perhaps, though," he continued, "we won't be needing your services after all. Perhaps you can get busy writing up the reports of your last several months in the field."

A score, finally. Krahl saw a muscle twitch in Hartmann's cheek: the field man's irrational disgust for paper work.

The phone rattled on Krahl's desk. His private line. That would be Berthold telling him that Inspektor Radok was in custody. He let it ring a second time before answering.

"Koenig here," he said into the receiver. He watched Hartmann as he spoke.

"Berthold, sir. At the scene . . ."

A pause. Christ! Somethng had gone wrong. Krahl could sense it in the man's tentative voice.

"Yes," Krahl said.

Berthold finally spoke again. "You'd better come over here, sir. I think he's given us the slip."

"You think so, do you?"

"Yes."

The goon has no ear for irony, Krahl thought. No nuances for Berthold.

"Sir?" Berthold's voice quavered.

"Tell me what happened."

Hartmann was sitting back in his chair. He seemed to be enjoying the conversation, Krahl noted.

"There was a light on in the flat and we followed standard drill," Berthold said. "Seems there was a fire stairs, though."

"And you did not apprise yourself of these stairs before moving in."

"   .   .   ."

"Am I correct, Berthold?"

"No way to know, sir."

Krahl could see the Gestapo goon on the other end of the line, fedora and black leather coat on, looking villainous as hell and about as effective in the field as a pregnant anteater. He inwardly cursed the Gestapo-SD treaty that forced him to liaison with such dogheads.

It took all of Krahl's will power not to scream at the

idiot. But he knew this would only give Hartmann satisfaction, only let him know how vital he now was to the operation. That was a card Krahl would not give to the undercover man.

"I'll be there," Krahl said and hung up without waiting for a response.

Hartmann was up now and had taken a book out of the shelves: reproductions of paintings and reliefs from Greek vases of interesting goings-on. The Lieutenant handled the book with surprising delicacy, like a true connoisseur. Still there was an unspoken insolence in the action which rankled Krahl.

"Whenever you're ready, Lieutenant."

"Yes, *sir*."

Hartmann got in the car first, snuggling in next to the door with no handle. It was just like Krahl to have a driver on call twenty-four hours a day, Hartmann thought; to have a six-wheeled Mercedes with one of the doors escape-proof. Hartmann had killed better men than Krahl. Frieland in Klagenfurt, for all his being a frightened rabbit at the end, was twice the man Krahl the Koenig was.

No foolishness of attempted conversation at least, he thought. No pretense of liking each other. Hartmann could settle back and take in visions of Vienna once again. It had been six months since he was last here, and then only for a night. The car made good time through the narrow lanes of the First District with no other traffic to slow them down. They arrived before Hartmann wanted: it would have been faster to hoof it than drive. Krahl was wasting precious petrol on an ostentatious show, Hartmann knew. An SD Lieutenant Colonel does not arrive anywhere on foot. And the Wehrmacht perishing in the East for want of a liter of fuel.

Krahl got out first, of course, and Hartmann found himself smiling at the man. He was so obvious. Waiting for them in front of the building was a thick-lipped Gestapo goon in the usual fedora and black leather greatcoat.

"Well, Berthold. Usual good work, I see."

Hartmann rolled his eyes at Krahl's stupid irony, but Berthold actually seemed to be impressed, to take it to heart.

"Somebody tipped the bastard, I'm sure of it now. Porter says his outside bell rang just before we arrived."

The porter, a fiftyish woman shivering in a light sweater, was standing on the street by the house door. Silly assholes wouldn't even let her put on her coat, Hartmann figured. They had blown it, and now others would have to pay for their mistake.

Krahl looked over at the woman, working his lower lip to show how hard he was thinking. Berthold stared hard at Hartmann who was, in turn, wearing the Bernau smile for him. The goon didn't know what to make of it, averted his eyes at the silly grin. Berthold was a simple shit, Hartmann figured, like every Gestapo station chief he had ever met, and the reason he worked on his own when out in the field.

"So there's a fire stairs," Krahl said to Berthold. "Leading where?"

"Cellar." Berthold looked back at Hartmann, staring him up and down as if trying to place him.

"And what exit from the cellar?" Krahl said.

Berthold's eyes traveled to Krahl now. "What?"

Krahl sighed, then exploded. "E-x-i-t! Means of egress! A way out, you shit-for-brains!"

Hartmann couldn't suppress a laugh. He'd never heard Krahl lose it before, and he thoroughly enjoyed being present for it.

Berthold glared at Hartmann. "None, sir. No exit. Just the door leading to the fire stairs."

"And you didn't wonder maybe where he got to. With no exit?"

"That's why I called."

Krahl shook his head, disgusted. "Show me."

Berthold stumped into the building through the front door, past the shivering porter, without giving her leave to go back to her snug apartment.

Hartmann brought up the rear, stopping by the woman first. Her cheeks were mottled with the cold.

"Listen, how long you been porter here?" he said, shooting her the Bernau smile.

Some of the fear left her eyes as she looked at his face. She didn't trust him, Hartmann knew, but not as much as she didn't trust the Gestapo ape.

"Ten years," she said.

"This building been here long?"

She shrugged, pulling the cardigan tighter around her front.

"What do I look like, an octogenarian?" she said.

Too much smile, he figured.

"Look, mother. No joking now. Simple questions, simple answers."

He rested a hand on her arm, then squeezed. She winced. Simple formula: cause and effect.

"How old is this building?" He released her arm.

She rubbed where he'd squeezed. "Not so old. There was another rickety old mess of stones here before."

Hartmann nodded. It was becoming clearer to him. Most likely catacombs below.

"Why didn't you tell Berthold about the cellar?" he said.

"Him?" she looked flustered. "He didn't ask."

"Thank you, *Gnaedige*." He doffed a nonexistent hat to her and followed the others into the building. Berthold gave him another menacing glance from where he was waiting with Krahl by the fire door leading down to the cellar. No more Bernau smile from Hartmann. Krahl began descending first, followed by Berthold. Hartmann tapped on the Gestapo man's back as he was descending.

"You want to know about me?"

Berthold turned and frowned. "I know enough about you. All you jerks who play at war. Goddamn glory boys."

"Good. I'm glad you know a little about me. That way you'll be aware that I'd just as soon eat your heart out as look at you. You mess with me and I'll insert that fedora of yours up your anus sideways. Got it? You want it rough, you'll get rough. You blew it here, and now I'm the fucking glory boy that's got to cover for you."

Berthold went red and Hartmann knew he had him. Berthold's right hand began to flex. Please do, Hartmann thought. I'll take your fat head off your shoulders before you even touch the armor. Give me the excuse, fatso. Hartmann's feet were spread; a good center of balance. A step higher than Berthold, as well. Leverage and precision. The bastard would never even feel the life going out of him, it would happen so fast. Please reach for the gun, prick.

"Are you two coming?" Krahl's voice from below broke the tension.

Hartmann kept his eyes on Berthold. No mediation

here, he told himself. Let the ape find his own way out of this.

Another flex of Berthold's right hand, then his eyes flickered to the right and left. A sigh. The hand relaxed.

"Well?" Krahl was impatient now.

Screw him, Hartmann thought.

"Okay," Berthold hissed at Hartmann. "You be the fucking glory boy. Just don't let me catch you alone."

I'm alone now, Hartmann wanted to say, but let it go. Let the bastard take the little face-saving he could and go down the stairs. Once below, Hartmann noticed the Krahl did not bother to hide an ironic smile. It was one of Krahl's joys to have his underlings at each other's throats: it kept the adrenaline flowing, kept him powerful and on top. Divide and conquer.

"It's down here," Berthold said, shining a torch into the dark cellar.

"Thanks," Krahl said. "Excellent observation."

Hartmann took one look at the corbeling over the cellar and knew his hunch had been right. It was now obvious how old this cellar must be.

"There's no way out," Berthold explained when they were on the dirt floor. "Fucking blind alley. The only thing I can figure, the guy hid somewhere here and my men missed him on the first look-see. Gave us the slip after we went back up the stairs.

"Exits?" Krahl said, his lower lip working again.

"Covered," Berthold said. "Houdini couldn't have slipped out."

"But our man did," said Krahl, turning the knife.

Berthold wiped sweat from his brow, although it was cold in the cellar; vapor formed in front of their mouths as they breathed.

"What's in the corners?" Hartmann said, peering into the darkness.

Berthold shone the flashlight onto a battered wardrobe. The doors had been splintered by the entrance holes of numerous bullets.

"Nothing there. He'd be leaking all over the floor by now if he'd been in there." Something approximating a nervous laugh accompanied Berthold's words.

Hartmann went to the wardrobe, then put his hand out for the torch. After a moment's hesitation, Berthold handed it to him. Hartmann knelt by the wardrobe, searching the hard-packed dirt. A pool of candle wax, white against the black earth, was where he'd expected it to be.

"He was here, all right," Hartmann said, shining the torch on the wax. "And he had time for some preparation before lamming it from his flat. Probably heard your car doors slamming when you arrived."

A telltale arced swath in the dirt in front of the wardrobe told him the rest of the story.

"You bother moving this thing?" he asked Berthold.

"I tell you, he couldn't have been in there or behind it. These Lugers pack a punch."

Hartmann looked up at Krahl, raising his eyebrows.

"You beginning to see the picture, Lieutenant Colonel?"

"Dammit, Hartmann, no puzzles tonight. What's on your mind?"

"We move this wardrobe and you'll see," Hartmann said.

Krahl directed Berthold to help Hartmann. It took some effort, but they moved the thing finally.

Krahl shone the torch in back.

"I'll be damned."

Hartmann looked around the back. It was the opening into the catacombs he'd expected.

"What the fuck?" Berthold gaped.

"Catacombs," Hartmann said. "Our boy's a clever one."

"I'll get my men," Berthold said.

Hartmann shook his head. "And do what? Get your asses lost in there so we have to send a patrol in after you? You know your way around these tunnels, do you?"

"But we can't—"

Krahl stopped him. "You already have. Radok's got over an hour's head start on us. Hartmann's right. He's gone by now, or lost in there. Post a couple of your men here in case he comes back. You can handle that, can't you Berthold?"

Chapter Fourteen

Once back at Headquarters, they went to Krahl's office. There hasn't been much change here in the past six months, Hartmann thought. Krahl's files have grown. There are six boxes of them now, where there had been only five before, all neatly arranged on a side table next to the desk. Krahl's bookkeeping system. Like a fussy librarian.

"In the event," Krahl said, easing into the comfortable armchair behind the desk, "it would seem fortuitous that I sent for you. Berthold and his henchmen are incompetent bumblers. Heydrich knows it. Himmler knows it. Yet nonetheless we are forced to carry on these joint actions with the Gestapo. The intent is to breed fellowship between the services. Absolute oxymoron, an intelligent Gestapo agent! If it were up to me, the Security Service would be the only intelligence service in the Reich. We'd incorporate them along with Canaris's bunch of prima donnas at Abwehr into the SD and the world would have an intelligence service to fear. Yet . . ."

He folded his hands in front of his face to show how helpless he was in the face of bureaucratic necessity.

"So we are forced to live with them, sir," Hartmann said. "That doesn't mean we have to sleep with them."

Krahl gave him a thin-lipped smile.

"Exactly, Lieutenant. Tonight was my fault. I underestimated this Radok. I thought even a fool like Berthold could take care of a simple pickup operation. Unfortunately, it would appear our friends at Gestapo are only successful when they come in the middle of the night. When they can catch a man with his pants down. Be that as it may, we are now left with the task of finding Radok as quickly as possible."

Krahl took a file from the top of several stacks of them on his desk and handed it to Hartmann.

"This should give you the pertinent details."

Hartmann opened the brown folder. Topmost was a photo of a young police cadet standing in a row of other like-uniformed men. A blue grease pencil circled the one: tall, a bit stoop-shouldered, well built, the face large and pleasantly proportioned. Not a smile on his lips; more a rueful glance at the world. Hartmann couldn't tell much from this picture.

"This recent?"

"No," Krahl said. "But it's the best we could do for now. He's been with Kripo for twelve years. He was a uniformed policeman before that. Lower middle classes; mother was a tobacconist. Father died young. Czech origins. That could prove interesting or merely coincidental. Another chap involved in this business, killed the other day, was Czech as well."

Hartmann picked through the papers: the Police Academy leaving certificate; a birth certificate from the Lainzer Hospital dated September 13, 1908, 5:30 P.M. Virgo, Hartmann thought. He used all details, all facts, even ones—such as astrology—that he basically distrusted.

"He has been married once," Krahl went on. "Divorced last year. Pretty ugly business, I understand. Infidelity. The wife, not him. Bit of a loner. A good service record, though. Decorated for bravery. He took some bird shot in the rump saving another policeman. There was also a brother who died last summer on the Eastern Front, leaving a wife and child. A boy. We're watching her flat. I doubt that Radok would be that dumb, however."

Hartmann continued looking through the accumulated detritus of Radok's life: an expired membership in the Alpinists' Society; honorary member of the Dachsteiner Club, people who have climbed the west face of that mountain. Hartmann was in the same club. He couldn't remember any Radok, though. Probably before his time, he thought. Also a boat registration: *Principia II,* a tiny five-meter job moored at the Alte Donau. Bit of a sportsman, then, Hartmann noted. It might come in handy, that sort of information.

Krahl picked through the papers in his in-basket.

"Wait," he said. "There's something new here from the Interior Ministry."

He opened the envelope; a black-and-white photo was
in it.

"Excellent. They had a picture on file from this year's
identity card."

Krahl handed him the newer photo. This was better.
Hartmann could feel his enemy now. The gray eyes.
Almost sad-looking—or was it melancholy? Hartmann
asked himself. Good. Made him easier to take. A man
with a capacity for melancholy had trouble steeling himself for real life-and-death action. Softness, too, Hartmann
could see in the face. The cheeks hid the man's bone
structure. Nothing hard or ruthless about that face. And
the mouth was full-lipped, rather sensual. A man who
liked his pleasures; a man who might do silly things for
love, even. Dark hair unkempt: an attempt at combing it
back off the forehead had been foiled by a thick lock
which dangled down. His tie was knotted carelessly and
the shirt collar badly pressed. The recent bachelor.

Radok has been lucky tonight, Hartmann thought. But
at best he's just a sheep among the wolves. Mere luck
won't see him through.

"One thing missing from the file," Hartmann said.

Krahl pursed his lips. "I believe it's all there."

"No. Something's definitely missing. I think you know
what it is."

"Well," Krahl sighed. "You'll need to know a bit of
the why, I suppose. It would come out soon enough,
anyway. When I give you the assignment, in point of
fact. So, our hero here has some papers we want. We
need. Quite valuable papers, as it turns out. Invaluable
to the Reich. I won't go into the reasoning on my part
that brought about this discovery. Enough for now to
know that it is imperative that our friend Radok does not
get these papers out to some foreign country."

"The Allies, you mean?" Hartmann said.

"Precisely. I have good reason to believe that Radok
came into possession of the papers in question during the
investigation of a double murder. General von Tratten
and a lowly black marketeer named Cezak. You may
have heard . . ."

Hartmann shook his head.

"No," Krahl said. "I quite imagine you were otherwise
engaged at the time. But these papers were funneled

through von Tratten from an Abwehr agent in Berlin. That man also is now dead."

Krahl waited a moment, then proceeded. "Von Tratten was killed in a setup for the black marketeer. Took his own life, in fact. Coincidence? Was he simply in the wrong place at the wrong time? So Kripo and Gestapo seem to believe. But I've taken a look at this Cezak's file. Radok personally tailed him for weeks before the setup. A thorough cop, Radok. Recorded Cezak's every move, his every urinal stop. Too much data for him, it would seem. But not for me. While examining the Cezak file late this afternoon, I noted an irregularity."

Krahl waited expectantly.

"What irregularity?" Hartmann finally said. It was required. He hoped his question would speed things up.

"Patience, boy. All in good time. The report on Cezak lists his religion as Protestant. Nationality, Czech."

"And Radok was a Czech," Hartmann said.

"Born here," Krahl said. "But his parents were from Bohemia. As I say, that could be coincidence or design. We'll find that out soon enough. More importantly, our Protestant black marketeer seemed to have a penchant for confession. Five recorded visits in the last two weeks to a certain confessional at Klosterneuburg."

Hartmann involuntarily shivered. Christ, it can't be! he thought.

"Are you chilled, Lieutenant?" Krahl was pleased at his reaction.

"Mayer . . ." Hartmann whispered. "He's mixed up in this?"

Krahl nodded. "Now you see your importance, Lieutenant Hartmann. Or should I just call you Wolf . . . ? Isn't that how your friends in the Mayer group knew you? Wolf? Yes. A bit of infiltration work for you. Re-infiltration, I should say."

"He's still around?" Hartmann said. "You never took him?"

"No, no," Krahl said. "You see, when we pulled you, it was thought by Kaltenbrunner that Father Mayer would be better left where he was. It was early days to be bashing priests back in thirty-eight. His case was handed over to Gestapo and they kept surveillance on him for a little over a year. Then came a change of leadership at the Morzin Platz, and Mayer's file simply slipped between the boards. There were more pressing matters at hand with the roundup of the Jews. Besides, he'd quietened down by then, no more fire and brimstone from the pulpit about the Nazis. The Gestapo figured that your faked arrest scared him. In fact, I think the bastard just quit being verbally subversive and instead went underground. I suspect he organized a resistance cell, that Cezak was somehow involved in it, and that the papers we so desperately need to recover might be finding their way to Mayer himself. Neat, eh?"

"And you figure Radok's working with Mayer?" Hartmann said, forcing logic into his mind; forcing out the sick feeling at the sound of Father Mayer's name and the thought of his near disgrace of four years before.

"Let's be kind," Krahl said. "Let's assume that Radok is simply a so-so cop who's had treason thrust at him. I think he's stumbling into this. He knew the General. He was in service to the von Trattens' with his parents. The Radoks were eventually pensioned off. You'll see in the file that the investment money for their tobacco shop came from the General."

Hartmann had already seen that connection, already made some of the same assumptions as Krahl.

"More than that," Krahl went on. "Let's assume that Radok is not a complete fool. That sooner or later he'll make the same connection that I did about Father Mayer. After all, he was the cop doing the tailing."

Hartmann looked straight at Krahl, willing his own eyes to be clear and straightforward; not to betray the fear he was feeling.

"And you want me to play returning prodigal son," Hartmann said. "You want me back in position as Wolf in case Radok turns to Mayer with these mysterious papers."

Krahl spread his hands on the desk: delicate, white hands. Too delicate, Hartmann thought. Too white. As if he had daily manicures, and soaked them in milk.

"Tomorrow should be time enough," Krahl said by way of reply. "You'll need to invent a story, of course. The daring escape from Dachau, that sort of thing. You've a fertile enough imagination for that, I'm sure. You know the standard drill. Report daily to this number.

And I mean daily. No solo flights on this one. It'll be too risky for you to stay here at Headquarters after tonight. Too compromising to your role as double agent. I'm sure you have a little hiding hole somewhere, haven't you? Someplace you feel safe from my prying eyes. Well, that place is safe simply because I have not yet sought it out. Go there, but report daily. I warn you, you'll end up in Russia if you play your usual tricks on this one. It's too delicate for the Hammer. Understand? It's Wolf again for this job. The Wolf whom Mayer and company know and trust. And I'm *Koenig*. I want you to remember that. Keep your ears open and get information, not scalps. Head-hunting we leave to the Gestapo. Above all, Hartmann, remember four years ago. Remember the mess you were in. Remember that you owe me."

Lieutenant Wolf Hartmann did remember now, cupped in a fetal position in a former maid's bed in the dormer-windowed room at the top of the SD headquarters. The circular nature of life. Retribution? Coincidence? A second chance? Lots of words for the same concept. The Red Priest, Father Mayer, would know of the concept. That was how they knew him back then. The Red Priest. A man of God and Marx, and Wolf Hartmann never really knew which one was stronger in the man.

The road to Mayer and his group had been a circuitous one. It started with his first mission for Krahl, when Hartmann had been fresh from Germany and the Special Section training at Bernau. Full of theory and knowledge of cyphers, poison, invisible inks—all that sort of thing, which Hartmann had never used since spy school. He was sitting in a scroungy café near the University, keeping an eye and an ear on a couple of students thought to be the control behind the CP students' union. This was in thirty-six, so Hartmann's job had been clandestine, deep cover, because in the Austria of that time the Nazis were still an illegal party. He'd been following these two students for the past week and had the better part of a graph-paper notebook filled with names and addresses of their contacts. These contacts were more rumpled and pampered student types like themselves.

But tonight it was different. There was a large group of students gathered at the café. The proprietor seemed to know them and tolerated their jokes at his expense with good humor. Fresh little shits they were, and Hartmann would have liked to break cover just long enough to show them how ineffectual they were; not the least because in the group of students was a special person tonight. Tall and lovely with cheeks aflame with good health, she was the center of the group's attention and was busily telling them how confused she felt and how out of sync with life she had been of late. Her studies suddenly had no meaning to her; she wanted to know the why of everything. Most importantly, why she was here. Answers were what she wanted and she kept asking why, why, why.

Her voice was low and melodic even when complaining. No trace of a whine. And she was dead serious. Hartmann could plainly see that.

The young boys around her—for she was the only female present—were all about Hartmann's age. They were listening, nodding occasionally, but none of them was truly serious. Not about her psyche, at any rate. Hartmann could see that they all wore the same faked expression of interest, and every last one of them looked at her legs every chance he had. They wanted to get into her knickers more than into her mind. Nice enough knickers they'd be, too, Hartmann thought.

Suddenly he took a deep aversion to the two Communists he'd been tailing. He wanted to hurt them. Oh, they'd eventually be hurt in the fullest meaning of the word when the Nazis took over Austria, but right now he wanted to strike a blow. To show them what miserable little creatures they were. He knew how to do it, as well. This was something they did not teach at spy school, but something for which Hartmann had a gift: insight into what makes a human tick. He instinctively knew how to reach the tall woman. On the back of a napkin on his table he wrote a short message:

You've got it backwards. There are no answers, only increasingly sophisticated questions. Keep questioning. Death is when you have all the answers. And forget those jerks. They just want to make you. They could give a damn about your pain. But I do.

A longish job of writing for Hartmann, who used words sparingly. He smiled at the message as he read over it. Not bad. Especially the last. "But I do." What? Want to make you, too, or give a damn? He laid some coins on the table, got up, put his coat on, and walked to her table. Thrusting the napkin into her unwilling hand, he turned and walked out of the coffee house. Voices were buzzing in back of him, but he never looked back.

A half a block was all he walked. Her footsteps clacked behind him. She called to him.

"Hey, you."

He turned. She caught up to him, breathing hard.

"Why'd you write this?"

"Better," he teased. "Now you're asking the right questions."

She smiled, then laughed. And he joined in her laughter.

They were inseparable for the next two years. What started as a lark, as a slap in the face to the smart-ass student boys, soon developed into real love. The only love Hartmann had ever experienced in his life.

To her he was Wolf.

Hartmann had used his contacts with his young lover and her soft university friends who played at dissidence to meet the infamous Red Priest, Padre, as his inner circle of acolytes called him. In those days the man had a following of young men and women who flocked to his sermons to listen to thinly disguised biblical parables condemning the godlessness of the Nazis. Hartmann's young lover was among those who listened wide-eyed to the priest's inflammatory Sunday preaching. It was difficult to admit, but Hartmann himself had also been drawn to the man; to his reckless heroics, to his unswerving belief in a higher morality than the state. Between the woman and the priest, Hartmann had almost become compromised. Almost sold out his true mission for the stupid intellectual virtues he was exposed to in their company. Krahl had saved him, that was true. Wolf Hartmann was in his debt. Also true.

Hartmann rolled over in bed, pulling the covers up over his head. He'd wanted to marry her. Lord, lord. To marry and be with her always. The slow ache caused by her absence came back to him now. He had told Krahl of his desire to marry; said that having a wife would not compromise his undercover work. That it would add intensity. It would give him something to fight for. But Krahl had not been convinced. He knew that a wife would weaken an operative, would make him think twice about putting himself in danger. Make him want to stay alive when an operative's ultimate directive was to give up his life happily if and when required. And Krahl went to his infernal files, dug and poked about until he'd found the trump card he needed. The Jew in the past. Hartmann's future wife a *Mischling*, part Jew. And that was absolutely forbidden for a man in the SS.

"You should be grateful to me," Krahl had said. "I've saved your career. If Berlin ever got word of you mixing with a Jew, well . . ."

And that had been Krahl's trump ever since. His assurance that no matter how much leash Hartmann was given, he would always have to come back to the master.

There were only memories and vile air in the dormered bedroom, as Hartmann put the Bernau smile on for himself, put all else out of his mind, and busied himself concocting an escape story for tomorrow to explain his miraculous return from Dachau. A history that would cover the past four years.

And still the bitter premonition was with him. He felt her near, now. Close and getting closer. After all these years.

Frieda. His part-Jew.

Chapter Fifteen

The first pearl-gray light was coming through the window. There were voices from below in the courtyard; the creak of garbage cans opening; the clank of them shutting.

Frieda woke up sharply, her heart pounding in a panic. It had been several months since she'd last stayed in this apartment, and the bedroom seemed strange to her. The man sleeping peacefully next to her was a stranger, too, though the stickiness at her middle made her remember that he was an intimate stranger.

Now the events of last night came racing into her mind. Surreal. The stuff of books, not life. She wanted to forget the cold fear of being chased by the Gestapo; the terror of the claustrophobic journey through the catacombs. Erase all of it but the man lying by her. His tenderness in the night. The feeling she had when with him.

She looked at his face and found it endlessly fascinating. A mystery to her; the sort of man she would never fully know. He was not traditionally handsome, but something in his sad, soulful expression—even in sleep—drew her to him.

He lay on his stomach, his head burrowed into a pillow, and she let her hands play across his back, feeling the strong muscles there, the thickness of him so unlike the narrow, boyish body of her Wolf. Always before she had been the one to lie docile, letting the hands play over her, discovering all the secret places, the soft places, the moistness. Now it was as if it were somebody else's hand tracing down the man's back, feeling every nub of his spine.

The man smiled in his sleep as her hand crept down to the sharp bone at the small of his back. An involuntary groan came from him as her hand moved lower, exploring the tight cleft between his buttocks. A nice, solid, muscular behind. She should be ashamed, but had no time to worry about propriety this morning. She wanted only to feel him, touch his flesh, know the hardness of his body. So strong. His muscles flexed as her hand moved lower and now she felt a strange roughness on his backside. A graveled and scarred terrain. She had to see. Pulling back the covers, she revealed a battlefield of tiny, puckered, pink scars on the cheek of his left rump: lesions that had healed into taut mounds of angry flesh.

"Old soldiers, old wounds," he said suddenly.

She jumped up to her knees on the bed, startled, the breath coming hard in her chest.

"Sorry to scare you." He rolled onto his back. "That felt good." He smiled at her through his sleepy eyes.

"How did you get those?" she asked, and felt damned stupid doing so.

He laughed, wrinkling the skin around his eyes as he did so.

"They're not as bad as they look. Buckshot. Nothing too heroic."

But she knew that there was something heroic associated with them. That he was the kind of man never to boast, always to hide his true self. It reminded her of her father's self-irony. The way he always played down his war experiences when her mother brought them up. The day of his funeral Frieda had discovered the Iron Cross among his cuff links, tie pins, and other jewelry.

She set her hand on Radok's chest, feeling the hair there. Not very thick, but black as night. He was watching her, still smiling. Drowsy and trusting. A simple animal trust. He allowed her to explore, not having to be the man in charge as Wolf had always been. Comparison made her feel guilty: she had sworn that there would never be another man after Wolf.

But her hands played a sweet melody over Radok's body, searching out his strange, secret places: under his arm and down his side, onto his belly. He flinched, his muscles tightening. The hand went lower, into his pubic hair and down the inside of his thigh. Her hand traveled under the leg now, touching the back of his knees and then moved up again, slowly, slowly . . . cupping his scrotum, so full and heavy in her hand. He was stiff and throbbing when she gripped him and then she heard her own breathing. Deep and raspy it was. She straddled him, putting him deep inside her; the foreign feeling. Letting her breasts dangle in his face as he lay on his back under her. She felt his tongue at her nipples and then she was lost in the sensation, moving faster and faster until she felt as if she would be torn apart. Faster and harder, their hips and bellies slapping together. Him going deeper into her until she screamed in delight. Then release. Darkness. Sweet oblivion, like a small death.

She lay on top of him and slept again, dreamlessly. Radok's fidgeting and wriggling awoke her. Bright light shone in the room now. Gray skies, but bright, mid-morning light.

"Sorry," he said, lifting her up and sliding out from under her. "Must just do a pee."

She sighed into the pillow, emitting a low laugh.

"Two choices," she said, turning to him. He stood naked and lovely by the window. "The *Clo* is down the hall. Chamber pot is in the nightstand there."

He opted for the chamber pot rather than the communal toilet, taking the pot into the sitting room out of modesty.

Words of her father came back to her as she listened to him urinating. She'd been only twelve at the time, just going into menarche, and her father had felt himself compelled to go over the facts of life with her. Something her mother had never attempted. Embarrassed and ill at ease, he'd attempted to sketch out the biological realities and quickly grown angry with himself.

"I make it sound like a biology text," he had said, disgusted. "Sorry. It's so much more than that. The sweetest thing in the world, if it's right and done with the right person."

Then he'd fiddled with his pipe, tamping down the tobacco with his callused thumb, flustered that he'd grown romantic and idealistic about it.

"What I mean to say is . . . well, you can sleep with all types of people, but you'll know it's right when you can wake up to him, too."

She now knew what her father had meant.

Radok came back into the bedroom, tall and a bit stooped, a sheepish grin on his face. She held out her arms to him and he lay by her again. She took his right hand, examining the thumb.

"You don't smoke a pipe, do you?" she said.

"Mistress of non sequitur."

"Just a question," she said. "Silly."

He shook his head, seeing she was serious. "Too much fiddling about with pipes. I never had the time."

She held his head, running her hands through his rumpled hair, graying at the temples.

"Dear Inspektor Radok."

"Sweet Fräulein Lassen," he whispered. "What are we going to do about this?"

And there it was, she thought. The real world once again. But without her realizing it, her subconscious had been working out a plan, a course of action.

"You stay here. By now, every cop and Gestapo agent in Vienna will be looking for you. I'll go to Klosterneuburg. Father Mayer will know what to do."

He said nothing. She sensed he did not like the idea of inactivity.

"I won't be long," she said. "And we can't just go running about without some plan. Eight days are all we have left, now. The documents are too vital for us to waste time. We need organization. A group plan."

"The documents," he said. "Are they all that's important?"

"Okay, okay. And we are, too," she admitted. "But who wants to get maudlin first thing in the morning?"

This brought another laugh from him and seemed to smooth things out.

"I'm putting you in danger," he said finally. "It wouldn't have taken them long to connect me with von Tratten."

Another silence; a radio played in a neighboring flat. Waltz music to make the people forget the world was falling apart.

"But what I can't figure out is how they got on to the papers so quickly," he said. "Maybe we're just being paranoid. Maybe the raid wasn't for me at all. A Jew in the same apartment building?"

"Keep on dreaming," she said. "I should have put two and two together yesterday when I was at Frau von Tratten's making sure about your story. As I was leaving the villa I passed a man getting out of a six-wheeled

Mercedes. I didn't give it much thought then. But it makes sense. I should have realized then that such a car means only one thing."

"Describe the man."

"He's tall and thin. Dapper, like his clothes come from Knieze's tailors and not off the rack. Blond hair. About your age."

Radok went on with the description: "A thin-lipped guy with eyes too close? Long, straight nose?"

"Yes," she said. "Who is he?"

Radok frowned. "They're on to it, all right. SD. Security Service of the SS. That'll be Lieutenant Colonel Krahl."

"So you see I'm right," she said almost proudly. "They'll be after you. It isn't safe for you to show your face."

"But what if they saw you?" Radok asked. "If they traced you to me?"

"The street was clear when I arrived last night," she said. "I do know the basics of the business. I may not be a pro yet, but I'm not a total idiot, either."

"You're right," he said. "They're on to me."

They said nothing more about it. Frieda dressed and got a reluctant promise from Radok that he'd sit tight until she got back to him. There's coffee in the kitchen, she told him. No cream, but this was real coffee brought back from Switzerland on her last tour. No use spoiling the taste with dairy products. The porter was the nosy type, she explained, so please just stay put in the flat.

At the door—he naked, she fully clothed—he held her hard against him. She felt him growing against her leg and her knees began to buckle.

"I love you," he said.

"You don't even know me," she said in his ear, but she knew she loved him, too.

"What I know, I love. I'll take the rest as it comes," he said, his breath hot and urgent in her ear. "Be careful. Come back soon. I'll be here."

He kissed her hand.

She decided on public transport as it was less conspicuous than a taxi. Less chance of spot-checks on a tram and bus than in a car. The tram stop was a block away. She had tickets in her purse. Father Mayer would know what to do. He'd devise a plan. She trusted him, believed in him. Suddenly she realized she felt the same about Radok.

It took ten minutes for a tram to come, time enough for her to go over last night, every detail of it, once again. She felt no shame at what she and Radok had done in the night and the morning. If morality is what one feels good after doing, then their love was highly moral.

But thinking this, she felt the heat of guilt at her throat. Only now did she begin to look at what had happened last night as a betrayal to Wolf. What if he's still alive? she thought. If he was, then what she and Radok had done in the night was highly immoral, no matter how good it felt.

Is that why you tore up the picture of Wolf this morning? she asked herself. The lovely alpine scene, flushed down the toilet. Eradicating all traces of Wolf, because of the guilt you feel?

The 49 tram finally came and she boarded, telling herself not to be foolish. All hope of Wolf's safe return was futile. And Wolf would not want her to sacrifice herself to his memory, she knew. Wolf would want her to snatch what happiness she could from the world. The conductor punched her ticket and smiled at her.

Frieda changed trains at Schottentor, took the D tram to Nussdorf, and waited a half hour there for a bus to Klosterneuburg. Getting off in the main square of that village, she checked her wristwatch: she'd been gone over ninety minutes already. Radok would most likely be frantic by the time she managed to get back to him.

She took the back way up to the abbey, up Schlosser-strasse, and then the rickety wooden steps up the steep hill by the Golden Horn Gasthaus. Snow was still on the ground here, and the wooden steps, in the shade, were covered in black ice and slush. She held on to the railing for all she was worth, happy just to make it to the top. The name kept recurring in her mind like a prayer: Father Mayer, Father Mayer. . . .

The side chapel was empty when she entered; she went into the main church from this chapel. Morning service was over. No light showed in Father Mayer's confessional. He would be in the vestry, then. She went in without bothering to knock.

The Father was talking to another man, who was seated and partially blocked from view by the Father's robes.

"Sorry," she said, trying to cover up her entrance in the presence of the stranger.

Mayer rose now, moving toward her.

"Frieda . . ." He looked agitated, but happy. "He's come back."

She could see the other man now, still seated. His eyes were wide in surprise, his mouth half open in exclamation. It didn't sink in for a moment. She could not recognize him; did not want to.

"Frieda," Father Mayer said, taking her arm. "It's Wolf. He's escaped."

Everything went black for her; the room spun and she felt herself slumping to the floor.

Chapter Sixteen

Hartmann ran to Frieda, still lying limp in Father Mayer's arms where she'd fallen. His premonition had been right—this operation would bring her back into his life—but he hadn't expected any such immediate verification of his forebodings. His young lover; the only woman he'd ever wanted to marry. But now Frieda represented a complication he neither wanted nor needed. Hartmann had hoped that any connection Frieda had to Mayer's group would have ended with his disappearance four years ago. Thus, Frieda was not the only one surprised at this sudden reunion.

"The bench," Father Mayer said.

Hartmann helped him carry her to the pew-like bench against one wall, her ankles in his hands, so thin and delicate. The Bernau smile failed him for the first time, and he could only look at her openly, honestly. With longing. His part-Jew.

"Feet up," Father Mayer commanded. "Here." He took a brocade pillow from under her head. "Put this under her feet to get the blood to the head."

Hartmann did as he was told; it seemed natural that he be in this role vis-à-vis Father Mayer once again.

Father Mayer took a handkerchief from his pocket, tipped a cut-glass water decanter, wetted the cloth, and put the compress on Frieda's forehead.

"I think she's coming round," Father Mayer said.

Hartmann took his eyes from her feet, following the contours of her legs up to her middle, then to her hands across her chest, and to her face. Her eyes were open now, staring into his.

"It's you," she whispered. "Really you."

He nodded.

"You've come back."

"Yes," he said.

She made to sit up.

"Easy does it," Father Mayer said. "Not too quickly. You've had a shock, child."

And more to come, Hartmann thought, trying to recover, trying to impose the discipline of duty on himself by use of cynicism. Hold nothing sacred but duty.

"How?" she said. "Where were you?"

Hartmann sat on the bench next to her, taking her hand in his.

"All in good time," Father Mayer said. "Wolf's been telling me of his exploits."

And a good thing I've started already, Hartmann thought. It would be hard for him to lie to Frieda, though he'd done enough of that in his time, also. The story he'd concocted of his escape from Dachau would ring hollow, he knew, when related to her. The adventures with a partisan band in the Waldviertel would carry no authenticity. Mayer had bought the pack of lies, for they had been told convincingly enough, the details clear and horrific enough to be true. The slain camp guard who'd tried to rape him; the burden of confession. Father Mayer exulted in such things. A secret so awful that it could not be shared with many.

Hartmann could feel the Bernau smile at work once again. He patted Frieda's hand.

"I've missed you," he said simply.

She blushed. Still his Frieda, to do with as he pleased.

"And we've missed you, as well," Father Mayer said, covering up the silence from Frieda. "Quite given up hope, I must confess. But this gives us cause for optimism. Especially so now."

Hartmann continued to hold Frieda's trembling hand, but looked into the priest's face.

"Why especially now?" he said.

Mayer put a large, pudgy hand on Hartmann's shoulder.

"No time for business now. This is a time for rejoicing. A time for a prayer of thanks."

Father Mayer took Frieda's free hand in his left, Hartmann's in his right. He bowed his head, closing his eyes. Hartmann looked at Frieda; her eyes were on his. So many things to read there, but among them fear or guilt. He was not sure which. His impish grin flashed for her now, nodding toward the praying priest. Their old joking manner behind Father Mayer's solemn back. She smiled, and for an instant, they were transported back to four years before. To their old connection. The priest finished his silent prayer, lifted his head, and the magic was gone.

Frieda squeezed Hartmann's hand, then inched it out of his grasp, looking at Father Mayer.

"I've got news," she said. "He's waiting for us. He wants to join us."

Mayer looked concerned. "Radok?"

She nodded. "And he's got the papers. They're awful. The Nazis are going to kill all the Jews in Europe. The papers show how and where."

The Padre scoffed at the idea as Hartmann continued to watch Frieda, fascinated. The contents of the papers sunk in only after a further comment from her.

"They're calling it the Final Solution. It's real. I saw the pictures." She went on to explain their deadlines: fifteen days until the transports began; eight for them to get word to the Allies.

"We've got to stop them," she pleaded. "Alert the Polish partisans. Blow the rail lines. Do something."

Mayer patted her hand.

"We will, my child. Don't worry."

Mayer was beginning to come around to believing her, Hartmann noticed. He watched her closely as she spoke of this man Radok and of the papers, wondering now if she had not been the secret caller at Radok's last night before the Gestapo arrived. Just how far was she involved with this man?

Hartmann put these thoughts out of his mind, quickly replacing them with more important considerations.

So now he knew the importance of Krahl's infernal documents. These were not just some insignificant military secrets out on the market to the highest bidder—the stuff of most espionage. No. These papers, if Frieda's description was anywhere near accurate, were very big fish indeed.

". . . photos, orders signed by Hitler," Frieda was saying, her eyes shining. "The whole panoply of proof. He has them and wants to get them out."

"This Radok fellow?" Hartmann said innocently.

She nodded.

"And he's a cop?" The moment he'd said it, Hartmann knew he'd overplayed his hand. Had that been mentioned yet? But neither of them seemed to notice this slip-up.

"Kripo," Father Mayer said.

"But he can be trusted," Frieda said. Then she related her story of the events of the night before: of her visit to Frau von Tratten to check up on Radok; of her arrival at the Inspektor's apartment just moments before the Gestapo arrived to arrest him; of their flight through the catacombs. The story ended with their arrival at her old apartment. The apartment Hartmann and she had spent so many nights in four years ago. And Hartmann had the feeling she was holding something back. He knew the signs when she was holding back part of the truth: her eyes gave her away, shifting back and forth like the lowest criminal. Her eyes dodged back and forth between Father Mayer and Hartmann now. What had been the sleeping arrangements at the apartment? Hartmann knew the luxury of her oversized double bed; the discomfort of the sagging couch in the living room. Were sex and betrayal the ingredients she was holding back from him?

Thinking it, Hartmann knew that it was the truth. Anything you thought had already been done. The bitch.

Hartmann met her eyes and she looked down automatically. Then he was certain his suspicion was right. She and the policeman had been lovers last night. Fine. It made what he had to do easier.

"I guess we have to go to him, then," Father Mayer said.

"He's waiting for us," Frieda said.

Lovely, Hartmann thought. Simplicity itself, for he knew the apartment building. One way in, one way out. No fire stairs this time.

"They're going to be looking for him," Hartmann said. "Half of Vienna will be out after him." He turned to Frieda. "And you too, maybe. You might've been seen."

"I'm sure I wasn't," she said.

"Wolf's right," Father Mayer said. "You may be in danger, too. I'll go."

"Father." Hartmann put his hand on the man's arm. "Forgive this poor sinner, but I think you're just a bit too high-profile for this job. Me, I'm long gone as far as the authorities here know. Besides, I've got an idea how to bring him in. I'll need one of these." He tapped the priest's cassock.

Mayer understood immediately, nodding.

"Yes. Very good," he said. "I see what you're getting at."

"But he won't know you," Frieda said. "He'll never believe you."

"He'll believe me," Hartmann said. "I know how to talk to policemen."

Father Mayer laughed, but Frieda looked at him wonderingly, almost warily, Hartmann noticed.

Father Mayer got a fresh cassock out of the wardrobe and blessed Hartmann. He in turn gave Frieda a timid peck on the cheek and was off.

"Be back in an hour," he said from the vestry door. "Not to worry."

Once out of the church, Hartmann stowed the unnecessary cassock beneath the side steps. It was only a cover story to explain his ease of movement around Vienna despite being a supposedly wanted man. Hartmann would retrieve the cassock when he returned. After this Hartmann went to a café to use their pay phone. Only a few customers around at this quiet time of the day: he could talk openly to Krahl. He dialed the well-remembered number and waited. Two rings; of course Krahl would wait for at least the second before answering. Hartmann hung up. Redialed. Two rings again. Krahl would know who.

"Koenig."

"Our man's at the Stieglitzgasse, Third District. Meet me there in a half hour. Full squad of SS. No Gestapo."

Hartmann hung up before Krahl could ask for the house number. That way they'd be sure to wait for him.

After Frieda had left, Radok puttered about her apartment, trying to ignore the obvious: that he was not used to waiting, or to letting a woman do his dirty work for him. He brewed a pot of real coffee, putting too much water in the pot, and had it percolate all over the stove. Cleaning up that mess took five minutes. Checking out the von Tratten papers another five. The photos did not shock so much today at second inspection. Everything was there, nothing misplaced or damaged from their flight through the catacombs. Another twenty minutes passed in disassembling and cleaning the Walther PPK. Only twenty rounds on him; not enough for much of a firefight, if it came down to that.

Ten more minutes were passed in making up his mind. It hadn't gone eleven in the morning before Radok stuck his nose out the green door of Frieda's flat.

Radok was the kind of man who could become completely unnerved by not having planned an escape route. Stuck at the top of the house with no fire escape, he was a sitting duck.

Just a quick look-see, he told himself. It's not really going back on my word to the girl. Wouldn't make her any happier if I followed the letter of my promise and was taken with my socks off, splayed out on the old sleeping couch.

There was no one in the hall, but he remembered Frieda's warning about the nosy porter, so went back into the flat. He didn't go back to stay, however, just to develop and augment his cover story if seen by someone. He strapped on the Walther, humped his overcoat on, gathered some loose change from the table, and put it in his pocket. Then he stuck the von Tratten papers into the inside pocket of the overcoat.

Into the hall again, where there were sounds of washing-up behind one door, a baby crying in another flat.

He thought of his brother's widow and his brother's son. The nephew. The continuation of the Radok line. Too late to worry about that by now. SD would be crawling all over Lombardstrasse by now: stakeout, the usual drill. Her phone tapped, mail opened. His brother's wife would have to take care of herself. Choices would be made without really making choices. She would find a likely young mechanic or some such to provide for the necessities. While Helmut fed the worms in an unmarked grave in Russia.

Can that, Radok. Take it step by step. You've got more to live for now than you had two days ago. Be happy, son. You've got a purpose again. A mission. And a woman.

There was no other way down but by the main staircase, just as he'd thought. No fire stairs this time. Ge-

stapo wouldn't fall for it a second time, anyway. If they
somehow got on to him again, the stairs would be covered. A bit of a ledge on the courtyard-side window, but
it led nowhere. Three-story drop from the window. Great.
The goon's delight: one way in, one way out. Escape
here meant a meat-wagon plunge.

My luck, I'd just break my fucking legs, he thought.
Land on my feet, not my head.

He went down the stairs anyway, hoping that there
might be an empty flat on another floor, some door he
could pick his way into. Names were on all the doors,
sounds came from behind most, but unless he wanted to
go knocking up everybody in the house he could not be
sure of a safe, empty flat. There was one likely-looking
one on the first floor, the floor just above ground level.
It was a corner flat; maybe a window in there faced onto
the alley, an easy drop to the street. The door needed
painting and its nameplate was about a century old. No
light came from the transom; no need for one, either,
this time of day. It told him nothing.

The door suddenly opened and he jumped back. An
old woman in a brown wool coat with a sheared beaver
collar came out, shopping bag in hand. Radok tried to
smile at her, but it probably came out a frown, for she
frowned back at him. That meant nothing, however: all
old Viennese women frowned. National pastime. Old age
frowning at youth, at health.

She passed him, looking back once from the top of the
stairs, then she descended.

Nice work, Radok, he told himself. Not even a polite
"Küss die Hand" from him to allay her suspicions. The
words had caught in his throat.

He followed her after a few moments, going into the
courtyard and through to the entrance hall, checking the
names on the wall board, looking for any blanks on other
staircases. It was becoming an obsession with him, finding a bolt hole for an imaginary escape. But he could not
stop now. Thoroughness might save his life, he told himself. Not paranoia, Radok. Just method. But he had no
luck. All the apartments in the house had names next to
them on the board.

"What are you doing here?"

The voice came from a large woman in white coat and kerchief. Cigarette in her mouth, garbage pail in hand.

"Just checking for vacancies," he said.

"There aren't any."

She stood between him and the courtyard. The street door was open in back of him: at least his story would appear true to her. The curious porter, he reckoned. Curious and belligerent. Not the type of woman he'd care to leg-wrestle with.

"Yeah," he said. "I see that now. Too bad. I could use an apartment for when I'm on leave. . . ."

She said nothing, standing there with her white metal bucket full of slop in her hand, furry house shoes over heavily veined feet.

"Nothing coming up free then?"

She shook her head. "The front door should be closed." Sullen.

"It was open when I came in," he said.

"Shut it when you leave."

She wasn't moving, waiting for him to go first. He did, for she was the sort to call the cops about anything or anybody suspicious. He thought quickly as he moved to the door, looking back once. She was still watching him. He nodded and went out, grasping the door handle firmly. It twisted in his hand. Good. The lock wouldn't engage unless he let go of it. He shut the door firmly, making it echo inside, and held the handle, waiting for the shrew inside to get lost. He counted to twenty, then another twenty just to be safe. Opening the door slowly, he figured he'd have to move quickly now to get back to Frieda's apartment without being seen. He couldn't just tell the porter he'd been staying with a friend. Or maybe he could have at first, but no way now would she buy the story. More work well done, he told himself. Excellent cover story.

The door opened silently on heavy hinges. A crack, then more.

The porter was standing inside, glaring at him.

"Just making sure it was locked," he said.

But she wasn't listening. She pushed the door shut in his face. It locked securely. Him on the outside.

Radok gave up on reentering the apartment building. Breaking-and-entering, on top of all his other mistakes,

would be too much for one morning. Instead he found a
window seat at the café across the street from the house
and waited for Frieda's return.

Two cups of ersatz coffee and three illustrated magazines
later, his wait was rewarded, but not by the return of
Frieda. To begin with, he saw the "Green Henry" park
at the end of the street, a black-tuniced SS man at the
wheel. Then a six-wheeled Mercedes arrived a few minutes later, parking at the other end of the street. No
movement from inside the car.

She's sold me. This was Radok's first thought. He
discounted the possibility of Frieda's having been picked
up and turned in such a short amount of time. Gestapo
let you cool your ass at Morzin Platz for several hours
before they began an interrogation; same with SD. No.
There was no other alternative. She had sold him. Frieda
was a double. He should have known it last night when
she'd led them through the catacombs. Knew the place,
she did. Trained in it. He'd been set up. Made to trust
her. Stuck his shaft in her and sown seed, which meant
she owned him.

Radok felt disgust at himself. So easily fooled. A little
screwing in the night and you're ass-over-heels in love.
Easy work for her. Pure chance he was sitting in the café
now and not in the apartment waiting for her little surprise party. You jackass, you idiot, he chided himself.
The old betrayal game. You should know that one well
enough by now. The betrayal is always there waiting for
you. Open up to someone and you'll get it. The General,
Helga his wife. Now Frieda. Misnomer there: from *Friede*,
meaning peace. No peace to be found in her; or, at best,
only the peace of the dead.

Still no move from the asshole in the Mercedes. Doing
a little wait-see. Or maybe just waiting for somebody
before starting the action. If so, that somebody must be
damned important. Some mastermind coming to coordinate the show. It couldn't be Krahl. If Radok's instincts
were right, the prick in the Mercedes was Krahl, smoking
a cigarette in an ivory holder, most likely.

Radok put the change he'd found in the flat onto the
table, ready to move. He did so not so much out of
charity as wariness. No need to call attention to himself,

and the waiter would scream murder if cheated out of his tip.

A taxi pulled up alongside the Mercedes. A small, compactly built man in a brown suit got out the passenger door, talking through the rolled-down window of the six-wheeler. Money was handed over to brown-suit and from him to the taxi driver.

And this is the mastermind they've been waiting for? Radok thought. Running around Vienna without a groschen in his pocket. What kind of a prick does that? Besides me, that is. But Radok knew. An undercover prick, that's who. Counterinsurgency with the SS. A glory boy, busting apart radio sets, riding the trams listening for gossip.

Krahl was getting out of his car now, crisp and chinless in the daylight, skin the color of death. Radok had seen him several times before at lectures given at Kripo HQ. Thorough, soulless. Krahl waved to the "Green Henry" and a full squad of armed SS piled out. Radok took another look at the glory boy: even beyond the brown suit, similar to one that Radok himself had once owned, there was something familiar-looking about him. A wiry little bastard with a mean face underneath a pasted-on grin. Christ, the grin! Radok thought. The boy in the alpine photo with Frieda! The final connection was made for Radok. It all made sense now. In it together, they were. A fine little duo. He sends his little lady out to screw the troops, then he comes in for the kill.

There were no lingering doubts for Radok now. Betrayal on the grand scale. Mayer's group was compromised for certain. Infiltrated. So that option was out. Radok was on his own.

He got up from the table calmly. Outside, the SS were converging on the apartment house. He wouldn't wait around for the finale. Into the Gents for him. The back window was stuck. He took his shoe off, wrapped a towel around it, and shattered the glass, then picked the jagged fragments out of the frame before crawling through the window to the alley.

Radok was two blocks away by the time he figured they'd gotten to the apartment and found it empty.

He flagged a passing taxi and had the man drop him at a tram stop, paying him with almost the last of the

change from Frieda's apartment. His mind was working
well now, remembering how easy it is to sniff out the trail
of a taxi. He wasn't going to make it easy for them.
Patience, that was the ticket. Take the circuitous path.
He'd lead the bastards all over Vienna, flashing his Kripo
ID at conductors through several tram transfers. That's
the ticket. Give the SS bloodhounds something to sniff
at, he decided. Give them too damn much to sniff at.

After the fifth transfer, Radok paid for his ticket with
the last of his change. No Kripo pass this time. This was
the real trip. The one to Hietzing. The one back home.
Dangerous, but the only place to go for a man out on his
own.

Chapter Seventeen

Later that afternoon, pimply-faced Adjutant Muellhausen brought the bad news. In ancient Greece they killed messengers for less.

"It doesn't copy, sir," the kid said, trying to lessen the blow. "Must be an alias. No police registration card for the owner of the apartment in Stieglitzgasse . . . nothing. A nonperson."

"Christ!" Krahl's face stayed the same livid red color it had been ever since they'd discovered the empty apartment. He sat stiff and irate behind his massive desk.

Sitting in a chair across the desk from him, Hartmann let go of his thigh where he'd been pinching it: a point of concentration to keep his face from giving him away. He'd blown it; hadn't thought past point A when calling in Krahl and company to bust the Kripo man. He hadn't considered that the trail would ultimately lead Krahl straight back to Frieda. Now, for the first time since returning to HQ, Hartmann was beginning to relax; beginning to see that maybe she'd covered her tracks herself.

Krahl ripped the report out of the frightened adjutant's trembling hand, motioning the youth out of the office.

"Waltraud Berger," he read from the report. "And there's no official trace of this Fräulein Berger."

It was the alias Hartmann himself had convinced Frieda to use four years before.

Krahl sucked on his lower lip as he took out the tiny black leather notebook he'd had at the scene and opened it.

They had traced Radok to the café across the street and to the lavatory window he'd knocked out. There the trail had ended. The stupid-ass of a waiter was complaining all the while about the small tip the guy had left and the cost of repairing the window. There were a couple more leads from tram conductors about the city, but Hartmann had a feeling these were red herrings. The bugger flashing his Kripo ID to ride the trams: no one was that dumb. He was having them on.

"It's not a complete washout," Krahl said, consulting his black notebook. "The porter gave us a positive ID of the woman who rents the flat. Tall, blond, mid-twenties. Infrequent use of flat. Prompt payment of rent, in cash. No bank transfers to check on. Pity, that."

Hartmann had been lucky with the porter: she was new since his time with Frieda. But he wasn't safe yet. He didn't trust this logical, methodical Krahl. The man was getting ready to blow: quiet before the storm. His face was still beet-red.

"Not much to go on from the inside of the flat. Looked like a student flat with all those posters. . . ."

The fucking posters, Hartmann thought. One even with Frieda's name on it. But it did not seem as though Krahl had picked up on that clue. Not yet.

"Black-market coffee. That implies that our blond friend is a traveler. Switzerland perhaps? But where does one get travel documents these days? She's not a private citizen, at any rate."

Hartmann was going over mental checklists: games within games. He had good reason to, for he was not simply protecting his former lover. No. Hartmann was protecting his own ass. Four years before, when telling Krahl of his plans to marry Frieda, Hartmann had of course not mentioned her connection with the Mayer cell. They had been two separate entities as far as Krahl was concerned. And now Hartmann needed to protect that lie.

"She likes music and decadent art, by the looks of the posters she hangs. And playing the animal with two backs." Krahl grinned. "She likes that overmuch, by the looks of the sheets. Enough semen stains there to fertilize half of Poland."

Hartmann's fingers bit deeper into his thigh at this comment, but his face was expressionless. He would pay her back for that betrayal.

"We have a positive make on Radok, too," Krahl continued. "This suspicious apartment-hunter the porter mentioned. Most likely it was Radok himself, searching out the fire stairs. He bumbles another escape on us. A lucky man, Herr Radok. . . . So, what do we do now? The tall blond was Radok's visitor last night, most probably. Taking him to the safety of her apartment, which is listed under an alias."

Hartmann knew it was coming now.

Krahl's voice was suddenly high and shrill, like that of a woman mourning the death of her husband.

"So who is she, Hartmann? They're your people. Whose apartment?"

"Mayer just gave me the address. A safe house, is all he said. He's gone pro in the last few years. Runs a tight ship. Cutout system at work. No more Sunday picnics. It's on a need-to-know basis now. So I just got the address and called you."

"I don't buy it," Krahl said.

"Nobody's selling."

"It's time to lift that bastard priest," Krahl said.

Hartmann shook his head. "There's a simpler way. I need a day. That's all. Mayer's the kind of fool to die under interrogation rather than talk. If they've got Radok hidden someplace, I'll find out where. If not, then I'll hand Mayer over to you on a platter."

"I want our man," Krahl said.

"You'll get him. Nobody's luck holds out forever."

A knock at the door. Adjutant Muellhausen peeked in.

"Sir? Scramble call from Berlin, sir."

Krahl frowned at the youth.

"Wait here," he ordered Hartmann, and went to the scramble phone in Operations.

Radok's not the only one with luck, Hartmann decided, as Krahl's footsteps receded down the hall. He waited for them to die away before going to the file boxes on the smaller table. L was in the first box and Frieda Lassen's card was still there. Age, sex, birthplace, all recorded in Krahl's precise penmanship in black ink. At the bottom was a notation in blue ink: "Hammer's girlfriend. A security deposit to hold over him in the future."

Hartmann pocketed her file card and was back in his chair by the time the door opened and Krahl entered. The red was gone from his face, replaced by an unhealthy paleness. The spring was out of his step, as well. He slumped into his chair as if falling into bed.

There was absolute silence for several moments, and Hartmann was not going to be the one to break it.

"Berlin," Krahl finally said in a reverent whisper.

Hartmann nodded. That much the Adjutant had told him.

"Himmler's office." Krahl's eyes came down from scanning the mahogany paneling on the ceiling to search out Hartmann's face.

"It seems some bright boy at SD headquarters is on to the von Tratten connection, too. Himmler's got a bee up his behind about the papers. He's convinced they're here on my turf."

"Well, he's right for once."

Krahl scowled at him. "Yes. But him not knowing made it easier. The pressure's on now, Hartmann. It's no longer just a glory-boy stunt. The operation's on a must-do basis from now on."

"Those papers are that important?" Hartmann said.

Krahl's eyes went upward again.

"Please, Hartmann. By now I'm sure your friends have let you in on the secret. Ingenuousness does not suit you."

A long sigh, and Krahl's fingers formed another steeple in front of his face. Hartmann did not like the direction Krahl's mind was going in. Krahl sighed again.

"Look," Krahl said, "I still don't buy this bit about Mayer. His cutout system and all that nonsense. The man's far from being a pro. A Bible-thumping malcontent is closer to the truth. I'll see him scalped before all of this is over. But you've obviously got your own methods. Better finesse then brute force. In the long run it's more productive. With that premise I agree. But I can hardly be expected to give you a full day now. Not with Berlin breathing down my neck for results. No. You've got until six this evening. You report back to me by six or I'll damn well move in on you, as well. Understood?"

Hartmann nodded his head perceptibly.

"That's all, then?" Hartmann said. "I've got work to do."

"One thing more," Krahl said. "Don't play with me, Hartmann. Your Bernau training doesn't impress me. I was there, too. Remember? What I told you earlier about solo missions goes double now. I want this Kripo dolt and I want those papers. Anything less and you take the fall with me. You think I'm a fool. I *know* you're a deceitful bastard. Let's call a truce on that for now. Just don't underestimate me."

"That's all?" Hartmann stood. His mind was already

improvising the story for Frieda and Mayer. It would be a close game, but that's what made it worth playing. Radok would fall, that was clear. Radok was a bumbler who had relied on luck, and luck is a bad tactician.

Krahl sat at his desk for a time after Hartmann had left, gazing at the mahogany inlay overhead; the Gobelins tapestry on the wall; a red leather couch opposite his desk; the cut-glass sherry decanter on an oak stand; and a Chinese carpet on the floor—with the delicate robin's-egg blue coloring one could no longer find commercially.

Krahl pulled the crumpled apartment registration form out of his pocket.

He thought for a few more minutes, working his lower lip in and out. Something was wrong here, but he did not know what it was. It would come to him, however, this missing piece of the puzzle. It always did. But for now he had to arrange the raid on Father Mayer. There would be no mistakes this time. Plain clothes all the way. No scene. No tip-off with the "Green Henrys." Just a clean sweep with five of his best men. And he would not wait until six, either. Four-thirty, the raid would be. A good time. Just before evening mass. Mayer would be in his study or the confessional.

Krahl was not going to wait for Hartmann on this one. The little blighter was only interested in protecting his cover, anyway. Obviously he didn't want Radok's disappearance and the arrest of Father Mayer to coincide too closely with his own homecoming. Coincidences like that make people suspicious. Well, fornicate the weasel, Krahl thought. Let Mayer get suspicious. Maybe the group would even put out a contract on Hartmann as a result. Let Hartmann play the game for the same high stakes everyone else did.

"Something's gone wrong. I know it," Frieda said.

Father Mayer busied himself with his esoteric research in Greek texts.

Frieda watched and listened to his pen scratching across the note paper.

"Dammit," she said. "It's been hours since Wolf left. Don't you care what happens?"

Mayer closed the books.

"Yes. But we all have several lives. You of any of us should know that. Would my worrying make it any better?"

"I'm sorry," she said. "It's this waiting. I hate it."

Mayer looked at her closely. "It's more than that, isn't it?"

He had always been able to see into her soul. Before, this insight had been a source of comfort to Frieda. She wasn't so sure she wanted its intrusion now.

"Would you like to talk about it?" he said.

She would, but could the Padre help her with this? With the guilt she was feeling now that Wolf was back in her life the very day after she had cuckolded him? Could Padre lead her out of the maze of confused feelings she had for Inspektor Radok? Could he, a professional virgin, begin to fathom the connection one night had created between her and Radok?

"Talking is a therapeutic thing, my child," he urged.

Before she could respond, the door opened without a knock and Hartmann entered. Alone. Frieda knew immediately that there had been trouble.

"He wasn't there?" she said.

"No. But half the SS in Vienna were," he said, looking frightened and just a tiny bit vulnerable for once. He was holding the crumpled cassock in his hand.

"They took the Inspektor?" Father Mayer had risen to meet the man.

Hartmann slumped into a chair; Frieda could see how exhausted he was. She suddenly felt the same way; she'd never been so tired in her whole life. A pleasant sort of numbness was taking over her mind.

"Let's be logical," Hartmann said. "How were the SS to know his whereabouts so quickly? Why were they lying in wait? They weren't high-profile; no simple raid was in progress. No. They were laying a trap. Waiting to take whoever came to bring our friend in out of the cold. Let's face it. The son of a bitch is a double. He set us up. And that means they'll be here any minute."

Frieda was caught up in events; she felt she had no free will. An emotional whirlwind was swirling within her. Too fast, too fast . . .

"It can't be," she finally said.

"I was there," Hartmann replied. "If I hadn't taken up watch at the café across the street, I'd be at Morzin Platz right now. They were waiting, I tell you. All set up. The street was subtly sealed off. Plain-clothes were on the street, and the boys in black were waiting in the apartment house. I saw a pair of them at a window. All too organized. Laid on, not just a lucky shot. He's running with the hounds, I tell you, your precious cop is."

Father Mayer spoke before Frieda could say more.

"What do you suggest?"

"We have to clear out. Radok's been playing for time, trying to win trust, hoping for a big score, to infiltrate and take the entire cell. But his master won't give him much more leash, now. They'll sweep here, and soon. Just as soon as they figure nobody's coming to pick up the Inspektor. So we have to disappear. Go underground."

"But the papers . . ." Frieda felt hopeless. Nothing to hold on to.

"Don't you see, woman?" Hartmann said. "They've already got them. They were just using them as bait to lure us in. . . ." He turned to Father Mayer. "Have you a place to go?"

Mayer thought a moment. "There's an abbey in the Waldviertel. The monks there know me."

"Good," Hartmann said. "Frieda and I can vanish in Vienna for a time. I know a safe house."

"It will take some time to pack my things," Father Mayer said.

"No packing," Hartmann ordered. "No things. Just change your clothes and off you go. They wouldn't let you take your things to Dachau, would they?"

Father Mayer nodded passively and left the room to change.

Frieda slid her trembling hand into his. It was firm, masculine. He gave her hand a reassuring squeeze. It was all she could do; there was no thinking possible. Thinking might bring up the image of Radok. How he'd obviously used her. And that hurt too much. That was for later, not now.

"It'll be all right," Hartmann said to her.

Frieda believed it; wanted desperately to, anyway. She wanted also to imagine that what had happened last night was only an aberration. She had been tricked by a con man, tricked into trusting and opening. But perhaps that was all for the good. Perhaps that had prepared her for Wolf's homecoming.

She was beyond more thinking, now. Much too late for that creaking apparatus of the brain to go into gear now, anyway. Padre was right: one night does not constitute love. Wolf Hartmann she had known over several years. At least he wouldn't betray her.

Father Mayer returned and was out of his surplice now, looking diminished and strange in a baggy street suit, fidgeting with a tie that would never be well knotted. She'd never seen him without the white collar of his faith, and now he seemed very mortal-looking.

Hartmann tugged at her hand. "Time to be off."

Father Mayer turned soft, moist eyes on them, making the sign of the cross. A sacrament, a blessing.

"Good-bye, children. Go with God."

"And you, Father," she whispered in automatic response. The ritual from the parochial school her mother had insisted she attend.

Hartmann's and her feet clattered on the flagstone floor of the empty church. So loud and hollow. She held tightly to his hand, when suddenly he stopped.

"Just a minute," he said. "We have to arrange a rendezvous with Padre."

Oh yes, she thought. Not to admit it was all over. A rendezvous would give hope for the future.

"Wait here," he said.

She obeyed, holding her hands primly in front of her as she had been taught to do when in church. Hartmann went back to the vestry, and she caught a glimpse of Father Mayer's surprised face before Hartmann closed the door in back of him. It took forever; she measured time with her heartbeats. She felt excluded. But of course, dummy, she thought. The cutout system again. What you don't know, you can't tell. Other than about the abbey in the Waldviertel. She felt uncomfortable with even that bit of knowledge.

Hartmann finally came out, smiling brightly at her. She expected the Father to poke his head out of the door and wave another farewell, but there was no sign of him.

"We must go now," Hartmann said, taking her hand.

His hand in hers cold as ice.

Chapter Eighteen

Radok walked three times around the perimeter, circling in, circling in. He wanted to make sure the villa was not being watched. It's an imperfect world, he thought: the hunters make mistakes, too. Thank God or whomever for that.

No one was watching the villa. Birds sat in the trees; begonias between double windows. An old, bandy-legged retainer was out washing a pre-war Daimler. No cops. No SS. No Gestapo. No shadows lurking in doorways. No assurances either, but it looked safe to him.

Up and down the street twice more went Radok, on both sides, before going to Number 186 and pushing the bell. Home. It was the only place left. Frau von Tratten was the only family he had in the world. Nowhere else to go. Not helpless, mind you, he thought, just in need of help.

The maid took her time getting to the door. Two more rings, him sweating out in the cold, glancing over his shoulder for a prowl car passing by. Infrequent checks were a possibility; no regular stakeout, but the occasional drive-by. That should be the drill.

Open the door, damn you.

It opened. The maid's moustache was more pronounced today. She's been too busy to pluck it, he thought.

"She's dressing." No good-days from the maid. "We have to leave for the funeral soon."

There was distrust and hostility on her face. Probably she thought he'd laid on Krahl's little party here yesterday. He could well imagine the SD man doing some thorough questioning. Hadn't Frieda said she'd seen Krahl arriving? Frieda. Put her name out of your mind, he told himself. Do your catechism, now; say it one hundred times followed by a chaser of fifty Hail Marys: don't trust women, don't trust women, don't trust women. Frieda the plant. Frieda the double. Frieda the betrayer of good causes.

The maid continued to glare at him.

"I'll make it quick," he said, brushing past her, heading for the stairs. He'd forgotten that the newspapers said the General's funeral was scheduled for today.

A sound like a growl escaped from her throat: protecting her mistress, protecting her job, protecting her ass.

Boxes were turned out in the foyer, in the bedroom. He could see the Frau in the back bedroom.

As he entered Frau von Tratten stood facing him in a high-collared black silk dress, a strand of pearls around her neck.

"They were here?" He looked at a litter of perfume bottles on the floor by a Jugendstil dressing table.

"Need you ask?" Her voice was a cold whiplash. "I assumed you sent them."

He shook his head, feeling anger rising in his chest.

"They're after me, now," he said. "After these." He patted his pocket. "The papers your husband was trying to get out. You know about them?"

She turned to look in a bureau mirror, her back to him, arranging the string of pearls around her neck. She watched his face through the mirror.

"Augustus did not include me in such decisions." Turning again to face him, her hands were still at the pearls. A short strand; nothing ostentatious for Frau von Tratten. A fold of skin under her chin, touching the collar of the black dress, reminded him how much she'd aged.

"Are those the papers they were looking for?" she said.

"Yes. He thought it was important to get them out of the Reich. I do too."

He looked straight into her eyes; silence for a full minute. A floorboard creaked in the hall where the maid lingered.

"Why should I care?" she finally said. "Those papers got Augustus killed. Killed for some foolish spy adventure. He was too old to play such games, Paganini. . . . What do you want of me?"

"Help."

She snorted. It was the first bit of inelegance he'd ever witnessed in the Frau.

"And get myself killed, as well?" she said. "You shouldn't have come here. A decent man wouldn't have exposed me to the risk. But I forget your antecedents."

It cut him, as it was meant to do. And fueled his anger. He took her by the shoulders and shook her.

"Dammit! Don't you realize that your old life is over? It's over for all of us! They're killing the Jews! Did you know that? Killing them by the bushel-load."

She shut her hands over her ears.

"Lies!" she spat out.

"Not lies! I have the proof. Your husband had the proof. He died for the proof. We've got to stop them, and we've only got a few days to do it in."

We now. And did he really mean it? he wondered. Did he really care? You'd better care, he told himself. You're selling your life for these documents. Better damn well care.

He shook her once more. "Do you understand?"

"You just want to destroy us. To bring us down to your level. Augustus was misguided . . . an old man. . . . He shouldn't have left me alone and unprotected."

"We're all alone. Born alone and die alone. But we don't have to live our lives alone. Trust. It's what separates us from the lower animals."

This was a close paraphrase of the General's favorite saying. He'd repeated it often enough to Radok as a boy. The familiar words struck home. She recognized them.

"Words," she said. But she was weakening.

"More than that," Radok said. "The General lived by them. He died by them. Alone."

"Oh, Paganini." Suddenly she was in his arms, sobbing against his throat. "I miss him so. I still think he'll come home in the afternoon with his twinkling eyes and stories of his latest schemes. But we can't bring him back."

"I loved him," Radok said.

She stood back from him, drying her tears with arthritic hands.

"I know," she said. "And he loved you."

"Then why? Why did he send us away?"

Why the need to know? he asked himself. It was better left unsaid. Better left in the dark night of ancient history. Better to keep pressing for advantage; win her and her help.

"I was a poor wife to Augustus, I know. The hothouse flower he plucked from the nobility. He was so alive. So . . . so virile. It scared me. We could never have children. I suppose that's why."

"Why?" He shook his head, not understanding.

"Augustus wanted a child. Wanted it more than anything in the world. It was the one gift I could not give him. He was kind about it. Augustus was always kind. But it was a trial for him. It clouded our years together."

"What are you trying to tell me?"

She fidgeted with the pearls once again.

"He was a deeply sensual man. He found love where he could. Your mother . . ."

No. It was better to let the dark night remain unlit, Radok knew now. He wanted to stop her, but she went on remorselessly.

"There was a pregnancy. He knew how it hurt my pride. How it compromised me. Promises were made. Your family was set up in the tobacco shop. Augustus never saw his son."

"Helmut . . ." Radok felt a world dissolving; a tidy world of his childhood. And a mystery unveiled.

"My brother . . ."

"Yes," she said. "No one ever knew, but we three: Augustus, your mother, and me. Your father never knew of it, and so could not be hurt by it. Of that Augustus made sure. The money for the tobacco shop was a loan as far as your father knew. Until the day he died, he believed Helmut was his own. Your mother was very brave. And Augustus vowed to me never to make contact with you or your family after you left our employ."

He should hate the von Trattens for this, but the knowledge only served to bring Radok closer, to make him feel more a part of the family.

"I know Augustus wanted to tell you," she whispered, as if full voice were beyond her powers. "You were like a son to him, he always said."

"But Helmut was his real one."

A sigh from her, almost a whimper.

"When he died last summer—your brother, there in the gore of Russia—it almost killed Augustus. He couldn't bear it. Though he never saw your brother, still he knew his blood lived on somewhere. Then, when it was extin-

guished like that, well, Augustus just didn't want to live.
Not long after, he made a trip to Berlin and then everything changed. Secrets, whispered phone conversations."

Radok had heard enough. Get on with it, he commanded himself. Quick and incisive. Get her help or get
out.

"Will you help me?" he said.

"It's hopeless, Paganini. If what you say about these
papers is true, then they'll never let you get out of
Austria with them. They'll seal off the borders and hunt
you down."

"Will you help me?"

"It's pointless. Futile. Can't you see? They're bigger
than us. They have the rights and power of the state
behind them. To them and most other citizens of the
Reich, you're a traitor. Worse than the lowest criminal.
They'll track you down and end your life. Is that what
you want?"

"There's no going back now," he said. "The hunt's
already on. Will you help me? I have a plan. It can be
done."

There was a glimmer of smile from her as her hands
fell from the pearls to her sides.

"You sounded just like Augustus then. Full of his old
enthusiasm . . . his optimism. 'It can be done,' he'd say.
'Everything you can imagine, you can do.' "

"I know," Radok said, recalling those days.

A knock at the bedroom door.

"*Gnaedige.*" The maid's voice. "We must be going
now."

"Later, Mathilde. They won't start without me."

This was the high, confident voice of the Frau von
Tratten he had once known in palmier days. Then the
humor left her face and she looked at Radok for a silent
moment.

"What is the plan?"

"I'll need a guide," he answered. "A man who's familiar with the western Alps. More than that you neither
need nor want to know. I want you to put me in touch
with your gamekeeper, Max."

"You plan to just walk out of Austria. Is that it?"

"As I said, you don't want to know. All I need is the
contact. I'll figure it out from there."

"It might put Max in danger?"

"If I get out of Vienna. . . . When I get out of Vienna and make it to Tyrol, most of the danger will be past."

"And what if he won't help?"

"Won't, or not want to?" Radok said. He'd thought of this himself and hoped the question wouldn't arise.

"Either," she said.

"Max is no friend of the Nazis. That I remember from the summer of hunting we did with him in Tyrol. And he works for you, doesn't he?"

She laughed ironically, shaking her head.

"I'm afraid, dear Paganini, that this request would be a bit beyond his simple gamekeeping assignment."

"Just get in touch with him, please. I'll take my chances from there. If necessary, I'll only get directions from him."

"And you think your plan will succeed?"

"I'm betting my life on it."

There. It was said, finally. The stakes he had not wanted to bring up before. The absolute enormity of the task he had taken on, and the risks involved.

"All right then. I'll call," she said. "I can't promise about Max. But I will call. Anything else?"

He shook his head automatically, without thinking. But there *was* something she could do; something for him and for the memory of the General.

"Yes. There is something else. It's . . . delicate. I really don't know how to talk about it. My brother . . . Helmut. He was married."

Frau von Tratten nodded. "Augustus kept track of his progress."

"Then you'll know he also had a baby, a son."

She shook her head. "No. We didn't know. A son. A grandson. It might have made a difference to Augustus. After your brother's death, that is."

Neither spoke for a moment. He did not want to go on, hoping she would understand his unspoken intent.

"The baby was born after Helmut died in Russia. They're alone now," he said. "I won't be here to look after them."

"I think I take your meaning," Frau von Tratten finally said, her jaw set, her lips turning almost white as she pursed them. It couldn't be a comfortable position, playing distant nursemaid to the General's grandson by a bastard. "I'll see to them. They shall have a monthly stipend. A von Tratten, after all. A male of the line." A laugh, low and ironic.

Radok would never know if her better self had won out, or if she was only being true to the General's wishes, even after his death.

He kissed her cheeks, awkwardly, even though it had always been their form of adieu when he was younger. Age makes all things more complicated, more heavily laden with veiled meanings and fear of misunderstanding. But Radok had wanted badly to kiss her cheeks again, to establish the old intimacy. His lips came away tasting of rouge and cold cream.

"One more thing," he said, holding her at the shoulders. "I wasn't here today. You didn't see me after my preliminary investigation."

"That's easy enough," she said brightly.

Maybe not, he thought. Maybe it's the hardest request of all, if they trace me to the villa once again.

He smiled at her, giving no indication of these internal doubts. He did not look back as he left the bedroom. Mathilde was fuming quietly in the hall and shot him a look of thinly veiled contempt. Age had brought on no complications for her: she still wore her emotions openly on her face. He passed by her wordlessly and let himself out.

It was gloomy outside at mid-afternoon, and the streets were slushy. It wasn't cold, but a wind was up out of the east, off the *pussta*, the eastern plains, which meant more cold, perhaps more snow. A smell of fresh water was carried on the breeze, straight from the Danube. A good day for leisurely walking, but not for Radok. He put his collar up, looking up and down the street for tails or drive-bys. Clear. He headed quietly toward the tramline. Next stop, the Prater.

Radok felt the car before he heard it, and thought his imagination was just running away with him. Then the car splashed in a puddle in back of him and he knew it was for real. He did not turn around, not even as the car slowed. Don't give them the face, he reminded himself. No positive ID, not until the last minute. His right hand

sneaked into the coat, to the butt of the Walther in the
shoulder holster. He tripped the safety, ready to draw it.

Just hope they don't call in the cavalry first, he thought.
They can't do a positive make on me from the back, for
Christ's sake.

The car hovered in back of him, tagging along like a
tame dog. They'll be running the usual spot-check on me,
he thought. Two of them, standard drill. Take the prick
at the passenger window first, the one who'd have his
hands free for weapons. Just turn when they call and
start firing. Second, you take the asshole at the wheel.
But fast, and high. No body shots. Too much metal
between them and you. Head shots this time. Splattered
brain on the windows. Point-blank into number one, and
then start spraying the second bastard. You've got a full
clip for it.

The car slowed almost to a stop, pulling alongside him.

"Radok." A familiar voice.

He swirled, the gun in his hand ready to drop number
one, know him or not. But there was no number one
there, only Radok's partner Hinkle behind the wheel.

"Jesus Christ, boy!" Hinkle said. "This is getting to be
a fucking habit with you. Why don't you just shoot now
and quit troubling me?"

"What're you doing here?" Surprise in Radok's voice.
Fear also. He didn't want it to end this way. Not with his
partner. Not with the man whose life he'd once saved.

"Looking for you," Hinkle said. "What else?" He
reached across and opened the passenger door. "Get in."

Radok hesitated.

"Lunch hour," Hinkle joked. "Not official business.
So, get in."

Radok did as he was told; the leather upholstery felt as
cold today as it had the other night at the stakeout.

"Don't they ever put heaters in these bastards?"

Hinkle laughed at the old complaint.

"No," he said. "And this particular bastard is my own,
so I'm the guilty fucker, okay?"

"What'd you do, trade in your push-bike for it?"

The old banter felt good to Radok, as if the last two
days hadn't happened and they were just a couple of cops
out cruising. They lurched away from the curb. Hinkle
was the worst driver on the force.

"You didn't show up for work today," Hinkle said.

"No."

"Some other boys came looking for you. Very un-nice sort of boys."

"I know," Radok said.

"What'd you do to piss off such big bad boys, partner?"

Radok took his eyes off the road. They were not headed straight back into town. Cruising. Just a couple of dumb cops on lunch break. He turned to Hinkle, looking at the paunch on the little guy and then at his mirthful face. Radok relaxed a bit.

"You don't want to know what I've been up to."

"No?" Hinkle ground gears shifting down for a stop sign. "Probably not."

"Why are you here, Hinkle?"

"Looks like you're in trouble. I owe you."

"Bullshit. That was line-of-duty stuff. There are no debts in the service."

Hinkle turned off of Rodaun Allee onto a quiet street and parked the car along a row of equally quiet houses. He shut off the motor and turned deliberately to Radok.

"Kiss me in the valley of wind, friend," he said. "I say I owe, I owe. I want to help, okay?"

"You'll get your ass nailed, Hinkle. I'm poison."

"Too late to worry about that. I'm a good cop—I'd have you halfway to the station by now. But I don't. We sit here under the frigging elms and argue about who's helping who. So my ass is already nailed. How can I help?"

"Serious?"

Hinkle nodded, then: "No, fucker. I just want to put the make on you. Thought maybe you'd go down on me for old-time's sake."

"Okay," Radok said. "I need money."

"Christ, Radok! I've heard some good stories. Even used a few in my time when I was broke. But you don't have to go this far just to work me up for a loan."

He chuckled and pulled out a wallet stuffed with Reichsmarks.

"I figured you might need some money," he said, counting off crumpled notes. "Heard you left your flat in a sort of hurry last night."

Radok took the fistful of money Hinkle shoved his

way, stuffing it in the coat pocket next to the Final
Solution papers.

"And you can drop me in town," Radok continued,
"across the Danube. I'll tell you where. Don't worry. It
won't be my final destination."

"Okay, okay. One thing. You didn't kill anybody, did
you? That's not what they're after you for?"

"No," Radok said. "I'm trying to stop some killing.
That's on the level."

"Okay. That's all I need to know. Cause killing never
stopped anything. Only starts it."

"Since when the piety, Hinkle? You with the tough-
guy reputation. How many have you killed?"

Hinkle looked around, as if fearful that a concerned
citizen might be eavesdropping.

"Secret?"

Radok nodded.

"I never even shot at a bastard."

"Bull."

"No. That's the truth. The other's just a crappy story
they make up for you on the force. Hinkle the mean
bastard. Everyone's got one, right? The old funny story.
The nickname. Hell, some call you Paganini. When's the
last time you finger-fucked a violin?"

"Point taken. How about we move on? Parked cars
make me nervous."

"Just don't kill, Radok. Not worth it. You can't kill to
save lives. Cockeyed reasoning, that is. And don't get me
wrong. I'm not religious. But the old man, my father, he
was in the first war. Worst butcher shop you could imagine, he told me. And for what? Just so we could dress-
rehearse an even bigger war this time around."

They drove into town, neither of them speaking. Going
the back streets, it took them over half an hour to get to
the spot Radok had in mind: out on the Canal in the
Second District. It was fifteen minutes by foot from here
to the Prater, where he was headed, the giant amusement
park where he could get lost for the rest of the day until
it got dark. Hinkle didn't want to know the final destination. Nobody should know anything about Inspektor
Radok, he thought. He would be the original invisible
man from now on.

Hinkle went up on the curb with his right front tire

where Radok told him to stop. He left the engine going: no long good-byes.

Radok opened the door.

"Thanks, Hinkle. I won't forget this."

"You'd better, asshole, if they catch you."

They both laughed. Radok got out, ready to close the door.

"And hey, Radok. You been a good partner, you know. But next time, keep your ass covered."

Hinkle was off, a trail of cackling laughter and diesel behind him as he ground his way into second gear.

On your own now, Radok, he told himself. On your own and you'd better hope your plan works. Time to get your ass to the Prater now. Time to look for a likely double with appropriate traveling papers: phase one of the plan.

Eight days left. Eight days to try to stop the carnage before it began. The papers in his pocket suddenly felt very heavy, as if he were carrying the weight of the world with him.

Chapter Nineteen

He raised himself over her. It was this moment he relished: the instant before entry, with the body beneath him quivering, expectant. Her buttocks were taut. Deep depressions formed on the sides from the flex of muscle, and continued down into her flanks. A pink flush of her skin where he'd spanked. Hartmann prolonged the instant until she relaxed, her rump going flaccid. And then he plunged. This would pay her back for her betrayal with Radok.

Frieda's scream was muffled, her face digging into the pillow. She fought his entry; tight, oh so tight, he thought. And dry there. No lubricant. She deserved none. This was sweet revenge for him. He plunged again. Another scream into the pillow and he was partly in.

So good, her whimpering under him. The more she fought, the deeper he penetrated her anus, until—with Frieda flailing and crying beneath him—he'd managed to impale her on him. Hartmann felt his orgasm building, the power of it, and her pleas, whimpers, and squirming only served to drive him on and on, harder and harder. Deeper and deeper.

All whores, they were. All of them. She had proved this last night, he knew. But a man needed the periodic release.

Hartmann was at the brink of orgasm and suddenly she stopped moving beneath him. She made no more protests at the brutal rape, only a spasmodic humping of her shoulders as she cried. The bitch! He was there, and she was denying him this last instant of pleasure.

"Move, damn you!" he hissed into her hair, biting at her neck. Then raising up one hand, he struck the side of her head open-handed.

"Move or I'll rip you apart!"

He thrust into her harder; another scream. She began

to move again at the hips. Oh, so good. The fucking tease. The bitch . . .

She lay whimpering beneath him for several minutes afterward, her head still down in the pillow, blond hair spilling about her shoulders, damp at the ends from sweat. A trail of moisture glistened along the down on her spine. Some blood down lower, Hartmann noticed, but nothing serious. No doctor needed.

Her damn moans finally died away and then her breathing went deeper and more rhythmic until she was asleep. Thank god for small favors, he thought.

It was as if he floated for a time on the mattress, weightless and free. He felt his chest rise and fall with his breathing. Not a sound in the room; not even the ticking of a clock.

Why did she have to betray him with that rotten cop? A common slut . . . And he had kept her memory with him these last four years as something precious. A multi-faceted gem, which he would take out to admire only at special times; a memory like a diamond, which he would not sully with continual inspection. All the while she probably had been fornicating with anything in pants. Obvious, wasn't it? If she'd slept with the Kripo pig after knowing him only a matter of hours, which men hadn't she slept with? She had fucked her way onto the concert stage, most likely.

Well, he'd got back at her good and proper. Paid her back in the coinage she could understand. He felt a heat in his groin now, remembering the terror on Frieda's face after he got her to this cheap room. A whore's room in a whorehouse for the whore Frieda. She had tried to hold him at first, to kiss him. "Wolf" she'd called him. Wolf. His first name sickened him.

Wolf is dead and you've helped kill him, you bitch. No more softness from your "Wolf." I'm Hartmann now, the hard man. Or Hammer. Wolf is dead. Dead and buried where that soft part of me belongs.

Frieda's face had gone white when Hartmann pushed her away from him and told her to strip. She stood mutely for seconds before his slap woke her up to reality.

"Strip!"

Hartmann had stood watching her disrobe; she was a thing, an object, his to do with as he pleased.

Her pleading began as he bit a nipple, threw her on the bed and tore off her panties.

"No, Wolf. Please!"

God, he'd loved the screams.

Then he'd taken her, taken her every way he'd ever wanted to. He'd even used his belt on her backside. No more softness from him. No more Wolf . . .

Now Frieda shivered in her sleep, curling into the fetal position with her back to Hartmann.

He heard the door open to the room next to theirs, then the mumble of voices: a man and a woman. This was the second time that room had been used since Frieda and he had arrived an hour ago. A half-hour hotel, not an hour hotel, he thought. The woman's voice was high and wheedling, haggling over the price. Dagmar. He knew the voice; knew her drill.

Hartmann knew most of them that worked the mean streets near the Prater. It was a regular homecoming with Hartmann back at the Hotel Paradis, where he'd spent too many nights on one of his earlier "heroic" operations: bordello duty, spying on the jerks who quivered with the whores. He'd been looking for fifth-columnists in the spasm of orgasm. Knew most of the girls, and them sniggering at Frieda when they'd arrived today. Even Madame Flo was grinning like a hedgehog when they'd come in the front door, sitting behind the counter in her kimono and pouring through magazines as usual.

Dagmar's voice was louder now; distinct.

"Oh God! Harder! Harder now! Suck my nipple. . . . Yes . . . That's good. Like that . . . Oh, you're great. You really know how to fuck a woman. Oh yes . . . faster . . ."

The bugger's getting his money's worth from Dagmar, at least, Hartmann thought. He could finish the scene for her; had written the script, in fact, during the month he'd run the voyeur scam here. That had been Krahl's brainstorm. The room with the one-way mirror and microphones. Recruited Dagmar, Hartmann did, and her friend Lisalotte. A dandy pair they were; lovers when away from work. Lesbians always made the best pros; no danger of them losing their heads or their hearts over any of the pitiful clientele. The house had dealt with the officer class then, mostly: see what kinds of beans they'd spill to a tart, or maybe just gather a portfolio of nastiness to hold over some poor bastard if and when the time came that the SS needed their cooperation. But that show had been closed down for years here, moved to the Café Lido in the City where the better class of customer was to be found these days.

"Yes, yes! Oh, my God!" Dagmar yelped.

Over, finally.

No farewell kiss for Dagmar; she was up and out of the room before the man even had his socks on, by the sound of it. Hartmann knew from the faint sounds he was hearing that the client was making a careful inspection of the bed and chair where his clothes had been to make sure he would be leaving nothing but a load of sperm behind. He departed a few minutes later.

Quiet now. Hartmann could think. It was going according to plan thus far. He'd have to call Krahl soon. He'd probably be back from the abbey by now. Back and fuming.

Hartmann knew Krahl would hit Father Mayer early; it was the prick's way. No subtlety at all. The shit-eating grin had let Hartmann know that Krahl had an alternative to their stated plan. But it was best to stick to schedule, he told himself. Wait until six, he reminded himself. Let Krahl smolder for a while at what he found in the abbey. Let him go jerk off to his dirty books or take afternoon tea to that disgusting lump of maternal flesh he kept hidden away in his mansion.

Not much about Krahl that Hartmann did not know. Krahl was a book, open for the reading. Hartmann had made a study of the SD man since the time Krahl had made a fool of him over his projected marriage. He had vowed he would not be caught at the short end of the information chain again; he had forged a pact with the devil inside himself to stay one step ahead of the Krahls of the world.

A knocking at the door. He tensed on the bed, but checked his panic. Madame Flo and her girls were the only ones who knew of his presence here. Frieda slept on through the knocking.

"Herr Hammer . . ." A voice whispering on the other side of the door. "It's me, Madame Flo."

Hartmann swung his legs off the bed and pulled on his trousers before opening the door.

"Sorry to interrupt you," she said. The stale odor of sweat reached his nostrils, heavily disguised by her perfume and the powder she put on her cheap blond wig to keep it from shining.

He said nothing, waiting for her to explain. But he had a sinking feeling in his stomach that he was once again at the short end of the information chain.

"It is the one who calls himself Koenig. From the old days."

He put his finger to his mouth to shush her. Looking to the bed, he saw Frieda was still asleep. He moved Madame Flo out into the hall, where they spoke in whispers. Quiet time now, no customers traipsing along the halls.

"He's here?" Hartmann said.

"No. He phoned. Told me not to bother lying. That he knew you were here. To give you this message, word for word: 'Koenig wants his vassal. Immediately.' "

Hartmann looked at his wristwatch. An hour to go until rendezvous. That meant that Krahl must have hit the abbey at four or four-thirty. And then traced Hartmann here. Or did Krahl have a tail on him all the time? Not likely. Hartmann could spot a tail blocks away. No. More likely it was just a lucky guess. But once again Krahl had scored the first point. Then Hartmann thought of what Krahl had found at Klosterneuburg. Make it a tie game, he thought.

"Thanks, Madame Flo. I'll have to go for a time. All right if I leave my friend here for a few hours?"

The old madam smiled, enjoying the role of duenna.

"But of course."

"Right, then. You didn't actually tell him I was here?"

"He didn't wait to hear. Just charged on ahead with his silly message. Are you the vassal, Herr Hammer?"

Hartmann didn't answer her. They talked for a few more minutes about the good old days and when he went back into the room to dress, Frieda was still asleep. He watched his former lover as he dressed, her back toward him, the curve of her buttocks peeking out from under the comforter as she hugged her knees to her chest.

Hartmann felt like having another go at her. After all, best not to respond immediately to Krahl's blasted command, or the man would be sure to know where he was camping out. No use confirming Krahl's lucky guess. The sight of Frieda helpless like this, open in her sleep, stirred Hartmann's lust. He wanted badly to have her again, to feel her squirming beneath him, crying into the pillow.

It would have to wait till later, however. For now, he had plenty to do covering his tracks before calling on Krahl at six. All innocence and what's-this-about-Father-Mayer-being-dead? Suicided-out, did he? The good Catholic? Well, you could never tell about these priests. That's the game he'd have to play. His role the innocent one.

He got dressed, knotting his tie while looking into the leprous mirror over the sink. It had lost all its back-coating, all its reflection.

No more delaying. Hartmann went to the bed and patted Frieda's arm. She yawned, stretched, opened her eyes at him. Another stretch.

"Did I sleep long?" she said. It was as if she were trying to reestablish their old intimacy, trying to forget that he'd just raped her.

He was having none of it. "I've got to go for a while. You'll wait here."

"Where to?" Something like fear in her voice.

He shook his head.

"I'll be back soon. Just stay here. In the room."

She said nothing, gathering the sheets around her nakedness.

"Understand? You're not to set foot out of this room. I'll be back as soon as possible. I'll bring some food."

He squeezed her chin hard, as if playing, but it made her wince. Frieda understood, all right. She was going nowhere.

She waited in terror as the sound of his footsteps receded down the hall. Her body ached all over and the burning in her rectum would not subside. Frieda wanted to run away somewhere and hide; to forget that she could ever have loved an animal like Wolf Hartmann. The Wolf she had once loved was dead, or perhaps had never lived. All that was left was this awful creature, Hartmann.

But there's no running anymore, is there? she asked

herself. Nowhere to run; nowhere where the danger wouldn't be present, for she was beginning to sense the truth about Wolf Hartmann.

For Frieda had been awake when the hideous Madame Flo came to the door, awake and dreading that Hartmann might want her again. She had heard the first part of Madame Flo's message: "Herr Hammer," the woman had called Hartmann. And then: "Koenig . . . from the old days." Frieda wasn't sure exactly what that could mean, but she was coming to understand that Hartmann had many contacts, and that he was capable of anything.

She'd had to act swiftly once Hartmann was out in the hall with Madame Flo, and she was amazed at how quickly her decision had been made, as if her subconscious had already been at work on it. There had been some instinctual mistrust of Hartmann growing deep within her over all these years, which now had surfaced as a result of the brutal way he had used her sexually. No one could love another and treat them so.

As Hartmann talked with Madame Flo, Frieda had pulled his jacket from the end of the bed and gone through the pockets. There was a ticket stub from Klagenfurt. He'd said that he was in the Waldviertel just before returning to Vienna, yet this ticket was from yesterday, from an entirely different part of Austria. No time to dwell on this fact, but she plunged her hand into the inside pocket. A cleaning stub from a Linz cleaners. That meant nothing; the suit was old, the ticket could be part of the former owner's history. Her mind was racing, as if trying to avoid the obvious conclusion. But not for long. She found what she'd feared she would find in the left outside pocket, along with a bill from a café in Klagenfurt. The other piece of paper was stiff, a file card, with a black metal hoop at the top. She heard Hartmann outside in the hall:

"Thanks, Madame Flo. . . ."

Only an instant to skim over the writing on the card. All she needed. The file card was headed with her name, age, place of birth. An asterisk next to "Race/Religion" to indicate her part-Jew status, and she went to the corresponding note in blue ink at the bottom of the card: "Hammer's girlfriend. A security deposit for the future."

"Herr Hammer," Madame Flo had called him.

A stamp at the top, the eagle and swastika emblazoned under the words, "Hauptamt SD-Wien."

Now, as she lay in bed once again, these observations took some time to filter down to her understanding, but when they did they struck her with real physical force and all but took the wind out of her. Frieda hoped that Hartmann would take his time with Koenig, whoever that might be. The longer he was away, the longer her head start would be.

Again she was amazed at how events had simply taken over, leaving her to follow them automatically. There were no questions to be asked; this was simply the new and changed course of events. This, therefore, must be her new course of action.

Have I always suspected Wolf? she wondered. Always doubted him; known that he was hiding another life from me? A nagging doubt now came to mind, one to which she had never before given voice. When Wolf—Hartmann—was taken four years ago, Mayer and the entire group had expected a rash of arrests in their ranks. Wolf had seemed to be a brave young man, but few can withstand Gestapo methods. Surely he would break under questioning and name names, they had all thought. But although they had waited in terror, no arrests ever came. Mayer had attributed this to Wolf's devotion, his loyalty. But Frieda had always wondered.

She had reasons to doubt him now, good reasons indeed.

She tried to get up, but her legs were still weak and twitching from where he'd used the strap.

Frieda wanted to wash now, to bathe all the traces of Hartmann from her. Standing was better than sitting, and she found that after the first step the rest followed more easily. There was a washstand in the corner by the sink with one empty water bottle on it and a soiled towel draped over one edge. The water from the tap was cool, and it soothed the places where he'd forced his way into her.

What are the logical conclusions? she thought as she bathed, forcing her mind to work rationally. The obvious one was that it was Hartmann, and not the policeman, Radok, who was the double. How else to explain the card from the SD in his pocket? Wolf Hartmann was Hammer. So he even had a code name. He was clearly an SD agent. All this would certainly explain his miraculous return just as she and Father Mayer were preparing to receive the Final Solution papers.

Father Mayer! She had to warn him. Hartmann knew where he was headed. Father Mayer . . . An evil thought passed through her mind: she wondered why Hartmann had returned to speak to the priest just as they were leaving. Why it had taken so long. Why Father Mayer hadn't waved good-bye to her afterward. No . . . Not even Hartmann was capable of that. . . . He'd let the Gestapo do the dirty work for him.

The towel she was using was rough from many washings, but she used it to scour the feel of Hartmann out of her skin.

Her clothes were scattered on the floor where Hartmann had thrown them once they were in the room together. The room where he had humiliated and hurt her. That would not happen again. Ever again. She dressed quickly, then listened at the door for a moment before attempting to leave. Silence. She opened the door a crack. The hall was empty. Easy now, but with a purpose. . . . She stepped out into the hall and a hand gripped her arm.

"Going somewhere, little angel?"

Hartmann had her arm in a vice-like grip, hurting her; smiling as he hurt her; digging his fingers into the top of her arm so that it felt as if she were being burned.

"I thought you were gone. . . ." she began.

He wore that awful, skull-like smile, as on a jack-o'-lantern at Halloween, and said nothing.

"I was just going to the toilet. . . . You're hurting me."

It was as if he recognized the lie, for the grip tightened and she felt tears building in her eyes.

Hartmann pushed her back into the room, onto the bed.

He shut the door silently and paced back and forth in front of the bed.

"What am I going to do with you?" he asked. "You make things very awkward for me with your silly damn spying."

"I don't know what you mean," Frieda said. "I was just going to the toilet. . . ."

He came right up to her, shaking his head in disgust.

He took her face in his left hand like a tomato he was testing for ripeness and slapped her. Then he struck her again backhanded with a swipe that cut her upper lip; she tasted the salt of blood in her mouth.

"Please," he said. "No more lies. As I was leaving I checked the little file card in my jacket pocket. You returned it right-side-up, you silly bitch. I had it in upside-down. You see, this is no game we're playing at here. If you want to be in the big leagues, at least know the basic rules."

He let her face go, pushing her back down on the bed.

"I repeat," he said. "What am I going to do with you now?"

She drew up all the hatred she could and spat at him. It did not provoke; he merely wiped the saliva from his suit coat with the sheet.

"Do to me what you did to Father Mayer!" she screamed. For she knew now that her wild fear was not so wild, after all. Hartmann was capable of anything, even of murdering their friend.

He turned that ugly, skull-like smile on her again. "Not to worry about our Padre. Quite painless. A little suicide pill. Better by far for him than answering Gestapo questions. . . ."

"Why?" She held back the tears. She must know everything. This was not a time for sorrow but for hatred. Hatred could save her, make her strong. This she knew instinctively.

"Still looking for answers, I see. Didn't I once teach you that only the questions count? Why did you sleep with the glorious Herr Radok? Answer me that one."

So, he knew everything. It was all over now. Over, and she was almost happy it was so.

"Because he's a real man!" she spat out.

Hartmann could not wipe this away; instead he jerked her to her feet and slammed his fist into her stomach. She crumpled onto the bed and was sick into the sheets.

"You bastard," she said, once she had stopped vomiting.

"Yes I am. And your life is in my hands. Remember that."

"Kill me. Do it now, or I'll kill you." The pain swept over her as she said this, until she could no longer speak.

"I'm not going to kill you yet. We have some things

to talk over when I return. Think about that. About our discussion later tonight. And think about your man Radok who I'm going to enjoy killing. You shouldn't have betrayed me. . . ."

So many things she wanted to say—to scream at him that *he* should talk of betrayal—but the nausea overcame her and she vomited again, the sour, stinging mass sticking in her mouth and nostrils.

"Bastard," she tried to say, but the word came out garbled and thick. He continued to smile at her like death.

"I'll be back," he said, moving to the door. "Think about that. Of course, there's always the window for you, if you want to emulate your Jew father."

He shut the door in back of him and turned a key in the lock. Frieda looked at the window and knew that he had destroyed that option for her by mentioning her father's suicide. Voices out in the hall. She forced herself to listen.

". . . that little tart? Why not visit a real woman now, Hammer?"

"She's resting, dear Dagmar." Hartmann's voice, with the reassuring tone Frieda knew so well.

"Imagine she'll need her rest if I remember right about you." Dagmar laughed tight and high.

Hartmann joined in with her laughter, as if at a dirty joke.

"Do us a favor," Hartmann said. "Listen in every now and again to make sure the slut's not up to any mischief."

"Like the old days, eh, Hammer? More undercover work. Things have been dull here since you left."

"There'll be something in it for you, Dagmar. Don't worry. Just give a listen every once in a while. I'll be back in a few hours."

Another laugh from the one called Dagmar. Frieda remembered her from when they arrived. She was the only one besides the Madame whom Hartmann had addressed by name. And Frieda also remembered the look Dagmar had given her: an appraising glance that held more than contempt. There had been enough of those looks from female singers whom Frieda had accompanied, even from her sometime piano teacher, Frau Madame Lasky, to let her know what it meant. Yes, Frieda knew that look and knew how she could use it.

Frieda did not want to die; she wanted revenge. Revenge for Father Mayer, for herself, and for the dying Jews. No leap from a window for her. Thank you, Wolf Hartmann, for making that impossible, she thought. You have sealed your own fate with that gift.

She lay on the bed for what seemed hours, the afternoon light dying at the window. Waiting and planning and stoking her anger until it was white-hot. Steps came to the door and stopped. High heels. Frieda moaned loudly. The steps were silent: Dagmar with her ear to the door. Again Frieda moaned, investing the sound with both pain and eroticism.

The steps moved down the hall after a few more instants. Frieda cursed to herself.

Another few minutes and the steps approached again. And again Frieda moaned, the sound coming almost as an orgasm.

The woman remained outside the door this time and Frieda moaned more loudly, forcing a whimper afterward. She partially unbuttoned her blouse and drew off her skirt, leaving only her panties on. Then racing to the washstand, she fetched the water bottle, returned to the bed and hid the bottle under the pillow. Another whimper and low moan as she lay back down.

"Hey, you!" Dagmar shouted from the door. "You okay?"

"No," Frieda said piteously. "He hurt me. Bad. Filthy pig."

"Stop the caterwauling," Dagmar said. "You'll be okay."

Frieda moaned in response.

A key at the door. Frieda tried to repress a smile: she'd been hoping there'd be more than one key to rooms such as these.

Dagmar opened the door and looked with undisguised interest at Frieda, lying half-naked and seemingly helpless on the bed. She came in, a big woman, and strong-looking, with makeup thick on her face. A smell of cheap perfume preceded her like a calling card. In her hand the woman held a bottle of French marc. Spoils of war. No Drei Sterne brandy at the Hotel Paradis.

"Maybe this will help." Dagmar held the bottle up

with one hand, then turned and locked the door in back of her. Frieda bided her time. The woman was too big to jump. Patience. She was playing this like Hartmann would. You want to play in the big leagues, you have to know the rules.

Dagmar took two grimy glasses from the wash basin and splashed brandy into them, then sat on the edge of the bed and handed Frieda one. Frieda looked at her dark eyes, her broad Slavic face.

"Thank you," she said to the woman. "You're very kind." The ingenue, an easy role for her to play. She pretended to gulp at the brandy, letting half of it trickle down her chin to her chest.

"Slow, now," Dagmar said, patting at the dripping liquor with the sheet.

"Christ!" she said, seeing the vomit on the bed. "What's been going on here?"

"He hurt me," Frieda said meekly.

"The bastard. They're all alike."

Dagmar rose, rolling Frieda first one way and then the other like a patient in a hospital bed, while tearing the soiled sheet from the bed. She crumpled the sheet into a ball and threw it at the wash basin.

"Let me help you," Dagmar said, standing rather unsteadily on her feet, Frieda noticed. Already a few drinks in her, she figured.

Dagmar wove her way to the wash basin, ran water on a towel, and came back to the bed. She wiped at Frieda's mouth, then her chest, letting her hand trail down to her partly exposed breasts.

"He's a real pig," Dagmar said. "You roll over now. I know what he's about."

Frieda allowed the big woman's hands to roll her over onto her stomach and draw down her panties. She must have bled more after washing herself, for Dagmar cried out:

"Jesus! He had a field day. Never did know the proper hole, did your friend Hammer."

Dagmar was surprisingly gentle as she washed Frieda's buttocks. A hand moved lightly between her legs and the warmth from the towel was reassuring. Dagmar got up again and rinsed the towel, then returned to the bed.

"Now, off with that top. I'll wash you off proper. The beast . . ."

Frieda made as if to protest, coquettishly, but rolled onto her back, allowing Dagmar to unbutton the blouse completely and slip it off her shoulders.

"It was awful," Frieda whispered. She let her arms trail up languorously over her head, her right hand searching under the pillow for the empty water bottle.

Dagmar traced the wet towel over Frieda's breasts, softly, softly. The woman was licking her lips. It was a pleasant sensation for Frieda and this rather frightened her. Her right hand dug under the pillow for the bottle.

"Who needs them, anyway?" Dagmar said. "Men are all alike. Animals."

She put the towel down and looked hard into Frieda's eyes.

"They don't understand women, do they, dearie? Not about what we really need."

"No," Frieda whimpered, finding the bottle finally and gripping it tightly, like a lifeline.

Dagmar began unbuttoning her own blouse now.

"Don't understand the softness a woman desires. See."

She wore no brassiere and her breasts were large, veined, and flushed.

"I'm just like you," Dagmar said. "Soft. Soft and gentle."

She put her hand on Frieda's breast, let it trail down to her belly and then to her blond pubic hair. A finger searched out Frieda's cleft.

"So soft," Dagmar sighed. She bent over and licked at Frieda's left nipple. It responded, stiffening, and Dagmar's lips sucked at the taut flesh.

Dagmar's left hand trailed up Frieda's side, along her arm, and suddenly yanked out her right hand, the bottle still firmly in its grip.

"What's this, then?" Dagmar said, gripping her wrist.

She looked hard at Frieda, then let her wrist loose.

"You were going to hurt me. You don't want my attentions, all you have to do is say so. I'm not some mean old dyke going to rape you."

Frieda could not speak.

"You want out of here?" Dagmar said.

Frieda nodded her head.

"Okay," Dagmar said. "Let's screw the little weasel over. I can't fucking stand him. Him and all his type who think sex is something dirty you do in the dark. Here's the key. Knock me on the head with the bottle. Not too hard, just enough for an alibi."

Frieda couldn't hit her now, not like this.

"Quickly, woman. You're losing time."

Frieda closed her eyes and struck. Dagmar cried out and slumped over on the bed.

"An alibi, not an obituary notice, you cow," Dagmar groaned.

"I'm so sorry. . . ."

"Disappear, now," Dagmar said. "I'm going to sleep."

"Thank you," Frieda said, but Dagmar's eyes were closed. A trickle of blood showed on her forehead.

Frieda quickly dressed, unlocked the door, and let herself out. Going down the stairs, she heard steps coming up. There was nowhere to hide, so Frieda braved ahead past a Wehrmacht private lurching drunkenly on the arm of one of the habitués. This woman was too busy maneuvering her client to give Frieda a second glance.

Down the final landing, and she hoped the madam would not be sitting at the front desk as she was when Hartmann and she had entered. But Madame Flo was still there, and looked up from a magazine when she heard Frieda approach. Too late now for subterfuge: Frieda simply ran blindly toward the front door. Madame Flo shouted at her, cursed, got up and gave chase. But Frieda was out the front door now, and the fat madam in her ridiculous kimono and mules could only scream at her as Frieda hurtled down the street, loving the feel of her limbs moving swiftly, the cold air as she sucked it deep into her lungs. She smiled as she ran.

Chapter Twenty

Like old times, Radok thought. Another familiar neighborhood; another old beat. His first. Every Viennese cop's first. After three months at school, they shove a nightstick in his hand, a badge on his chest, and drop him into a world where crime is a way of life: the narrow streets of the Second District near the Prater. Partnered with an older guy on the force, but they mean it to be a test by fire. Separate the wheat from the chaff. Get the piss-their-pants brigade out of the force first thing.

It was a human comedy out here on the streets, Radok thought. Whores calling out: "Schatz, I have something for you"; haggling at sidewalk stalls that offered half-rotten potatoes; the blind lotto salesman still geeking about, sporting colored glasses and the yellow armband with the three black dots in a triangle to show he's sight-impaired. The bastard had the keenest eyes around, Radok knew; a damn good shot, too. Radok would see him off duty scoring kewpie dolls at a shooting gallery in the Prater.

Radok heard shouts now, a high, angry scream: "You cunt! Get back here."

He recognized the woman screaming, even from the back. No one could mistake the kimono, nor the platinum wig. Madame Flo was still at it, and looked now to be giving chase to some customer. The bugger was probably skipping out on his bill. That was a ripe one. Madame Flo had always been the cautious type; had her girls get the money up front before any of the pleasantries began.

Radok laughed. It made the trip here worthwhile just to see Flo getting flimflammed. But Radok cut short the peepshow, ducking down a side street. There were too many familiar faces here, and his might be one of them. Even out of uniform.

Radok entered the Prater by one of the side gates,

going into the grounds rather than the amusement park. Wait for a bit of darkness before venturing into the arcades, he thought. The lowly Order Police were on duty out here. Dumb bastards mostly, but no sense giving them the advantage of good light to get a make on him. He was hatless; Radok never wore hats, but he would've loved one now to hide beneath. Find a copse of trees, he told himself; keep your ears open and ass down. Hinkle's advice.

He felt safer in the woods of the park, as if he belonged there and not on the asphalt streets. He sat on a bench under a bare plane tree and thought. Not much of a plan he had, but about the best he could do. His mind wanted to go elsewhere, back to the bed and the girl. That seemed so long ago, but it was only a matter of hours. Time's a relative bugger, he realized. It takes a man only seconds to die, and that's all the time in the world.

"What would you do if I ran away from you?"

The teasing words of his first love came back, stinging him, cutting into him as they had when she had said them so many years ago.

"What would you do . . . ?"

"I'd forget you, bitch," he said aloud. His voice seemed to echo in the little glade of trees.

He watched the daylight die, the slow creep of dusk settle over the park. It was cold now and there was just enough light left to see his watch; gone half-six. Time to move on.

Lights came on in the amusement park. He could hear the screams from the passengers out of control on the roller coaster, the pop of the guns at the shooting galleries. The strong garlic scent of frying *Langos* reached him, and he remembered he hadn't eaten all day. He walked up warily to the stand, watching for any police about, placed his order, and ate three of the potato pancakes. Immediately he felt a burning in his stomach from all the grease. The beer gardens were now full; oompah music drifted over the park. Blinking lights and laughter and pink daubs of cotton candy in the night. No war here. No dying Jews here. Still the pleasure garden of the bourgeoisie; give them their circus. Keep them happy, he thought. Opera shut down tighter than a nun, but business as usual out here.

There were uniforms, too. Radok, now that his hunger was assuaged, strolled away from the food stand, keeping his eyes on the uniforms, looking for the right one. Soldiers on leave milled about, stealing a bit of make-believe before the reality of the front. Their eager eyes looked not quite right; over-large, protruding. Startled at the pop of a rifle in the shooting gallery. Haunted eyes. Radok didn't want those, not the ones who reminded him of Helmut home on leave with the look of death upon him. And nothing above *Feldwebel*. There were plenty of noncoms here; officers took their pleasure elsewhere. Officers had a reputation to maintain; a stature to measure up to. They couldn't be seen larking it in the Prater with the other rough-and-readies.

It didn't take Radok long to find the right soldier. He was about Radok's size: a big, loping, country-looking kid. A tit-pulling dairy farmer, by the looks of his massive fingers as they curled around the butt of a rifle in a shooting gallery. The kid would be fresh from training camp, Radok figured, for he was still getting a hard-on from popguns. No action yet for this one. Still sleeping with his teddy bear. A private without even a sign of a service stripe. The only problem was the cap—this boy had a head like a melon. Oh well, Radok told himself. You can't wait for the perfect lamb. He was a piss-poor shot, too. Pulled right every time. Must have driven his DI mad at training camp. No teaching tit-pullers. Milking's all they're good for.

Radok was trying hard to create a nonperson out of the boy so he would be able to do what he had to do later. Another fifty pfennigs laid down for the second shoot. The kid counted it out carefully: two twenty-pfennig pieces and a ten. The kind of kid not to have much spare change on him; his private's wages next to nothing, and less than that coming from home. He pulled off the rounds angrily, like he knew he was going to miss; feeling no connection with either target or rifle. Just a pulsing finger. The sort of kid who would be impatient with all the subtleties of life.

"This fucking thing's rigged!" He threw the rifle down on the counter.

The man behind the counter, he'd seen them all come and go and paid no attention to this one. Little guy. Nice smile. He looked like he smoked too much and his pants were too big for him, Radok noted, but he wasn't going to take it out on the world, not like this ignorant dairy farmer from the country.

"You hear me, old man? I say this fucking shooting gallery is rigged! I don't even think you've got bullets in there!"

The little guy behind the counter just kept smiling, Radok noticed. He pushed a fresh clip into the rifle the kid had thrown down, keeping his eyes open all the time for new customers.

The kid slapped down another fifty pfennigs on the counter.

"I'll give it one more try, bastard. This time there better be bullets in there."

The little guy just kept looking at the kid, shaking his head. His small, wizened left hand held the rifle, the other hand went under the counter.

"What's this shit, man? I want to go again! Here's my money! What's the problem?"

"No problem," the little guy said, still shaking his head. "Just walk. I don't like the way you handle my rifles."

"Your fucking rifles! I got a right to use 'em, just like everybody else!"

The other people at the gallery were doing their damndest to ignore the scene. Viennese, they were expert at the maneuver.

Sent from heaven, Radok thought. Orchestrated just for him.

"Look, you bastard," the kid said as the little guy kept shaking his head at him.

The little guy started to bring something out from under the counter.

Radok moved quickly from out of the shadows, into the light of the shooting gallery. He tapped the kid's shoulder.

"Hey, Mueller!" He slapped him on the back now like long-lost friends.

The kid spun on him, fists clenched.

"What the hell?"

"Oh, sorry, friend," Radok said. "I thought you were a buddy of mine. Christ, you could be his double. You from Steiermark?"

The kid looked suspicious at this. Too good a guess, Radok, he thought. Slow it down.

"How'd you know?"

Hell, son, Radok thought, seven-to-one odds where tit-pullers come from in Austria.

"My friend Mueller, he came from there," Radok said. "From down around Leoben."

The kid shook his head.

"No, not me. I'm from the Lake Country. Bad Aussee."

Radok tried to look astonished. "Well, sorry to bother you. You're a real double. Look just like old Mueller."

Radok looked over the kid's shoulder at the little guy, then back to the kid. He nodded his head for the kid to come closer. The kid did so but kept a step away, turning an ear toward him.

"That little guy, he's about to clip you one, see? Got a fucking crow bar under the counter. You don't want any trouble, not on furlough."

The kid looked menacingly at the little guy.

Radok grabbed his arm. "Just let it be. You don't want the military police screwing up your leave."

The kid shrugged. "What's it matter? I go back tonight, anyway. Bastard traveling orders." Tapping his tunic pocket.

Thank you, whoever, Radok said to himself. Heaven-sent. The kid's making it too easy. But go slowly; he could be undercover. He's so obvious. Christ, he thought. And your aunt could be your uncle if she had balls. The kid's a dumb-ass farmer. Just enjoy the setup. Enjoy.

"Come on." Radok tugged at his arm. "I'll buy you a beer. Let the guy have his rifles."

"Yeah." The kid looked over his shoulder as they were leaving. "Asshole!" he shouted at the little man.

The Prater Beer Garden was packed, inside and out. Radok led them to a free table outside.

"I can't stand the shut-in feeling," Radok said, explaining his choice. "A man can't breathe inside."

"Yeah, I know what you mean," the kid said. "Same with the barracks for me. I can't get used to sleeping with all those guys. It stinks at night."

A waitress built like a sumo wrestler plopped two stoneware mugs in front of them without waiting for their order. Beer was all they served in the place: frothing mugs of it. She notched a coaster for their bill and shoved off bearing a tray full of beers without spilling a drop. Her legs were like fire hydrants and she had an ass on her that made Radok wince. The kid watched with hungry eyes as she moved away. He wasn't doing what he really wanted to do the last night of his leave. Radok filed that observation away for later.

They clacked mugs, and Radok watched over his foam as the kid downed half of his double liter in one gulp.

"Thirsty?" Radok said.

"There won't be much of this where I'm going. Shitty damn frog wine instead." But the kid shut up after this comment, as if he realized he'd said too much with his first sentence; his DI's warnings about fifth-columnists most likely clicked in his head. Radok could almost hear the rusty cog wheels of thought-process grinding in the kid's skull.

"Who'd you say your friend was?" the kid asked.

"Mueller," Radok said. "Hannes Mueller. Leoben boy. In the First Deutschland Regiment. We served together at Prague before I bought this." Radok tapped an imaginary leg wound. "Fucking partisan sniper."

"Bastards," the kid growled, and finished his beer. "We'll show the fuckers who's who. Sort 'em out soon enough."

"Do one for me, huh, kid?"

The farmer brightened at this, feeling like an old soldier. Suspicions dissipating.

Two beers later they were old friends. Radok knew everything there was to know about the Wolfgruber's dairy farm near Bad Aussee: the number of milkers, how many calves they were expecting this spring; about Bertha the crazy cousin, who helped out with the milking and let wonderboy here stick his sausage-like finger up her midline orifice one rainy day in the barn; about Vater Wolfgruber and how he severed his big toe, by shoving a post-hole digger onto it one summer afternoon; and about how the old fart walked the four kilometers home after the accident, his boot full of blood and the severed toe.

And the kid knew nothing about Radok other than his story of the stint in Prague.

When the waitress brought the fourth round, the kid made a grab for her ass and she pounded him on the ear with the back of her hand. Other drinkers laughed and the kid turned scarlet.

"Hey," Radok said. "A young guy like you, he needs some action before going off to fight the bastards. Know what I mean?"

The kid stared at his beer.

"You know," Radok went on, "a bit of the soft stuff. I know a place. It's safe. The girls are young and saucy. Just your style. How about it?"

The kid took a wooden match and threw it on the foam. It didn't stand up in the froth.

"Christ! The shit they're passing off as beer here. Crappy city, Vienna. Foam won't even hold a match."

"Look," Radok said. "This place, they got girls who'll make your match stand up. My treat. One soldier to another."

"No. I couldn't do that."

"Bullshit," Radok said. "Do me a favor, make me feel less guilty I'm back here in civilian land while you're out there fighting the bastards. It'll do you good, too. A guy needs some release before shipping out."

Radok stood up before the kid could object again and threw some bills on the table to cover the cost of the beers. Two of his were still untouched. He tugged at the kid's arm.

"Come on. The girls are clean there. No worry about taking a little friend with you to the front. Fresh country girls. They've got those milkmaid's hands."

The kid chuckled, lost in a dream of Bertha, Radok figured, and allowed himself to be maneuvered out of the beer garden.

"I shouldn't really." The kid's step was unsure. "Sarge, he warned me about . . ."

"Bugger him. I was a sergeant before I bought a discharge ticket. I told the recruits the same shit. And where do you think I spent every free evening?"

"You didn't?"

"Secrets of the trade." Radok winked. "I didn't want to have to wait in line. Scare all the young buggers silly with stories about their peckers falling off. Never trust a sarge about women."

"Bastard."

"All's fair," Radok said.

Radok avoided the lighted amusement park and made for the woods and the side entrance to the park.

"Hey," the kid said after a time of silent trudging. "Are we going for a fucking hike? Thought we were headed for the women."

"A special house," Radok said, keeping a grip on the kid's arm. "We don't want that grubby Prater snatch. This place is exclusive. Out of the way. Special mirrors, nurse costumes, you name it."

"God!"

"You'll be saying more than that soon. Just through here now and out to the street."

They went into the copse where Radok had hidden earlier. The path narrowed and Radok let the kid take the lead. Two paces in back of him, Radok let his hand go to the shoulder holster and draw out the Walther. The kid was stumble-drunk and reeling ahead. Radok waited until they were near a clump of bushes and then raised the pistol by its barrel, preparing to strike the kid over the head with the heavy butt.

A groan sounded from the bushes. Thrashing about. Radok quickly thrust the pistol out of sight in his coat pocket as the kid whirled around.

"What the fuck's that?" he mumbled.

Radok shrugged. "Squirrels?"

Another groan. They heard a woman's voice and then the panting of a man. Through the bushes Radok caught a flash of white thigh in the dark, a half-moon of naked, hairy ass pumping up and down.

Great. Rites of spring. Keep calm, he told himself. Shepherd the kid on.

"What's going on there?" the kid said.

"Come on. I expect they want some privacy."

"Fuck off, you!" the man's voice growled at them from the bushes.

"Pleasant dreams," Radok said as they moved on.

"Were they doing it in there?"

The kid was amazed and beginning to sober up suddenly.

"About the size of it," Radok answered.

"Christ. Like animals."

"How else is there?" Radok said, and for a moment his mind played tricks on him, taking him back to last night with Frieda.

They continued on through the damp grass, Radok waiting for his opportunity, but the kid seemed on guard now, shaken into sobriety by what he'd witnessed. The kid was likely a virgin, Radok figured, and he'd drunk heavily to get his nerve up for the imaginary whores Radok was taking him to. There was no time to reassure him, for they would soon be out of the woods and back into civilization. Still, they had to get far enough away from the couple in the bushes so they wouldn't hear anything. It was too late to back out now, Radok knew. The kid had a make on him. There would be no second chances. This one would have to be a go-ahead for Radok.

Radok could see lights ahead through the trees. No blackout tonight. No such luck. You have to manufacture your own luck, Radok thought. He pulled out the pistol again just as the kid turned around to say something to him. The kid saw the gun, was dumb silent for a moment, and then made a jump at Radok, hitting him hard in the chest with his thick head. Radok felt the wind go out of him and his legs lift off the ground, but he managed to swing out wildly with his gun as he was falling.

"Fuck!" the kid yelped.

The butt of the gun had caught the kid behind the ear, and he fell on top of Radok, still conscious but stunned. Radok managed to bring the gun down again on the kid's head and heard a sickening crunching sound. A gush of hot, beer-scented breath blew onto Radok's face from the kid's mouth and then he lay still, half on top of Radok in the middle of the path.

Radok could hear voices behind him. A man and woman's. The couple from the bushes. They had finished now and were coming his way. He slid out from under the inert body, his sternum aching where the kid had head-butted him, and began tugging at the heavy weight of the body. Shit, the kid felt as if he were dead: limp and heavy as a sack of coal. The voices were nearer now and sweat dripped from Radok's nose as he lugged the body, dragging it off the path and behind a stand of trees. None too soon, either, for the couple walked by then, arm in arm.

"But I thought you had one on," she was saying in a whine.

"Not to worry, dearie. It never happens the first time. Sort of a grace period, you know?"

"But you should've worn one."

"Can it, will you?" the man said.

The kid began to stir at Radok's feet, emitting a low moan. Radok clapped his hand over the kid's mouth.

"What was that?" The woman's voice trembled.

"You ought to know." The man laughed. "Same as we were doing a minute ago." Then, his voice raised and directed at the woods, the man said, "Prong her once for me, buddy!"

The couple walked past, out of the trees, toward the street.

The kid was coming around now. Radok held the gun on him and the kid's eyes opened, staring straight into the barrel.

"What do you want?" No drunkenness now. Just fear.

"Out of your clothes. And quiet, or you're a dead man." Radok felt the absurdity of his position. There was nothing louder than a gunshot in the still night. Poor threat: quiet or I shoot. But the kid didn't pick up on it.

"Are you some pervo?" The kid's voice broke. "Look, I got no money."

"Shut up and get out of your clothes." He shoved the muzzle against the kid's nose.

"Okay, okay. Just don't hurt me. I didn't do nothing to you."

"Make it fast and shut up."

The kid obeyed, stripping down to shorts and socks, shivering in the cold night air.

"Those, too," Radok ordered.

"Come on, mister."

"Now." Radok shoved the barrel against the kid's chest.

He did as he was ordered and stood with hands cupping his genitals.

Radok motioned with the gun. "Turn around."

The kid was frozen. Not moving, just shivering in the cold.

"Turn!" Radok hissed.

Blood was trickling onto the kid's face from the head wound. His eyes looked wild with terror and Radok thought, he's going to make a move, do something damned stupid, if I don't say something.

"I'm not going to kill you. Honest. I just need your clothes."

The kid's eyes shifted to right and left. No way out.

"I'm not a killer," Radok said.

The kid turned slowly.

"I've got to get . . ." the kid began saying, but Radok would never know what the kid had to get: his train? his courage? Radok brought the gun down again on his head and the kid sprawled out on his belly in the undergrowth.

Radok quickly changed clothes, bundling his own in his overcoat, and stuck the kid's travel documents along with the money from Hinkle and the Final Solution papers in the army tunic he was now wearing. The Walther went in the heavy overcoat the kid had been carrying.

Radok rolled the kid onto his back. Now was the hard part. But you're a fool if you don't go through with it, he told himself. Turn the tables: this kid would pull the trigger at your firing squad. What's got to be done, has got to be done. Time gained is time won. Time is the only thing you have on your side.

Radok put his hands around the kid's throat, digging his thumbs into his thorax, and squeezed. A curious gurgling came from the youth's throat; his unconscious body thrashed, fighting the suffocating hands.

Keep it up, he ordered himself. Keep it up. You or him. Old training came back from a distant corner of the mind. Police cadet school. Forensics. It takes two kilos of pressure to compress the jugular; five to do the carotid; and fifteen to finish it off with the trachea. The kid's trachea felt ridged and hard under his thumbs. Push, damn you, he told himself. Fifteen kilos worth of push.

The kid's leg kicked up spasmodically. Hinkle's words came unbidden: *"Just don't kill, okay, Radok? Not worth it. . . . Can't kill to save lives. . . ."*

Radok's hands loosened involuntarily. The unconscious body gasped for air. Radok tried to tighten his grip again, but no go. He had been right when he'd told the kid he was not a killer.

The hell with it then, he thought. Play the humanitarian. The kid's been bunged on the head several times. He's not going anywhere for a good long time.

Okay then, hero, he thought. Get out of here, and fast. You've got a train to catch.

Radok left the kid unconscious in the bushes and carried his bundle of clothing to the street, feeling damned uncomfortable in the uniform of a *Feldwebel*. A trash bin stood in the street in front of an apartment building waiting for garbage pick-up in the morning. He stuffed his clothes under a mass of potato peelings and old newspapers.

Right, Private Radok. Off you go. Step lively now. At a tram stop under a streetlight he pulled out the travel orders for Private Wolfgruber: the kid was headed to France. Heaven-sent, just as he'd suspected. Go west, young man. A tram came, and Radok got on. He dug in the wool uniform for change to give the conductor.

"Enlisted men travel free, son," the old conductor said as Radok placed sixty pfennigs in the coin tray.

"Oh yeah," Radok said, flustered. "Forgot."

You're in the army now, he reminded himself. Don't forget it again.

Chapter Twenty-One

Krahl watched the ordeal for a time: it gave him no pleasure. It was slow, arduous work. First they had strapped Hartmann to the metal chair; the chair was in turn bolted to the floor. The barber chair, it was called. Then Berthold started on the body, in the ribs and groin. Hartmann was naked and sinewy, taking the first blows silently, which was silly, of course. It only upset Berthold. And in front of Krahl, which made it even worse for Hartmann by calling into question Berthold's efforts in front of the boss. It angered the man and he slammed his fist into Hartmann's face twice, dislodging a tooth with the second blow. Hartmann blew out blood and the tooth onto the floor.

"Not the face," Krahl ordered. "Not yet. Take your time. Work him over methodically."

Berthold apologized, rubbing the knuckles of his right hand.

Krahl left after the first time Hartmann passed out, still wordless. No protests; no recanting.

Now sitting in the interrogation room next door, Krahl was thinking of Hartmann and about the senselessness of violence. After all, it always ended the same way: confessions and pleading and messed pants. Lord, if they'd only be sensible at the outset, all this could be avoided.

But Krahl knew better than to expect miracles from a man like Hartmann. He'd not even bothered to present the agent with the charges yet. For that, he'd wait until Berthold had done some softening-up work. For that, he'd wait until Hartmann himself had tumbled to what was up.

Lesson One in terror: let the victim imagine his own crimes, his own punishments. Nothing is so fertile as man's imagination, Krahl knew.

Go on, Hammer, he thought. Go on and create your

own scenario for this one. You've got a wealth of sins I'll never even begin to discover. Do the hard work for me, Hammer. Write your own warrant.

Berthold came into the room sweating and holding his right hand tenderly in his left.

"He's passed out again. The third time. Shall I give him the electricity?"

Krahl waved a bored hand at him.

"No. Not yet. Let him come to by himself this time. Let him crawl back into consciousness slowly and painfully."

Berthold snorted.

"You make it sound like a science," he said.

"It is, you oaf. A very precise science. You've left the face alone?"

Berthold smiled. "Sure."

Shithead, Krahl thought. Save me from the shitheads of the world.

"Listen and learn," Krahl said. "It might make you boys at Morzin Platz more effective in future. The secret of diplomacy is that you always leave your adversary with a way out. A face-saver. You get what you want, but you give a little, too."

"This ain't diplomacy."

"Shut up. I'm explaining by analogy. And that is not something you rub on sore muscles. The principle holds true for interrogation as well. Always leave your man some undamaged area. Something to preserve. Something he'll want to protect later on. A hold on life. With Hartmann, it's his head, his mind."

"Good thing it's not his balls." Berthold chuckled. "Won't be using them much anymore."

Krahl felt a wave of revulsion at the man.

"Lesson's over," Krahl said. "Report back when he comes to."

He thought a rib was broken, perhaps two. As a kid he'd had his appendix out, otherwise it would have been ruptured by now. Hartmann did not want to let his mind examine anything beneath the waist. The pain was immense; focused upon, it would engulf him, wash over him like waves in the ocean and take him under.

Let me focus on one thing only, he told himself: that of killing the pig Krahl and his pet, Berthold. Each blow he suffered was only another hammering of the nails in their coffins. Focus on hate, not on pain, he told himself. That was all that mattered. Survival and revenge.

"Your mind's working overtime," Krahl said, standing in front of Hartmann now. "Wondering, 'What's this barbarity got to do with me?' Right?"

Hartmann met Krahl's eyes and looked into and through the man.

"Shall I tell you?" Krahl said. "Would you like to know why you're going to die?"

Hartmann kept himself from responding to this.

"I'll tell you." Krahl turned his back on the prisoner and began pacing back and forth.

And he's left my face for a purpose, Hartmann thought. Not because he likes my looks, but because he wants my mind functioning, so it can feel the terror, create it for me. Because he wants something from me. Something he doesn't know. Otherwise I'd be dead already.

Krahl began to speak in a monotone as he passed back and forth in front of Hartmann.

"I underestimated you, Hartmann. That is my fault, of course. I thought you were just a glory boy. That you enjoyed the killing. Bit too clever for your own good, but essentially a loner, an action boy. Seems I've been wrong about that from the start. Where I went wrong was back four years ago. The little incident with your Jewish girl. I should have fed you to the hounds back then."

Of course, Hartmann thought, catching the reference to Frieda. The bastard didn't need to put a tail on me. He had his insurance policy: the fucking file cards. There must have been another cross-reference entry for Frieda that Krahl tumbled onto, one that Hartmann had not pulled from the files.

"I wonder if you ever gave her up," Krahl continued. "If you ever cut loose from the Mayer group. I think you're doubling on me, Hartmann. Damn stupid of you."

Hartmann did not try to speak. It was too early for denials; too early even for the truth. But he did not like the direction in which Krahl's logic was taking him.

"You see how my thoughts run, of course," Krahl said. "When we found Mayer's body this afternoon, I knew immediately that it was your work. Priests do not take their own lives. They're much too frightened of that ultimate act of independence; scared deathless of the hereafter. No. There shouldn't have been a tight little smile on the priest's lips, nor the smell of bitter almonds about him. Obvious then that it was an attempt to cover up homicide under the guise of suicide. Did you dissolve the pill in his afternoon sherry, or hold him down and force the cyanide into his throat?"

Krahl stopped pacing and stood directly in front of Hartmann now.

"I imagine it was the latter," he said. "Knowing your style. Bruises on our man's chest, as well, forensic tells me. Clumsy, that. But I imagine you were playing against time and subtleties were lost."

Hartmann breathed deeply through his nostrils. Pain shot up from his groin and he fought it, remembering the look of . . . what was it . . . terror; surprise; compassion? That look the priest gave him as he struck Mayer on the top of the sternum, paralyzing him momentarily, then throwing him soundlessly to the flagstones and crushing the death pill between Padre's teeth.

"And," Krahl went on, resuming his pacing, "that made me begin to piece things together. Why you'd bother to kill the bastard. Quite a gamble. Crude, but barely plausible that in my haste I would mistake murder for suicide. But it was a big risk, and I began to wonder what could make you take that kind of foolhardy risk. And it was, when once discovered, quite simple. Father Mayer had something to tell us that would compromise you. So I went back to the files and pulled your card and found what I was looking for. The Lassen girl. Your Jewish fiancée. Yet *her* card was missing from the files. Another damn stupid oversight on your part, Hartmann. I assume you lifted hers when I was out of my room this afternoon. If you're going to mess about in such matters, at least be up to the job. But you're a field man. You take orders and do the dirty work. I should hardly expect you to be a brainy type. Annoying, really. You've been pesky, like an insect. And now I'm going to squash you."

A lost feeling swept over Hartmann: all due to his own mistakes, his own clumsiness. He had neglected to pull a card all right: *his own.* The cards were obviously cross-referenced. For the first time, he thought he might not get out of this alive.

"I do believe you're a romantic, Hartmann. That's the most surprising thing about all this to me. A foolish romantic, selling yourself for the love of a Jew."

"You're wrong," Hartmann said. He had to say something, to assert himself somehow or he would be lost.

Krahl swung around to him. "Just shut your mouth, Hartmann! I don't want to hear from you yet. Later . . . There will be time to tell me what you know later. For now, listen and realize how irrevocably you're lost. So . . . where was I? The Lassen girl. All those years you hid her involvement with Mayer from me. Protecting her. And it was so easy to blow that lie. My men took a picture of her to the porter of that safe house where friend Radok was hiding this morning. Most instructive. Frieda Lassen turns out to be the mysterious Fräulein Berger."

"What is it you want?" Hartmann said.

"Excellent! That is the spirit I was hoping for, Hartmann. Cooperation. Acknowledgment of defeat. You see, I can make the dying easy for you, or difficult. What is it the philosophers say? Count no man lucky until his death. The last moments of life, those are the important ones. They can, if horrible enough, erase an entire lifetime of happiness. I want what I have wanted from the start. I want Radok and I want the papers he carries. I believe you can help me with that."

Hartmann had expected a demand for Frieda; the request for Radok was a surprise. He wanted no surprises at the moment. He tightened his abdominal muscles, and the pain again licked through him like fire. His mind raced for an out: promise Krahl anything. Anything to buy time. To think of a way out. There would be no convincing Krahl of the enormous mistake he was making; no way to make the Lieutenant Colonel believe that he'd only been protecting himself by this cover-up; no way to make Krahl trust him, to make the man see that self-protection had been the extent of his double game. To argue the fact he was not a double agent would only anger Krahl, would only make him send for his cretin Berthold again, would only serve to recommence the agony of his beating.

But what to tell Krahl? Hartmann wondered. What can I give him to appease his hunger? Of course. So simple. The girl. Shop Frieda. Sell her with the story that she was the only one who knew where Radok had gone; that he'd been working on her at the brothel, trying to slap some sense into her and get the information himself.

"You find something amusing, Hartmann?"

He must have been smiling at the thought. One last use for the bitch.

"I think . . ." Hartmann began, but was interrupted by the young adjutant, who barged into the room after lightly knocking at the door.

"Lieutenant Colonel . . ."

"Out, damn you! Didn't I say no disturbances?"

"But this is important, Lieutenant Colonel. Vital."

The boy said the word vital with such religious fervor that he won even Hartmann's attention.

"Quickly," Krahl said.

"There's an Order Police officer here, sir, with a young Wehrmacht private. I think we've got a lead to Radok."

"Show her in then, Mathilde."

"But my lady. I think she's in trouble. She has that look about her. . . ."

"All the more reason to send her in at once," Frau von Tratten said.

Night. Gloomy night, the lampshades filling the room with amber light. Frau von Tratten had wanted bright lights since Augustus's death. Bright lights and company in the evening. Especially today after the horrid funeral; all those ghastly people saying silly eulogies over his grave. How poor Augustus would have hated it. They had laid him to rest in the family plot: a tight circle of distant relations. He had hated silly pomp and lugubrious phrases. That banker Thaler—how he'd gushed on about the fallen warrior, while in Augustus's lifetime he was not only a rival in business, but a backbiting cad, as well. She reddened thinking of the time Thaler had once whispered salacious words in her ear in the gazebo during a summer garden party.

And Prokop had looked like death itself for having to be present with all those SS men around. For once their hideous black uniforms were in the proper taste. The absurdity of it all: that those who had killed Augustus, who were his enemies, should give him the hero's fare-

well. Obscene. The world was a frightful place, really,
when the veil was drawn back. A thin veneer of respect-
ability hiding the black bile beneath.

Mathilde clucked disapprovingly as she showed Frieda
in. The girl stood by the door tall and quite magnificent-
looking, Frau von Tratten thought, but real terror showed
on her face.

"You may go now, Mathilde," Frau von Tratten said.

"But my lady . . ."

"Mathilde." She used that gently rising tone of voice
which meant she was not to be disobeyed. Mathilde left.

"Now my dear, come sit by me. What is it?"

Frieda seated herself in the armchair next to her, but
was not relaxed; rather she sat on the edge of the chair
with legs pressed primly together, hands on her knees.

"I'm so sorry to bother you like this," she said.

"Nonsense, child. How may I help you? You do need
help, don't you?"

Frieda sighed. "Yes."

Yet the girl couldn't seem to bring herself to the point,
Frau von Tratten noticed. They sat in silence for a few
moments until suddenly the Frau rose, put her finger to
her lips to still Frieda, and went to the salon door.
Throwing it open suddenly, she revealed Mathilde waiting outside.

"About your duties, Mathilde. We don't want any
eavesdropping in this house."

"But my lady, I was afraid . . ."

"I don't care about your fears. Off with you now. I'll
ring for you when I need you. Do not interrupt us."

"Yes, madame."

"She does mean well," Frau von Tratten said, turning
back to Frieda. "Always trying to protect the family
name and reputation. This has been a difficult business
for her. More so for her than for me, I daresay."

Again the silence.

"It's about the papers, isn't it?" the Frau finally said.

Frieda reddened. "I thought you might know," she
said.

"Oh yes. A friend told me of them. Not Augustus, of
course. He wouldn't have trusted me with such men's
business. Not to worry my pretty little head over such

things, he would have said. But what else have I a head
for? Surely not just for decoration."

Frieda smiled at this, seeming to relax.

"And I assume," Frau von Tratten continued, "that
this person who informed me of the papers is a mutual
friend. Your coming here yesterday was no coincidence,
was it? Just as your arrival now is not a matter of hap-
penstance. It's Paganini. Are you in love with him?"

Frieda's befuddled look told the Frau that Radok's
nickname had not been understood.

"Radok, I mean. Gunther Radok."

She watched recognition sweep over the girl's face as
sun coming from behind a cloud, and knew her assumptions were correct: that if this girl was involved with the
same papers as Paganini, then she would also be involved
with the man himself.

"And you want to find him," Frau von Tratten said.
"Are they after you?"

The "they" need not be specified. The memory of the
horrid Lieutenant Colonel Krahl was only too vivid in the
Frau's mind. It would be he or others like him who were
after the girl. The decision was an easy one; she gave
not a moment's thought to suspicions of the girl. No
wondering about her motives. About such things as personal integrity, Frau von Tratten was an uncanny judge.
She knew instinctively she could trust this Lassen girl.

"I can help you," she said.

This is luck! Krahl thought. The first positive make on
Radok since losing him yesterday. Some quick-witted
Order Policeman with promotion in mind had found a
bare-assed and bloody-faced army private unconscious in
the tall grass at the Prater. First thing the cop does after
reviving him is ask for a description of the assailant—
which turns out to be a match for Radok's, distributed to
military and civilian police that afternoon. Voilà! A fix.

Luck was on Krahl's side, now.

Krahl gazed for a time in silence at the thick-necked
youth whom he'd been questioning now for the past ten
minutes. He looked pathetic with his bare shins sticking
out of the bottom of the coat someone at Ordnungs
Headquarters had loaned him. From time to time he

pulled the coat tighter around his legs, like a woman fidgeting with her skirt on a train.

Why hadn't the fool Radok simply killed this kid? Why leave him around to give a description and travel information?

Because Radok *is* a fool, Krahl finally decided, accepting the tautology. Because he's soft and playing at being a damned humanitarian. And that's why I'm going to catch him. This is not a case of a red herring laid on by a pro, but of a foolish mistake made by an amateur.

"The travel documents?" Krahl said again. It had not registered with the kid the first time he asked about them.

The kid looked up from the brass button he'd been fingering. A trickle of blood was still caked on his temple and there was a glassy look in his eyes, but he was competent enough to answer a few questions. No time for mollycoddling now, Krahl thought; a doctor would come later for the kid.

"Yeah," Wolfgruber said. "He got them. Orders and travel pass. All that."

Patience, Krahl told himself. Bluster won't get what I'm after; it'll merely send this private into a tizzy. The kindly uncle role needed here.

"We'll get you some clothes," Krahl said. "You can't go round in that coat. Someone will mistake you for an exhibitionist."

Smile now, Krahl commanded himself. Look reassuring; friendly.

But the kid stared at him stupidly. A fifth-grade education on top of a ten-year-old mind. He didn't even know what an exhibitionist was!

"Berthold," Krahl said to the grinning Gestapo man sitting in on the interrogation. "Go see what we can do about some clothes. My adjutant should be able to help."

Krahl wanted to get rid of the buffoon, anyway. The man looked at the boy in the coat like a butcher examining a prospective carcass. There was only one technique Berthold knew for getting information, and the kid sensed the possible danger. He has animal cunning in him, at any rate, Krahl thought.

Berthold shuffled out of the room, the back of his blue suit coat bulging at the shoulders.

"Don't worry about him," Krahl said to Private Wolfgruber. "Just a little liaison arrangement we have with Gestapo. But this is soldier to soldier, now."

Trading confidences; trading on uniforms. Krahl was wearing his gray-green SD tunic tonight.

"Now, about those travel orders. Where were you headed?"

"France," Wolfgruber said after a momentary hesitation. "Guess it's okay to tell you. Even though Sarge warned us not to tell anyone."

"Very wise of him," Krahl said. "But of course you need to tell me. Everything."

Until the damned Wehrmacht officer comes to pick you up, that is. And gets all huffy about territoriality. An Abwehr matter, he'd said on the phone earlier. The stupid, blasted Order Police were too thorough. They had called up the military police in addition to SD. Everybody would be in on the show at this rate. But Krahl could keep them away long enough that they didn't mess this up. There'd be a long wait for any interviews with Lieutenant Colonel Krahl tonight.

"What exactly do you need to know?" Wolfgruber said.

"The pass was for the West Wall, you say. France." Krahl spoke as calmly as possible; there was no need to excite the kid at this point. Delicate, now. "And you were entraining tonight. With your company?"

Wolfgruber shook his head. "Uh-uh. Not with my company. I had special leave, you know. To visit my grandmother in Burgenland. She's . . . she's dying."

The kid looked down at the brass button again; he had trouble with that word. Most do, Krahl thought.

"Awful. Sorry to hear that," Krahl said. "But, it happens to all of us, doesn't it?" Brightly.

"She's old."

"Yes," Krahl said.

"Cancer."

"Ah. So you were in Burgenland, and then . . . ?"

"Then, what?"

Krahl had a sudden urge to strap the kid in the barber chair and let Berthold have his fun.

"Then," he said, controlling his anger, "when were you scheduled to leave?"

"At night."

"*Which* night, dammit!"

The voice startled Wolfgruber.

"Tonight, sir. Tonight. The pass ends at 2400 hours."

Perfect, Krahl thought. He went to his desk, ignoring the kid, and picked up the blue, buckram-covered Reichsbahn train schedule.

Chapter Twenty-Two

Radok sat on the hard wooden bench of the third-class compartment and sweated into the heavy woolen fatigues. It was rough wool, the kind that scratches right through your underwear. He glanced out the window of the compartment: a pair of initials scrawled in the grime of the window—B.B. + P.M. Proclamation of love in translucent dirt.

The train had not yet left the West Train Station and the heat was on in the compartment, intensifying the smell of late-night travelers and flatulence. The cramped compartment had been full even half an hour ago. Four men sat on the bench opposite his, three next to him.

A shot of steam from the brakes, the whistle of the caped platform conductor, and at last the first lurch forward. They were moving. He felt his spirits rise, for he'd not seen any sign of SS or Gestapo. That dumb private must still be unconscious or wandering bass-assed around the Prater. An incredible lightness overcame Radok.

Then, in his peripheral vision, he noticed rapid movement on the platform, a man running, chasing the train, catching the last door, and swinging his heavy body up the steps. The blue-sleeved arm of the conductor helped the man aboard. The lightness left Radok; he tensed, ready to head for the Gents, to find some hiding place. The newcomer passed down the aisle outside of Radok's compartment. He looked to be only a ridiculous businessman with briefcase in hand, seriously out of breath, red in the face. Hatless. He was wearing an unbuttoned, crumpled Burberry.

There's something familiar about the face, Radok thought for an instant; something about the thick features, the massive shoulders. But then he decided he could be any of a hundred provincials, all with the skeletal grace of a dray horse, up in town for the day on business and now catching the last train out. Familiar, but only because all these types had a wurst-and-wine look to them. They began to take on a porcine animus. Eat enough of the stuff you'll start looking like a piggy, too, old son.

Gathering steam now, the train hurtled through tiny suburban stations, bewildered faces on the platform watching the express howl past. To Radok, it was all a blur of signs and lights. First stop, Wiener Neustadt, fifty-five minutes away. First railhead out of Vienna.

Radok tried to sit back in his seat comfortably. Impossible. The wool was scratching the hell out of him. The little inconveniences that drive you crazy. Hardly on a scale with the firing squad they'd set you in front of if they caught you with these papers, he told himself. The relativity of discomfort. But it was enough of an annoyance, the scratchy wool, to steal his attention. You should concentrate on the fellows out beating the bushes for you instead, he thought. On what they want to do to you. Makes a rough wool uniform seem like favoritism.

The conductor came, breaking the silence of the full compartment. A private first class to begin with; checking his papers, clicking his teeth in approval. Then, crawling over the legs of a couple of Waldviertel farmers and a frog-eyed man who had the wooden seat opposite Radok's, he finally came to Radok himself. The conductor held out his hand for Radok's ticket. Wolfgruber's papers had no photo and all the proper stamps, but still, when handing them over to the conductor, Radok felt as if the whole compartment were looking at him, waiting for the conductor to see through the game. And the conductor seemed skeptical now, too. Taking his time with the pass, reading it carefully, pulling out a great thumping pocket watch and sucking his teeth while looking at the time.

Finally the conductor handed the pass back. "Cutting it rather fine, aren't you?"

Radok looked up, trying to smile.

"How do you mean?" he said.

"The pass," the conductor replied. "It runs out at midnight. You take the 11:50 train for Salzburg. Looks like you're using up every minute of your leave."

The private's eyes bore down hard on him now, as if in condemnation. But the conductor was gone before Radok could answer. The man picked his way around the cog wheel of interlocking male legs in the compartment, and was off to the next compartment.

There was nothing for Radok to say. By the time he had gotten to the West Train Station, there was only this one train left that was heading west tonight. He had been stuck with it. Radok had passed a nervous hour waiting at the station for this train, but there had been no sign of his pursuers there. No sign of them on the train, either.

But wait, he told himself. His mind suddenly made a connection. The face! The one who'd gotten on late. Now Radok knew why he'd looked familiar. Because he damn well was. He was the Gestapo baboon at the Cezak and von Tratten stakeout. The coarse bastard Radok had had words with. And it wasn't just evil coincidence that had brought him onto this train, Radok knew. He was babysitting, most likely, until the first stop. No show of force in Vienna; they didn't want to scare the rabbit off. And Radok had led them to him by letting the private live.

Slow down, he told himself. Easy. Nerves, that's all. The joker could be an undergarment salesman for all you know. It was dark that night, remember? You didn't even get a clean look at the geezer's face. One way to find out, he thought. Get up and stick your nose out in the aisle; the boy's there, he's babysitting, all right.

Radok rose through the legs, excusing himself. Poking his head out barely into the aisle, he made himself look first to the right, the direction from which the man had come. Now to the left. Bingo: there he was four compartments away, leaning against a windowsill on his elbows, his fat ass pressed up against the window of the compartment in back of him. Bingo, indeed. A quick take.

How could I have missed him before? Radok wondered, pulling his head back in the compartment. But of course. No fedora tonight. No enormous black coat. Disguising it tonight, he was. Looking normal. A hard thing for this ape to do. A man with a body frame like he's got, he only looks right in laboring clothes. No suit's going to fit right if you're a guy whose ass is as wide as his shoulders.

Berthold was picking his nose with his thumb. Busily

engaged in this operation, he had not noticed Radok, who now made his way through the outstretched legs, and into his corner seat.

So what now? Radok said to himself, sitting on the wooden bench again. What indeed? One goon meant that there were certainly two or three on board. They never travel alone. There'd be another one, at least, working back from the engine. Maybe a third coming forward from the caboose. Radok could take out one, maybe with luck, two. But how long could this go on before raising a general alarm? That was exactly what Radok had to avoid.

Keep them babysitting me, he told himself. That's the thing. Don't let them know you're on to them, or else there'll be no more casual nose-picking, no easy waiting for the troops at Wiener Neustadt. Nose-picker and company, if they get suspicious, will just get obvious, Radok realized. They'll begin blasting away; set the whole train on me.

So, no panicking. Think it out slowly, carefully. Still twenty-five minutes, maybe half an hour to Wiener Neustadt.

He sat motionless for a full three minutes: the goon walked by his compartment once, cutting his eyes toward Radok, then turned around and headed back to his original position in the aisle.

When Radok finally moved, it was all very slow and considered. Not a great plan, but then the world's an imperfect place.

He took the coat off the rack above him. It was heavy with his Walther PPK in its pocket. He put the coat over his arm, hand in the pocket, and gripped the gun, flicking the safety off.

Slowly now, Radok, he told himself.

He excused himself once again through the seated men. Gruff looks were shot his way this time; they'd had enough of this musical chairs. He went out to the corridor; the goon was still lounging with his ass against a compartment window, elbows on the sill of the outside window opposite.

Radok turned to his left and walked deliberately up to the goon. Smiling. Shaking his head. Berthold didn't catch on until he was only a step away, but Radok was already talking by now.

"No sign of him," Radok said. "It's got to be this train."

Berthold's hand dug into his inside pocket, but Radok kept smiling, making no move.

"Looks like they got half the force out on this one. I hate this damned undercover work. Like to get my hands on the prick Radok. Wife and I had tickets for Lehar tonight, but I get to wear this damn scratchy uniform, instead."

Berthold gawked at him like a sprung accordion.

"Say," Radok blathered on. "You remember me, don't you? From that shootout the other night. Black marketeer and the old General."

Berthold's hand was still on his hardware, but now there was a new sort of doubt written on his face.

"Too bad Radok didn't buy it then," Radok said. "Save us all a lot of trouble. I mean, I was his partner and all, but if what they say about him is true, a bullet in the head is too good for him."

Berthold's head was nodding like a yo-yo.

"That's where I seen you," Berthold said. "The partner." But his hand was still in the coat pocket. Another wave of suspicion crossed his face.

"Yeah. Name's Hinkle." Radok put out his hand to shake, but Berthold ignored the gesture, studying his face instead.

Radok knew that Berthold didn't quite believe it yet that the man he had been tailing looked familiar *not* because he was the one in the picture they showed him before sending him on the train tonight, but only because he had run into him at the von Tratten shooting the other night.

Radok nodded, leaning against the compartment window, shoulder to shoulder with Berthold. "I told them it was useless sending me. Radok, he'd spot me right off. They think this uniform's going to throw the bastard off. Not a chance. I'm just glad I haven't seen him. You had any luck?"

Berthold went red and shook his head.

He's buying it now, Radok thought. The fool's embarrassed at being caught watching someone who turns out to be a fellow watcher.

"Maybe the other boys spotted him?" Radok suggested, indirectly digging for information about how many other watchers were on the train.

Berthold nodded solemnly. "Maybe."

"Look-see?" Radok nodded toward the rear of the train.

There was a baggage compartment next to this one, Radok had noticed when boarding the train. A secluded spot to do what he'd have to do. Pick them off one at a time, beginning with Berthold here.

Radok turned first, leading the way, with Berthold in back of him. Build the trust, he told himself. He felt vulnerable as hell with his back to the goon, but he had to convince Berthold that he was one of the chasers. Had to get some straight information from him about how many babysitters there were before disposing of him.

"How many of you got on?" Radok said over his shoulder.

But the goon was too busy counterbalancing the jostling motion of the train to answer him. They bobbed back and forth down the corridor as the train hurtled through the night. The tracks were bumpy as hell after nearly three years of total war: over-used and poorly maintained.

They reached the end of the car, Berthold still tight in back of him. Radok opened the adjoining doors and they stepped out on the open platform between cars. Cold air whistled around them; the wheels thrummed on the rails. A glimpse of track blurred by underneath, as sparks from the wheels illuminated the undercarriage.

Radok braced himself, ready to step over the open space to the baggage car. He made a split-second decision to lose Berthold, information or no. Better to get rid of the goons one by one than to play this trust scenario any longer, he thought. Instinct told him this was the proper course; he couldn't expect anybody, even one as dumb as Berthold, to go along with this deception much longer. He would catch Berthold mid-step, moving from carriage to carriage. This was the perfect spot for it. Send him under the wheels. Squash him like a bug. Just a well-placed kick as the bastard came across the open space after him.

The muzzle was cold against the nape of Radok's neck.

"Nothing cute now, Radok. Else I'll leave bits of your head all over Lower Austria."

Berthold nudged the barrel to let Radok know he meant business.

"We both just step over, nice and easy like," he said.

No, Radok thought. It obviously isn't the best plan.

They stepped over the hitch together, the barrel never leaving the back of Radok's head.

Berthold opened the heavy door to the baggage compartment and shoved Radok in. He stumbled over a wooden crate just inside the door and fell heavily to the floor. Looking up, he saw the Luger leveled at his head.

"Smart boy," Berthold hissed, kicking his shin with a heavy boot.

Pain shot through Radok's body and he wanted to lunge at the fat bastard. To have done with it.

"Thought you'd fool me with that load of bull about being your own partner. But you didn't, did you? I'm too smart for that. Thought I wouldn't recognize you. Well, you shouldn't have tried to pump me about other agents on the train. That wasn't smart. I'm playing it solo on this one. No backup. So, maybe Kripo would send you along, but they'd tell you that much, at least."

Radok stared into the eye of the gun. The searing pain in his shin had become a dull throb.

"What were you planning on, smart boy? Huh? Push me off the train back there. That it?"

Berthold kicked higher this time, hitting Radok in the meaty part of the thigh. Radok gripped his leg, rolling into a ball. Wrong, he thought. It just opened up his kidneys to the man's boots. Berthold struck once, twice. Again.

"I should kill you now, asshole. Even though they told me to bring you in alive. Kill you and have done with it. You just lay there, smart boy. Lay there real still and you'll live until Wiener Neustadt."

After what seemed like several minutes, Radok could finally see again. The bloodred of pain and anger was left in his eyes. He turned over and saw Berthold sitting on the wooden crate, smiling down at him. He had Radok's, or rather Wolfgruber's coat in his hand and had just pulled the Walther out of the pocket.

"Cute little gun." He opened the door and tossed it out into the night.

Radok watched him closely, waiting for any chance, any opening.

"Don't even think of it, Radok," Berthold said, seeing his look. "You're dead before you make a move. You almost fooled me there. But like all smart boys, you overplayed your hand. What kind of dumb bastard you take me for?"

"A very dumb one," Radok answered, feeling the coolness that for him always preceded action settle over him.

Berthold's eyes bulged and he rose to kick at Radok again. Radok was ready for him this time, and thrust out a leg as Berthold got up from the wooden crate, hooking his calf. Berthold was caught off-balance and began falling backward. The gun was no longer pointing directly at Radok and Berthold let off one shot, chipping the floorboards by Radok's head. Radok pulled the foot hooking Berthold's calf and twisted toward the goon all in one motion. Another shot now just as the train screeched into the Wiener Neustadt tunnel.

Berthold was down, using the gun now as a club; the butt of it caught the back of Radok's neck as he rolled on top of the Gestapo man. Berthold shot once more, into the ceiling, and tried to bring his knee up into Radok's groin, but Radok deflected the thrust with his leg. He was a machine now. He knew what he was about. All drill and training.

He caught Berthold's gun arm and brought it down to the floor, slamming the man's wrist against the wooden planks. Berthold let out a cry of pain, and Radok swung the arm up and then down once more, jarring the Luger loose. Berthold went for the gun; Radok went for his face. He brought his fist down on the bridge of Berthold's nose and heard the crunch of cartilage as the big man yelped. Berthold lay stunned for a moment, and Radok struck out again, precisely and without any feeling. This time the blow landed just as in training. No mistaking the sound of broken bone at the nose. Berthold lay inert now, gurgling blood as he breathed. Radok rolled off him, picked up the Luger, and set it at Berthold's temple.

The coolness of action suddenly left Radok and he was

swept by the heat of anger and repulsion. Radok's leg throbbed where Berthold had kicked him. The back of his neck was cramped and his kidneys ached with each breath.

It was fat man's turn, now. Radok's finger nudged against the trigger.

"And so you see, yours was a foolish game," Krahl was saying.

Hartmann watched the prick strut and prance in front of him.

"Foolish and rather senseless," Krahl continued. "You simply do not have the abilities to carry off a great deception. Only the soulless trick of eliminating enemies of the state. And even for that, you require direction. One must point out the enemies for you. You demonstrate a crude animal cunning in the elimination of these people. Efficiency, even. Nothing more, however. You overreached yourself in this, Hartmann."

Hate, like a sudden palpable being, raged in Hartmann's breast. He sat handcuffed to a chair now in Krahl's office at headquarters, his old brown suit covering the body blows that disfigured his trunk. He breathed shallowly to avoid the pain of fractured ribs, of mangled testicles.

"But you cannot say you were not duly warned. I gave you ample verbal assurance of my expectations. But you played the smart boy, the glory boy. Did they pay you highly, your resistance friends? Or do you actually have a drop of nobility in you? Some level of loyalty I have not before measured in you? Perhaps neither. Perhaps it was only the warm wetness between your Jew-girl's thighs. Is that it? The great Hammer only a prisoner of three square centimeters of a woman's flesh? Quite droll, that is. I strike close to the truth with that, don't I? The core of it: Wolf Hartmann's fixation on the hairy part of a female. Sickening."

He came to where Hartmann sat handcuffed in the chair and struck him across the face once, twice. Without anger. Without haste. The blows stung Hartmann's face, but still he stared silently at Krahl, as a hunter will watch its prey before making the kill. He was thinking:

There are so many ways I would like to destroy you, Krahl. So many methods I would employ to achieve your death. I shall sit here considering them, for they give me strength.

Hatred empowered Hartmann, and he wished for even more reasons to detest the man.

"All so senseless," Krahl said, stepping back from him and wiping the hand he'd struck him with on his sleeve, as if removing contagion.

"We shall soon have your colleague Radok," Krahl went on. "And your lover, the Jew Lassen. She shall play in the Auschwitz orchestra. If she is lucky. Or perhaps serve a more useful purpose in the camp brothels. . . ."

"You're a stupid bugger, Krahl," Hartmann said, no longer able to restrain himself. "A pompous, silly bastard. Why would I give you Frieda's safe house this morning if I was part of her group? Why present you with such a lead?"

Krahl thought for an instant. "Jealousy. The pig Radok slept with your woman. . . . Or maybe it was a cheap sales job on your part. To protect your position with me. Give me a tidbit to keep suspicion off of you. I don't give a damn why, all I know is that it signed your death warrant."

"But you called me back here from Klagenfurt," Hartmann said. "It was you who sent me to Mayer again. I didn't want the assignment."

"Because you knew of your weakness."

Krahl's voice was shrill, almost hysterical. Hartmann saw that he had scored with his sally; that he had wedged a sliver of doubt into Krahl's logical system.

"More lies will not save you," Krahl said. "You're a doomed man, Hartmann. Doomed unto death."

But Krahl said it less convincingly than before.

"As I have already stated, the only leniency you can expect from me is an easy death. We virtually have Radok in custody. The creature stole papers off a Wehrmacht private that are only valid until midnight tonight. The trains going west are covered. Berthold himself is on the last one out from the West Train Station. He has a score to settle with Herr Inspektor Radok. I have arranged it precisely: no show of force at the station, only a watcher for each possible train. The troops will be waiting at Weiner Neustadt. No stops in between.

No way out for your Inspektor Radok, this time. He will be taken at Wiener Neustadt and brought back here for interrogation. You see, your absurd game is at an end."

Hartmann saw only that Krahl had made a major tactical error. He was still underestimating this Radok. Hartmann's mind was working at breakneck speed, searching for any possible out for himself with all this. Negation of life was not in his syllabus; not at the hands of a man like Krahl, at any rate. Hartmann himself would be the one to determine when and how that last act was played out. So he thought of Radok, the only man he hated as much as Krahl. Radok had stumbled into good luck so far, it was true, but that was not the full story. Hartmann was beginning to sense that there was more to the man than he had thought, and he knew for certain that Berthold alone was no match for Radok.

But he said none of this. Krahl would learn it for himself soon enough.

What he did say was: "You want the girl? I can give her to you."

"That would be nice," Krahl said. His irony was heavy, like too much lemon soda in a summer beer.

"She is at a certain hotel near the Prater. Where you called, in fact. I imagine you were making quite a few of those calls," Hartmann said.

By the look on Krahl's face, he knew this was correct. Back from Klosterneuburg and fuming at Mayer's death, he'd put out an all-points on Hartmann. Tried every nook and cranny he could think of. But there had been no follow-up. There was none needed, for Hartmann had brought himself into custody.

By shopping Frieda, Hartmann knew he was playing his last card. She was the only one who could convince Krahl of his innocence. Her hatred of him now was strong enough so even someone as thick-headed as Krahl would recognize it as sincere.

"She is nothing to me," Hartmann said. "I confess one thing only. I have kept her out of your way only to preserve my own skin. That is my one crime. I was stupid enough to once be in love with her, to try and protect her from you four years ago. That one mistake has dogged me and finally caught up with me. I was never a double agent for anyone but you. That's the simple truth."

Krahl smiled. It was as if Hartmann were looking into a mirror, for it was the Bernau smile. Krahl had warned Hartmann about that, as well. Cut from the same bolt of cloth, they were. Except for this: Hartmann knew when he was wearing the mask.

"Nice parry, but hardly convincing," Krahl said. "We shall, however, see about the girl."

Chapter Twenty-Three

It did not take long for the SS dogs to come back from the Paradis empty-handed. Hartmann soon learned that the fucking girl had done a skip: Madame Flo's indignation and reports of Dagmar's contusion had been the only news.

Lost, Hartmann thought. Fucking lost, but he refused to show it, even as Krahl began to rant at him, even as he backhanded him once more across the left cheek as Hartmann sat, still handcuffed in the chair.

The ringing of the phone saved Hartmann from more immediate abuse. Krahl shook his head at Hartmann as he picked up the receiver. He listened for a moment, and his expression brightened.

"Excellent," Krahl said. "Bring him in at once. I shall be waiting."

He laid the receiver back in its cradle, drawing in a long breath. A look of smugness settled across his features.

"Good news?" Hartmann said.

The handcuffs bit into his wrists and his body wanted to slouch, but still he would not allow himself to assume the aspect of defeat.

"Very good news. They have Radok in Wiener Neustadt. The SS are bringing him in now. It's only a matter of hours now until this whole business is cleared up. I'm sure your friend Radok will be able to educate us as to the whereabouts of your missing girlfriend. For your sake, I hope you are not lying about that."

And now Hartmann did slump in his chair. It seemed well and truly over. His only hope, since the news from the Paradis had reached them, was that Radok would prove so elusive that Krahl would have to turn to Hammer to bring the Inspektor in. No matter how much he distrusted Hartmann. But now that final hope was gone.

"I see it's finally sinking in on you, Hartmann. The impossibility of your situation.

"You know, I almost feel sorry for you," Krahl continued. "Men like us, like you and me, we should never allow such bourgeois emotions as love to get in our way. The closest thing to that tawdry emotion I allow in my life is the care I give Maman. I imagine you've made it a job of yours to look for my weak spots, as I have for yours. And if you've been thorough in your researches, then you'll know that I am all but irreproachable emotionally. My only failing is an aged and rather vexing parent. But then you'd know about that, wouldn't you? The vexing parent, I mean. With the mother you had. No secrets now, you see."

Hartmann wanted suddenly to have this all over and done with. His body ached, his soul was empty. He was betrayed, misunderstood, and alone. Self-pity swept over him; a moroseness he had not allowed himself since childhood when his mother had brought one of her visitors home on his birthday, forgetting her promise to have a little party for him after work. And in the morning, seeing his pitiful face, she had denied him even the twisted intimacy of the strap. Indifference, that was what she gave him as a tenth birthday present. And he'd vowed then never again to let self-pity debase him. Never to wallow in that senseless emotion.

And here he was in the last moments of his life tasting its bitterness again. A fitting preamble to death.

"Yes," Krahl said. "I almost feel pity for you. You were a good operative. About the best I had, in point of fact. That's why I allowed you your little peccadilloes. But you turned against me. Cheated me. That is unfortunate. And, like a dog in sheep country who begins to savage the livestock, you must be put down. I'm sure you understand the logic to this. After all, you've put down enough people who tasted the metaphorical mutton. Those who turned against the Reich or against the sanctity of orders."

Is that what I've been doing? wondered Hartmann. Putting down mad dogs? Is that what those dumb bastards in Klagenfurt were? Was I protecting the sanctity of orders by blowing them into bite-sized chunks?

Since going to cadet school in Bernau, the concept of

duty always had been the one thing he had to live by: it represented the order he'd never had in his own life.

Yes. In a way Krahl is right, Hartmann decided. Pompous phrases aside, duty and following orders are what this is all about. A higher sanctity than individual lives.

"I know," Hartmann said, unwillingly. Yet it had needed to be said. Not an act of remorse, contrition, or confession. Simply a statement of fact.

"Yes," Krahl nodded. "I'm sure you do now. I'm sure you realize your mistake and that you must suffer for it. That's what makes this all the more pitiable. Absurd, really. You do know. But you have failed us all because of a petty emotion. Tricked by a vile Jewess who in the end deserted you. Yes. I believe she really did fool you in the end by fleeing that hotel. To see the look on your face when my adjutant came back empty-handed . . . You are not that good an actor. You simply could not disguise the bereft way you felt. So senseless. Absurd . . ."

It was all Krahl had to say. He set about going through nightly reports from Vienna Station, waiting for the arrival of Radok in company of the SS and Berthold. Hartmann was left to his own thoughts. He dozed for a while, still bound to the chair. He did not know he'd slept until a sudden noise awakened him.

A loud rapping at the door, sounds of protest from outside. A familiar voice. Hartmann woke with a start and suddenly had hope again. The voice. The protesting voice was not as it should be.

But Krahl did not notice anything amiss. Looking up from his papers with a satisfied smie on his face, he shouted:

"Enter!"

The door was thrown open and the doorway was suddenly filled with black uniforms and a shuffling and scuffing of feet. Above the din the voice sounded again, bellowing and insistent.

"Leave go, you bastards! You'll soon learn of your mistake!"

One of the SS soldiers stepped forward.

"Scharfuehrer Obermaier, Lieutenant Colonel. We have brought your prisoner." A crisp salute and click of his heels from the long-lipped sergeant.

Berthold, dressed pitiably in the uniform of a Wehrmacht

private and dragging a couple of soldiers with him, hurtled into the room.

"Krahl, for God sake, tell these fools who I am!"

There was blood streaming from his nose; his voice sounded as if he had a very bad cold.

The SS sergeant cast an ironic glance Krahl's way. "He's been trying the same weak trick on us all the way to Vienna."

Krahl slumped wordlessly into his chair. His mouth seemed to try to make sounds, but nothing would come out.

"Telling us," the SS sergeant continued, "how he's with the Gestapo and that you sent him aboard the train."

A chortle from one of the nameless guards.

"It's true, you idiot!" Berthold shouted.

"Silence!" Krahl had found his voice and it came out high and piercing in the wood-paneled room.

Hartmann was definitely perking up now, seeing his chances were not completely lost. There was a glimmer of hope; a tiny seed of it alive in his breast. He watched the scene carefully. If he died now, at least he'd had the gift of seeing Krahl disgraced, for the fool had already sent word to Berlin that Radok was in custody.

"He *is* a Gestapo agent," Krahl said, almost in a whisper.

"But . . . he couldn't be," Sergeant Obermaier said.

Hartmann watched the perspiration break out on the sergeant's too-long upper lip.

"Your agent came up to me properly as you please," Obermaier said. "Flashing his Gestapo ID disk and telling me where to find the criminal. He was expecting us."

"I didn't tell him!" Berthold pleaded. "I swear! It was our friend here." He nodded at Hartmann. He couldn't point; he was still handcuffed to a guard. "He must have got word to Radok. I was set up. He spotted me right off."

"Shut up, you ignorant ass! You blundering, stupid ass!" Krahl got to his feet, crossed to Berthold, and spat in the man's face.

"You incompetent pig!"

"I'll report you for this!" Berthold shouted. "My chief won't stand for this insult to one of his men!"

Krahl turned to the SS leader.

"Sergeant, I want you to dispose of this thing here. Back at Wiener Neustadt would be preferable. Make it look as though our rogue Inspektor did it. Shot in the line of duty."

Krahl turned to Berthold. "I'm going to make a hero of you."

Terror showed on Berthold's face. "I'm Gestapo, damn you!"

"Silence him," Krahl ordered.

There was the crack of a pistol butt against Berthold's head, and the room became quiet, almost peaceful. Berthold slumped, unconscious, between the two guards supporting him.

"So, Sergeant. I'm not concerned about your methods. But make it look as though there may have been a shootout. Nothing too obvious."

"But . . ." the sergeant began.

"No buts," Krahl said to him quite calmly. "Kill him. That's an end to the discussion. Leave him by the tracks. And not a word of this to anybody or you'll all end up in Russia."

"Yes, sir." Obermaier saluted again, not quite so crisply, for the starch had been taken out of him by the crude realities of the situation.

"We have no need for bunglers on this operation. Understood, Sergeant?"

"Yes, Lieutenant Colonel."

"You may go now," Krahl said.

"Yes, sir. Heil Hitler!"

Krahl returned the stiff-armed Nazi salute laconically, his arm bent at the elbow.

Berthold's feet dragged along the floor, crumpling a corner of the Chinese carpet as he was moved out of the room. When the door closed, Krahl bent and smoothed the carpet.

Hartmann watched all of this, a smile on the inside, his face a blank.

Only then did Krahl remember his presence.

"Did that amuse you, Lieutenant Hartmann?"

Hartmann sat silently, pondering. It was time now. Time to buy his freedom.

"He'll have taken another train by now," Hartmann said finally.

Krahl returned to his chair looking dazed, as if in shock. Immobilized by this latest fiasco, he did not hear Hartmann.

Hartmann spoke again, louder. "He'll have taken another train by now."

Krahl looked up. His face held the disoriented eyes of the profoundly lost.

"Where?" Krahl asked.

"To the west. That's pretty clear. He's heading for Switzerland. Look at the schedules. Find trains leaving Wiener Neustadt at about the time ours arrived."

"Ours?" Krahl said.

The implication that he wanted back on his team did not escape Krahl, Hartmann noticed. Perhaps he is not as devastated as I thought. Krahl reached for the Reichsbahn schedule, examining it with the care of an Amsterdam diamond-cutter at work.

"There was a Salzburg local train departing at about the time Radok's express arrived in Wiener Neustadt," Krahl announced.

"That'll be the one," Hartmann said.

"How can you be so sure?" Krahl said. His voice sounded hopeful now.

Hartmann saw a crack in his door to freedom and put his foot solidly in it.

"I know Radok by now," Hartmann said. "I have the feel of him. He's making his way for the West Country. That's obvious. He's going for the hero stunt. Taking the papers out by himself. Right over the border to Switzerland."

Krahl stared hard at the rows of times and train numbers in the schedule, a Persian pouring over the poems of Hafiz, looking for meaning, inspiration.

"We'll have the train stopped," Krahl said. The light from the green-globed desk lamp turned his skin a corpse color. His right hand trembled on the margin of the schedule.

"Too late," Hartmann said. And it probably was, at that. "Put yourself in his shoes. He's not the amateur we thought he was. Not just waiting for luck to happen. He's creating luck. So, his train's passed through Linz by now.

He'll have got off there. Changed trains. But he'll be moving west. That's for sure. Milk runs, little-traveled lines at first. But westward."

Krahl did not look at Hartmann for a time. He sat staring at the *Reichsbahn Fuehrer*.

"He could be anywhere," he finally muttered.

Hartmann spoke with an authority he hardly felt. "Have the Salzburg train met. Question the conductor. We have a description. He'll be wearing Berthold's clothes now. Maybe he flashed the Gestapo ID along the line somewhere." But Hartmann doubted now that Radok would be so stupid.

"We'll pick up his scent soon enough," he assured Krahl.

Krahl did not look convinced, but took Hartmann's suggestions, calling in the adjutant and relaying the orders to him.

Time trickled away; there was nothing to do until they heard from Salzburg. Linz SD Station was also alerted, sent out to make inquiries at the train station there. The waiting was always the hard part, especially for a man of action like Hartmann. But he still did not know if these were to be his last hours; he did not wish for a rapid passing of time.

The phone call came through at one in the morning. Hartmann was just nodding off again when the harsh jingle shook him awake. Salzburg Station had questioned the conductors on the local train from Wiener Neustadt; one of them remembered a guy in a trench coat fitting Radok's description who got on at the last minute in Wiener Neustadt without a ticket. He bought a second-class to Salzburg, paid the surcharge ungrudgingly. Accommodating chap.

"He would be," Hartmann said. "Wants to blend into the wallpaper, does our man. No scenes for him."

"But he wasn't on the train when it arrived at Salzburg," Krahl said, relating the rest of the phone conversation to Hartmann.

"It was searched thoroughly," he went on. "All passengers stopped." Dried flecks of saliva at the corners of Krahl's downturned mouth. Tired eyes. He repeated the phone conversation like a seventy-eight record played too slowly.

"And one of them turns out to be a *Gau* functionary mad as a hatter that someone had pinched his charcoal tweed overcoat."

"The ID of this man was certain?" Hartmann said.

"Salzburg Station knew him personally." Disgust in Krahl's voice.

"Switched coats again," Hartmann said. "A worthy opponent."

Krahl got up slowly from the leather chair; took a long time doing it, like someone with arthritis or a heavy burden.

"I think you're having me on," he said.

Hartmann shook his head. "I want the bastard as badly as you do. Different reasons, perhaps. But I want him, too."

Krahl looked into Hartmann's face now the way he had earlier looked at the train schedule. He moved cautiously toward him and Hartmann had a sinking feeling as the man approached. His one chance and he'd blown it. Hartmann expected the bastard to take out his bile on him rather than Berthold now, for surely his slow-motion movements were a calm before the storm. He loomed over Hartmann, an ambulatory cadaver, and reached into his tunic pocket. Hartmann expected to see the officer's blunt-nosed pistol in his hand. Make it quick, bastard. Hold your pansy hand steady for once. Hartmann wondered what it would feel like, the last instant of life. The last touch of indifference from the world. In an infinitely indifferent universe where all truth is relative, where relativity itself is the only truth, Hartmann had managed to invest his own existence with meaning. Yet now that that meaning was cracked, if not irreparably shattered, Hartmann almost longed for the final touch of cold metal that would extinguish indifference.

But there was no pistol in Krahl's still trembling hand. A key instead, and Krahl kneeling before him, unlocking first the ankle bonds and then the cuffs at Hartmann's wrists. Wordlessly. Then Krahl returned to his desk, to the soft lamplight. Hartmann made no move, but felt the blood rush back into his extremities; felt the rent in his invested meanings begin to repair itself.

"We'll hear something soon from the Linz trace," Hartmann said. "Meanwhile we should seal the borders."

Krahl nodded.

"Seal them tight as wax," Hartmann said.

Another nod from Krahl; he sat straighter in his chair now.

"We can still get him," Krahl said.

"*Yes.*" Hartmann put all the conviction he could muster into the word. Make yourself indispensable; it's your one chance. But Hartmann knew how hard it would be to catch the man. There were hundreds of kilometers of possible border-crossing both to the south and to the west. Radok could double back on them, go over the Glockner into Italy; try to hook up with partisan bands there and head for Switzerland through Lugano. Or head through Voralberg into the Drei Ecke, the three corners of high mountain passes, almost impossible to patrol, tucked into a Swiss, Italian, and Austrian pocket to the southwest.

"We'll need to coordinate this one from the field," Hartmann said. "No more relying on the office boys to do the work for us."

Krahl looked hard at him again.

"Keep talking," he said. "You might just buy yourself a pardon."

"We'll need some coffee. And I'm starving," Hartmann said. "Any food around here?"

Krahl pressed the button on his desk intercom, summoning Muellhausen. Steps echoed in the hallway outside the door as the adjutant approached.

It had been a short and dreamless sleep. Too short, and Frieda's mind was disoriented when Frau von Tratten shook her shoulder.

"It's time," Frau von Tratten whispered in her ear. "The truck awaits you downstairs. They are trusted drivers. I told them only that you are a Jew."

Frieda looked up at her with unblinking eyes, trying to remember what in the world Frau von Tratten was doing waking her; what all this nonsense about a truck was about.

"Hurry, child," Frau von Tratten coaxed. "No time to waste."

The Frau's hand on her shoulder felt comforting. Frieda was in need of it.

"They have done such things before," Frau von Tratten continued. "For Augustus. As a personal favor. But they are nervous. They have families to protect. So hurry now. No time to lose."

Alone in the guest room, Frieda dressed rapidly in the rough gardening clothes the Frau had provided. These had been long unworn, judging by the smell of naphthalene and the sharp creases and folds in the clothes. Packed away for other gardeners. Not a bad fit, though a bit tight.

Frau von Tratten was waiting in the dimly lit hall, wearing the same clothes she had had on earlier in the evening, as if she had not been to bed at all. She put a forefinger to her lips, nodding her head toward Mathilde's room down the hall. Let sleeping dragons lie.

Frieda followed the Frau out of the house and down the stairs into a clear, crisp night, with constellations overhead the names of which Frieda did not know. As they passed through the carriage house Frieda could hear the rumbling of a truck engine outside, smell its diesel exhaust. Out of the front door now to the waiting transport: a cab with a trailer in back covered high on the sides with dark tarp. VON TRATTEN PAPIER was stenciled on the tarp in Gothic lettering as white as the stars above. The Frau left Frieda by the back of the truck and went to the man standing on the running board, saying a few words to him. He peered over the Frau's shoulders for a better view of his passenger. He was a big man, towering over Frau von Tratten like a wrestler. He initially refused to take the money she held out to him, and continued shaking his large head even as she stuffed the notes into his jacket pocket. A light, warm wind was up. The *Foehn* off the mountains bringing pine scent. It ruffled the lank hair on the big man's head.

Frau von Tratten patted his arm and turned back to Frieda.

"So, in you go. All arranged," she said brightly.

Frau von Tratten held more paper in her hand now and passed it to Frieda. For a moment Frieda thought she was pressing money on her, too. But it was better than money.

"It's a letter," Frau von Tratten said. "To our game-keeper, Max. He won't like you at first. He's a confirmed bachelor. But he knows where Radok is. He'll take you to him. You can trust Max."

They embraced like mother and daughter, and Frieda nimbly hopped up and over the cloth tailgate. Inside the trailer were boxes and boxes of toilet paper. A cubbyhole of sorts had been prepared for her among these. She reached out to Frau von Tratten and they squeezed each other's hands wordlessly.

The truck suddenly bumped into gear and their hands parted. The Frau smiled, her eyes closed. Frieda's attention was diverted for a moment to movement in the upstairs apartment: a curtain falling closed in one of the street-side rooms.

And then they were gone, jostling over the cobbled streets.

Chapter Twenty-Four

Pure damn luck, Radok thought as he paced the cold platform at the train station in the little town of Steyr, reviewing the incredible happenings of the past few hours.

Radok's coolness had returned in time to keep him from killing Berthold outright. There was a much better use for the goon. He had changed clothes with the man by the time their train reached Wiener Neustadt. Berthold was still unconscious. Radok could see the troops waiting on the platform outside.

Sweat had poured into his waistband as he got off the train in Wiener Neustadt. Thinking of it now, after the fact, Radok could still see the long upper lip of the SS sergeant waiting with his troops. Radok had brazened it out, striding right up to the bastard, decked out in the Gestapo goon's clothing, telling the sergeant where to find his man, where to take him. And the fool SS man gave a Heil Hitler to his stolen Gestapo medallion as if it were a chunk of the True Cross. And afterward Radok had slipped into the night to find another train. He had still been able to see the turbulence on platform one, the SS boys pouring through the train, a glimpse of the semiconscious Berthold in Private Wolfgruber's kit being hauled out of the baggage compartment.

There had been loud voices on the platform then, and Radok stared at it all, transfixed, as his new train pulled out of the station.

That was another bit of the luck or whatever you wanted to call it, he thought: another train making up two platforms away, heading for Salzburg; a milk run, but heading west. He'd got on ticketless just as it was leaving. Not even a thought of flashing the Gestapo ID in lieu of playing full fare plus surcharge. Blend in, he commanded himself. Become part of the crowd. Even in the damn stupid trenchcoat he'd been wearing, crumpled

241

as it was, giving him the appearance of a Hitler doll from the rough early days in Munich.

He'd found a half-empty compartment baking with too much heat, but was not going to risk animosity by opening any windows. A snoring businessman type sprawled in the window seat, drool running down his chin. A heavy charcoal tweed coat hung from the hook over the seat. There was a pair of farmers playing Schnapps on the seat opposite, slapping the cards down on the wooden bench as if playing around their favorite table at the local inn. At home here on the train. Too damned ignorant to feel estranged anywhere in the world. Give me the gift of such ignorance, Radok had thought as the train steamed into the night.

An hour out of Wiener Neustadt, the heat overtook the others in the compartment and they slept. The businessman woke up then, swiping at the drool on his chin with sausage fingers, and stumbled out of the compartment to water the horse, giving Radok the chance he'd needed. The man's tweed coat looked awfully tempting on the hook. Soon they'd be in Linz where he would detrain, and he'd need to look different. He waited until the businessman had gone down the corridor, checked to make sure the two farmers were sleeping, then took the charcoal tweed coat off the hook and hotfooted it out of there, moving along the corridor in the opposite direction from that the businessman had taken, to find a seat many cars away where he could await the arrival in Linz. On his way, Radok popped into a lavatory, changed coats, and tossed Berthold's out the window. Ten minutes later, with Radok seated in a new compartment, they arrived and he got off without a hitch, then bought another second-class ticket on yet another milk run, this one to Steyr.

And now, two hours later, his mouth dry and nose stuffy, he was clumping up and down the cold, empty platform of the Steyr train station, waiting for the overnight train to Innsbruck, reviewing the escape so far. No mistakes yet. Smooth.

Correction. One possible mistake. He'd bought a first-class ticket in Steyr, and knew it was wrong the moment he'd requested the ticket, for the sleepy old man behind the ticket cage woke up at the mention of first class, eyeing Radok's fairly disheveled appearance with the gaze of an offended tailor. It had been too late to change, though; the damage was already done. And Radok knew he'd need the comfort of first class; knew he'd need the sleep. A big day tomorrow.

He stumped up and down the platform, waiting for the train, trying to stay warm. A Wehrmacht officer lounged in the first-class waiting room, his brown boots on the low table in front of him: they were highly polished boots, shiny in the harsh overhead light of the waiting room. Radok wanted no conversations, so he stayed on the platform alone. The train made up on time, originating in Steyr. It was a goods train, ammo train, with only six passenger wagons. Radok's first-class section was in front, directly behind the engine. He waited for the Wehrmacht major to board and saw him take an empty compartment at the engine end of the car. Radok then boarded, choosing a compartment at the opposite end of the first-class car and pulling the curtains closed on windows and door.

The conductor came by ten minutes after they were under way, the same suspicious old man who'd sold the ticket. He punched the ticket now, looking at the overhead rack as if wanting to see the luggage that Radok did not have: the look of a night clerk at an hour hotel.

Staying long? the look said.

Radok made no comment. The man left, and then it was dark and close as the engine pounded rhythmically in the night, rocking Radok as he stretched out on the velour-covered, first-class seats, the armrests raised on his bank of seats so that he could spread out fully, luxuriously. The cradle action of the train soon put him to sleep, but there was no soft sliding into it, rather a plunge as into a warm ocean.

Mathilde felt better after having made the call. It had needed doing. She only regretted that she had not done it while the girl was still here. But the name was actually announced on the radio this morning! That had sealed it: Mathilde had no choice after hearing the announcer's bland, nasal pronouncement that police were seeking information as to the whereabouts of the concert pianist, Frieda Lassen, twenty-six. The announcer went on to tell of Frieda's successes, but Mathilde had stopped listening. She had used the phone instead.

She stood in front of her bedroom mirror now, the one framed in baroque Cupids and billowing clouds done in gilt, and straightened her hair. Have to look presentable for the guests, she thought. She brushed her thick hair with the boar-bristle brush her mistress had given her last Christmas.

The old world is slipping away, she thought. The world of aristocracy and privilege. Slipping away and nothing but chaos to replace it. If, however, Mathilde were made to choose between being the hammer or the anvil, it would be the hammer for her. She would not wait for the world to come crashing down around her ears. Would not wait to be led away like a common criminal.

Mathilde finally managed to subdue the recalcitrant hair behind her left ear. A car pulled up outside. She heard the door open and thump shut. Harsh voices sounded in the new morning. Mathilde thought she had heard the Frau get up just now, as well.

I must go down to meet them and explain to them how things are, Mathilde told herself. Why I found it necessary to inform upon my own mistress. I had the von Tratten name to protect, of course. That was it. The blond woman had tricked the Frau, certainly. The Lassen girl had won over the Frau with guile and deceit into sending her off somewhere, lord knows where, smuggled in the back of a company truck.

Mathilde had seen her leave this morning while it was still dark, after the whispering voices below awoke her. Not that she could sleep with that young tart in the house, who was sure to bring ruin down upon them, Mathilde knew.

The little witch was sure to be caught; sure to be traced back to the Villa von Tratten. And then it would mean prison or worse for all of them. Much better this way. The blond would be caught anyway; why not salvage something out of it, like their skins?

Knocks sounded on the metal clapper below: insistent and loud. Suddenly Mathilde wanted to undo what she had done. An evil premonition swept over her.

She thought of how, when children, she and her sister had used to laugh at their old grandmother from Burgenland.

The woman was stooped, and was knobby at every joint; had a moustache as thick as a hussar's; and was more Hungarian than German. Mathilde and her sister had laughed at her impossible, halting movements, and laughed at her prophecies. It was said she had the gift of seeing in her, yet the children only laughed, Mathilde could remember.

But Mathilde herself was feeling more and more like the grandmother every year. She felt she was beginning to move like her, to speak like her. Yes, even the hideous fuzzy fringe on the upper lip was reminiscent of the old woman. And now Mathilde was also beginning to feel her grandmother's gift of seeing in herself. She did not like what she was seeing now: grief and sorrow framed in bloodred. It had been a terrible mistake, calling in the police. She must explain that she had made a mistake.

What had she told them? That there was funny business going on at Villa von Tratten? No, nothing so general, unfortunately. She'd mentioned the presence of the Lassen girl; had even identified herself over the phone. What else could she have done? Mathilde had panicked after hearing the name mentioned on the radio this morning. All she could think of then was how to save herself and the Frau.

And now, how to take it all back? Was there a way? The rapping at the door was insistent, impatient. No time to think. She must answer them; they'd be smashing the door down next.

"Coming!" she yelled, reaching the carriage house. Her voice echoed back at her in the cavernous old garage.

She wrapped a shawl around her shoulders and hurried down the stairs.

The rapping continued, louder and louder until its sound blotted everything else out of her mind, and, opening the door, she was sweating and nervous even before seeing the visitors. She recognized the tall one rapping at the door: he'd been there the other day, the one who'd led a search for some papers. The short, dark one in civilian clothes next to the tall one was new to Mathilde. He stood hunched, hands in his pockets as if in pain.

"Fräulein Mathilde," the tall one said.

"I'm afraid there's been the most awful mistake," she said.

The tall one's eyes were red-rimmed, as if he had not been to bed at all that night. At her words, the eyes squinted together in a sort of angry scowl that frightened Mathilde.

"Mistake?" he said.

Cowardice won out: "I . . . I shouldn't have called. It wasn't my place."

He placed a fatherly hand on her shoulder, even though he was young enough to be her little brother.

"Nonsense. You have done your duty to the State. You have been a brave woman. Now let us take care of the rest."

The short one stared at them, Mathilde noticed, eyes black but with a smile on his lips. She did not like the smile; it was cruel, heartless. The eyes looked through her into the very gate of hell.

Shut up, old woman, she told herself. You're getting as bad as your ridiculous grandmother.

She remembered the tall one's name and rank suddenly: Lieutenant Colonel Krahl. That reassured her somewhat. He led the way toward the upstairs suite of rooms. Mathilde had to trot along in back to keep up.

"Where is she to be found?" Krahl said over his shoulder to her.

Mathilde wasn't sure to whom he was referring—the Frau or the Lassen girl?—and said nothing as they began ascending the stairs.

"Your mistress," Krahl said. "Where is she?"

"In the morning room, sir."

They mounted to the top landing, the short one breathing hard as if the act of walking cost him not only energy but pain.

Entering the upstairs apartments, Mathilde made to show the Lieutenant Colonel into the morning room, but he took her hand off the door latch, smiling at her and shaking his head, no.

"I'll call you if I need you," he said to the short one, who was left out in the hall with her.

Mathilde caught a glimpse of her mistress's surprised face before Krahl shut the door in back of him: the Frau's glasses had slid down over the bridge of her nose as she was reading the morning papers; her mouth a bit open as if about to say something. Her eyes went quickly from Krahl to Mathilde herself. There was knowledge in those eyes. The mistress always knew everything. And now she knew that Mathilde had brought the police into her house. Then the door closed.

Oh, it was all a mistake, but how to explain it? She was only doing it for her mistress, but would the Frau believe her? Even this short, dark man standing next to her in the hall probably misunderstood it. Thought she was just doing it for the reward.

"She was here last night?" he suddenly said, as if reading her mind.

His voice was quiet, raspy, and, like his walk, seemingly used at great pain, and it startled Mathilde. The voices were loud now from the other room and Mathilde had the impression that this one meant to distract her.

"Fräulein Lassen," he said. "Last night."

Mathilde turned away from the door, from the increasingly angry-sounding voices, nodding her head.

"She left in the middle of the night," she said. "In a company truck."

"She was alone?" he said.

"Just the driver and his friend," Mathilde answered.

"I mean while here."

Mathilde thought she heard the sound of a slap from the other room.

"My mistress."

She made to move to the room, but suddenly the short one had an iron grip on her left arm.

"Was she alone while here?" His eyes were intent, emotionless.

"Yes. Let go. You're hurting me!"

He let her arm go and Mathilde was glad for it; his grip really had hurt. He knew just where to catch one in the fatty part of the arm, which was quite a feat considering Mathilde's thinness.

Now came an unmistakable sound: fist meeting bone and cartilage, and high, whimpering moans.

"The pig!" Mathilde exclaimed. But again she was restrained by the short one's vice-like grip on her arm.

"You called it down on her yourself," he said. "If you don't want the same, you'll tell me what you know. All you know."

The sounds were horrible from the other room. He

was actually beating the Frau! But she was a von Tratten!
He couldn't behave so with a von Tratten! And now
Mathilde knew that she had been wrong; that no one was
immune from the State. They were all vulnerable, and
just because of that blond woman, Frieda Lassen, all the
powers of the State were going to come down straight
upon their heads here at the Villa von Tratten.

"Where was she headed?" the short one asked.

"I don't know."

The grip tightened on her arm; she felt tears come to
her eyes, when suddenly there was a scream from the
morning room, followed quickly by the sharp percussion
of a gunshot.

Mathilde's arm was dropped free as the short one burst
into the morning room. She followed, peering over the
man's shoulder. Krahl stood sweating, his hair rumpled,
holding his right hand to his mouth. He looked stunned,
as blood poured from a wound on his thumb.

"She bit me! The bitch actually bit me!"

He held the thumb out to them.

"The bitch . . . Now look what she's done. Just as I
was getting somewhere."

Mathilde looked at the Lieutenant Colonel, smelled
the gunpowder in the air, and then saw the body of the
Frau sprawled on the floor. Her morning gown was torn
open, revealing welts on her flaccid breasts, and there
was a tiny pistol still in her hand. The front of her head
looked quite normal, but the back had been ripped away
by the explosion of the bullet, throwing pink flecks of her
onto the rosewood Biedermeier desk. Blood pooled on
the Turkish carpet underneath.

"The cow! Bit me, then ran to the bureau before I
could stop her. She was just going to tell me where the
Lassen girl had gone."

"She already did," said the short one, turning his eyes
away from the body. "She had something to hide, all
right. She killed herself to keep it hidden. That tells us
something."

Mathilde thought she was going to be ill. Impossible
that this could be happening, but the tight grip on her
arm again awakened her to the reality of the situation.
The short one was dragging her into the sitting room,

toward her mistress's body. No . . . She couldn't speak, could only resist physically. But he dragged her on.

"You did this," he said, pointing down at the body. The poor, ravaged body.

"No! He did it!" She almost spat the words at him.

"Yes," he said nodding. "But you signed the death warrant. The same can happen to you. So tell me what you know. Where was she headed? Where was the Lassen woman going?"

"I don't know. . . ." Mathilde said, faltering, looking for anything that could be salvaged out of all this hideousness.

To salvage anything at all . . . What she'd heard the mistress saying to the girl last night. Anything. Give them anything. "The truck had Tyrol plates," she said. "I think I heard them talk about the Brenner Pass. . . ."

The short one looked to the Lieutenant Colonel.

"That'll be south into Italy, then," he said. "They're crossing at the Brenner."

Krahl looked unimpressed. "I know my geography, Hartmann! Now get me something to staunch this wound with! I'm bleeding to death!"

His voice was high, almost hysterical, Mathilde thought. Not at all what she would have expected from an officer. She suddenly realized that it was Krahl, not Frau von Tratten, who had screamed just before the shot. Screaming like a woman at a mouse. She felt great contempt for the man, but also a greater fear.

"She talked about some papers," Mathilde said, trying to ingratiate herself with this hysterical man.

This seemed to take Krahl's mind off his bitten hand.

"What papers?" he said.

"I'm not sure, but I think they were the ones you were looking for yesterday. The Inspektor knew about them, as well."

"Inspektor Radok?" Krahl said.

Mathilde nodded. "Yes. Him. The one that was in service to the family. I think they're both going to meet up at the Brenner Pass. From what I could overhear, that sounded like the plan."

"Christ, Hartmann! We've got to get reinforcements on that crossing."

"Yes, sir," the one called Hartmann said, but Mathilde

did not like the way he continued to stare at her with blank eyes and smiling lips.

The thing she hadn't considered was the cold. Potential danger, potential tedium, yes. These she had known to be possibilities. But not this continual gnawing of the cold in her very guts; not the pain without release, so that she thought she would have to pass out at any moment to escape it.

There was no such easy release for Frieda, however. The clothes the Frau had given her were warm, but there was no clothing that could keep her warm while inactive in the unheated, canvas-covered trailer. Cold air whistled through the flaps from all directions. There was no protecting herself from it. She was conscious enough to mark the progress of her chilling trip by the changing of smells: the diesel stink of the city and outskirts; the fresh loamy smell of newly tilled fields in the plains; the sting of pine, resin, and snow as they climbed into the Alps.

She had no idea of routes, only of destination. And even that was clouded now by what the Frau had said as she'd escorted Frieda to bed last night. The Frau had talked suddenly of the Brenner Pass as they moved down the silent hall at the Villa von Tratten, the curious maid long since having gone to bed. She mentioned how Radok was to meet her there, at the Brenner, and then put her finger to her mouth to shush Frieda when she made to say that she thought she was going to the von Tratten estate above Innsbruck.

But not to worry about that now; destination was unimportant. Surviving this trip was now the only important thing. Frieda trusted Frau von Tratten. Whatever plans had been made, Frieda believed they would turn out all right.

No. Do not use up any energy and body heat worrying about destinations. What the Frau said about the Brenner may have been for the curious maid's ears, anyway, she thought. In case her curiosity was of a more than common variety. Save that energy, that body heat, to keep yourself from freezing. Her fingers in the heavy wool gloves, and toes covered in sturdy mountain boots, were almost without feeling. She thought she was moving her toes, but was unsure.

The men up front had said to knock at the cab only in case of emergency. Was this an emergency? That you could not feel your toes? If you have to ask that question, she told herself, it means that it is not an emergency. Wait until it is no longer a question, but a directive. Meanwhile, dress yourself like a mummy. There's enough toilet paper in here to wrap a hundred pharaohs. And she did, ripping open one of the large cartons, then starting at her feet and working up, she wrapped herself in the paper, even her face and head, leaving a visor of clearance at nose and eyes. Then she unrolled more of the paper, fluffing it up like a goose-down comforter over her. She could actually lie now for a time without her teeth chattering.

She did not sleep, but lay somewhere in the interstices between dream and reality and, once again, began wondering about her true destination.

Chapter Twenty-Five

The train arrived in Innsbruck at first light, and Radok had been ready for several hours. Little sleep, but still he was refreshed and eager. His breath formed large white skeins in front of him as he got off the train unnoticed. Not even a glance from the stationmaster, standing rheumy-eyed on the platform by the incoming train.

Radok walked from the station down slushy streets, looking for an open café; finally found it in the center of the city, on Tiroler Platz, from which point he could see snow-capped peaks surrounding Innsbruck, now turning pink in the sunrise. The city still sleeping. A metal shutter clattered up, as a store opened across the square. A solitary policeman on patrol passed the café just as Radok was arriving there, but did not examine him too closely.

Radok ducked into the open café and took a snug booth at the window giving onto the square. Random panes of this window were leaded, so that the scene outside had a weird jigsaw-puzzle quality to it. The tall, thin, rather frightened-looking waiter brought coffee, almost good, and a butter *Kipfel*, almost fresh. Radok ate and drank greedily, settling the dyspepsia brought on by his night journey. Sour stomach, sour times.

Before he could wonder about the next move, a military transport braked noisily outside and three SS troops leaped to the pavement, side arms drawn. Radok froze; he had not checked on escape routes and his guard was down. The waiter stood near the kitchen door, wringing his hands, for he'd seen the truck, as well. The soldiers were in the door before Radok could do more than grip the butt of the Luger he'd taken from Berthold. Christ! Was it even loaded? Did he know how to take the safety catch off? The first SS man glared at Radok, his pistol held out from his side and pointing at the floor.

"That's him."

A voice from the door, a short, squat man in plain clothes. He was pointing at the waiter. The poor bastard tried to make a run for it through the kitchen, but the young boys in black had caught him before he even got to the sink, twisted his arm behind his back, and hauled him out of the place, protesting that there had been some sort of mistake, that it was his cousin they were looking for; he could tell them where to find his cousin.

The plainclothesman came up to Radok and tipped his fedora at him.

"Sorry for the inconvenience." The man's piggy eyes surveyed Radok suspiciously. "A Jew, you know. And notorious black marketeer. We must be harsh with such ones."

Radok nodded. "I'm sure you'll know how to deal with him." The combination of hatred for and fear of the SS made Radok feel like vomiting, a trickle of bitter bile coming up his throat. He took a deep breath, forcing the nausea away.

The plainclothesman squinted even harder.

"Early to be abroad," he said.

Radok knew that the request to see his papers would be next. The pig's suspicions were up. Looking for more truffles. Radok decided to take the initiative rather than wait it out.

"Innsbruck Station, I assume?" Radok said. "Vienna," he continued, referring to his own supposed Gestapo affiliation, and he flashed the oval identity disk which Berthold had so helpfully loaned him. It was possible that it had been traced by now, but that was a risk he had to take. Brazen it out, he told himself. Take the offensive. Show no fear; fear makes these people strong. They feed on others' fears like vampires.

Pig-eyes brightened at the sight of the magic oval.

"Actually," Radok continued, "I'll be looking you fellows up later today. I'm down here on a fact-finding mission. But hush-hush, you know? I don't want you people laying on the special treatment. Just between you and me, of course."

"Certainly, sir." The man was obsequious now.

Thank God for Berthold, Radok thought. Gestapo rank was a matter of identity number. The lower the number, the longer you'd been in, ergo, the higher the rank. Berthold's disk bore a low five-digit number, which made Radok, by implication and possession, a "sir" to Pig-eyes.

Radok rose.

"I'll be going now. Good work this morning . . . ?" He made searching sounds for the man's name.

"Brandstetter, sir. Wilhelm Brandstetter."

"Yes . . . well." Placing some coins on the table. "Shan't leave a tip, I suppose," he said.

Brandstetter thought this damn funny: his eyes disappeared totally, choked by his round cheeks as he laughed.

Out in the street Radok and Brandstetter stood side by side, watching them load the wretched waiter. Brandstetter bid adieu with a Heil Hitler, returned smugly by Radok. As the van pulled away, Radok felt his knees buckle and grabbed hold of a gas lamp at curbside to steady himself.

It took several minutes of simply holding onto the cold metal before he could move again. Before he could think. Nice morning's work, he chided himself. So now they'll have a trace on you right to Innsbruck. Most cooperative of you.

But by that time Radok planned to be well away from the town. Workers were out on the streets now, walking and pedaling to work. He followed the flow of them back toward the train station. He should have stayed there in the first place, he now realized, even though it was the most obvious place for the chasers to hunt for him. But he had desperately wanted a moment of normalcy in this strange world he was entering. He had felt he had to have it to survive. A little warm breakfast. Was that asking too much?

But there were no safe places anymore. The Gestapo and SS would have a new description out on him by now, probably; they had perhaps even discovered the last coat switch and knew to look for a man in a heavy black tweed coat.

Radok waited across from the station, watching women park their bikes, trailing off to the suburban trains, to the munition and metal works south of town. Dutiful lemmings off to their appointed duties. All part of the fabric of daily life, outside of which Radok now operated. Outside the quotidian.

By eight in the morning the flood of workers had turned into a trickle. Rows of bikes stood unguarded, unlocked, and he chose a sturdy new Puch. He walked up to it assuredly, as though he were the owner, and pulled it out of the metal rack where it was parked. Flipping up the kickstand with this left foot, he mounted, the horn of the seat pressing uncomfortably into his scrotum. Wobbly at first, for it was many years since he'd ridden, and the cobbles here were making an obstacle course for him, but soon the rhythm returned and his tweed coat billowed out in back of him as he pumped. He began to enjoy the pleasant sensation of self-propulsion. Took the taste of fear out of his throat. Radok felt outside of time for the present; outside of history. Free and gliding.

He knew the way as if he'd been here only yesterday and not twenty-five years ago, the summer he'd been a gun bearer for the General. But the euphoria left him about four kilometers outside of Innsbruck. The roads had not been cleared here recently; the slush and roadside snow were still piled high. A line of wetness soaked through his coat in back from the spray off the rear wheel. No mudguard, no luxury of fenders over the wheels.

He was pumping uphill now, as well, into the highlands and out of the valley of the Inn River, past farms with thick coils of smoke coming from their chimneys. No one was working in the fields this time of year. Soon, though. Spring tilling and planting. Soon. But for now, only the crows pecked through the crusty snow for the odd worm or grub. Tufts of hardy winter wheat poked yellow through the white covering. Radok's breath was cold and harsh in his lungs as he pedaled uphill. The road narrowed; trees impinged on the fields. Out of agricultural country and into the upland forests. Several times Radok dismounted and walked the bike up steep grades. One time he lost control going downhill and around a tight curve, and ended ass-up in a snow bank, with the front wheel spinning crazily in front of his snow-covered face. He picked himself up, brushed off the snow, and pushed on. No traffic along the road. Nobody was silly enough to be about at this time of the year; even the army was staying in today.

Fifteen kilometers out of Innsbruck he reached the von

Tratten estate. He caught glimpses of the big house up the rough country road: a yellow cupola through the green and snow-laden branches of pine. Walking the bike now, the crunch of hard-packed snow underfoot, he shivered. It was colder up here, high above the valley. A chicken hawk swept by overhead. Suddenly a rifle shot broke the serenity of the walk; the hawk faltered in midair for a moment and then plummeted to the earth in a dizzy spiral.

Max. Protecting his damn chickens. Fighting off mountain solitude and winter boredom with a little target practice.

Radok saw the old man now, stooped but spry, trotting toward the fallen bird, a green hunting hat on, loden half-cape and elk-hide breeches connected by gray felt gaiters to heavy mountain boots below. The same clothes he was wearing twenty years ago. Max, like the mountains, was unchanging. Eternal. This fact made Radok feel safe, at home.

The old man noticed him now, wheeling the bike up the steep drive. The rifle came up in the man's arm, leveled vaguely at Radok, who was now waving frantically at the old man. No response from Max.

A shouted hello.

Max levered a shell into the chamber.

"It's me! Gunther Radok! From Frau von Tratten!"

Radok had no chance to duck as the old man fired off a round. The shot went high over his head and a moment later another hawk dropped almost at Radok's feet. A clean shot that had taken the head off the bird, staining the snow deep crimson. The smell of gunpowder lay heavy in the mountain air.

"You'll be the young fiddler the Frau spoke of," Max said as he ambled nearer. "The one that was here that summer."

The nickname, or reverberations thereof, was still holding, Radok thought. Obviously nothing else was memorable about him from that faraway summer when he'd met Max, acting as the General's gun-bearer, for Max did not seem to recognize him. Radok remembered suddenly how amazed he'd been at the weight of a rifle the first time it was thrust into his hands.

"It's been a good many years," Radok said. "I'm glad to see you so fit."

They were the wrong words, of course, for they only served to rankle the old man.

"And why shouldn't I be fit? Still run *your* ass ragged over the mountains, I'll warrant."

Radok did not rise to the bait, but instead smiled, patting an imaginary paunch at his stomach.

"No doubt you can," he said. "City life makes a man soft."

Notwithstanding the daily regimen of sit-ups and push-ups he forced himself to do, simply to maintain a slowly diminishing physical status quo. In fact, Radok's thighs were still twitching from the bike ride; he was beginning to feel soreness and pain in parts of his body he'd forgotten even contained muscle fiber.

"The Frau tells me you're after taking a hike. Inclement weather for such adventures."

Max's rheumy eyes went heavenward to a patch of herringbone clouds that looked to contain snow. Radok could smell the fragrance of it now: the thick, sweet water smell of snow over the harshness of cordite and pine resin. And over Max's own peculiar odor, as well. The unwashed sweat of years, so that the old man must wear a patina of grime next to his skin like a suit of long underwear. This odor had been there those many years ago, also.

The scent took Radok back to the three-day chamois stalk that had climaxed that summer's hunting. Radok struggling half a kilometer in back of the grown men, desperate to keep up pace. Desperate not to allow his youth to be a physical liability. It had been Max, not the General then, who'd waited up for him, who'd saved him from embarrassment by taking most of the load from his backpack and putting it into his own. Max with the same bandy body, stooped shoulders, and knobby fingers even then. How old was the man? And was his extreme old age as much a detriment now as Radok's extreme youth had been then? This was something for Radok to take stock of, to measure at the proper time. Which would be very soon now. Very soon, indeed.

"I imagine you'll be hungry," Max said, turning agilely on his heels and heading off toward a low hut which served as his residence. The big house, ocher in the afternoon light, rose grand and fearsome on the crest of a hill several hundred meters distant from this humble lodging. In the main house there would be porcelain, electricity laid on, and a cook/housekeeper to keep all in readiness against the event of the owner's infrequent visits. Infrequent, hell, Radok reminded himself. Never again.

"You know about the General?" Radok said to the back of the old gamekeeper, pushing his bike along the rutted track. Max was busily outdistancing him, just as he had done twenty-some years ago. *That* question was answered, at least: the old man was fit enough for what Radok had in mind.

But Max only shrugged his shoulders in answer to the stated question, not slacking his pace one whit. Dead birds hung on rusty hooks along the eave of the hut, a shamanistic warning to other creatures to beware. Stay clear. Radok rested the bike against the cabin under one of these birds.

Max threw open the plank door and entered the cabin, setting his gun into wooden notches over a stone fireplace. Radok followed him into the dank interior, in which small windows were curtained in filthy gingham. A simple bed stood in one corner; no sheets, only tattered blankets.

"He was a good man." Max's eyes filled with moisture. It was to be his only pronouncement on that tragedy.

"The Frau says you're helping the General," the gamekeeper said, blinking the tears away. "That's good enough for me. How can I assist?"

Simple eloquence from Max. Few words, used sparingly. They sufficed.

"But we'll talk of that later," Max quickly said, not waiting for Radok's response. "Now for some food."

A cast-iron pot of stew containing some wild, gamy meat, simmered on the coals of an open fire. The old man placed the pot of stew on a rough deal table, not bothering to protect the wood surface from the hot metal. He dished out large helpings in tin-ware and set to greedily, not waiting for Radok.

Max's teeth had been ground down to brown, triangular pegs, which ripped into the potatoes and the meat. Chamois, the meat was, Radok thought. Max wrapped his left arm around his plate warily; wiped the plate clean with the dimpled heel of a two-kilo loaf of rye bread.

The gamekeeper smiled at Radok through the spaces in his teeth, belching extravagantly.

"A dump, huh?" he said. "But it's home for me. I've got other accommodations for you."

No more explanations. Lunch finished, Max led the way a kilometer distant to the stationing lodge, where the local gentry gathered in the summers for the steep mountain ascent to the chamois hunting sites. *Lavine Huette,* Max called it, the Avalanche Hut, for it was situated just at the base of the Joachim Alp, with rocky crags overhead that had the nasty habit of dribbling the odd avalanche of snow onto the hut below during the spring melts. This was to be Radok's temporary headquarters until they set out in the morning.

There had been no melting yet this year; in fact it had started to snow heavily now, and darkness at midday gathered like a palpable presence. It was not the absence of light, but rather the presence of darkness.

Radok remembered the staging hut from that summer he had been up here with the General; he thought it a good idea for Max to put him up away from the main house and enquiring eyes. As they trudged toward the distant hut, Max explained that in case of visitors of the wrong sort, he would give two warning shots to set Radok off on his way. Max the old warrior, suddenly. More facets to him than a cut diamond, apparently. A good man to have along.

Finally they arrived, Radok wet and cold from the snowfall. The stolen charcoal tweed coat was not much good in the country. The Avalanche Hut was cavernous and cold; the damp smell of vacancy was heavy in the air as Max opened the door—like opening a tomb.

Max put a match to a kerosene lamp in the sitting room; the pitiful battling of one flame against the darkness at noon.

"The nobs' place," Max said. "Don't think it's wise to have a fire here. You might just as well announce yourself formal-like to the neighborhood. But there's plenty of blankets. You'll be snug enough until we leave."

Max pulled an oilskin bundle from an inside pocket of his mountain cape and placed it on the table.

"Frau von Tratten said maybe you'd need these, too."

Radok slowly unwrapped the bundle with fingers numb

from the cold. Inside were several maps of the Alpine passes in the 1: 50,000 scale. Old maps, wrinkled and reinforced with heavy tape at the folds, but the passes did not change. The trails stay the same for generations.

"I'll come back later," Max said. "Keep your ears open for the two shots. If you hear them, head for the high mountains and don't wait to ask questions. You'll have to use these maps and your own intuition in that case."

Max looked around the room closely before leaving, as if to take inventory in case the new lodger felt like a little friendly thieving. Old habits in the old die hard.

Radok took off his wet coat, exchanging it for one of the gray, pressed-wool hunting jackets on wooden hooks by the door. Elk-hide hunting bags hung there, too, stained rust with old blood. He looked around at his accommodations, wondering vaguely if he could trust the old gamekeeper. But then the SS would already be here if the old man were not be trusted.

Radok was exhausted from the bike ride and knew he needed rest. There would be little enough of it soon. No cots in the main room, only the enormous river-rock fireplace, so empty-looking without a fire. A door in the far corner led to a sleeping room: rows of bunks where the gentry, after a day of hunting, would bed down, away from the prying eyes and ears of their wives, where they could belch, fart, and tell tall tales of serving wenches they'd had, chamois they'd shot.

Stairs led off from this room. Radok took the lantern with him and climbed the stairs up to an unfinished attic. Old habits die hard in cops, too. Sniffing out the gremlins under the beds, the ghosts in the lumber rooms. At the top of the stairs, Radok could see huge cobwebs dangling from the attic rafters like banners in a medieval dining hall.

Three wooden packing crates sat in the middle of the attic floor. He went to them, set the lantern down, and found upon examination, that the crates yielded up a small treasure trove: two of them contained books and records along with an ancient gramophone. The third held an Armageddon stash of food, including canned cling peaches from France and a case of 1938 Heidseker *Sekt*. Next to this German champagne, wrapped carefully in cotton wool, were ten sticks of dynamite, their fuses and percussion caps stored safely in a separate oilskin pouch. The dynamite would be used to set off avalanches in those years when the thaw came dangerously late.

Radok, kneeling by the crates, smiled at the absurd necessities stored by the gentry. He would love to be able to hole up here, listening to Beethoven piano concerti, reading Shakespeare in Tauchnitz editions, supping on peaches soaked in bubbly, and setting off fine fireworks displays in the mountains with all the dynamite.

The wonderful arrogance of gentry like the von Trattens: the same sort of unconscious chauvinism and fancy that allowed men like the General to own an Alp. How different they were, thought Radok, those who stored champagne against the coming cataclysm, who could own a mountain like the Joachim Alp! It was part of what had drawn Radok to the General in the first place.

Thinking of the General now, he let Frau von Tratten's information sink in for the first time. All those years feeling betrayed by the General, when actually the old man had been trying to protect his wife and the Radok family. All those years of misunderstanding. Perhaps the world was not quite the simple place Radok had imagined it to be? Not black and white at all, but many subtle shades of gray.

Betrayal. Was Frieda another such case? Was her supposed betrayal just another shade of gray? Another misunderstanding? Radok would love to share this silly cache with her; closet themselves off from the world and let the snow fall. He would love to be wrong about her, as he had been about the General. For she had touched him, touched a part deep within him. How could he have been so wrong about her?

The lantern next to him guttered, spluttered, and then leaped back to life. A draught from downstairs: a door opening and closing.

Beautiful. And me with my back to the wall, like a dumb-ass captain retreating up a hill, he thought. Max should have fired warning shots . . . but have you been listening? Have you given it an ear at all? Or have you been so caught up in your explorations and daydreams that you missed the boom, boom?

He had the Luger in hand at least. That reaction had

not been compromised. But he fumbled with it, still not knowing where the safety catch was. There was no hiding place up here; a quick survey told him that.

The safety off the weapon now, Radok was crawling on all fours to the top of the stairs. I'll have a fair bit of pot-shooting before it's over, though, he thought. Enough clips of ammo to make it cost them. He looked back to the center of the room. Shit, the light! He scrambled back to the lantern, cupped his hand over the glass chimney, and blew. The glass was hot on his palm as the smell of kerosene reached his nostrils. Black darkness now, and back to where he hoped the stairs ended. A glow of light from below; sound of footsteps, a mumbling of voices.

"Radok? Where the hell are you?"

Max. There was pique in the old man's voice.

"I'll be damned," the old man spluttered from below. "Gone off strolling, the damn fool."

Radok listened for a moment, keeping an ear open for the ruse; the other voice that would mean the old fool had given him away.

And there was another voice now, indistinct. But not the gruff official voice he'd been expecting. This one was soft; fearful even, though Radok could not make out content. High and soft. A woman's voice.

"Up here!" Radok yelled. "I'm coming down! Give me a light!"

Shuffling footsteps from below as he rose, brushing at the dust on his clothes. The ocher orb of light coming from the downstairs landing illuminated Max's wrinkled features and glinted off the blond hair of the woman standing half concealed behind him.

"Reunions," Radok said mirthfully as he descended, the Luger still in hand. He was feeling anything but mirthful. Nauseated was closer to the truth, as if he were about to come face to face with his own fate. His mouth was dry and coppery-tasting. He felt as if he might be dealing blows and not words soon enough.

"Damn strange rabbit hole you found," Max said. "This one," he held the lantern to Frieda now, lighting her anxious face, "she says she knows you. Bears a letter from Frau von Tratten."

"Interesting," Radok said, picking his way down the

remaining steps, none too anxious to reach the bottom, like a suitor fearful of tripping in front of his girl, fearful of the onions he's had for lunch, fearful of the smell he can discern rising from his armpits. Fearful and anxious. An unaccustomed feeling for Radok.

A smile flickered across her face as if she recognized the anxiety in him, the same that resided in her.

It was a homecoming, and words were not needed. The open look on her face said it all. He knew that his suspicions about her had been wrong; that somehow it had all been a terrible misunderstanding, a subtle shade of gray, and that now they had been given another chance with one another. He knew simply and instinctively that he could trust Frieda; explanations would come later. For now, all he wanted was to be near her.

They stood together on the landing staring at one another, and Max soon grew fidgety.

"She's to be hiking with us then, is she?" Not a question but a complaint.

"Yes, Max," Radok said, his eyes not leaving Frieda's. "She's to be hiking with us."

After the old man had left; after their long silence; after slowly undressing each other; after lying close together in one of the narrow beds of the sleeping room; after meeting and joining and parting and meeting again; after going beyond words, there was time for words:

"I don't deserve you," she said.

Warm breath in his ear as she whispered it. No explanations; only this admission. No feeble kerosene lamp in here; only the soft afternoon light filtering through the unwashed windows. His hands continued to play over her, touching the moistness of her skin, moving over the welts on her buttocks. A mirror image of how she had earlier touched his wounds. She winced in his arms.

"He did this?" Radok said.

She sighed, her entire body rocking in his arms, as if to say yes. The rocking made the ancient springs of the bed squeak. Muffled stillness outside; the snow still falling.

"He was my friend once. I *thought* he was my friend."

"Shhh." He held her tighter, feeling now the tenseness in her back. He rubbed at the muscles to either side of her spine, her shoulder blades, her shoulders.

"No need to talk about it now," he said.

But she could not stop; she had to tell Radok about her history with Wolf Hartmann so that he would understand and would not blame her. Radok listened, breathing slowly, trying to keep his anger at bay.

"And he was always one of theirs," Frieda said in concluding her story. "Their pet monster. All these years. Lying. Me believing. Thinking he was wasting away in a concentration camp. And then he came back, the very morning after I'd been with you, and I felt so guilty. That I'd betrayed him after so many years of waiting for him. I felt so awful, I told him everything."

Wet tears fell on his shoulder.

"And he told his master," Radok said, piecing it together now. "Lieutenant Colonel Krahl."

"Father Mayer." As Frieda said the name she was almost weeping. "Wolf killed the Padre. With his own hands. I want to destroy Wolf."

"No." Radok rocked her even harder. "No. Enough destruction. Forget Hartmann. That's the destruction he deserves."

She was quiet for several minutes. Finally: "I love you. Love all of you."

Radok laughed, lightly in his throat; merrily.

"What?" she said, stiffening at his laughter.

"No, my love. Not laughing at you. Just at life. At coincidence. Fortunate you love me, else I'd have to *make* you love me. I feel all a piece of you."

Say it, you coward, he said to himself. Why were the words so hard? This was no time for irony. He felt her drawing back from him, misunderstanding.

"Because I love you, too," he said.

Words he'd never believed before.

Chapter Twenty-Six

It had been an awful morning for Krahl. The bite had taken seven stitches, and then there were the shots. The young SS doctor wore comical, round tortoiseshell glasses, and muttered on and on about the septic quality of the human mouth, spitting as he talked. A shower of flecks flew across both the stitches and Krahl's sleeve.

With the last stitch needled in, the dreaded call came through from Berlin. Colonel Boelhaven, second to Heydrich at Berlin SD, making a personal call. No intermediaries, secretaries, or adjutants. Congratulations were in order, Boelhaven said; the full colonelcy could be expected as a result of the efficient handling of this most delicate operation. The pig Radok was in custody by now, no?

No. Krahl had taken the call in his office, the doctor packing up his bag, while Hartmann was in the outer office getting the flight arranged to Innsbruck and warning the Brenner patrols to keep a lookout for the Lassen girl. Thank God he had taken the call somewhere semiprivate, for once Krahl had confessed that Radok was still at large, Colonel Boelhaven began such a tirade down the phone line as to turn Krahl's ears crimson. Naturally, he shooed the SS doctor out of the room as soon as it began.

"You fool!" Boelhaven boomed at him over the crackly line. "How could you let him slip away again? Don't you comprehend the magnitude of this operation? Has the importance of these papers completely escaped your imagination? Viennese!" And the full colonel made a noise as if hawking down the line, spitting at the stupid Viennese.

"What are we to do with you besides relieve you of duty?" Boelhaven asked rhetorically.

Krahl felt his bowels loosen at the suggestion of demotion and disgrace. So much for the warm, well-staffed villa in Penzing. He could never face Maman again.

"We'll get him," Krahl said. "It's only a matter of time now."

"You've been saying that for two days. Your words are becoming a rapidly devalued currency here in Berlin, *Lieutenant* Colonel."

The emphasis on "Lieutenant"; the scant half-step in promotion separating the two men was becoming as significant as the very physical distance between Vienna and Berlin.

Hartmann was at the door as Krahl hung up the phone, smiling his news that the Junker was ready and waiting for them at Schwechat Airport, and that the border patrol at the Brenner had been alerted. For if the maid's overheard bit of information was correct, that was where both Radok and the Lassen girl were headed.

Krahl's right arm was cradled in a sling, and he found it awkward to move without the balancing effect of the arm in its normal position. He had trouble getting up out of his chair, pushing himself ineffectually with left hand only. Hartmann merely stood by the door watching, a half-smile turned on Krahl.

Why should I give a damn, Krahl thought. He's only here on sufferance, anyway. One step out of line and he'll be back on the chopping block at the Justice Palace.

But Krahl did care; he interpreted the half-smile rightly as Hartmann's comment on this morning's action. So what if the old cow had killed herself. Her suicide saved the ratepayers a lengthy and embarrassing trial, after which the good lady would have been executed anyway.

Cheeky damned bastard, Hartmann. He was all but whimpering in front of me a few short hours ago, Krahl thought, ready to sell anybody for his own freedom. And indeed he had. He'd shopped his lover, just as the maid had shopped Frau von Tratten. But she'd already done a runner on him. Ironic, that. It had been worth all this fuss just to see Hartmann sweat and fret. Krahl hadn't planned on killing him, it was never in the cards. Well . . . If Radok had been caught on the Wiener Neustadt train, the temptation would have been rather more than it was at present, when Hartmann's help was still needed.

Krahl would need every experienced operative, as Colonel Boelhaven had so kindly reminded him.

"Wipe that fucking smile off your mouth!"

Hartmann squinted, obeyed.

"Sorry . . . sir."

The too-long delay between the words to show his disdain, but not long enough or obvious enough for Krahl to do anything about it.

"Let's catch a plane then, Lieutenant."

Krahl led the way out of the room, losing his balance at the door and brushing into the wall. Hartmann's hand was at his back, solicitous as if to a blind man crossing a busy intersection.

"I can manage very well on my own, Lieutenant."

"Yes . . . sir."

The plane dropped a few hundred meters in a downdraft as it circled over Innsbruck, and Hartmann watched Krahl go as white as the snow on the mountains below, tightening his death-grip on the left arm of his seat. White face, white knuckles. Terrified, as he had been at the Frau's early this morning looking at his bitten right hand. Terrified and screaming. Like a damn woman, Hartmann thought.

Hartmann looked at the scene below: Innsbruck surrounded by snowy alpine peaks. He felt an incredible clearness in his head. The mountain heights and airplane heights: these were places where he could truly see and feel. The only places he felt real at all. He worked on his dream again. When all this was over, he would buy himself a piece of one of those mountains. He would have the money then, for he would be a national hero. And he would purchase himself a hideaway; a refuge. The pure whiteness of it. And he'd dig a moat all by himself; construct a drawbridge. No one would enter his pure realm without his say-so.

When this was over. If it was ever over. He suppressed a sneeze, fearful of what the jarring would do to his body. The numbness was wearing off in his ribs and in his groin, replaced now with almost unbearable spasms of pain. Hartmann had never been beaten like that before. Never suffered that kind of humiliation. He feared a part of him below had been ruined forever by Berthold. What a joy it had been to see that pig's demise. The only thing better would have been for Hartmann himself to pull the trigger.

They began descending for the landing.

"How far from here to the Brenner?" Krahl asked, as if trying to distract himself from his fear of the descent.

Hartmann inclined his head. "Half an hour by car. Not far."

"What if we're late?" Krahl looked worried as the runway sped upward to meet the wheels of their plane.

"We won't be," Hartmann said. "If the maid was telling the truth, we'll have them in custody by this afternoon."

The wheels touched down; a bumpy landing.

"*If* she's telling the truth?" Krahl said through clenched teeth.

"I've been thinking about that," Hartmann said, shaking his head. "It's too easy. Much too direct a route for Radok."

"You like things difficult, Hartmann. Makes you feel important."

They were taxiing to a stop now; Krahl can talk confidently once again, Hartmann figured.

"I have the feel of him," Hartmann said. "And I don't think he's heading south. Nothing so obvious. He'll go west, I figure. Toward Switzerland. And by foot. He won't risk being spotted by our recon planes. He's a patient son of a bitch. He'll head west and wait for us to commit our forces at one of the likely crossing points, then he'll try to change direction on us."

"You've given it some thought," Krahl said, unbuckling his seatbelt.

Hartman nodded.

"It's what you'd do?" Krahl said.

Another nod.

"And I've been thinking about Frau von Tratten, as well," Hartmann said. "About what her death tells us. What was she trying to protect? What information? She spoke of the Brenner crossing last night in such loud tones that the maid could easily hear. Well, the old woman would hardly die for secrets that weren't really secret, would she?"

Krahl looked interested now, as they made their way

down the steps from the plane directly into the onset of a snowstorm.

"In point of fact," Krahl said, wiping snow from his eyes, "the Brenner may be a red herring. Is that what you're suggesting?"

"Exactly." Hartmann smiled, a snowflake landing on his nose. "And she killed herself rather than risk divulging the real whereabouts of our man."

"*And* your girlfriend," Krahl said. "Don't forget her. I'm not."

Hartmann tried to ignore this, but he was still stewing and squirming about her escape and how she had put him even deeper under Krahl's power. She would pay for her treachery.

A car was waiting for them, its engine on. Once settled in the back seat, Krahl turned to Hartmann.

"An interesting surmise," he said. "But I think that we shall leave a contingent on guard as planned at the Brenner."

They drove to the old Art Institute in the city which now housed Innsbruck Station, and it took only ten minutes to learn of the two possible Radok sightings: a stationmaster from Steyr reported seeing someone matching Radok's description on a local run into Innsbruck early in the morning. And a tap on the local Gestapo headquarters had caught a message to Morzin Platz in Vienna asking about a visiting Viennese agent, a chap flashing an ID number that was a match for Berthold's.

Krahl, seated in an armchair in the elegantly appointed visitor's room, a log fire crackling in the fireplace, looked pleased. He sipped on a sherry an adjutant had poured for him from a cut-glass decanter.

"So much for your theory, Hartmann," Krahl said.

"He could still head west as easily as south," Hartmann argued.

"They, not he," Krahl reminded. "Your Jew bitch is surely with him by now."

"I still don't trust the Brenner route," Hartmann said.

"Give me alternatives, Hartmann. Not vague suspicions."

"It goes back to von Tratten. All the ties. Back to the General, to his wife. . . . Aren't they from here originally? From Tyrol?"

Krahl looked unimpressed. "I believe so. But what has that got to do with . . ."

"They probably still have an old country seat or a shooting box, or some such folly. No?"

Krahl set his glass down on the green marble top of the side table.

"You're beginning to make sense, Hartmann. Check on it."

Another ten minutes, and Hartmann was back to the visitor's room with the address of the von Tratten estate, located some fifteen kilometers west of Innsbruck.

"Permission to investigate, sir?" Hartmann said after informing Krahl.

"Permission granted." Krahl was sipping on his second glass of the excellent sherry, well ensconced in the brocade wing chair.

Hartmann turned to leave. Permission my ass, he thought. He'd already phoned the local constabulary to meet him and assist at the von Tratten estate.

Chapter Twenty-Seven

Radok moved his long, thin index finger over the map, tracing a line now on red routes, now on yellow, secondary routes, out of the valley and into the mountains, and finally off the colored lines altogether.

"It'll be the trails from this point," he said, jabbing his finger at the map spread out on the dining room table in the Avalanche Hut. Frieda sat watching the finger trace her destiny.

"To the west," she said. "Why not south from here? Over the Brenner? Time's running out on us. We need to get these papers out quickly. You said so yourself, earlier."

She spread her thumb and forefinger over the distance between Innsbruck and the Brenner Pass, then using her thumb like the point of a compass, swung the distance around through Tyrol and Voralberg as Radok had traced their path.

"Your way must be three times as long," she said.

"That's right," he said. "But remember, we still have seven days left to get these documents out of the Reich. Time enough to be cautious."

He smiled at her and then looked at the map once more. His finger pointed to the dot on Bludenz.

"By foot from there," he said. "Plateau walking. It's hard stuff at first. You'll be up to it?"

"You didn't answer my question," Frieda said.

The softness was gone from her voice now, Radok noticed. No more of the helpless female for her. She had left that behind in the sleeping room. Now, with afternoon dusk lowering around them, she had once again become Radok's equal. He was surprised to find that he liked it. Not a hardness, really; just an evenness. A fairness seeking fairness from him. She had a right to know. It was her life, too, he reasoned. But how much to tell her?

271

"Okay. We're not going directly south from here because that's where they'll be expecting us. If they've traced us to Innsbruck by now, and they may well have, the Brenner would be the closest, most logical crossing. . . ."

"Is that how you arranged it with Frau von Tratten?" she said.

Radok looked at her, puzzled. "Arranged?"

"Yes," Frieda said. "Before I left, she mentioned that we would be meeting up at the Brenner. Earlier she'd talked of meeting you here at the estate."

Radok took this information in; considered it for a moment. It was so like the Frau to make an impressionistic judgment of Frieda; to know instinctively that she could trust her. Just as Radok now did. How could he not have? But another thought intruded now.

"Did Hartmann know?"

She shook her head at him, not understanding.

"I mean, did he know about your visit to Frau von Tratten?"

"Yes. I told him and Father Mayer that I'd gone to check your story out there. Why?"

But she obviously knew now, for she went on. "You think they went there? To the Frau's?"

Radok nodded. "If the guy's as professional as he seems, yes, he'd probably tumble to the connection. The only person between you and me. The Frau. It's all too likely."

"No . . ." Frieda's voice trailed away like smoke. "I don't want to think of that. That I might have set them on her, as well."

"She was already in it," Radok said. "Her husband, remember? She had no choice in the matter. She was in it if she wanted to be or not."

He caught her glance: her surprise at this hard edge to him, as he had been surprised at her demand for equality just before.

"And no, I don't like to think that what I do or what you do puts another in danger. But it's a fucking imperfect world. We're all in the water together; the ripple effect of human actions. It's not the way I'd choose it, but it's the way it's laid out. . . . So it's plausible, even probable that they are questioning Frau von Tratten at this very moment. And she obviously had a story arranged about the Brenner. It holds water. . . ."

"But it's not true," Frieda said.

Radok shook his head.

"We're heading due west from here. Perhaps a feint to the south, to throw them off. But basically it's westward to Switzerland for us."

"Then he'll know," Frieda said. "Wolf will know. He always knows when someone's lying."

Radok averted his eyes from Frieda's, looking down at the map, at the dot of Bludenz just above which his forefinger still rested. He jabbed the dot once more and thought of the cache upstairs, the peaches and sekt, books and records. He'd shown them to Frieda after their lovemaking, sharing the treasure trove with her, as well as his dream. Seductive. Snow falling outside, the dumb, numb quiet of it. Cotton-bandaged away from the world, hidden away snug in the cabin eating peaches all day, listening to Beethoven concerti at night. Seductive, to both of them, for then she had told him of her passion for the "Emperor" Concerto, her signature piece. They both wanted suddenly to steal a couple of days away from the world, to play hooky from reality, if only for a day.

Radok jabbed the dot of Bludenz again on the map. The end of the dream. Not even one day would they have. Perhaps not even one night. He'd have to talk with Max.

Just then the old man charged into the room carrying a gust of snow with him.

"She's dead!" he exclaimed. "The bastards killed her."

"Hold on," Radok said. "Who? Who's dead?" But he knew.

"The bastards. The evil fucking bastards." There was snow on Max's shoulders, on his hat. "First the General, now her."

"No . . ." Again the moaning escape of voice from Frieda.

"The cook's cousin just called from Vienna," Max went on. "The Frau is dead. This morning. The villa's crawling with SS and police. The cousin was due down here for holiday; stopped by the villa to pick up some supplies cook wanted. And there you are. Dead! Shot! By her own hand, the police told her. Christ! The pigs!"

Dark as sin up the narrow driveway. Snow was still falling out of the blackness. Their running lights were on, headlights off. The driver cut the engine several hundred meters from the house.

Birkau, the thick-boned man from the local constabulary, sat in the back next to Hartmann. He was familiar with the von Tratten estate.

"The main house is up the drive a piece," he said, breathing heavy onion fumes into the close space of the car as he spoke. "The cook'll be there. Gamekeeper, he lives in the cottage over there."

Hartmann peered out into the darkness and saw nothing but dollops of snow.

"Our men are in place around the main house," Birkau said. "No one gets in or out without our say-so."

This was exactly the sort of cocky attitude that rankled the professional in Hartmann.

"Any other out-buildings on the estate?" he asked the constable.

Birkau didn't seem to hear Hartmann's question; he had one of those stupid peasant faces that showed hardly any emotion.

Finally the man answered the question, long after Hartmann thought he had not heard it.

"There's an old knocked-together hut sort of affair," Birkau said. "Right under the Joachim Alp. It's closed this time of year. Avalanches, you know. They used it as a staging camp for mountain hunts. Not likely, that one. Not with spring thaw."

"It hardly looks like a thaw to me," Hartmann said.

Birkau made no reply.

"Have your men secure the main house," Hartmann said. "And the gamekeeper's cottage. Then bring along two more men and show me this hut."

There would be nothing obvious for Radok, Hartmann knew. Eschew the commonplace. Go for the risky, the daring. Living under the shadow of avalanche; that was Radok's style.

Birkau did as he was told, but was damn surly about it; put out that he was forced to miss the big action at the estate, that he had to trudge through the fucking snow on a wild goose chase just on the whim of this evil-looking son of a bitch who gave orders like he was born to it. But he did as he was told, getting out into the heavy snowfall and talking to his men staked out at the estate. Then he returned to the staff car with two more constables in tow and Hartmann got out to join them.

"This way," Birkau said ungraciously, and they set off into the darkness and falling snow.

Hartmann pulled up short after a few minutes of hiking. He glanced from Birkau to the two look-alike constables the man had picked to accompany them.

"You men ever do any mountain stalking?" Rhetorical question: Hartmann knew everyone in this part of Tyrol had hunting experience in the mountains.

The two nodded their heads vigorously.

"Chamois?" Hartmann asked.

More nods, enthusiastically.

"You like chamois meat?" he said.

Oh, yes. More than pussy, their nods said.

"Right." Hartmann leveled his automatic at them. "You fucks want to set foot in the mountains again, you'll damn well take this operation seriously. Or I lose you right here, right now. You stalk this bastard like he was the biggest damn chamois in the world. *Verstehen*? Like he was the godhead of all chamois, and you're all good religious boys, right? So no shuffling along the trail, no banging of guns against ammo belts. Not even a fart out of you. Get it? You're hunters now, not gawking farm boys pissed off and cold."

Hartmann slid the safety off his PPK Walther so that it clicked in the silent, snowy night.

"Do you read me?" he said.

They understood, nodding as enthusiastically as they had for the chamois. They all moved off together. A team. Spread out. Silent. On the hunt.

It took ten minutes for Birkau to find the hut. Hartmann knew they'd been lost for a time, but said nothing. His eyes had adjusted to the darkness and he made out the bulk of the wooden hut before Birkau's meaty hand on his shoulder confirmed its presence. No lights on inside. No smoke from the chimney. No surprises there. Instinct told Hartmann this was where the action would be, at the most removed building. An escape hatch; a bolt hole.

There was a flicker of movement from within. Hartmann was sure of it. A curtain dropping, ever so imperceptibly. He wanted to be sure of it, but the darkness swallowed vision. Still, the reflection off the snow gave him some

light, some hope. Well screw it, he told himself. The
curtain *had* moved; it was enough for him. He motioned
the two constables to his side. One thing in their favor:
the bastard hut was built smack into the base of the
mountain. Once inside, the only way out seemed to be
back again through the front door. No smoke-out, however. Too crude. They would destroy the papers if they
were given time; never know if they had had them or
not, that way. No, Hartmann thought. I want to catch
them face-to-face. Take them fast and hard. No tricks or
strategy for this bastard. No opportunity to think.

"They cover the windows," Hartmann whispered to
Birkau, meaning the two lower officers. "You back me
up. We go in shooting, low. Through the front door. Me
left, you right. Tuck and roll."

"Fucking cowboy maneuver," Birkau murmured.

Hartmann moved him toward the door. "You've got it,
friend." They approached slowly, waiting for the other
constables to get in position. Finally they were at the door.

Hartmann nodded at Birkau to make sure he was
ready; the other returned the nod.

No sounds from within as Hartmann's boot kicked just
above the latch mechanism. The door flew open and
Hartmann hurtled into the blackness of the room, rolling
onto the floor. Birkau behind him, no shots, but onto the
floor, right on top of him.

"To the *right,* asshole!" Hartmann whispered, but did
not know why he kept his voice low, after the crash of
the door.

They scrambled for cover, but none was needed. There
were no shots from within. Hartmann waited a long
minute, then was up and firing into the blackness and
rolling onto the floor again to the far wall. A patter and
splat of fire came from outside now, whistling over
Hartmann's head.

"Hold your fire, your shits!" he screamed. "You there,
Birkau?"

"Yeah." Exhaustion and fear in the voice.

"Think it's clear?"

"Yeah."

"You going to shoot if I stand up?" Hartmann said.

"Piss off," the constabulary officer growled.

"All right. Let's check things out."

Flashlights now playing through the rooms, yellow arcs in the darkness. Nothing to find in the main room. The two other men were inside now and up the stairs, and going ga-ga over the sekt they found in the attic.

Hartmann found it in the sleeping room: a thin, tortoiseshell hair clip that Frieda wore. He knew the type; she always bought them at the same shop just behind Stephansdom Cathedral. A big damn tortoise shell rested in the window as an advertisement. She had laughed at these specialty shops, comparing them with Macy's in New York. Making a living off of buttons and hair clips seemed quaint to her, coming from the new world of department stores and chain groceries.

They'd been here, all right, Hartmann could see. On the bed. On the musty fucking blankets. He shone the torch on the blankets and moistness glistened under the light. Leaving their pecker tracks over half of Austria like a slug trail, he thought.

"Find anything?" Birkau was behind him now, two bottles of sekt in hand.

"They've gone," Hartmann said.

"Right," Birkau replied. "They aren't fucking here, is what you mean."

Hartmann put his hand on the blanket stain: still moist, still warm. Not long gone from here. He put the fingers to his nose: ammonia smell. Semen and the pungent, earthy scent of a woman's sex.

A bloodhound, sniffing his prey.

From the other room came a scream; a man's voice. A shot.

Hartmann and Birkau were out there in an instant, weapons at the ready.

"Bats!" one of the men yelled.

A bat darted about the room, in and out of the beams of the flashlights like a bomber through searchlights.

So that was the phantom at the window he had seen, Hartmann realized. More shots as the men emptied their pistols at the bat.

Movement and action, Hartmann thought. Not to confuse the two.

Chapter Twenty-Eight

They'd had to leave the von Tratten estate in a hurry; there was no time to argue about the initial destination. The hunters could have been there at any moment, Radok knew. Out. That was what had been important. Just out and away from any place associated with the von Tratten name.

Radok had delayed only long enough to stuff the maps into a pack, along with a few sticks of the dynamite from the General's strange cache of goods in the attic. No telling what might come in handy along the trail. Max took care of food supplies and weapons, not trusting Frieda enough to let her assist.

Max had said he knew of a mountain hut hidden in the vicinity. Some place they could get to in a few hours of walking. Enough for Radok. Snow fell down on them as they walked, trudged rather. Thank God for that, Radok thought. It would cover any tracks they left behind. Max took the lead, proving his worth.

Now at the hut, with everyone tucked into bunks, Max was snoring nonstop, and farting occasionally and quite contentedly, as Frieda and Radok shivered against each other in one bunk like ice cubes in a tray.

"You sleeping?" she whispered.

"Does it feel like it?" Ass-freezing, ball-breaking, bone-chilling cold. "I'm stiff as a corpse."

"In all the wrong places." A giggle from her.

"Not funny," Radok said. "My testicles feel like they've taken refuge somewhere near my liver."

"Maybe we should have waited until morning. How likely was it that they'd find the estate so soon?"

"Very likely," Radok said. He wanted to keep this banter alive, but knew that he couldn't. He knew that when the solace of words ended, then the grief of Frau von Tratten would begin. As it had just days before for her husband. Grieving for them, or for the death of your own past? he wondered.

Yet he was not one for public displays of grief. Like a dog, Radok needed to find a quiet corner and grieve on his own.

"I think I'll take a walk," he said. "Too cold to sleep."

"I'll go with you." Her voice was bright, hopeful.

"You'll need the rest," he said by way of discouragement.

"But I can't sleep without my portable foot-warmer," she joked.

"I'll only be a few minutes."

"Sorry," she finally said. "Rather thick of me. You want to be alone. I'll manage without the foot-warmer. Hurry back."

He leaned over her face: it was only a black silhouette in the gloom. A peck on her cheek. He could feel the softness of her skin-down on his lips.

"I love you," he said.

"I'm not going to get in the habit of answering that all the time, okay?" she said. "I want to keep it spontaneous."

For which he had no answer. Just a gentle cupping of her buttocks with his palm before leaving the narrow bunk. Outside the door of the ramshackle hut the snow was still falling, tumbling out of the sky. It looked artificial, like the bits of paper confetti used on stage at the Volkstheater. Radok stared into a patch of it as it descended, creating vertigo in him: suddenly the snow was ascending rather than descending. Without a fixed reference point, the flakes seemed to defy gravity, and Radok felt dizzy, swept away.

No tears. Grief is not solely a matter of tears, he told himself. Anger there was, though. And a sharpening, a honing of that anger. A directing of it, as well. To the agents of the Frau's destruction: to the pig Krahl and the other animal, the one with the animal name—Wolf.

Under the snow-filled sky, Radok made a simple promise to himself and to the memory of the von Trattens; to the memory of the unknown millions who were scheduled to die under the yoke of the Nazis. One cannot hate a system; one must concentrate that emotion on a few individuals. Vengeance cannot be wrought upon a bureaucracy; its representatives must be brought to account.

So, Radok's vow was a simple one: he would have the asses of Krahl and Wolf Hartmann.

It was no longer enough simply to evade capture and get the papers out of the Reich; Radok wanted to get even. He wanted to stop being the hunted and start doing the hunting. But this he could not let the others know; not yet. The cutout system at work. He employed the need-to-know tactics of life in the field.

Snow clumped in Radok's hair, melting, dripping into his face.

"You're going to catch pneumonia this way, boy."

Max stood behind him, rolling a cigarette with one hand, spreading the tobacco evenly on the paper with thumb and forefinger.

"Just going in," Radok said.

"Wait a minute, okay? Keep an old man company while he smokes."

Max lit the cigarette with an ancient flint and cotton-stuffing lighter—no fluid. There was the rank smell of singed cotton wadding as it smoldered.

"Lucky about the snow," Max said.

"It'll give them a run for their money," Radok agreed. "No tracks. They should be expecting us at the Brenner."

"And you don't want to go that way," Max said.

"Right."

"You want to take us over the passes through Voralberg, that it?"

"Something like that. Except you do the taking," Radok said. "We follow."

Max flicked the half-finished cigarette away; it cart-wheeled orange sparks into the dark.

"It's not going to be easy," the gamekeeper said. "Hard enough we got two men in reasonable shape. A woman along, what kind of chances you think we got?"

"We need her, Max. She's the key. We've got some very impressive information here. About how Hitler and his friends are killing all the Jews in Europe. Understand? I don't mean just randomly; a pop on the head here, a shot in the neck there. Christ, Max! They're rounding all these people up, all across Europe. Systematically. Herding them into cattle cars like livestock, shipping them across Europe into Poland or Russia to huge camps where they're going to gas them."

"All right." Max held up a gnarled hand. "I get the picture. But I'm no Jew-lover. I'm doing this for the General. Because it's what the General wanted."

"It's not a matter of Jew or Gentile, Max." This was a new voice. Frieda stood behind them in the door of the hut.

"Killing like this," she went on. "Exterminating. It murders us all. It's humanity dying, not just the Jews. The humanness in all of us. I guess maybe we need to get this straight before we go on."

"No choice now, anyway," Max grumbled.

Radok was about to reply, but Frieda did instead.

"You have a choice, Max. You can go back home now. No one's the wiser. You don't know anything yet about our plans. Only where we overnighted. So we kidnapped you at gunpoint and you managed to escape. Tell them what you know. It won't hurt us. You see, you do have a choice. I . . . we don't want you along unless you feel as though you have choice. When it comes down to it, when it's do or die, that's the only attitude that will keep us from each other's throats."

Radok looked at her with something like a smile on his face. It was exactly what he'd been thinking, but not how he would have said it. He'd none of her directness.

"Easy for you to say." Max was unconvinced. "But I didn't have any choice about you, did I?"

"No," she said. "I'm not just excess baggage, though. You do need me. Think about it. I was born here in Austria, but I lived for many years in America. I'm one of them, in a way. You two take these papers to Switzerland, approach the Allies. Great. A rogue cop and a veteran of Kaiser Bill's war. You think they're going to believe you? At least with me we have a chance of getting past the front-door guard."

"She's right," Radok said. It was what he'd been getting at earlier, except that he hadn't really believed it before. It had only been an excuse cooked up for Max. The truth was, Radok was taking Frieda along because she was a part of him now. He might as well try to leave his legs behind as leave her. But now he saw the real logic of the argument. She was right. And she was damn strong.

"We're a team," Radok said. "We have to feel like one and act like one."

"But she's a woman, dammit." From Max's mouth, the description sounded like an epithet.

"I'll keep up. Don't worry about me. And I'll carry my own load."

Max sucked in cold air. "We'll see."

Back in the cabin, Max went to sleep again almost immediately: the deep, regular breathing of the guiltless.

In their shared bunk, Radok spooned about Frieda.

"You were great," he whispered. "Ought to run for Parliament."

"It wasn't rhetoric." Her voice had a sharp edge to it.

"You don't have to convince me."

"Sorry." She rolled over to face him, kissing his lips, his closed eyes.

"You see," she said, "I really do believe what I said. We each have our reasons, Radok. I doubt it's really a matter of humanity for you. The General asks this of you. You love the General and his memory. That's reason enough for you. Me, I'm a Jew. And I've got my own memories. But none of this matters. Only that we're committed to the mission, believe in it, for whatever reasons. And that we go into it by choice. Is that okay, Radok? A bargain?"

She held his hand close to her body.

"A bargain." He shook her hand. It was strong, dry, and warm in his.

Radok woke first in the morning, Frieda still wrapped around him as they'd slept last night. The musky smell of sex rose from the sleeping bag.

Max was gone. Sleeping bag, pack, and rifle with him.

"Shit."

Frieda awoke. "What is it?"

Radok nodded at Max's empty bunk. "The old one's done a scamper. Guess he finally chose."

Silence for a time.

"We don't need him," she finally said.

Radok grinned. "I'm afraid we do, old girl. But we'll have to do without him."

"I came on too strong."

Radok shook his head. "Maybe. But you were right. It

needed saying. And we are better off without him if his guts weren't in it."

"So what do we do now?"

Her pelvis was still against his, wrapped in the sleeping bag. He knew what he wanted to do and so did his penis.

"I mean constructively," she said.

"It's very constructive. Kept the world populated for millennia in this manner."

The door burst open and Radok scrambled out of the sleeping bag toward the rifle, his penis dangling out of his long underwear, half tumescent.

"Max!" Frieda yelped.

"Tuck it in, boy," Max said to Radok. "Godawful sight."

Radok started fumbling with the fly on his underwear.

"I've been reconnoitering," Max said. "It's a beautiful damn day. Takes months of cobwebs out of the brain."

Radok wanted to shout "Thank God!" that the man hadn't left, but didn't. He swallowed the comment, and finally got his penis tucked away as directed.

"Snow's stopped," Max went on. "Bright, sunny son of a bitch out there. And you two making like rabbits in the warren. It's time to be off. No sign of patrols. No air traffic. We've got the mountains to ourselves today, by the looks of it."

"Maybe we ought to check the maps now," Radok said as he stepped into his trousers.

"Maybe we ought to," the old man said.

Max had made his choice.

Radok pulled out the maps while Frieda got a simple breakfast of cheese and bread together. No coffee; there would be no fires, no smoking chimneys, until they were well away from the von Tratten estate.

"Yes," Max allowed, examining the planned route on the map. "It may be do-able. Much depends on the border crossing itself, however." Squinting at the tiny writing on the map, nodding his head.

"We should have a better idea of that once we're close to the border," Radok said. "Local gossip. Troop movements. Perhaps there might even be a partisan group at work in the vicinity to link up with. I've seen police reports on groups working in the Drei Ecke."

Max nodded more. "I've heard of such things. But I

know that area, and I know the passes there. This snowfall will make them impassable for weeks."

They ate the bread and cheese hungrily, silently. Max
did not bother to wipe away the crumbs at his mouth, but
pointed a gnarled, nicotine-stained finger at the map, at
the northern tip of the Austrian-Swiss border near Lake
Constance.

"Bregenz. Now I hear that is some town," Max said.

"You're crazy," Radok replied. "That's valley terrain
there. There's no cover there and it's heavily patrolled.
We'd have to cross the Rhine. Be sitting-bloody-ducks
there."

Max ignored the comments.

"Yes, a lovely town," he said. "So I have heard.
Flowered walkways right out onto the lake, it's said. An
old quarter that will take one's breath away."

"Gestapo will take our breath away for good," Radok
said, "if we go sniffing around there. The town is crawling with SS and Gestapo and all the rest of it. Bregenz is
the major staging ground for the western provinces. Like
walking right into their parlor. Dumber than crossing at
the Brenner."

Max folded the map neatly.

"Perhaps," he said with dignity. "We shall see. No
need to decide today. Westerly movement is called for
now. Next few days, that's what we need. Due west.
Nothing fancy."

Nothing fancy, just as promised. The first day out they
slowly ascended the high mountain plateau, pulling through
knee-high powder snow that had all but obliterated an
old forest road. Max took the point, knowing almost
instinctively the route. A friend to the mountains. At one
with the mountains. He was as much a part of things as
the eagle circling overhead or the tall pine trees shrouded
in snow to each side of the trail.

By midday they had made it well up the north side of
the Joachim Alp, into the first of a series of high alpine
meadows or *Alms*. Panting breath was the only thing to
be heard in this mountain fastness devoid of other hu-
mans. Frieda had done well, keeping up with them all
morning, digging through the fresh snow as if it were the
most natural thing for her to be doing. Max looked

disappointed that he hadn't been able to say "I told you so" about her holding them up. She gave nothing away by the way she looked, but at lunch ravenously ate wurst and bread. Also a carrot as special treat. Packing had been hurried and haphazard the night before. Provisions were not the best.

"I hope you brought enough food along," Radok said.

Max looked up from his half-gnawed carrot.

"Enough for about a week," he said. "If we ration it. Plenty of water up here."

"Right," Radok said. A week was about how long they'd be traveling.

Slower progress in the afternoon. They were still up in the *Alms*, above the tiny world of valley and cities, but snow was piled deep here, almost waist-deep, and turning slushy in the strong afternoon sun. Radok's clothes were soaked through, and the boots he'd found at the Avalanche Hut were beginning to leak, as well. There'd been no frog oil to work into them. But at least the climbing was done with for today. Level, high-meadow hiking. The deep snow was the only encumbrance. Yet it was so damn pretty up here above the tree line, Radok thought, so pure and clean, that he could almost forget these discomforts, almost forget that they were running for their lives and for those of millions of others.

They talked little this afternoon, as if none of them wished to spoil the natural stillness. It was still light when they arrived at the second in a series of high mountain huts Max knew of. These huts were used in the summer by the Alpine Society, but were closed in the winter months. Primitive wooden structures with a main room lined with bunks. There was usually a wood-burning stove, as well. This one, the Magdalen Hut, was no exception. It was easy to break into, a potbelly stove stood in one corner with a stock of wood at the ready, the walls were taken up with single bunks, and a deal table was in the center.

"I hope I won't have to listen to the young lovers again tonight," Max joked. "Get some sleep, thanks be to God."

Frieda blushed and it was only now, looking closely at her face, that Radok realized how exhausted she really was. She had hidden the exhaustion all day, but the pose was too much for her now. Only one day out on the trails, and she was done in. What would she be like after a week of this? Radok wondered for the first time if Max hadn't been right about taking a woman along. And now, also for the first time, Radok felt like a man without choices. No way to leave her behind. No way to go on without her. A prisoner to his love for her.

They tried sleeping together for a time on one of the narrow pine-slat beds, but Radok needed to stretch out, needed to make plans for vengeance, and so moved to the bunk above. Frieda seemed to fall asleep immediately, while Radok lay on his back, his mind spinning, fabricating the animal trap he would spring on the animals chasing them.

He fell into a deep and dreamless sleep, his muscles luxuriating in the stretch, but awoke sometime in the darkness to a whimpering sound. Disoriented at first, he had to put together where he was; what the sound might be. Suddenly he realized the sound was coming from Frieda in the bunk below him. He looked over the edge of the bunk and could see her outline in the penumbral light, seated on the edge of her bunk, gently peeling off her walking socks. They stuck at the heel; as she pulled the wool away from blistered flesh, breaking the caked bond of blood, she whimpered.

Radok did not reach out to her or speak. She had waited for this privacy of the deep hours of night to minister to those blisters; he would not interfere with that.

Hartmann sat on the edge of the bed, naked. He felt lost. He was losing it all, he knew; could feel it slipping away from him. Maybe he had never had it? Never had the real stuff of a field man; had only been up against amateurs and fools before. They were staying one step ahead of him, consistently. One step that Hartmann could neither guess nor divine. That worried him. Radok and the whore, Frieda. Beating him. Leaving a track of semen and dead bats for him to follow.

And now this humiliation, as well. Not being able to perform. An ache in his groin, but no other sensation there.

"Don't worry," the woman on the bed in back of him

said. "Lots of fellows have trouble that way, you know? It passes."

She winked a heavily made-up eye at him when he looked around at her, then rolled over onto her back, picking his pubic hairs out of her mouth.

Hartmann surveyed the whore in disgust: breasts sagging into her armpits like melting pats of butter; blue veins streaking her upper thighs. She reminded him of his landlady in Klagenfurt. What was her name? It seemed so long ago, but it was only a matter of days.

"Injuries like that"—she pointed a chipped, red-lacquered fingernail at his swollen and blue testicles—"what do you expect?"

He wanted to make her quiet, to silence her grating, whisky voice as he had silenced the landlady in Klagenfurt. How had he come to such grotesquerie? Another exercise in self-abasement?

She ran a puffy hand down his flanks, gently touching her ass where he had been at work.

"Give you an A for effort, though," she chuckled. "Set my old buns tingling, you did. Some of you boys like the weirdest things. Only yesterday this soldier comes in . . ."

So easy. Just stuff the pillow over her hideously rouged face, he thought. Stop those bright red clown lips from moving. He looked at his limp penis: a red circle of lipstick left there as on a cigarette butt. She should die.

What was he doing here, anyway? He should be out on the trail of Frieda and Radok. But he had reached a dead end with that, as with this. No sign of the two at the Brenner, and they had already come and gone at the von Tratten hunting lodge, disappearing into the Alps and taking the old gamekeeper with them, apparently. Which was good: the old bastard would slow them down. Frieda would slow them down. Frieda. The name sounded like betrayal. The cunt.

Hartmann had spent a miserable day after returning from the von Tratten estate empty-handed. He knew he needed to make something happen, not just wait for Radok to make a mistake. Not wait on the edge of this whore's bed without being able to get his dick up. Not allow Frieda and Radok to make a fool of him or Krahl to smirk at his mistakes. There must be something more he could do.

". . . and after that he asks *me* to roll over," the whore was saying, but Hartmann shut out her words.

Borders to the south and west secured at major routes; alpine passes blocked with snow. It was melting in Tyrol, but in Voralberg, where the bastard might cross, the snow was still ass-deep. All public transport in Austria was being watched, as well. No more switching of coats could save Radok now. No more ignorant Gestapo baboon to ruin their plans, either.

But what else? There had to be something more he could do; something that he'd overlooked. . . .

". . . Bang. Just like that. It was over." The whore continued her story. "I mean, just that fast."

"I'm not really interested in your other clients," Hartmann said, getting up from the bed.

"You're not going?"

His back was to her as he searched for his clothing scattered next to the bed on the floor of this dreary Innsbruck flat. A picture on the nightstand of a young boy in uniform. Whores have kids, too. Hadn't his own mother had one?

Suddenly Hartmann was struck with the realization, the terrible understanding, that in fact his mother had been a whore. An old, bloated prostitute like the one lying in back of him. That all her men friends had only been clients, paying for their bit of flesh. Why had he never seen it so clearly before? His mother the whore. Just like this old bag of bones sprawled out here.

And with this realization came a sense of loss; the pure white dream was suddenly gone. His mountain retreat. What did any of it matter? he wondered. In the face of this kind of sudden insight, why should I keep up the orderly facade?

She placed a hand on the back of his thigh, squeezing and crawling upward to his buttocks.

"Know what I think?" the whore whispered. "I think that you've been a naughty boy. That's what."

A wave of heat like a searing pain flashed through his abdomen, down to his groin. The hand cupped his left buttock, pinched it. He felt his hips convulse.

"A very naughty boy." A hissing chuckle from the whore. "What should we do about it?"

A thumb probed him, the other hand roughly kneaded his right buttock. He involuntarily twitched again at the hips.

Her first blow made him shiver exquisitely, stinging his ass, drawing the breath from him. He felt himself harden, moving spasmodically as he stood.

"Such a naughty, naughty boy," she repeated, seeing the reaction she was getting. "You've got to lie down and take your punishment."

He closed his eyes and let himself be pulled down on the bed, facedown into a limp pillow smelling of talcum and booze, just as his mother's had.

Chapter Twenty-Nine

Frieda's foot suddenly sank in the melting snow. She stumbled and fell sideways. Snow encompassed her, crushed in upon her, filling her ears, her nostrils. There was no air. Frieda opened her mouth to scream and it filled with snow, as well.

Something hard touched her now; substantial. Hands gripped her legs, her arms. One was on her breast, but that was released quickly.

Max and Radok pulled her out of the snow, and she coughed and spluttered back to life.

Then they continued.

Day two.

Away from the level *Alms* now, and up and down the jagged peaks of the Stubaier Alps. The hot mountain sun glistened harshly into her eyes, melted the deep new snowfall down to the hard-packed level in places, and exposed crumbling "snow caves" in others, such as the one Frieda had tumbled into. Westward they were headed today, for a dot on the map called Landeck.

By noon they had reached the first summit, the Acherkogel, at three thousand and ten meters. The weather was again clear and fine, with snow glistening all about them. The views were glorious, but daunting, as well, when they looked at the wilderness of forest and alpine peaks through and over which they must cross to reach Switzerland.

A short stop for lunch at the Acherkogel and Frieda, in charge of the lunch today, knew the provisions would not last another day. She wondered if Max had been sneaking extra rations in the night. All she wanted was to be able to maintain her dignity in front of the crusty old man; to be allowed to plod on as best she could without his condemning eyes on her.

After lunch they plunged ahead, down into the valley

of the Oetzl. The melt had progressed here: most of the snowfall had become mud in their path. New muscles in Frieda's legs began to ache with the descent, but at least they no longer had to deal with the drifts. Once in the valley, however, there was nothing for it but to come off the old logging roads and mountain trails for a time and cross a secondary road going north and south. To make a diversion around where the road dead-ended to the south would cost them a full day of walking. That, balanced against a few moments out in the open on the road. A simple equation, but one Frieda was happy that she did not have to solve.

Their one strength, she figured, now lay in invisibility. Keep to the mountain trails where no passersby could identify them. Keep Krahl and Hartmann guessing even about the general direction in which they were headed. That was all they had on their side for the moment, as far as Frieda could see. Soon enough, as they approached the border and civilization, that element of concealment would be denied them, Radok had told her. The question now was whether they should risk throwing down their one ace long before they were close to the border.

They all stopped in the trees at roadside, looking at the narrow strip of pavement as if it were a serpent.

In the event, Max made the decision.

"I'll go first," he said.

It was a winding country road, overhung with branches and traced on the other side by a swiftly flowing creek. They could neither clearly hear nor see if someone was approaching from either direction.

Max crossed quickly on his short legs, without incident, and reconnoitered the opposite side to find the best crossing of the creek. He disappeared for a time into the woods on the far side, then came out smiling about a hundred meters south of where he'd gone in. A wave of his arm beckoned them: he'd found a ford to the creek.

Radok and Frieda looked at each other wordlessly and then began crossing the road. When they were halfway across, a truck appeared around the bend to the north, almost on top of them. Gray-green; military.

"Run!" Radok pushed her ahead of him and she stumbled across the road to where Max was, his rifle at the ready. There was the sound of brakes in back of her. She turned, saw Radok standing his ground dead center in the road, his rifle, too, whipped off the shoulder sling.

But this was no military vehicle, Frieda noticed now, despite its color. Or at least it was no longer. Perhaps in the first war it had carried troops into the Italian Alps, but had long since been used for more peaceful purposes. A load of manure steamed in the open flatbed where once untested combat troops had shivered with cold and terror.

"You all right?"

It was a loud, booming voice from the driver in the cab. He jumped down now that the vehicle was stopped just in front of Radok. He was a giant of a man in ragged loden jacket, wool pants, and heavy boots, and his head was as big as a helium birthday balloon.

He moved toward Radok. "I almost didn't have time to stop. Not many hikers hereabouts. Not lately, anyway."

He looked Radok up and down now, from muddy boots to sunburnt face, then back to where Frieda and Max were.

"Fucking farmer. . . ." Max muttered.

Frieda felt a fool. She and Max should at least have looked for cover; not let the yokel get a good look at them. With her hair up in the blue woolen stocking cap, she might pass for a youth, but she somehow doubted it. The man's eyes searched out hers, then traveled down to her chest where his gaze rested on her breasts. No. There was no hiding those, not even under the hunting jacket she had taken from the estate.

"Out hunting?" the man said. Irony in his voice. "Good weather for it."

Radok nodded. "It is that," he said. He stood his ground, apparently not wanting to appear too eager to be gone.

We're going to have to kill him, Frieda told herself. He's seen too much. He can identify us.

"Nice old piece you've got there." The man nodded at Radok's Maennlicher.

Another nod from Radok.

"I used to own one myself," the man went on. "Before Hitler's boys took it away from me, that is. Thirty-eight or thereabouts."

Frieda didn't want to listen to this silly and rather

mysterious discussion. She only wanted to be off, away from here, even if it meant climbing again, with her thighs aching every step.

"He's one of us," Max whispered. It was not necessarily meant for Frieda; it seemed more like something forced out of him.

"Bad years, they were," Radok replied.

Frieda wished she knew what was going on; it seemed everyone was talking in code. But one thing she sensed: the farmer's stock had somehow gone up. A subtle change in the power balance among the four of them had occurred.

"We used to go into the mountains then, too," the farmer said. "But never this early in the year. No game about now."

"Maybe we just like to walk," Radok said.

The big man laughed. It echoed in the narrow valley, along with the rumble of his engine. It was startling, also, for his laugh was high and almost hysterical, hardly the sound Frieda expected from one so large.

"Maybe," he said, still chuckling. "Maybe you like walking, and maybe you wouldn't mind the offer of a lift, either. By the looks of your group, you could use one."

He looked directly at Frieda, and she felt a hot flush of anger and shame creeping up her throat. At this rate, the fool will make it easy to kill him if need be, she thought.

"Where you headed?" the man asked Radok.

"West."

Another laugh, less genuine this time, Frieda reckoned. She heard the click of Max's bolt. The sound was not lost on the farmer, either.

"Well, I guess it's none of my business. West is a good enough place to be going. If you want a ride, it's been offered."

"Good of you," Radok said. "But it'd be a bit crowded with four in the cab."

"Nonsense, man. It was built to hold four easy. We'll just snuggle up. You're in luck. I'm headed west, too. After picking up a load of the black stuff here for the spring potato planting. My brother has a dairy farm back up the road. I'm on my way to Landeck now, if that'd be any good to you."

Of course it would, Frieda thought, and had to check herself from jumping with joy at the offer. She knew

what Radok's answer would be, though; what it had to be.
They could not risk taking a ride, no matter what the man's
political affiliation.

"Sure," Radok said.

Frieda nearly fainted.

They were stuffed in the front seat like double liters of
wine in a crate, bouncing against each other as the ancient truck—had it ever had shocks?—rumbled along.
The wind whipped against their faces, for the truck had
no windshield. Max on one side of her, Radok on the
other.

Out came the inevitable bottle of schnapps, and Frieda
was the only one not to tilt the bottle back and let the air
bubbles sound in the upturned bottom. Amber-colored
schnapps. Slivowitz.

Ice crystals bit at their faces through the open wind-
screen. Perhaps it was not a drunkard's nose she had
noticed on the farmer earlier? More probably a case of
frostbite.

"So you're out hiking," the farmer said, effusive after
a few rounds, obviously wanting to be brought in on their
secrets. "By the looks of your hands"—he was speaking
to Radok—"you come from the city. You're not Jews on
the run. So what are you?"

The question brought an intense and uncomfortable
silence in the truck.

"Austrians, like you," Max finally said, in a dialect so
thick that Frieda at first did not understand him. It was
the first thing that Max had said directly to the man, and
the use of the shared dialect made it very direct and full of
unstated meaning.

The farmer seemed to catch some of the implications,
especially that of "Austrian" rather than "German," and
for the rest of the ride he was quiet, seemingly content to
let Max's answer stand.

Frieda tried not to look at oncoming cars. It was a very
vulnerable feeling being so completely exposed on this
busy highway. There might be physical discomfort for her
in the mountains, but that was nothing compared to what
she felt in the cab of this truck, naked and defenseless.

Houses appeared now; they crossed a bridge over the
river Inn to the north of its frothing course and continued

on, past a ruined castle and over another bridge back to the south side of the river.

"I don't suppose you want off in the marketplace?" the man joked.

Radok remained cool, refusing to be tempted by the farmer's attempts at intimacy, at secret-sharing.

"Actually," Radok said, "we'd rather be closer to the trail-head. We can still make some time this afternoon."

The farmer nodded, jostling and scattering chickens as they sped through the village streets of Landeck.

"West, huh?" the farmer said.

"West," Radok said.

"Okay. How about I drop you a few kilometers outside of town? Near Pians. The trail from there heads back into the mountains over the Peziner Spitze up to the Hoher Rifler. Good old peak, that one is. Over three thousand meters."

"Be a good hike," Max said.

Useless, Frieda thought. It was obvious the farmer did not believe their story of hiking; he had said as much. It was clear to her at least what needed to be done. No use keeping up the verbal subterfuge. It was all very well to cry about what was happening to the Jews, but when it came down to it, they needed to be as ruthless as the Nazis to stop the butchery. The farmer should die. Surely the others could see that?

Pians proved to be a tiny, wood-framed village spread out along both sides of the road, topped off with an onion-domed church on the hill above.

"In back of the church," the farmer said. "The trail leads off from there."

He turned off the ignition; the engine rattled and sputtered to a stop. Stillness all around them suddenly. The silence was almost palpable, Frieda thought. And the others recognized it, too. The near holiness of the silence, and no one wanting to be the first to break it. Max stirred next to Frieda, but checked himself from speaking. Then there was a low rumble, as of distant thunder.

"Down!" the farmer ordered. "Onto the floorboards!"

His massive right arm swept the three of them off the seat, stuffing them under the dashboard, crumpled onto the floor like broken dolls. No time to ask why, only the crazy pounding in Frieda's chest and the adrenaline rush of fear.

"What is it?" Radok said.

"Quiet!"

The rumbling grew louder and the truck began to rock and rattle as if caught in an earthquake.

"Stay where you are," the farmer said. "Down. Not a word."

The warmth of Radok's and Max's bodies, between which Frieda lay, was reassuring. Even the old man's harsh, metallic breath was friendly, like old shoes.

"Shit," Max said. "Tanks. We've had it now."

"I said *quiet*." The farmer got out of the cab, his back to the road, and the truck door open. The farmer was not looking at Frieda and the men but at his trouser's fly, which he was busily unbuttoning. The crunch and rumble was almost upon them, deafening. Frieda could no longer tell if she was trembling or being shaken by the shock waves of the giant tank treads, tied to their awful rhythm by the ripple effect.

But she also watched, fascinated, as the farmer reached into his fly and drew out his penis: enormous, dark red, and angry-looking. Like a weapon. Holding it in his hand. She did not understand what he was doing, only watched as he held it gently between thumb and forefinger, aiming it at the side of the truck.

He gave a quick check over his back; the tanks were just coming into sight around the curve. He fired: a high and elegant golden arc that caught the sunlight, and now that the tanks were in sight he began hopping about as he urinated, acting as if embarrassed at being caught in the act. The men on the lead tank began whistling and laughing at his antics, as he urinated on himself in an effort to get his penis back in his pants. Three, four, five, six tanks in all, Frieda counted, seeing them pass through the field of vision she had between the farmer's legs.

"You shitheads laugh!" the farmer yelled, shaking his fist and fumbling with his penis.

"Laugh, pricks, and be gone!" he cried. His voice did not carry over the rumble of the Panzers.

It was a wonderful performance. Frieda felt like laughing, applauding, running to him and hugging him.

The tanks drew out of sight, their evil rumbling swallowed somewhat by the great silence of the forest. The farmer buttoned his fly, kicking slush over the yellow puddle by the truck. No one moved from the floor. There could be more coming, Frieda thought, and knew the others were thinking the same. Another minute. Frieda felt she could maintain this almost bent-double posture not a minute longer.

"Okay," the farmer said. "You can get up now. Best to be off, though. No dawdling."

None of them felt like dawdling.

"You get a look at the uniforms?" Radok asked the farmer as he uncoiled his long body from the floor of the truck.

The farmer nodded. "Waffen-SS."

"That's what I thought," Radok said. "What brings them here?"

The farmer shrugged.

Frieda could no longer restrain herself.

"That was marvelous!" she said.

The farmer grinned shyly. "Most of the women think so, ma'am."

She grinned as Max and Radok almost fell over laughing.

"I meant the performance," she said.

"They like that okay, too, ma'am." Deadpan.

More hoots; a physical release from the moments of extreme tension.

"But hardly necessary for us," she braved on. Someone had to at least try and cover their tracks. "I mean, it's not as if we're wanted by the authorities, or anything."

She realized immediately how artificial it sounded, but it was too late to take the words back. Better to have said nothing.

"No, ma'am," the farmer replied. "No one said you were wanted. But those fellows"—he nodded his head in the direction the tanks had passed—"they get awfully curious about nothing at all. Best not to arouse their curiosity, if you know what I mean."

"I do," she said. "And I thank you." Said regally; she'd take her dignity away with her, at least.

They humped their packs on their backs as Radok checked his maps.

"Just behind the church there?" he said to the farmer.

"Right. Lovely walk, it is. I'd come with you myself,

but I've got spring planting, once the snow completely melts."

They all shook hands with the man, Frieda the last one.

"It's been a pleasure, ma'am. Perhaps we could have another performance sometime soon?"

"Perhaps," she said, pinching his bristly cheek, catching him off guard and breaking through the tough exterior. He smiled like a puppy being petted.

"Wait," he said as they were leaving. "A going-away present."

He dug under the driver's seat and brought out the double liter of slivowitz, or what was left of it.

"You'll need this to warm yourselves up there." He handed it to Max, and now the old gamekeeper was the one caught off guard. He almost broke his face smiling.

"Good luck, comrades!" he shouted at them as they neared the church. "You'll need it!"

A laugh, dry and hearty, carried on the wind to them.

It was sunset by the time they reached the peak of the Hoher Rifler back up in the snowy world. Today, after the ride, Frieda found the climb exhilarating. There were aching muscles, sure, but she was slowly beginning to recall how good it felt being in motion. The sturdy boots she wore felt as natural to her as her fingers on the ivory keys of the Bechstein grand.

Max had again taken the lead on the ascent, setting a brisk pace, the pack on his stooped back swaying back and forth like a large metronome. She found herself responding to the rhythm, keeping up with the men this afternoon after such a rotten start this morning. Was it only this morning she'd felt like giving it all up? Only last night she'd been peeling skin off a blistered heel? Clearly it was not a matter of pure agony today as it had been yesterday. She even had enough energy this afternoon to admire the natural artwork of snow on rock formations, to gulp down great greedy breaths of the tangy pine scent, to look above at the hawks and curlews circling dizzily in updrafts. Gorgeous is the world of nature, she reminded herself, and how terribly blind we all are to it most of our lives.

Radok was directly in back of her, carrying the heaviest load: he'd been the only one with room enough for the two-liter bottle of schnapps. The neck of the bottle bulged out the top of his pack. All the way up Radok said not a word, and Frieda was beginning to feel him somehow distancing himself from her. As if he were holding something back. There was something on his mind that he felt he could not share with her. But she shut this doubt out of her mind and concentrated on the tapestry of landscape unfolding below and all around them as they ascended ever higher.

A silent climb up to the Hoher Rifler, then, but not sullen. And the hut came into view just as the sun was going down. There was a feeling of magic in the air because of this coincidence of arrival and sunset; before entering, Frieda knew something special would be awaiting them there. And indeed there was: stacked cord wood by a massive cast-iron stove, and in a neighboring room a larder full of potted meats and canned vegetables. This was a sight seemingly too tempting for even Radok to pass up. The possibility of a warm meal and a sit-down around a hot stove broke down his resistance to having a potentially revealing fire, Frieda figured. An indulgence, but they'd earned it today with the territory they'd covered. Radok and Max lit the stove while Frieda started preparations for dinner.

An hour later they were eating hot stew for dinner, with Max complimenting Frieda on the cuisine, and then Radok brought out the slivowitz. Frieda at first declined.

"Come on, girl," the old one said. "Puts hair where you'll need it."

He slapped his knees with delight.

So she tried a shot, and after the fire had left her throat and her eyes stopped watering, she tasted the sweet plum flavor deep back on what was left of her palate, and held her shot glass up to Radok for a refill.

Max nodded with something like approval on his face.

"She's a mountain girl," Radok said proudly as he poured the amber liquid. "I keep telling you that, Max."

The old one pulled out a dog-eared and sticky pack of playing cards from his jacket pocket, and for the next hour they played cards by stovelight and by the glow of a lantern found in the larder.

Max rose finally. "Call of nature," he said, and then he was out the door to any bush he could find.

Radok got up too, and looked out at the night through the open door. The sky was filled with stars. Frieda rose unsteadily; the powerful drink had gone straight to her head.

"Do you know the names?" she said, coming up behind him at the door and looking up at the constellations. She put a hand intimately on the small of his back; he stiffened at the touch.

"I did once," he said. "Long ago." He moved away from her, out the doorway. His voice sounded forced, artificial. "Let's go see."

She followed out into the moonless night, across the great *Alm*, away from the hut and the light. The stars were even brighter now. Closer. Both their heads craned upward.

"That's Orion there," he said. "The easiest to pick out." Radok's voice was low and indistinct in the great night.

They both heard the drone at the same time. Close by, flying low. They froze for an instant.

"No!" Frieda yelled and began running. "The lamp!"

But it was too late. The sound of the plane was overhead now as she approached the door, and she could see blue running lights blinking overhead. Max came stumbling up to the door now, too, buttoning his fly as he moved. Both of them were caught in the rectangular spill of yellow light that came from the open door. The plane circled once overhead and then was away. Frieda pulled the door shut.

Footsteps sounded in back of her: the crunch of the snow as Radok caught up with her.

"He must have seen the light," Frieda said, but there was hope in her voice. She wanted to be convinced otherwise.

Radok did not answer, nor did Max.

"Well?" she finally blurted out. Radok's fatalistic, almost blasé attitude about this, and about the farmer earlier, was making Frieda nervous and angry.

"Well what?" Radok said.

"What do we do now?" she said.

"We get some sleep and get the hell out of here at first light."

Max grunted an assent. The festive air was gone from the room when they went back in, and they extinguished both the lamp and stove before curling up in sleeping bags in three separate bunks. Radok did not even attempt to curl up with her before going to sleep.

For the first time since leaving Vienna, Frieda felt lonely and afraid. The vastness of the Alps and the night sky were no longer her friends, but now frightened her. A breeze clapped a loose shutter against the side of the hut. Sleep came hard for her that night.

Chapter Thirty

The recon plane, a Junker 445, flew into a dense fog as it left the Hoher Rifler, losing its bearings. The pilot was a green flier, fresh from aviation school in Stuttgart, and had little experience with alpine flying. He ended up in Bregenz rather than Innsbruck where he belonged, and when he finally reached his destination, his CO there was so angry with him that he chewed his ass for a good half hour before even listening to his report. By the time news of the possible spotting on the mountain peak had been reported to Innsbruck Station of the SD, it was almost dawn, and it was thought better not to wake the Lieutenant Colonel with such a vague report, especially so after last night, with the inroads he had made into the bottle of Amantillado.

Thus it was that Krahl was not informed of the possible sighting until early that morning, when he was brought coffee in his temporary quarters at Innsbruck Station. Much too late to drop parachutists in to investigate. But not too late to do further investigating to confirm the sighting. Krahl controlled his rage that he had not been wakened immediately upon receipt of the sighting; repressed his anger and did what he could to salvage a bad situation. He contacted all SD and Gestapo stations and listening posts near the mountain in question, warning the local agents to keep their ears open for any news of strangers in their areas, with, as it turned out, some interesting results.

For the next two hours, Krahl sat in front of the maps pinned to the wall and tried to plot a course using the new information received.

And all this without the aid of Hartmann. Terrific field man. He'd simply disappeared for the past day and night after the fiasco at the von Tratten estate and was not even on hand this morning when Krahl so desperately needed his help. Nowhere to be found. The Hammer had better not have done a scamper, Krahl said to himself, for he would find him if so, and make Hartmann wish he had never sworn the SS oath. He'd make the little weasel squirm.

As if on cue, the door opened and Hartmann was shown in. He looked haggard; a day's growth of beard was on his cheeks.

"Reporting for duty, sir."

"You're late, Lieutenant. And you look awful. Where were you?"

"I had some private business to attend to, sir."

"What was her name?"

Hartmann's face twitched and Krahl knew he had hit close to home.

"I get the distinct impression you are not grateful to me, Hartmann. You should be dead. But I allowed you to survive because you are the great agent, the hero. Now when there's been a sighting, you're not even around. . . ."

"A sighting? Where?"

Krahl said, "A light was spotted last night atop a peak called the Hoher Rifler. That's near—"

"Landeck," Hartmann said. "I know the peak." He was at the map and located the position immediately.

"Impossible." Hartmann shook his head at the map. "They couldn't get that far on foot in two days. Not with an old man and woman in tow. It's almost eighty kilometers of mountain terrain, ass-deep in snow in some places. No. They aren't ours. Maybe poachers or deserters. Who knows. Resistance is active in those mountains, isn't it?"

"Oh," Krahl said slowly, "they are ours, all right. We've got a positive make on them. After the plane sighting was reported to me this morning, I ordered the Landeck Gestapo to keep their ears open. They have a well-placed agent, a publican at the Gasthaus zur Post. He'd overheard some farmer bragging about how he'd helped three 'freedom fighters' that very afternoon. He gave them a lift to Pians, a little village outside of Landeck, and dropped them off in the early afternoon. Said they told him they were headed west."

"That's all?" Hartmann said.

"Isn't it enough? He's not a very talkative chap, by all

accounts. But Gestapo is convinced that what he told them is the truth. They are continuing their interview."

"I mean, was that all there was about where they were headed? Just west? No other destination?"

"You didn't expect friend Radok to give the man an exact itinerary, did you?" Krahl said. "The room numbers they'd reserved for the night, perhaps?"

"You don't find it strange?" Hartmann said to Krahl.

"What should I find strange?" Hartmann could be an exasperating little shit when he began communicating in his didactic mode, Krahl thought.

"Strange," Hartmann went on, "that they came down from the mountains. Strange that they surfaced just in time to get a lift from a loud-mouthed Sunday resistance fighter. Strange that Radok would give away any destination, however vague. Strange that they would break the basic rule of night recon, and light a fire or lantern on a clear, moonless night atop a three-thousand-meter peak. Like a goddamn signal beacon. You don't find any of that strange?"

"They're amateurs," Krahl said.

"Yes." Hartmann nodded his head. "That's what we're counting on, anyway."

"So you have two map coordinates, Lieutenant. Plot me a route."

Hartmann took only a moment to examine the map.

"The most obvious route takes them through to Bludenz. It's clear enough. From Innsbruck they opted for the southern route. They're staying below the E17 highway. They could have gone north through the Lechtaler Alps and through the Bregenzer Woods on to Bregenz and Lake Constance. That would have been the logical thing to do this time of year with the far western mountain passes still clogged with snow. But instead, Radok chooses the southern route that will lead him to Bludenz. From there he's hoping to see where we commit, just like I said before. Simple strategy. He hears of large troop movements along the Rhine between Feldkirch and Bregenz, and he opts for the high passes of the Drei Ecke to the south, snow or no snow."

"So we've got him." Krahl could not help but smile again. "He can only bluff once he gets to Bludenz. He can't cross those mountains. He can only use the low-lands at the Rhine."

"We'll see," Hartmann said. "It's a long way to Bludenz, yet."

Hartmann put the fingers of both his hands to the wall map, as if divining it for a feeling, an inspiration. He traced a slender forefinger along the gray-ridged mountains of the topographical map.

"Here," he said. "We'll lay on a surprise party at Kalten Berg for Radok and friends. It's a nice peak. Radok seems to have a thing for peaks. He'll push on with the plateau walking today. No descent into the valley so soon after the last. Whatever his game, he won't risk being spotted two days in a row. There's a sturdy old Alpine Society Hut up on the Kalten Berg. The distance is about right for a day's walk from the Rifler. And another day's hike from Kalten Berg would take him into Bludenz. Yes. That'll be the spot. Just at the Voralberg-Tyrol border." He jabbed the peak with his finger.

"I think we should prepare a party up there for tonight. Did you bring your tuxedo?" Hartmann said.

Krahl remained seated, staring at the map.

Hartmann reached under Krahl's arms and lifted him out of the chair. He can be a charming bastard when he wants, Krahl reluctantly thought, feeling Hartmann's strong fingers on his body. Makes you almost forgive a world of his sins. Infectious enthusiasm. It's what attracted me to the bastard in the first place, he realized.

"Come on, Lieutenant Colonel. It'll be a good show. Worth the price of admission. You get us some troops and a light plane. We've got well over a hundred kilometers to do. We don't want to be late for this one, do we?"

Krahl smiled. He couldn't help himself. Impish little grin on Hartmann's face, too, he noticed. For the first time in several days Krahl was beginning to feel sanguine about his chances for promotion; optimistic again about bringing the Kripo man in and recovering the Final Solution papers.

Maman would be so proud. And the Penzing villa . . .

In the end, fear had won out. Radok wanted the hunters to track them, to extrapolate their movements and their possible course from sightings, but he did not want them in his backyard just yet. Krahl and his friend Hartmann might just set up a commando-type raid: drop some *Fallschirmjaeger* onto their mountain peak in the middle of the night and surround them in this draughty old hut.

Sightings, yes. It was part of Radok's plan. His design for vengeance. But not capture. No confrontations yet. That would come later, on his own terms.

So, after rolling about in the cold bunk for an hour or so after the recon plane flew by the night before, he rose and put on his soggy boots. The others weren't sleeping anyway. It took little prodding to get them up and out into the deep blackness of night.

Max led them by the stars. The whiteness of the yet unmelted snow lit their earthly route. They were cold, miserable, and silent until first light broke in the east. Radok took Frieda's hand at one point but let go soon afterward, too distracted to give her real attention.

Now, with the sun up and beginning to warm them at mid-morning, Radok could take his mind off the cold long enough to think; to plan.

There was much that he still had to plan. In the bottom of his pack was the dynamite he'd taken in the last frenzied minutes at the von Tratten lodge. The fuse and percussion caps were along with it. He'd tested a length of the fuse last night when setting the fire in the stove. It seemed to be in order. At least *that* section of the fuse was in order.

And how do you know they will be there at all? he asked himself. How can you be so sure?

They'll be there, he assured himself. The two coordinates I handed them . . . They'll be there with bells on.

No guilt about the farmer, then? No bad feelings about setting him up? his conscience nagged him.

If he's talked too much, like I figure he has, Radok thought, then he deserves anything he gets.

He took his mind off these thoughts by following the course of a plane high above as it cut its way west. A solitary machine, its thrum breaking the silence of the morning.

Freida couldn't see the plane at first, only hear its engine. The sun was in back of it, but finally she picked it out in the sky: a tiny wasp high above them. They did not bother to leave the trail for cover, for the plane was flying too high for reconnaissance. It was headed west, as they were. Frieda wished the going could be so easy for them: just fly to Switzerland. Instead of this madman's scheme of peak-dangling all the way to the border.

She had an evil feeling about today. She had an evil feeling about the whole mission, suddenly. Radok was hiding something from her and Max; she was sure of it. He was pinched, withdrawn. There was the feeling of something unsaid between them all. He had taken her hand just before first light, but she had experienced no solace from the touch before he let it go again.

Birds sang in the trees now, for they were once again below the tree line where the snow was almost totally melted. The path was clear, though muddy, the day bright blue, and the sun warm on Frieda's back. Yet she could take no joy from any of this. She wanted only to know what was going on in Radok's mind. She was beginning to feel not only neglected, but suspicious as well. The farmer yesterday, the light Radok had allowed last night. Crude errors in judgment . . . or were they something else?

A question she wouldn't have asked even twenty-four hours ago.

Chapter Thirty-One

They had made good time, even up the pitted, graveled Russian Road to the peak. There is ample time, Hartmann thought, to set up inside the Kalten Berg hut with care and intelligence. No slipups on this one.

There was a good field of fire from inside the mountain hut; almost three hundred and sixty degrees visibility. One blind spot to the rear of the hut where a granite outcropping afforded cover, refuge. But that was, after all, behind the hut. They would be coming in from the front, if they came.

No ifs, Hartmann told himself. You must will the bastards in here; you must bring them in by the sheer force of your mind. No ifs. This is a must-do operation.

What will you do when you come face to face with her? he wondered. Laugh. That would be best. Laugh all the way to her death. Maybe he'd do the killing himself. No. Better to have a masked executioner drop the guillotine. To see the fear in her eyes just before the order was given; to watch the blood spurt out of the severed neck and the head roll into the basket. How many times would the sightless eyes blink after the head was chopped? What grimace would the face show from the bloody depths of the wicker basket?

Sweet thoughts. But no hatred. No revenge. Keep it cold, as Mad Markl had always advised. Keep it professional. Keep it passionless.

The bitch . . .

The Lieutenant Colonel lay napping in a corner of the hut like a brittle Dresden doll, his face shiny in the diffuse light coming through the window, a cross thrown up on the wall over his head: the shadowed window sashing projected by the setting sun.

It's just as well he's sleeping, Hartmann thought. Stays out of things that way. The bastard can't move fast enough to be of use, anyway. A bloody nuisance. But there are others along besides Krahl. Seven of them in all. All we could fit in the Junker, the only size of plane that could land at the nearby Saafeld airfield.

"We try to take them alive," Hartmann whispered to the other men. "Remember that. Alive. First priority. That means we shoot low."

The men were positioning themselves beneath the windows. Hartmann had mentally run through the option of waiting for them outside, waiting for Radok and Frieda to trap themselves in the hut then moving in on them, but canceled that plan: once you trap a person you give him a chance to think, time to react, to feel threatened. Time to die. No. Hartmann wanted it simple. Let them walk right into us, he thought, guns pointing down their throats. No options that way. No time to do anything with either the documents or their own souls.

"Eyes below the window," Hartmann cautioned one of the Waffen-SS. "I'll do the looking. You do the ducking. Asses down and guns loaded." Another Mad Markl dictum.

Krahl snored contentedly in the corner, sleeping off the Amantillado he'd overindulged in last night. . . .

"Sergeant, if you will?"

Hartmann gestured to the man to pinch Krahl's nose to stop the snoring. The sergeant obeyed unwillingly, and Krahl spluttered and coughed in his sleep, rolled over to his side, and was silent once again.

"Don't you think . . . ?" the sergeant began.

"We let him sleep," Hartmann said. "That's the best help he can be to us."

The sergeant said nothing, but the other four men snickered at this as at a dirty joke.

Hartmann and Krahl were a bit of a myth to the noncoms, like a famous vaudeville turn.

It was bloodred now in the close hut, the setting sun almost touching the western peaks. This used to be the holiest of times for Hartmann when in the high mountains. The sun setting; birds swooping for their last meal of the day; an incredible stillness settling over all of creation. A high breeze overhead; soft and caressing.

Radok and Frieda would be here soon.

                    *   *   *

Radok was fagged. They had moved steadily all day; only a short break for lunch. Otherwise it had been continual, gradual movement. The backpack straps cut into his shoulders painfully. No more handing the heavy load over to Max. No longer was Radok the juvenile gun-bearer.

They were close now, approaching the Kalten Berg from the south, up the longer, more arduous route. They could have just taken the Russian Road in, built by Russian POW's during World War One. Or the easier north trail. But those were the very directions they would be expected to come from.

Radok knew the Kalten Berg. He'd approached the peak from both the north and south during his walking and climbing years in the thirties. He also knew the hut, knew how it was situated. They'd be waiting for him and Frieda in the hut. Krahl and company would have set up a lethal little welcoming party for them there, Radok was sure. From the von Tratten estate to the Oetz Valley to the Hoher Rifler. Just plot the line, he had tried to command Krahl and Hartmann. Stick your compasses in your pockets and put a ruler to the map. The Kalten Berg was obviously the next stop; any dunce could see that.

Radok could see the summit above them now. He looked at Frieda and Max. They were as done-in as he was. But if things went according to plan, they would be able to rest easy tonight. No more chases; no more hunt.

The high rock escarpment was exactly as he remembered it. Radok made sure to motion for absolute quiet from the other two as they approached the rock.

Radok had not expected anything obvious: no smoke from the chimney or indolent SS guards hanging about outside the cabin. But he was not prepared for the alternative, which was nothing. Looking down from the escarpment, he could see absolutely no trace of anything in or near the Kalten Berg hut. He felt suddenly bereft and hopeless. It's all been for nothing, he thought. All my clever maneuvering, the "accidental" sightings, the lies to Max and Frieda. All for nothing. Krahl and Hartmann haven't even put the coordinates together, the fools. The hut is empty.

The bastards! He wanted to shout out the words, but

suddenly saw movement from within: a flash of something in the dying light. Gun metal?

"What are we waiting for?"

Frieda was directly in back of him and he swung around to silence her.

"We're tired," she continued. "Let's go—"

He cupped his hand over her mouth to still any further words. She mumbled incoherently into his hand for a time, her eyes looking terrified, but finally she realized that he wanted absolute silence. He took his hand away.

They moved back down from the rock escarpment, Max and Frieda both looking bewildered.

"Somebody in there, Radok?" the old man said.

Radok nodded, moving them farther back down the trail, well out of earshot of the hut.

"Who?" Frieda said. "Mountaineers . . . ?"

Hopeful voice.

"I think they've set up an ambush," Radok said finally.

Frieda and Max were silent for a time.

"Let's get back down the trail, then," Max said.

"No." The word sounded final in Radok's throat. "We'll take the bastards out. I've got dynamite along."

Frieda looked unconvinced. "But how do you know who's in there? They might be just hunters or deserters. Anybody could be in there."

"No," he said again, and this time she seemed to understand.

"You set this up, didn't you?" Red at her cheeks, as rosy as the setting sun. "That's what the ride with the farmer was about. The light at the hut last night . . ."

"Set what up?" Max fingered the trigger of his rifle.

"You gave them our trail," Frieda said. "Hoping they'd jump one step ahead. That they'd lay an ambush and we could ambush them, instead."

Radok was listening to Frieda but not looking at her, too busy with digging out the dynamite from the bottom of his pack. Three sticks of it strapped together in a long triangle. Orange-red cardboard cases. Black stenciled letters no longer legible on them, but Radok knew the charge. He could feel the weight of it in his hand: enough to take out the wooden hut and all those within. Enough to scatter their bodies all across the *Alm*.

"You mean you're hunting the hunters?" Max said.

Radok looked up from the dynamite. "That's about the size of it."

"By God, son, that's a ripe one." Max was amused, but Frieda was not at all.

"You should have told us, Radok. Should have trusted us. We're in this, too."

"I didn't think you'd go for it," Radok said. "And it's got to be done."

"For the von Trattens," Max said. "For what those bastards did to them."

Frieda shook her head. "This isn't some private little vendetta we're playing at here. We've got bigger things than personal vengeance to settle. There are millions of lives at stake, not just the General and his wife."

Max was now helping Radok with the dynamite, his knobby fingers busily uncoiling the fuses.

"Looks good," Max said. He touched the end of the fuse to his tongue, held the taste in his mouth like a wine connoisseur.

"She's still good," he finally said. "Dry powder. Going to make a lovely boom, she is. Regular New Year's Eve fireworks."

"Frau von Tratten helped me," Frieda continued. "Saved my life. But it's too late for her or for the General. It's these papers now that matter. Getting them out. Not getting even. Let's just walk back down the trail, circle around this peak—"

"We'll approach from the rear," Radok interrupted her. "Their field of fire will be broken by the rock escarpment above us. And they'll never expect us to be coming from this direction. Max, you'll cover me from the escarpment. Frieda, you cover our rear. They may have a perimeter guard out, but I doubt it. The welcome's laid on inside the hut."

She grabbed his arm.

"Listen! Hear me!"

"Keep it low," Max cautioned.

Radok looked into her eyes, focusing on the left, into the gray-blue depths of it.

"Krahl may be there," Radok said. "Hartmann surely is. They need to pay. Now you can help us by keeping watch, or you can just sit here feeling betrayed. Either way what's going to happen is going to happen."

"Come on, boy," Max urged. "Light's dying. We aren't there by last light, they'll figure we overnighted elsewhere and they may up and leave."

"Let them leave," Frieda said. "Just let them go. I'm not trying to protect Wolf. I want him to pay as much as you do, Radok. But I've got a bad feeling about this. It's not right."

"Don't jinx it, woman," Max said.

He'd fitted the fuse to the wrapped sticks of dynamite and was now working on the percussion caps.

"I'll deliver the house-warming gift," Max said. "You cover *me*."

Radok shook his head.

"My idea. My gamble."

He bent to his pack again, pulling out the orange envelope of documents and photos, and handed them to Frieda.

"You keep these. If anything goes wrong on the peak, you and Max get the hell away. Get these out. Understood? No deliberation. No wondering. Just move. You too, Max. Don't stick around. Just get away. I'll take care of myself."

Frieda took the papers, stuffing them into her coat pocket.

"I'll be here," she said. "I'll keep watch."

Radok smiled at her. "Whistle if you see anything."

She nodded.

"Three times if you see someone coming. Max will be up top. You'll hear an explosion in a few minutes. Be ready to move out when you hear it."

The sun was almost gone. Hartmann didn't like that: took away the vision. If they weren't here in a few minutes, he'd have to give up on this ambush. Radok and friends would be here by dusk or not at all.

Were the pricks out there waiting? Had they seen movement in the hut and grown suspicious? Or had he, Hartmann, miscalculated? Was there another mountain hut they could have made for tonight? Had Radok, in fact, fooled them?

Krahl was awake now, looking damned put out.

"No sign of your friends," he said.

Hartmann made no answer. The other men were still low by the windows, keeping watch.

Again the nagging thought came to Hartmann: this is all too damn obvious. Like it was handed to them. Krahl said it was because Radok was an amateur; Hartmann was not so sure about that. Radok was a cop. Hartmann recalled the dossier: he'd been under fire and been decorated for bravery. Those weren't any amateur theatrics. And now another thought came to Hartmann's mind. Radok was, like Hartmann himself, an mountaineer. He knew the Alps, as did Hartmann. And he damn well might know this very peak; know this hut and the escarpment in back. This could, in fact, all be a setup: the hunted become the hunter.

"I'm going to take a look," Hartmann said. "Keep me covered. And for shit sake, don't shoot me."

Hartmann didn't wait for a response. He crouched to the door, opened it slowly, feeling the evening breeze on his face. Then he slid out into the shadows of sunset, staying in the crouch for a time by the side of the hut, looking out onto the bare patch of alpine meadow before him. He could see no movement. Nothing. Only a lone hawk circling above them, spiraling up and down in the updrafts of cooling mountain air.

There was movement behind him. He swung his machine pistol toward it.

"It's me," Krahl whispered. "Anything here?"

Hartmann shook his head, lowering the Schmeisser.

"Another miscalculation, Hartmann?"

Hartmann ignored this, listening to the sounds around him. No movement visible, but now he could hear something. The low hum of voices, he thought. A scratching of footsteps from somewhere. Sounds carried incredibly well up here; even the hawk's wings made a whistling noise as of a huge glider. He was certain of the sounds now. Krahl made to speak again, but Hartmann put his hand up to stop him.

Krahl heard it now, too. The soft scratch of footsteps on the scree. Now a rasping sound, a snap, and then a fizzle as of champagne bubbling or sparks igniting.

"Clear the hut!" Hartmann yelled, rushing from the side of the building, his weapon up in firing position.

It would be a short fuse, he knew. Christ! But no time

for that, now. Find the body. Find the bastard scampering away. Dusk now. Shadows only. Krahl standing with his mouth agape, then following Hartmann away from the hut, not knowing what the hell was going on.

"Radok!" Hartmann yelled.

Then he saw him, running up the back escarpment. He led him, had his back dead in the sights as the man scrambled up the steep incline.

He pulled off ten quick rounds and heard a scream just as the hot blast of air from the explosion knocked him over. The sound of it was deafening, a roaring in his ears that blacked everything else out.

He lay inert on the ground for minutes not knowing where he was, feeling as if he were floating in a warm bath.

Slowly he got up, feeling for broken parts. He breathed deeply. All in one piece. Krahl was stirring on the ground near him. Like Hartmann, he'd had the wind knocked out of him by the blast but sustained no major injuries. Those in the hut were not so fortunate. They were gone. Fragmented. Dead.

Hartmann found his pistol, looked around again for movement, pricking his ears to sounds in the stillness. And he heard them. Unmistakable. Making for the old road. He began running, racing across the *Alm* to cut them off.

Frieda heard the shout first: "Radok!"

Wolf's voice. She was sure of that. She wanted to cover her ears so as to hear no more. But shots sounded, then a scream. A ghastly, animal moaning. And then the explosion. It ripped through the gathering gloom. A flash of light from over the escarpment. Bits of wood landing by her. No one could have survived that. Not even Radok, she thought.

She could not move at first, immobilized by her fear. Where to go if they're all dead? Then a sound from above; a form by the rock

"Help me."

Radok's voice. It broke her trance and she went to him. He supported the old one with one arm, carrying the rifle with the other.

"The crazy old man jumped in front of me," Radok said. "Took the shots meant for me."

"Boom, boom," Max said, smiling wanly. "Great fireworks."

Blood was flowing down one of his arms, Frieda could see. But his bluff exterior fooled her into believing that the wound was not bad.

"We've got to move," Radok said, grabbing his pack with the provisions and throwing it onto his back with one arm, holding Max with the other. "I don't know if they were all inside the hut or not." He slung his rifle over his shoulder now, too.

No questions from her. She took Max's other arm and they hobbled down the trail, then circled around to the far side of the meadow, the opposite way from which they had ascended. No words: she just followed Radok's lead.

"Leave me," Max said. "It's all right. I'm an old man. I've had my life."

They ignored this and kept moving in the twilight, stumbling, catching themselves before falling. They were neither silent or stealthy as they tried to put distance between themselves and the hut.

Soon they came to a graveled track leading off to the right.

"The Russian Road," Radok said. "We don't want that one. We'll head for the north trail."

But Frieda saw something in the gloom that made her stop.

"What is it?" Radok said.

"I think there's a truck down there. In the boughs of that tree."

He squinted. "I'll be damned. You're right."

Max was mumbling about dying in the mountains, not in the valley, as they reached the truck.

"You're not going to die, old man," Radok said. "It's just a flesh wound."

They rested Max against one of the wheels while Radok swung up into the cab.

"Beautiful," he said. "Custom-made. The keys are in the ignition."

Frieda waited for a moment, then the truck spluttered alive. She clapped her hands and jumped up and down as Radok gave her the thumbs up from the window.

They put Max in between them and then Radok threw

the big truck into gear, rolling down the mountain road. Shots rang out in back of them as they cleared the first curve. Looking back, Frieda could make out the slight silhouette of Wolf racing after them.

Too late.

Radok knew that they could not risk taking the truck onto the valley roads. That would be suicide. Civilians in a military vehicle. They'd be picked up within an hour. Not far from the bottom of the Russian Road, he pulled the vehicle over, tore out the ignition cables and drained the oil.

Max was asleep. He would need the rest. Flesh wound or not, the old man had taken a bullet. That was hard work.

Frieda watched Radok destroying the truck's engine. She was silent, had been for the entire ride down the winding road in the darkness. No lights on. No telling if others would be waiting at the bottom.

Radok knew this terrain, knew it as well as he did the trails in the Wienerwald around Vienna. Just back up the road was a trail-head heading north. That was the new direction for today. Put the original plan into operation now, he told himself. Forget about the botched job up there. The truck would be left beyond the trail-head; the chasers wouldn't think they would backtrack, not with a wounded person in tow.

"Bleeding stopped yet?" he said to Frieda.

"He's dying."

"What do you mean? It's a shoulder wound. . . ."

"It's his chest."

Radok could see the blood now, soaking the blue jacket at Max's chest.

"There are at least two wounds in his lungs," she said. "He's dying. For what, Radok? For what? So you could feel like a hero? The great avenger."

"Let's get him out of here." He didn't want to deal with the guilt now; just keep busy, he told himself. Keep moving.

"Leave him," she said. "He'll be dead in an hour. It's no atonement to take him along."

"We'll make a stretcher," Radok said. "We can't just leave him."

"Boom, boom," Max mumbled in his unconscious state. A throaty chuckle followed by wet coughing. A blood bubble formed at his mouth.

Frieda nodded. "Okay. Let's build the stretcher."

And so they found two lodge-pole pines, sheared the branches off them, stuck them through the arms of Radok's coat, put Max atop the crude stretcher, and began walking back up the Russian Road a few hundred meters to the trail.

Radok knew the way from here. North to Germany. North into the heart of the Reich. No border patrols would be looking for them there, because Germany was a place nobody would ever suspect they'd go. And once there, they'd lie low a day, letting the chasers fret. Because chasers there still were. Hartmann had survived the blast, if not Krahl as well. And they would be on their trail again once support arrived at the Kalten Berg.

But there would be no more easy traces to follow. The snow was all but gone. At first, when running from the von Tratten estate, the fresh snowfall had covered their tracks. But ever since that time, they had worried continually about leaving a trail in back of them through the deep and melting snow. Well, at least that worry was over now. The melt had taken care of that. So it was north for Germany now. And then a little sail on Lake Constance. But from the *German* shore, where no one would expect it. A little moonlight ride across the waters to Switzerland. They still had two, maybe three days to get the documents out.

Max let out a groan on the stretcher as Radok and Frieda stumbled along the narrow trail. Keep your mind on the plan, on the route, on the tactics, Radok told himself. Save the regrets and sorrow for later.

"Fireworks," Max again mumbled.

Chapter Thirty-Two

He was fourteen, the son of a woodcutter, and desperate to get into the army.

He would complain to his mother almost every night that the war would be over by the time he was eighteen. It just wasn't fair. Life was no damn fair, he would say.

To which his mother, darning a sock with a wooden egg stuck in the heel, or pounding out dough on the marble kneading board, a dusting of flour on her cheeks and fleshy upper arms, would reply:

"Don't swear in this house."

That way she wouldn't have to deal with the question; wouldn't have to tell him how she hated this war, this evil machine that ate up all the good men and left only the weasels alive at home.

End of discussion, by reprimanding him for his foul mouth.

But Juergen, the son, grew daily more frustrated with such tactics. He was big—arms like a wrestler's—and his cheeks already bristled with whiskers, much thicker than those of boys three or four years his senior. He had worked a man's job since his father was drafted, but despite this his mother persisted in treating him like a schoolboy in short pants.

He was ready for adventure. Thus, when he saw the three in the woods near the stand of larch he was working on, he instinctively knew that they would provide adventure for him. Not much instinct needed for that, in point of fact, for his eyes told him everything he needed to know about them. Two of them stumbled along under the burden of a rough-hewn stretcher: two lodge-pole pines stuck through the arms of a coat. On top was an old man, his chest rising and falling very slowly, as if every breath were an agony. They stopped when they saw Juergen.

The man in the lead was the first to speak: "Are we far from Lech?"

It was a strange accent to Juergen. Nasal and full of gutturals at the same time. Not like the musical language he had grown up with. City slicker, by the sound of him, Juergen figured.

"He hurt?" Juergen looked at the old man on the improvised stretcher. Then at the two carrying him. Backpacks, hunting rifles strapped to their shoulders. Blood at the old man's chest, Juergen could now see.

"A hunting accident," the city slicker said. "We're trying to get him to Lech. To a doctor."

"He's shot?" Juergen brightened. "In the chest?"

The first man nodded. The other, who for an instant he had thought might be a youth about his age, was a woman. Anyone could see that by the bulges at her chest. And she looked impatiently at him now. Her look made Juergen redden.

"You think he'll die?"

"Look!" the woman almost shouted. She was straining under the load of the end of the stretcher she was carrying. "Can you show us the way to Lech or not? Is there an infirmary there? Are you a cretin, or what?"

Juergen broke out into a sweat at this; the woman reminded him of his former teacher at the Volkschule, Fräulein Paulus. She'd teased him like that when he froze up at the geography or mathematics questions she would pose him.

"It's that direction." Juergen indicated over his shoulder. "Trail's marked in blue through the stand of larch. Then along the old forest road to the left. An hour. Maybe a little more, carrying him."

The woman looked down at her load with something like terror in her eyes. Juergen knew the look: he had felt the same sort of panic at the loads his father used to prepare for him to lug down the side of a mountain.

"Maybe I can help you?" he asked. "Help carry him, I mean."

Frieda wanted to hug the boy. Her arms ached; her back ached; her feet and legs ached. There was not a muscle on her body that did not ache. Even her lips ached with the strain of pursing them at her heavy load.

Before he'd lost consciousness, old Max had begged

them to shoot him. Shoot him and bury him up in the mountains he loved.

"Don't let me die in the valley," he'd pleaded. "I don't want to die with valley folk. I want to die close to heaven. Do an old man a favor."

But they didn't shoot Max. They carried him like a communal load of guilt between them, Radok and she. It made no sense; none of it made any sense, but she was too tired now to wonder why. Too tired to do anything but put one foot in front of the other.

So when they came upon the boy, and he proved he was not a cretin after all but was even offering to help, Frieda felt deep relief. Yes, she needed help. She could no longer carry the burden of Max to atone for Radok's guilt. She was sure that the old man would die before they got to a doctor; he might even be dead at this very instant. No. She looked down at him: his chest was still moving up and down slowly; oh, so slowly.

"Really," the boy said. "I could help you. It's a long way to Lech."

She knew Radok did not want the boy to join them. It was their mission of atonement. He saw it that way, she was sure.

"I could use some help," she said.

Radok looked at her sharply for a moment, then, as if realizing the absurdity of the demands he'd made on her, he nodded. A look in his eyes again, as on that first night after he'd gotten her through the tunnel in the catacombs, and led her out of her fear of enclosed spaces. An acknowledgment that she had done the same for him now.

"Yes," he said to the boy. "We'd appreciate a hand. He's pretty badly hurt."

Max died just after they got out of the larch stand. He opened his eyes and looked directly up at the boy, who'd taken that end of the stretcher from Frieda. Max saw the young face, the unfamiliar features, and for a moment took them to be Radok's as a young boy. The General's gun-bearer.

"Tell the General good-bye," Max said to the startled youth. "It's late. I've got to go."

Max knew the darkness would fall before he got home.

He knew the forest, and was not afraid of making his way in the darkness, but he worried that the General might get lost.

It was his last thought. His eyes closed quite peacefully and breath rushed out of his body with a rasping wheeze. A slight jerk, and it was over. Max was gone before Radok could turn to see him. Suddenly the stretcher felt lighter, and Radok knew he was gone.

"He's dead," the boy said in wonder. "I've never seen anybody die before."

Frieda began crying. A sniffle at first, then building to a regular flood of tears. Funerals are not for the dead, Radok thought, somewhat cruelly. Mourning is not for the dead, either. It's ourselves that we're mourning. Our own mortality.

Radok set the stretcher down and took Frieda in his arms. Sobs racked her body, and they were not just for Max or her own mortality, Radok sensed. This had all been too much for her; too many close calls, too much scurrying about, messing up and moving on. He understood her need to crumble.

The boy watched them, his mouth open, lips cracked. A mouth-breather, Radok registered. They'd have to get rid of the kid before they got rid of Max. The irony of that one: the kid had seemed like a godsend coming along just as Frieda was spent. Turns out he's too little, too late. A complication. Ten minutes after joining them, Max is dead. And there's another witness. Here's another pair of eyes to know they were here. What direction they were headed. How done-in they were.

"I guess we don't really need your help now," he said to the boy.

You're a coward, Radok, he told himself. Do him. Do him now. Make the pain short and accurate. If not, it's sure to come back at you. So take him now; a shot in the back of the skull. What would he know? Up behind him fast, like a nurse with an injection; no time for thinking. Pull out the gestapo goon's Luger that you're carrying and put the muzzle to the soft depression at the joining of neck and skull. Then go on; go on, you bastard: pull the trigger.

"You going to leave him here?" The kid watched the sightless corpse: Max's eyes were still open.

"No," Radok said impatiently.

Frieda looked up into his face; she felt the tension growing. She's savvy enough to know what has to come now, Radok realized.

" 'Cause it's against the law," Juergen said. "You'll have to take him into town. Get a death certificate. It happened once cutting wood. Joachim, he was a tree-topper, and he fell right out of a tree on his axe. My dad saw it. Dead, you know."

"We'll take care of it," Radok said.

"And they had to carry Joachim all the way to town just to get a doctor to say he was dead, all official-like. Joachim, he weighed a hundred fifty kilos, easy. There was blood all over Dad when he came through the door. But Doc says it's a good thing Dad took the man in. Makes it legal."

"We'll make it legal," Radok said. "Thanks for the help. You can go on back to your work now."

The kid's eyes grew large at the word "work." He'd rather be helping out here than clearing brush and split-ting larch logs, Radok figured.

"I'll help you."

"No!" It was a scream from Radok, full of anger and frustration.

Frieda tried to restrain him. The damn kid is going to make it difficult for me not to kill him, Radok thought.

"You've been sweet," Frieda said to the boy, wiping away her tears with one hand, holding onto Radok's gun hand with the other.

"And we don't want to put you out any longer," she said. "Besides, we'd like to be alone with our friend here for a while to say good-bye to him. You'll understand that. This Joachim you mentioned . . . you know how the officials take over. Well, we just want to sit with our friend for a time before all that starts."

Juergen looked at her doubtfully, but tried to smile, Radok noticed. She had that effect on males. You wanted to please Frieda.

"Okay?" she said again, brightly. "And thank you. Thank you very much. You've been sweet."

"If you're sure . . ." the kid began.

"We're sure," Radok said.

"Yes," said Frieda, her tone softer and more reassuring than Radok's. "We'll just sit here for a time." She put her hand out to Juergen. "Thanks again."

The kid looked at the hand, sucked on his swollen and chapped lower lip for a moment, then took Frieda's hand in his own nut-brown, ham-shaped fist. He shook it twice then turned abruptly on his heels and set off back toward the stand of trees where he'd been working, without looking back, without saying good-bye.

"He came this close to dying." Radok held up a thumb and forefinger a centimeter apart.

Frieda nodded. "I know. Maybe we should have killed him."

"Like with Max," he said.

She did not reply.

Maybe they should have killed him, Radok thought. A kid. A mouth-breather. Who's going to listen to him, anyway?

"We'll need to dig a grave," Radok said.

But Frieda had already started preparing a grave a healthy distance from the old forest road.

Chapter Thirty-Three

The toe of Hartmann's black boot was scuffed. Only now, as it nudged on the mulch and bracken of the forest floor, uncovering the body hidden there, was he aware how worn the boot was.

The large scuff on the toe: he'd got that a day and a half ago atop the Kalten Berg, when the force of the blast had thrown him to the ground. No scuffs since then: nothing but cooling his heels, trying to find a trace of the bastards. The long walk down the mountain in the middle of the night, because the driver had been stupid enough to leave the keys in the truck at the Kalten Berg. Heaven-sent for Radok, Frieda, and the gamekeeper to make their getaway. Krahl had ragged him the whole way down the mountain for setting a trap that had backfired on them. And then finding the truck toward the bottom of the road, a sudden moment of jubilation until they discovered it had been ruined.

Hartmann had known then that Radok and Frieda had set off in another direction; he didn't expect them to continue on to the bottom of the road and run smack into the patrol bottling up that means of escape. But using the truck for a getaway, they had a couple hours head start on Hartmann. No telling where they might have got to in that time or what new direction they might have set off in. No use stumbling around in the dark looking for a trail. No snow left; no easy footprints to follow. So Hartmann and Krahl had had to wait for morning light to try to pick up the trail; had to stumble down to the bottom of the Russian Road and explain their presence to the pricks on guard down there. Embarrassing; very.

Hartmann knew he'd hit one of them. He'd heard the scream before the explosion. Taken him well and squarely in the chest region. At least two hits. Which one? Let it be Radok, he thought. Let it be finished.

The boot lodged against the body now. Hartmann bent over, using a twig to scrape back the leaves from the bloated gray face. He checked it against the photo he'd taken with him from the estate. Death had played its disfiguring games on the man, but the resemblance was clear. Disappointment swept over Hartmann. It was not Radok.

"That's him," Hartmann said. "The gamekeeper."

A sigh of relief from the kid named Juergen.

"Didn't I tell you?" he said. This to a florid-faced local Order Police constable in his cylinder hat, his nose magnificently red.

"I knew they were important," the kid whined. "I told you so, so you wouldn't listen. Now look what you done. Gave them a day head start."

The cop held out his hands to Hartmann, a pleading gesture.

"How was I supposed to know?" His beer-breath all but knocked Hartmann over. "Juergen here, he's got a new story every week."

"Not so."

"The old fisherman?" the cop reminded him. "You said he'd hung himself with a fishing line last month. We break down his door, it turns out the old guy's just visiting his daughter in Bregenz."

"He could've been in there, couldn't he?" Juergen looked to Hartmann to take up his case.

"Enough!" Hartmann's voice cut through the squabble like a siren. "We've found him now, that's what matters."

Hartmann turned toward the kid. "What can you tell me about those with the old man?"

"There were two of them." The kid spoke, looking triumphantly at the fat policeman. "A man and a woman. They looked knackered, done in. Been carrying the old bugger all night."

To this little shit, Hartmann thought, the old gamekeeper *would* be an old bugger.

"This would be at about what time?" Hartmann said.

"Let's see. . . ." Juergen seemed to be enjoying the attention and wanted to prolong it. "I'd been working a couple of hours already when I first saw them. Sweating, know what I mean? Work up a sweat even in the early spring. Cutting wood's not the simple job some say it is. . . ."

"The facts, for Christ's sake," the policeman coached.

Hartmann blinked both eyes at the man: leave it be, leave him to me, was the silent message.

"So you'd been working," Hartmann continued.

The kid smiled down at the body between their legs, his own greased woodsman's boot pecking at the detritus covering the body. A light breeze lifted the strong stink of the corpse to Hartmann's nostrils.

"Yeah," Juergen said. "It must have been about nine o'clock yesterday morning. I'd worked up a sweat already. And along they come, down the path there."

He pointed to a switchback trail on the mountainside above them.

"Proud as you please, they were. Till they saw me, that is. Then the guy, he just stops and stares at me. I think there's a boy with him at first, then I get a look at the hair sticking out of the stocking cap and, well, a closer look at what she's got sticking out of her chest."

Juergen gave a low, lewd laugh which Hartmann tried his best to ignore. He did not like this boy; did not like him at all.

"They were lugging this old bag of bones," the kid went on.

He actually kicked the corpse now, with enough power to force gas out of its rigored lips. More stink came to Hartmann's nostrils. No, Hartmann thought. Decidedly I do not like this one.

So new to death, was Juergen, yet already it held no mystery for him, Hartmann knew. He could speak of the display of entropy beneath them as some old codger, could boot him until evil gas escaped the bloated corpse. The kid put on the bravado act, scoffing at the last great mystery life holds in store for us.

Christ, man! Mad Markl at the Bernau cadet school should hear you rambling on, Hartmann told himself. Mad Markl would straighten you out soon enough.

But Hartmann suddenly realized that Markl truly had been mad. Hence the name. How much could one learn from a madman?

The kid booted the corpse again, and Hartmann lifted him off his feet with a powerful grip around his chest.

"Leave it off, you little prick! Understand?"

The kid nodded vigorously, his face turning bright red, his feet dangling centimeters above the ground.

"Yes, sir," he said. "Yes, sir."

Hartmann let him down.

"Are you quite done, Lieutenant?"

This was shouted from Krahl, snug in his six-wheeled Mercedes, parked on the forest road.

"Sir." Maybe a yes, maybe a question. Let the faggot sit and stew about it.

Like I am, Hartmann thought, like I am. Too little and too late, once again. They'd traced Radok and Frieda as far as Lech. That was something. But the scent was a day old.

"Then let's do be off, Lieutenant," Krahl called out, his face sticking out the back left car window.

"Yes, sir," Hartmann said. "Off." It was a direction, at least.

The sun was just setting, a dull pink glow on the western horizon. Radok and Frieda were a day and a half ahead of them. Somewhere.

She rolled on top, sliding up and down on him. Slowly. Radok lay beneath her, passively, letting her do the lovemaking tonight. She gripped his buttocks. Drawing her legs up under her, she pulled him deep, deep inside of her, touching the tip of her uterus. She sat like that for long minutes, feeling his pulse inside her, loving the floating feel of it, trickling sweat from her breasts onto his face. Radok's prickly beard set her nipples tingling.

The orgasm built in waves from deep within her. Neither of them moved; they lay almost glued together as the heat overcame them at the same moment. She whimpered into his ear as she felt his warmth flood into her, as hers poured onto him. A long, low sigh from Radok. She felt tears build in her eyes; tears of love and passion. Something had dissolved within her and melded to Radok.

No words. His breath came deep and rhythmically and he eased into sleep like a child, part of him still pulsing inside her. She looked at his peaceful face in the moonlight streaming through the cracks in the roof of the unused hay barn where they were hiding: freckled eyelids, laugh wrinkles at the corners of his eyes.

"I love you, Radok," she said, but he could not hear her. "I love you for always."

She continued to lie atop him, languishing in the feeling of a continued life together; not wanting the fairy tale of the last day to end. But she knew it would, later this very night. Radok had told her so.

They had walked into Germany yesterday, crossing the border with no difficulty, taking a bus fifty kilometers to the northwest with no questions asked. It was as Radok said: no one was looking for them in Germany. They had found this abandoned hay barn near the Bavarian village of Kempton, and here they had stayed, up in the hay loft, through last night and today and into tonight, as well. They had come to know each other in this hay loft; to forgive each other for everything that had gone before and everything that must come in the future.

It was an idyll, but one Radok said they needed. They were not avoiding their duty vis-à-vis the Final Solution papers; this was part of Radok's plan.

So enjoy.

They had.

In two hours they would be off again. But for now there was no duty but the two of them in this barn and the warmth and love they could give to each other. No guilt at this enjoyment, not even with Max dead and all. Max's death had only served to show Frieda how fragile life is, and how precious each day.

Just the two of them, Frieda and Radok, in this hay loft under a full moon in the south of Germany.

The last place on earth anybody would look for them, Radok said.

Full moon. Hartmann loved full-moon nights with all the fervor of a predator after prey. No little mice tonight, however. He adjusted the grenades in the arm braces, flexed his forearms to release them—this over and over, as soldiers oil their guns before going into battle.

The map of the western Alps was spread out on the wall in the temporary HQ in Lech. The borders of the Ostmark were delineated by a thick black line.

Where the hell were they? Hartmann willed up his darker, fanatical side:

You're the glory boy, Hammer. You tell me where the hell they've got to. Remember our bargain?

Piss off, wanker. I'm working on it.

Great work, Hartmann said. You've managed to lose five of your men and shoot an old gamekeeper. Gives you a thrill, doesn't it, Hammer? The impact of bullets in someone's body. The hard-on that comes with death.

Look, mama's boy, Hammer said to him. *I live by my own rules. I do what I can. I don't take pleasure in my job. Not the sort of pleasure you're talking about. Not the sort of pleasure that you need for enjoyment. I'm not sick. Not warped.*

You're a prick, Hammer. An egotistical asshole and you're reached the end of your usefulness. Krahl knows it. I know it.

If I go, then you go with me, little boy. And you're afraid of the dark, remember? You don't like the unknown. You talked of the bargain. Do you even remember what it was? Those nights when your Mutti the slut left you unattended. The whimpering little maggot begging for strength. For company. Remember the bargain we struck then? That I'd give you that strength. That companionship. I'd turn the frightened little boy into a man. Give him courage and balls. In return, you'd give me legs and arms. A face. You'd put me into the world with you. I've kept my part of the bargain all these years. . . .

I finally know you, Hartmann said. Know what you are. Who you are.

You've known all along. You were just too frightened to admit it to yourself.

It was an unfair bargain. I was only a kid. . . .

Don't whine now, Hammer said. *You liked the terms well enough when you were a whore's son. Anything to get you through those nights.*

But you took more than you gave, Hartmann said.

You're never happy, are you? You wanted strength; I gave it to you. You wanted to be able to hurt people the way you felt the hurt. I did your dirty work for you. You think I take any pleasure in this work?

It's your only pleasure. Destruction is all you know. I see you now, Hammer. I see you quite clearly.

And I see you, Wolf Hartmann. Squirming and screaming and shooting your wad while some droopy-dugged,

rheumatic whore spanks your lily-white ass. Quite a man you've grown into. Krahl half kills you, and now you're licking his toes. And if it comes to that, you'd lick more than his toes. You'd do anything to get back at Frieda and at the world. You'd go down on Krahl or his ancient mother just to get your way. That's the only trick you haven't played yet: the glory boy of the popsicle brigade. If I know you, you'll be down on your knees soon now. Very soon. Oh, a regular conquistador you are, chum.
. . .

What's the matter, Hartmann? Whore got your tongue? No argument for that one, is there? You know how empty you are, don't you? How desperate and hollow. Without me, you don't even know your own sexual preferences. Without me, you're just stale meat walking around looking for a grave to crawl into. You and every other lily-white ass disguised as a human being. Bunch of hulls lurching around the earth taking up space and time. Without me you're nothing. There's no getting rid of me, chum. I'm with you for the duration. Now you just be a good boy, and I'll help you figure out where the girl and Radok are. You want to know, don't you? Don't you?

Hartmann had no control over his muscles. His head nodded.

Good, Hammer said. *Then let's look at the map again.* . . .

"And so, dearest Maman," Krahl wrote, the gold-nibbed Pelikan fountain pen scratching across the paper, "I implore you to watch after your health, to get plenty of sleep, and eat nourishing, wholesome food."

Like marzipan, you cow. Would that it should stop up your heart.

The duty letter when away from Vienna, just as with the duty peck on the cheek at bedtime when Krahl was in Vienna.

"Things go well here," he continued to write. "Am involved in a most intriguing case, details of which I shall regale you with when back in Vienna."

Would that this case were gone, too, Krahl thought. Radok and all his fucking deceptions; his luck—his infuriatingly good luck!

Radok would cost Krahl his posting, that's what it would

come to very soon. No longer a question of promotion or of the new villa in Penzing, but of simply being able to hang on to what he already had. And the way this operation was headed, Krahl figured he might as well put in early for angora underwear. They had cold winters in Russia, he understood.

If only the son of a bitch would get out of the Ostmark; would be dumb enough to go to Germany, for example. Then he would be somebody else's problem, wouldn't he? No longer SD Ostmark's headache.

What a wish, Arthur, he told himself. Might as well ask for snow in August.

Despite this personal levity, Krahl was a frightened man. He did not want to go to Russia. Great unpleasantries occurred there, he was sure of it. And what of Maman? Where would she go if he were sent away in disgrace? Maman would be off to the poorhouse or to the Sisters of Mercy. Perhaps even a third-rate sanatorium in the Tenth District.

Such a possibility was indeed the only silver lining to this otherwise cloudy future. To be rid of Maman!

The door crashed open against the inside wall. Hartmann stood in the doorway, a wild expression on his face.

"We've got them!" he shouted.

Krahl ripped the letter with the nib of his pen. These were the words he'd been waiting to hear for so many days.

"Brilliant! Where were they caught? Who took them?"

"This time I know we've got them," Hartmann went on, light glinting in his eyes.

It slowly dawned on Krahl that the initial statement had been one of bravado rather than of fact.

"This is another harebrained scheme, isn't it?"

Hartmann looked him square in the eyes. "We have him now, I tell you."

He was carrying a file folder, Krahl now noticed. Hartmann threw it on the desk in front of him.

"It's on page five," Hartmann said. "I underlined the pertinent points."

Krahl looked at the manila folder suspiciously.

"This had better be good."

Hartmann continued to nod at the folder.

Opening to page five, Krahl quickly found the underlined portions: "Sailboat registered to Inspektor Gunther Radok, boat number 62D5NZ; moored at the Alte Donau."

Below this was mention of the von Tratten sailboat at the Wienerwald See, where young Radok had spent several summers; of a boating incident in which a local policeman reported that the teenage Radok had apparently proved himself an adequate sailor.

Krahl looked up blankly at Hartmann. "So? So the man likes to sail."

Hartmann grabbed the file off the desk, flipping through the pages.

"Can't you see?" he demanded. "Here!" Finding the page he was looking for. "All this garbage about Radok's mountaineering prowess. A red herring! We've been expecting him to hike into Switzerland. But all the while the bastard's had a different plan in mind. All the while he's been planning to cross by water. To *sail* into Switzerland. Don't you see?"

It was an idea that had validity, Krahl had to admit. It held—pardon the pun—water.

"Yes?" he said, indicating that he wanted Hartmann to continue.

"Another thing we haven't looked at because we've been so damn busy chasing after Radok. Time."

Krahl didn't catch this. "How do you mean?"

"It's on our side," Hartmann said. "Frieda said that the papers they've got talk about the first delivery to Auschwitz on the twenty-sixth. She was most adamant that they needed to get word to the Allies a week before then, by the nineteenth. That was their deadline. It's after midnight now, so this is already the eighteenth. There's only one full day left. Don't you see? They'll try and get the word out today or tomorrow to stop the operation before it really gets under way. It's Radok's deadline. He's the kind to set deadlines."

"You mean he's a glory boy like you, Hartmann? That he wants to single-handedly stop the carnage? That kind of scenario?"

"Something like that," Hartmann said. "My sense is that he'll make the crossing tonight so he can alert the Allies in plenty of time. A suicide bombing mission on Auschwitz; a crack squad of partisans attacking the installation. That sort of thing. He's the good guy, remem-

ber. The humanitarian who leaves witnesses living. He'll
have to get word out while the concentration camp is still
empty. It's the *humanitarian* thing to do. Meanwhile,
he's been leading us around like fools. All the time that
he was heading west, we beefed up the mountain passes.
Waiting for his move. But westward was only one of his
movements. North is the other. North right into the heart
of Germany where there will be no border guards or
police looking for him."

"Germany!" This was getting better, Krahl decided.

"Yes, Germany. Where we'd never expect him to hide.
Into Bavaria and to the northern shores of Lake Constance. Just look at his northward course to Lech. It's
clear. He's in Germany right now, most probably."

"Germany," Krahl repeated. "Excellent! Then he is
no longer our problem."

"And he'll take a sailboat at Lake Constance, at some
little village along the German shore where we aren't
expecting him. He's only got a day left."

"Did you hear me, Hartmann? If the man is in Germany, then he is no longer our problem. Let Stuttgart
Station take over from here. Let the sword be over their
heads from now on."

"Any boat will do. The man knows large and small
ones. And it's only a matter of eight, nine kilometers to
cross at the narrowest points. It's the last place we'd be
looking for him."

"You aren't listening to me, Hartmann." Krahl stood
up with some difficulty, his face directly across from
Hartmann's now.

"It's over!" Krahl barked at him. "He's in Germany,
that's all there is to it. We notify Stuttgart immediately."

The pronouncement seemed to cause Hartmann physical pain. His face pinched up, his eyes watered.

"One more day," Hartmann said, his eyes and voice
both pleading.

A luscious warmth spread through Krahl's middle. Hammer was utterly in his power again.

Krahl turned the knife. "It's too risky, Lieutenant. I
for one intend to get out of this war alive."

The expression changed in Hartmann's eyes. Krahl
read him like a barometer. Thinks he's going to get
around me, Krahl sensed. Outsmart me. But not this

time. Krahl would not be seduced again by Hammer's promises, enthusiasm, or exhortations.

Cunning in Hammer's eyes now, Krahl noticed. And something deeper: a somber, smoldering look such as Krahl had never seen before outside of his collection of erotica. Again the warmth, indeed heat, swept over Krahl in a delightful wave.

"Please," Hammer said. "It's important to me. We've got them this time, you'll see."

He dropped to his knees in front of Krahl.

"Don't be ridiculous, Lieutenant. Get up, now. On your feet." Krahl put his hands on Hammer's shoulders, feeling the rigid tendons there. Another spasm of warmth in his guts.

Hartmann was looking up at him now, no more the supplicant. His hands gripped in back of Krahl's knees.

"It's so easy, isn't it?" Hartmann said, looking up into Krahl's soul. "Isn't it, Arthur?" The "th" said in the soft, English manner as Krahl liked. "This is what you want."

There—the damn grin again, Krahl thought. The smirk; the skeleton head.

"No begging, Hammer."

But he knew the man was no longer begging. Krahl's mouth felt dry and he tried to lick moisture onto his lips. A deep silence in the room, punctuated only by a clock ticking, the rasp of breathing.

Hartmann's hands moved up the backs of his thighs now, drawing Krahl closer toward him.

"Stop this, you fool!" Krahl's voice broke. His hands, still on Hartmann's shoulders, dug into the strong sinews and taut flesh under the clothing.

"And afterward, Arthur, we'll take a little drive into Germany," Hartmann said, no longer looking up.

"Enough." But there was no force in the order. Krahl felt himself slipping into deep, warm water; felt fingers working at his fly, and held on to the shoulders beneath him as if to a life preserver.

Chapter Thirty-Four

Radok completed the connection by the waning moon-light: magneto wired to distributor, distributor wired to starter. A spark. The engine rattled, coughed.

"Give her gas," Radok whispered as loudly as he could. Frieda, sitting behind the wheel of the old Fiat, obviously heard him, for Radok could see the gas line jerking as she pumped the gas pedal. The cough of the engine turned into a rough idle.

"The choke," he hissed.

A muffled response from her; he thought she'd said, "It's on."

Radok hurried to the driver's side of the car.

"You're marvelous," Frieda said, scooting over to the passenger side of the front seat, Radok taking her place behind the wheel and pumping the car to life.

"Police training," he laughed. "Prepares you for every contingency."

"You're awfully gay for this early in the morning," Frieda said.

"Fine day for it," Radok beamed. "Or it will be anyway, when it gets light. Feels like it'll be the first warm day of spring. New growth. New life."

"Won't you tell me now where we're going?"

The car was in gear now and rattling down the cobbled, silent streets of Kempten, near where they'd stayed. Radok had dumped their packs down a well near the unused hay barn they had stayed in the last day. The rifles they had hidden in the woods before entering Germany. Traveling light now. Only the Luger for protection. No running lights on this car yet; wait till we get out of town for that, he figured.

"Where we're going?" he repeated. "Yes, I guess so. Can't see the harm of it now. Headed for Lake Constance, we are. A bit of a sail. Have breakfast in Switzerland. Fresh rolls and real coffee."

The moon was nearly down now, and the night would soon get blacker. Not much wind up, but there'll be enough on the lake, Radok figured.

"But I don't swim," Frieda said.

Radok shifted into third, letting his hand trail to her knee and patting it.

"Not to worry," he said. "We'll steal a boat with life jackets."

"We're going to do it tonight?"

"You don't think I have you losing your beauty sleep just so we can linger at the lake shore all day long, do you? We'll find our boat tonight and set sail immediately. Breakfast rolls in Switzerland, just like I said."

"And cream in the coffee," she said, catching his optimistic mood. "And strawberry jam."

"Fresh strawberries," he said. "From the greenhouses of the Vaucluse."

"Isn't that in France?" she said.

He drove slowly still, rounding a curve just outside of the town. Nobody abroad this early in the morning, or this late at night—however one wants to look at three A.M. Radok put the headlights on now and took a quick look in the rearview mirror, to see that no one was following them.

I really shouldn't feel so good, Radok thought. The hardest part is yet to come. But he couldn't help himself. He felt both confident and strong. They followed the course of the Ille River south, passing a couple of small lakes barely visible in the darkness now that the moon had almost set, and also through a couple of sleepy villages. In one, a local gendarme officer was up and about and gave a long look at the blue Fiat as it sped through town. Radok watched the man recede into a miniature in his rear-view mirror. Not to get paranoid over. The cop had nothing better to do than look at the only car to pass through his town all night. No paranoia, but Radok passed Immenstadt, his westerly junction, when it came up, by missing the right turn, then headed on, as if for Sonthofen to the south. A couple of kilometers the other side of Immenstadt Radok pulled over, shut off the front beams, turned around and headed north again, making the left turn just before the town, heading for Lake Constance. A kilometer down the road he turned the headlights on once again.

"Cautious, aren't we?" Frieda said. These were their first words in many minutes.

"You're looking damned lovely tonight," he said by way of avoiding the question. "Have I told you that yet?"

"Five times."

"Good. We'll make it an even six. Damned lovely."

Through Thailkirchhof, Simmerberg, and on to Lindenberg. He was beginning to smell the water nearby. Lindenberg was still sleeping when they pulled through the main square. No lights on yet in any of the houses.

"Are we going to need gas?" Frieda said. They passed a closed service station with a green and yellow marquee over the pumps.

"I stole one with a full tank."

A laugh from her as they headed downhill into the bowl of the lake. The sweetness of the water was all about them now, but nothing ahead to be seen except for a patch of earth illuminated by their yellow headlights. When the great blackness of the lake finally came into view, Radok pulled the car over and turned the lights off. The lake became a deeper blackness in the dark of the horizon.

"It's huge," she said. "I can't imagine us ever getting across it."

"We won't cross it, not here. Austria's on the other side at this point. We'll head further west along the lake shore. Don't worry. Sailing is quick. Finding the right boat is the hard part."

"That's what I've been thinking about," Frieda said. "I don't always want to be the nay-sayer or the one to find fault. . . ."

"But?" Radok said.

"Well, I mean about the sailing . . ."

"It's perfectly safe. I know what I'm doing. I've been sailing all my life. Trust me."

"That's not it," Frieda said.

"Okay. What is it?"

"It's early spring, isn't it? Almost winter, still."

"So?"

"I knew you'd be like this. That's why I didn't bring it up before."

"Like what?" Radok said. "And what didn't you bring up before?"

"Like a wounded bear," Frieda said, "if I found fault

with your plan. I don't know much about sailing, but isn't this a bit early for it? Won't the boats be stored away somewhere, off the water?"

Dry dock, he thought. Shit. He hadn't reckoned with that.

"I've taken it into consideration," he lied.

She looked at him hard, probably knowing he was lying, but not calling him on it.

"That's good," she said. "Just something I thought I should bring up, is all."

"Good thinking," he said. "But it's taken care of."

Everything's just dandy, he thought. Hunky-dory. If you can walk on water, that is.

Fifteen minutes wasted already at the fucking border crossing while this cross-eyed Austrian twerp tried to decide whether or not to let them pass on into Germany. They had no authorization for operating outside of the Ostmark. Lovely. Checking more lists now, while the Mercedes chuffed diesel into the chill four-in-the-morning air.

Hartmann watched the guard from behind the wheel of the car. Just Krahl and himself on this little trip.

Hartmann took another sip out of a brandy flask kept in the glove compartment. He'd been trying to get rid of the evil taste of semen in his mouth ever since Lech; trying to purge Hammer's laughing comment from his ears: *"You'd do anything. . . ."*

Mad Markl would love this one, Hartmann thought. Right up his alley, the silly bugger. The ultimate morale-flogger. Markl would file it, dole it out sparingly to cadets who showed promise: when all else fails, give the son of a bitch a little head. Does wonders for the pansy brigade.

Fuck. All the brandy in the world wouldn't get rid of that taste. Hartmann was beginning to wonder if it was all worth it, but did not want to start wondering about that absolute question. Not now.

"We've got to get going, sir." Hartmann looked at Krahl through the rear-view mirror as he spoke.

"The man has to follow his regulations," Krahl replied, watching the guard in his glass hut.

"Time," Hartmann said. "This is taking far too much

time." His fingers tightened on the steering wheel as the headlights shone through the barrier into Germany and the north shore of Lake Constance.

"Internal controls, Hartmann. A matter of policy. Not even I am above such things, I'm afraid."

Krahl's voice had a sudden softness to it which repulsed Hartmann. He flung the driver's door open. "I'll see if I can't speed him up."

"Hartmann . . ."

But he was out of the car before Krahl could advise or reprimand him.

Hartmann entered the hut and the sergeant looked up from the list of names he was busily checking with a magnifying glass.

"It'll be a moment still, Lieutenant." He looked back down at the ledger, not noticing Hartmann adjusting something in his right hand.

"The Lieutenant Colonel wishes to talk with you," Hartmann said.

"Look," the sergeant said. "I feel as bad as you about this inconvenience. But I've got my orders. The guy could be a full *Feldherr,* and I'd still have to go through the lists. Without a pass . . ."

"I know," Hartmann assured him. "It's always us in the lower ranks who get the blame, when all we we're doing is following orders for the big-shots."

The sergeant nodded. "Right you are, there."

"Me, I could care," Hartmann said. "I could sit here all night and it would suit me just fine. But the Lieutenant Colonel wants a few words. He's just out back." Hartmann stood in front of the window, blocking the sergeant's view of the Mercedes. "Had to relieve himself."

"Hope he didn't wander over the frontier. I'd have to arrest him in that case." The sergeant laughed at his own comment. He was a tall, thin man and his laughter made his narrow shoulders shake.

"A good one," Hartmann said, joining in the laughter. "Have to arrest him. Very funny." Strained laughter, but the sergeant wasn't looking any deeper than Hartmann's Bernau smile.

"Where is he?" the sergeant asked.

Hartmann nodded toward the back of the hut.

"Around there. Looking for a dark place to water the horse."

The sergeant returned Hartmann's polite laughter now. He was in a very festive mood. He moved away from the podium desk where he was working, walked to the door, and squinted into the dark.

"Can't see him."

"Oh, he's out there," Hartmann said. "Just in back."

Hartmann opened the door and let the sergeant out in front of him. The sergeant stepped out; he had an almost graceful stride, for his legs were long. It was the man's last step, for once outside, protected from Krahl's sight by the open door, Hartmann drove the knuckles of his forefinger and middle finger into the base of the sergeant's skull. It was a small act of physical violence, one requiring no great effort on Hartmann's part. Yet the hat pin held between Hartmann's fingers struck through the occipital bone into the cerebellum itself. The sergeant felt almost no pain, only the merest sting as of a mosquito bite. Even as the sergeant registered this tiny annoyance, he died, crumpling to the ground at Hartmann's feet.

Hartmann gripped hard on the pearl tip of the pin and pulled it out of the base of the dead man's skull, wiped it on the gray serge of the man's pants, stuck it under his lapel, and was back in the car in another four seconds, putting the auto in gear.

"Okay," he said. "We're cleared."

"Very good, Hartmann. You see, it didn't take so long as you thought. It's not always necessary to short-circuit the chain of authority."

"Right, sir," Hartmann said, driving around the still closed barrier.

Krahl did not notice the slight detour.

She was right. Radok had known it the minute Frieda had said it. It was too close to winter. In Lindau, the first town they came to on the lake and the warmest mooring to be found there, there were no boats in the harbor. A bad omen, for they had no time to waste looking in out-of-the-way places. Radok's plan called for an early start this morning, while it was still dark. They had to find a boat, secure it, and sail across the lake before first light. Which was about three hours from now. He had

set aside one hour only for the finding and securing
of the right boat, which would leave them a couple of
hours to negotiate the crossing.

The moon would be down soon. That's one thing in
our favor, anyway, he thought. But Radok knew they
couldn't just keep driving around Germany looking for
another bolt hole. There would be a make on the stolen
car they were driving quite soon, and so near the border
they would be terribly exposed, come daybreak. So, it
was either turn around now and get clear of the border
and the lake, or alter the plan somehow. Should they try
to cross the frontier by car or foot at the city of Konstanz?
Radok had no idea of what the border was like at that
point, but was sure it would be heavily guarded, with
Konstanz so close to the Swiss frontier.

"No sailboats back there," Frieda said after they had
passed out of Lindau, following the bank of the lake to
the west.

"No," he said. "I didn't think the plan through well
enough."

No reply; her face was lost in the gloom of the car.
Radok could only make out the glistening of her left eye
in profile directly after she blinked. On through Bad
Schachen, Wasserburg, Nonnenhorn, and Kressborn. The
tidy coziness of these villages all mocked Radok: he took
no sustenance from their vineyards, beaches, cloisters,
moles, and castles. Quaintness was, for once, lost on
him. The only thing he noticed was the complete absence
of small-craft moorings.

"If there's nothing in Langenargen, we may be in
trouble," he said after a long silence. Shimmering mist
hanging over the lake. "There's a lake research center
there, according to the map legends. If anyone has a
sailboat out now, it'll be there."

"Why a sailboat?" Frieda said suddenly.

"Because it's easier than walking on water," he said
peevishly.

"Sorry. I thought this was a team effort. My mistake."

Radok pulled over to the side of the road. They were
partly hidden by an overhanging hedge and he cut his
lights, leaving the engine idling. Rolling down his window, he took into his lungs three deep breaths of the
tangy air from the lake.

"I'm the one that's sorry," he said finally. He reached across the seat to her. "I messed this one up good, it seems."

She squeezed his hand as it rested on her thigh.

"Why a sailboat?" she repeated softly and tenderly. "Why does it have to be a sailboat?"

"I know how to handle them. I sailed with the General as a kid. Lord knows, it seemed right when I thought up the plan. Romantic."

Another squeeze of his hand.

"How about a rowboat?" she said. "Not romantic, but practical."

Radok nodded his head, his attention diverted out to the lake for an instant. Headlights suddenly shone in his rear-view mirror. Coming fast. A local gendarme wagon fairly flew by, the driver's eyes straight ahead on the narrow road, seemingly taking no notice of the parked Fiat along the side of the road.

Radok did not like the looks of the car on the road this early, but said nothing.

"So?" Frieda persisted. "What about a rowboat?"

"I know," Radok said. "I've seen a few dinghies turned over on the shore along here. It might have been a possibility two hours ago, but not now. I planned this lark as a sail across the lake, not for rowing. We start rowing now and we'll be sitting ducks once the sun comes up with us out in the middle of the lake."

"We could cross further west along the lake," Frieda said. "Where it's narrower."

"So what guidebooks have you been reading?"

"I played in Konstanz last year."

"It's an armed camp there, I figure," Radok said. "No good trying to cross there."

"I know. That's not what I'm saying. But on the way to Konstanz there are a few small fishing and tourist villages. Hagnau. That was one of them. Only about six kilometers across to Switzerland from there. And far enough east of Konstanz to avoid the heavy patrolling you find there. I mean, what choice have we got?"

"Okay." He put the car in gear. "We have a quick look-see in Langenargen, then on to your village." They pulled out onto the road once again.

"*My* village." Frieda laughed. "Okay, I'll take the blame if it doesn't work. Is that what you want?"

"That's what I like to hear, woman," Radok joked. "Can't let the poor men go about making all the mistakes."

"I love you, Radok. I said it to you in your sleep earlier tonight. I say it now when you are awake. I love you. I'll love you no matter what happens."

"You just like me for my body."

"That too."

"We'll be okay, love," he said. "It'll be just fine. Sunrise in Switzerland. You've never seen a man put oar to water like me."

"You can dip your oar in my water anytime, Inspektor Radok."

A heron landed on the still waters nearby as they sped along. It sent out a shrill call in the darkness. That bird, like the local cop who just passed us, is up awfully early, Radok thought. He took the bird as a good omen; the cop he put out of his mind.

The harbor master at Lindau was surly and blurry-eyed. He lived over the harbor offices, and Krahl had Hartmann pound on his apartment door until they roused him. It took the master a few moments to get to the door. A smoker, the man was. He has to have one of his obnoxious, cheap, oval cigarettes just to wake up, Krahl noticed. Like jump-starting a car. The man inhaled the smoke deep into his lungs, coughed wetly, and then seemed to perk up, to come alive.

Krahl explained the basics to him and the harbor master looked at them cunningly.

"A couple of things," he said. "One, nobody's reported any missing craft on the lake in the past few days, so I don't know how your friends could've got across already. Not unless they walked on water. And number two, there won't be no sailing this time of year. We've had a cold winter. There was ice out on the lake for the first time in thirty years. It's melted now, but still no sailors abroad yet."

Another cough, bringing up chunks of phlegm this time, which he hawked into a soiled handkerchief he kept in the breast pocket of the filthy tartan-plaid bathrobe he was wearing.

"Anyway," the harbor master said. "No one's going to be fool enough to try and cross at this point. They'd drive up the lake a bit. Get past the Austrian border on the south shore and to where there's a narrower crossing. Up toward Konstanz way. Meersburg or maybe Hagnau. That's where I'd try it. If I could find a little skiff or dinghy, that is."

Another wet hacking cough, convulsing him this time. He recovered finally, his eyes watering.

"Offer you guys a cigarette?"

No smokes for Krahl, but the harbor master did have the decency to fix them a pot of coffee. He busied himself banging pots and pans around in the kitchen, to show the SD Lieutenant Colonel just how industrious he was.

"We've really got him now," Hartmann was saying, an unhealthy glint in his eye. Like the look of a tubercular patient, Krahl thought.

"How is that, Lieutenant?" The irony in his voice was very thick, but Hartmann was too caught up in his own enthusiasm to notice it.

"We've got Radok boxed in here. There's nothing left for him but a rowboat to try and escape. Like the man says, he'll be forced to go further west along the lake to cross once he discovers his mistake about the sailboats. That makes the number of possible crossing points that much easier to patrol."

Hartmann's sheer bravado made Krahl grin. "And how can you be so sure that it is Radok's mistake, and not yours? What makes you think he didn't tumble to the winter moorings without having to come here to see for himself?"

"If I didn't," Hartmann said quite simply, "how could he?"

Krahl clapped his hands in delight at Hartmann's egoism.

"Or," Krahl said, trying to keep his true feelings under control in front of his vassal, "how can you be sure that our man's here at all? That he's not crossing into Switzerland at some other point?"

"No!" Hartmann's eyes flashed at the suggestion. "He's here. I feel him. Besides, there's not been time enough for that. First he'd feint to the north, deeper into the Reich to throw us off his scent. Well away from any possible border crossing. Then back down south. It's only been a day and half."

Krahl could not help but smile again. Hartmann really is so charming, he thought. So full of life and energy. It feels good just to be near him. Is this what I've always felt for the Lieutenant? Why I've tolerated his insolence for so many years?

After the coffee, and against his better judgment, Krahl allowed Hartmann to convince him to involve the local gendarmes in the matter. Calls were made to Friedrichshafen and Konstanz, respectively, alerting the police to be on the lookout for two strangers answering Radok's and Frieda Lassen's descriptions. Krahl would not say what they were wanted for, however, only that the two should be held for questioning if found. He found himself still hoping that this compromise would enable him to claim sole responsibility for the success, even if the gendarmes were the ones to capture Radok and his bitch. They placed the calls from the harbor master's phone and left while the man was still coughing in the kitchen, knocking the dirtied pots and cups together quite industriously.

Outside, the moon was just going down over the lake; melting, as Krahl imagined, into the coating of mist hanging over the water.

I'm becoming positively poetic, Krahl thought. Perhaps this is what affection does for one. . . .

"Where to, Lieutenant?" he said, once they had gotten back into the Mercedes.

"Where the bastard harbor master told us to go," Hartmann said. "West along the shore to Hagnau. We'll make a quick stop-off at Friedrichshafen along the way to see if any boats have been reported missing there. But I doubt there will be. Only a couple hours until daylight. We'll have them soon."

"And what will you do with your prize once you have her in tow again?" Krahl could not prevent the edge of jealousy from creeping into his voice.

"Simple," Hartmann said, looking in the mirror at him. "I'll kill her."

Krahl settled back in the leather upholstered seat for the ride, a satisfied smile on his lips. That suited him fine. So long as they got their hands on the papers, Hartmann could amuse himself however he wanted with the two criminals.

Chapter Thirty-Five

Andreas Volker still had an erection when he got into the green, four-cylinder gendarme car. The tumescence was uncomfortable, pressing as it did against his blue wool tunic and the steering wheel.

Andreas Volker was a very well-endowed man. He thought of himself as a stallion; the various women with whom he'd been more or less intimate would say he was hung like a horse. Which is not quite the same thing; not quite so complimentary as a stallion. These same women might use other adjectives as well, such as stevedore, coal miner, grunting hog.

Andreas Volker still had an erection because Uschi—Ursula Hauptmann, to give the skinny bitch her full name—because she was a prude. Wouldn't let him take her doggy-style like he'd wanted; said it hurt her. What the hell does a man have a mistress for if not to do those things his wife won't allow? Volker wondered. Well, fine then. He was off home to Moni in the early-morning hours. Monika, his wife. It had been several months since their last lovemaking, but he might as well try it on with her, now. After all, she couldn't refuse him *normal* sex, at least.

He was having problems steering, what with his hard-on interfering with the steering wheel, and he began thinking very unsexy thoughts so as to lose the hardness. Frau Boltzmann, the baker's wife, was his usual antidote: she had a wart on her nose just like a witch's, and hair popping out from under her arms in the white jumper she always wore when baking. Enough to make a man turn to his own sex for consolation.

The image of Frau Boltzmann was just materializing when the car radio crackled to life. Christ, who could it be this early in the morning? Volker had never wanted the damn radios put in, but the Chief Superintendent had

347

demanded it last year. Use the new technology, the Chief said, or be swamped by it. Andreas Volker would just as soon be swamped, but picked the receiver up when he heard his name being paged. It was Hofer, on night duty this week.

"Yeah," Volker said into the instrument, unsure that his voice would carry.

"That you, Andreas? Over."

"No, shit-for-brains. It's Hermann Goering. Who you think?"

"You weren't at home. Over."

"I could've told you that."

"Monika said to check your friend's house. You weren't there either. Over."

Hofer was enjoying this, Volker could tell. Calling all over kingdom-come where he might rest his bones at night.

He said nothing.

"Last place I'd look is your car," Hofer said. "Over."

"Over, your ass!" Volker said, finally losing his temper. "What the hell you want?"

"A little early-morning action for you. All points on a couple from Vienna."

Volker listened with half-interest as Hofer recited the descriptions. His shift didn't start for another two hours. Volker was no red-hot. Let the other boys chase these two. He was going home for some kip action. Moni had been looking pretty good lately.

"Chief says we're to get every available man out on this. So don't think you can just head off home for a little more shut-eye, Volker. Understand? This is priority. Over."

"What'd they do, steal Hitler's balls?"

"Very funny, Volker. But nobody's laughing on this end." It was the Chief's voice.

Hofer, the prick, had set him up for that one. He should have told him the Chief was with him.

"Okay. I read you." That's what they said in the movies when they talked on these damn things, Volker knew. It sounded savvy, like a guy knew what the hell he was about. "Over."

"Hold for questioning," Hofer repeated. "No stunts,

okay Volker? Some very important SD fellow called us on this. Report in on the hour. Over."

"Over and out," Andreas Volker said, and fumbled getting the receiver back into its metal notch.

One thing, he thought as he continued to drive the shore road toward Friedrichshafen, a call like that works as good as Frau Boltzmann to relieve a guy of his hard-on.

It took Andreas Volker two more kilometers of driving to remember the parked Fiat he'd passed near Langenargen. Parked at the side of the road, partly hidden by the hedge, lights off, and the engine still going. He had noted the exhaust in the air. How many in there? Two? One? Had he even noticed? But it had impressed him, this parked car so early in the morning and the engine rattling on. A terrible waste of gasoline, and that was uncommon what with rationing and all. At the time he'd let it pass his conscious mind, so intent he'd been on hurrying home to Moni before she'd had a chance to wake up and get out of bed. Now, after the radio message from Hofer, the parked car made more sense. It could be the very two everyone was looking for! And he'd gone smack past them. Get on the radio, he told himself, call up Friedrichshafen, give them a make on the Fiat.

He reached for the car radio but thought better of it. No way was he letting all the others in on this one. That's why everyone on the force gets promotion but you, he thought. Those two, they're waiting like on a platter for you, and you want to give them to some other cop. Just like that. No way. You turn this buggy around, head back, and see if you can't pick up their trail. They're supposedly headed west, Hofer had said. Okay. Set up a road block. I know where, too. Just at the Sankt Georgen curve: come on it blind around the sharp bend. No chance to turn around; they won't see me until it's too late, and then I'll have them covered.

You capture these two and who knows what's in store for you, Volker, he told himself. Captaincy, maybe. Wouldn't need a skinny little wench like Uschi, then. You could afford a strapping woman who'd let you do everything you've always wanted to do. Heroes always get their way, don't they?

He screeched to a halt on the wet asphalt, fishtailing in the middle of the road, and spun around back toward

Langenargen and the perfect curve for his little greeting party.

This can't be happening, Radok told himself.

But he wasn't convinced.

It was happening.

The damn Fiat was running out of gas. It lurched suddenly as they were driving toward Langenargen, spluttered, coughed once, then died, coasting to a stop alongside the road.

The gas gauge read full, just as it had when they started.

"It sounds like—" Frieda began.

"Don't say it," Radok said, pounding on the steering wheel.

"Well, we can't just stay here," she said after a moment's silence. "Let's get walking."

"I know you dislike details, but do you have a destination in mind?"

She opened her door. "Of course. Hagnau. We've got a date in Switzerland, remember?"

"You're crazy," Radok said. "It's got to be thirty kilometers to Hagnau."

"More like twenty," she said. "And maybe there'll be a lorry we can hitch a ride with."

"And maybe there will be another gendarme car, or the border patrol."

"What happened to all the optimism you started with an hour ago?"

"A distinct lack of sailboats and an empty gas tank have put a damper on it."

"Poor Gunther," she teased. "You should have stuck with the violin."

"Okay," he said. "Very cute. So let's start walking. But first we've got to hide this car."

A narrow forestry road led off from the main road just in front of where the Fiat had run out of gas, and they pushed the car up the track fifty meters off the highway, covering it with branches and brush.

"They'll find it," Radok said. "But we'll be eating fondue by then."

"Yes." She took his arm. "That's the Radok I love. Peeing on every fire hydrant, just like a big happy dog."

"At least we know things can't get worse," he said.

But they did. Five minutes from where they had left the Fiat they all but walked straight into a roadblock. Coming round a sharp bend, Radok spotted a cop on duty in the middle of the dark road and quickly jumped back out of sight, putting his finger to his mouth to still Frieda's question. Pulling her back along the road, he whispered what he had seen. When he felt they were safely out of earshot of the man, they stopped, both breathing hard, but not from physical exertion.

"How many?" Frieda asked.

"Just the one, I think. But I didn't get a close look. They usually work in pairs." His mind was working quickly, looking for their next move.

"I say we take him," Frieda said.

"You *are* a bloodthirsty one today."

"I don't mean kill him. I mean take him. And his car. A hostage."

It was the next move he'd been searching for.

"You're right. Roadblocks mean big trouble for us. Maybe they're meant only for us, maybe not. Whatever, we have to talk to this cop and find out. Right."

"And if there are two of them?" Frieda said.

"Deep, bad trouble for us," Radok replied. "So I'll do a little reconnoitering first. I'll climb around the road-block in the woods, get in position, check things out. When I see it's fine, and there's only one of them, I'll give a whistle like this."

He pursed his lips and let loose an exquisite rendering of some bird Frieda did not know. Yet she was sure it was a fine reproduction of the sound, its tone was so pure and high. So nonhuman.

"Okay?" he said.

She nodded.

"Meanwhile," he went on, "you stay here under cover, wait for the signal or my return. You hear the whistle, then limp around the curve like you've been hurt. When the cop sees you, he'll come running. Just take it slow so he doesn't panic and shoot. Tell him there's been an accident. Your car went off the road. Whatever. But keep his attention for a couple of minutes. That's impera-tive. If nothing happens in ten minutes, then you take the documents and get the hell away from the lake." He gave her the envelope that he had kept safely in the game pocket of his jacket. "Head back into Germany. Here's some money, too," he said, handing her the rest of the crumpled bills Hinkle had given him. "Wait until things cool off. Maybe crossing the border will be easier later."

As Radok reeled off these instructions, the reality of the situation suddenly struck home for both of them. It was no longer a lark, as it had been for the last day and a half. They were once again faced with the possibility of death, as on the Kalten Berg; with the possibility of losing one another.

"You better stay safe, Radok. . . ." Her eyes were full of tears. "You stay safe or . . . or I'll never speak to you again."

He laughed, pecked her cheek, and was off into the woods.

Volker was cold. He needed a drink, or at least a cup of coffee. With his luck, the jerks would light out in the opposite direction from him. Good-bye major stripes, good-bye doggy-humping with some new and big-breasted mistress. He checked the Walther PPK in his hands: loaded, safety off, and bolt slid back. Lock and load, Volker. Lock and load. Just let the bastards come along his stretch of highway now. They'd be sorry they ever heard of Andreas Volker. He would have felt better if the weapon in his hand were a Schmeisser automatic machine pistol, like the field police of the SS carried, but the Walther was a trusty weapon, a proven weapon. A friendly gun.

Hartmann drove the car quickly and expertly. Ten kilometers out of Lindau a roadblock held them up. The gendarmes were already in position along the north shore road.

We've got them now, he told himself. They're out there; I can feel them. And their luck is running out on them. Hartmann pulled the Mercedes up to the police van parked crossways in the highway; two traffic cops stood in back of the van, carbines directed at him, looking as if they were ready to shoot.

Hartmann quickly rolled down his window.

"We're with you!" he yelled. "Lieutenant Colonel Krahl of the SD!"

One of the guards hotfooted it around to their car, saluting smartly.

"Sorry, sir. Orders are to shoot on sight."

Krahl sat up in the backseat. "Who gave you those orders, Corporal? I said to hold for questioning."

"Yes, sir." The corporal saluted again, addressing Krahl now. "But word just came in from Lindau, sir. The two suspects killed a border guard in Leiblach. They're considered highly dangerous. Shoot on sight."

"You've got the description of the two?" Krahl said.

"Yes, sir."

"Then get back on your radio and tell your superior I say no shooting. The two are to be handed over to me, alive. Understood?"

"Yes, sir. But . . ."

"Thank you, Corporal. Now carry on."

Hartmann drove onto the shoulder around the roadblock. Krahl tapped his shoulder as they sped up.

"Nice work, Hartmann. You just kill for the hell of it, don't you?"

"No, sir." Hartmann slammed it into third and sped around a curve toward Langenargen.

She shivered again, heard a sound, and was ready to get on with the action, then decided it was merely the hooting of an owl. But from this distance would she be able to distinguish Radok's whistle from other night noises?

How long had he been gone? Wait ten minutes, he'd told her. Should she be gone already? There had been no gunshots, no sounds of a fight. She didn't want to be waiting uselessly here while her lover might be dying elsewhere.

Dying. But he couldn't die.

Yes he could. Her father had. The Padre had. Radok could, too.

The whistle finally came, high and as piercing at this distance as it had been close up. She moved off into the road from the brush where she had been hiding, then stopped, remembering something. An accident . . . Well, she must look as if she'd been in one. Picking up red clay from the roadside, she smeared it on her forehead, messed her hair, then unbuttoned her overcoat.

Her heels clacked on the asphalt as she walked, and she thought the whole world would hear her coming, but she was the one to finally have to shout to the policeman waiting in back of his car.

"Thank God!" she cried out in what she hoped sounded like elation. "Help us! Help us!"

His head jerked up and he held a pistol out in a triangle from his body, aiming directly at her. For a moment she thought he might shoot. There was no sign of Radok.

"No! Don't shoot!" she said.

"Who are you?"

His voice was so guttural and so full of the West Country dialect that she could barely understand him.

"There's been an accident. Please. It was terrible."

She approached his car slowly.

"Stay there!" he commanded. Suspicion was in his voice.

"I think I may have broken a rib," Frieda said. "My husband . . . the car . . ."

"Okay, lady, easy." He put the pistol down and came to her. She noticed that he walked awkwardly, bow-legged, on the outsides of his feet. Come on now, Radok, she thought. Make your move now while he's got his back to you.

But there was no Radok to be seen.

The policeman was next to her now, shining a flashlight into her face so that her peripheral vision was ruined.

"Where you headed?" the policeman barked at her.

"Friedrichshafen," she said, picking a name off the top of her head. "But my husband . . . he's still in the car."

"You were driving?"

"My husband, officer. He's hurt! Couldn't we save the questions until later?"

He thought about this for a moment, or at least was noisily silent for a time, breathing hard and clucking his tongue as he played the light beam up and down her body.

"Where you hurt?"

"The ribs," she said. "I think I might have fractured one."

"You were limping."

"Yes. My ankle, too. But that's nothing. My husband!"

"Okay, okay, lady. Let's get in the car and see."

Now, Radok, she thought. Make it now. Be here now and take over. I don't know what else to do. . . .

The policeman's hand was on her arm.

"Come on, then. You're in such a godawful hurry, let's go."

Frieda stumbled along beside him as he half led her, half dragged her to the car. Panic set in: no Radok. He had not made his move and now she would get in the car and it was all over for her. What had happened? Was it his signal she had heard, or had it actually been some wild animal calling in the night?

"What are you waiting for?" the policeman said. "Get in."

She opened the door and slid onto the passenger seat. Nothing to do now. Where would they go? How was she to explain the missing car, the absence of the injured husband she had been screaming about? Blood was pounding in her temples as the cop got in the other door.

Chapter Thirty-Six

"All cozy-like," Volker said, putting a fat hand on her thigh. "Maybe I ought to check that injury of yours right now."

Metal clicked against metal in the darkness. The barrel of a pistol touched the policeman's right temple.

"Just behave now," Radok said, crouching in the backseat. "Behave and you'll live."

"Thank God, Radok!" Frieda couldn't restrain herself.

"Jesus, mister, don't shoot! I was just trying to help the lady!" The cop tried to turn, to get a look at Radok.

"Eyes forward!" Radok dug the barrel of Berthold's Luger into the man's scalp. "Take his pistol," Radok said to Frieda.

She reached across the man, plucked it out of his shoulder holster and handed it back to Radok.

"I'm glad to hear that you're the helpful sort, friend, because we need your help."

Radok left off for a moment. Let the man come up with his own solutions, he thought.

"What kind of help?" the policeman finally said.

"There. That's good," Radok said. "Demonstrates the correct spirit. Well, helpful friend, I'll tell you. Let's get this little buggy safely off the road first. I'll tell you where to pull in. Nothing fancy. Easy does it. Be helpful and you'll live. Tricks, and you die. Simple, huh? Now let's go back down the road."

The cop said nothing. He started the car, put it in gear, and drove where Radok told him to.

"There, to the left," Radok said when they arrived at the spot. "Pull onto that forestry road."

The car bounced over the deep ruts in the track, the headlight beams dancing into the sky, over the camouflaged Fiat they'd abandoned earlier.

"Further," Radok said. "And cut the headlights. There. That's fine. Now the engine. Good."

None too soon, either, for headlights showed on the highway in back of them, approaching fast. A large car, possibly a Mercedes, rushed past. A six-wheeler, Radok thought, looking back for an instant just as the car passed. Staff car, possibly. There might have been flags on the front fenders, but he couldn't tell in the moonless dark.

He jabbed the pistol into the back of the man's head.

"Name," Radok demanded.

"Volker," the man said. "Andreas Volker."

"Rank."

"Lieutenant."

"You scared, Andreas?" Radok asked.

No response.

Another nudge with the Luger barrel. "You should be. I'm a mean bastard. You know that?"

"You the ones they're looking for? The ones from Vienna?"

"Who's looking?" Frieda said.

"Big boys," Volker responded. "SD. They first say to pick you two up for questioning. Now it's shoot on sight."

"We must be very bad," Radok said.

"Hofer, he says you did the border guard at Leiblach. Killed the poor sod. He had a wife, three kids."

"You're making me weep, Andreas."

Radok played his role as broadly as he could. The only thing a man like Andreas here will understand is terror, he figured. Raw, straightforward terror. Thoughts jumped around in Radok's mind like ping-pong balls. Too much data. The search for them here at the lake had been initiated by SD—the staff car that just passed by, for now he was sure it had been a six-wheeled Mercedes. The death of a border guard laid on their shoulders. All of this had the feel of Krahl and company; of Frieda's friend Wolf. Somehow they'd tumbled to the lake crossing.

"They tell you where we're going?" Radok said.

"Look, mister. I don't know you from anyone. I just don't want to die. Okay? You tell me what you want. I just don't want to die."

"Nobody does, Andreas. But they do every day. There's a war on. Hear anything about it out here?"

But irony wasn't going to help.

"Direction, Andreas," Radok continued. "Where are they looking for us?"

"West," Volker said. "Out toward Konstanz. Maybe Meersburg or Hagnau."

"Right." Radok thought for a moment. "You know what we're wanted for?"

"The border guard . . ."

"Before that," Radok said. "Why they put out an all-points on us?"

"You sound like a cop," Volker said.

"I might be one," Radok said. "So talk straight with me. Bullshit me and your brains will be wall decorations."

Come on, Radok told himself. Enough with the tough-guy act. But it was out of his control now: Radok had become his role. Irony was something he might wake up to again one fine morning, but not now. No time for it.

"Speak, Andreas."

"I don't know," Volker mumbled. "They only said you were wanted for questioning. Not why. Just to hold you for the SD boy."

"They know," Frieda said.

Radok nodded at her. "And they also know we'll have to cross by rowboat at the narrowest point of the lake."

"Cross?" Volker said. "You planning to escape to Switzerland?"

"That's about the size of it, Andreas, old sport. You got any recommendations for us?"

"You'll never fucking make it. They got roadblocks set up all along the road between here and Konstanz. Every harbor and mooring is being watched. This lake is closed down."

"So what are we going to do now, Andreas? We die, you die. Simple enough."

"Look, I'm trying to help! It's not my fault!"

"Easy, Andreas. Calm down. Think. There's got to be a way."

An idea was forming in Radok's mind as he spoke; beginning to take both shape and dimension. A long shot, but Frieda had said it earlier: what choice do we have?

"Does that radio you have transmit, too?"

Volker looked at the set as if noticing it for the first time.

"This? Yeah. I got to report in every hour."

"That's good. You're going to get a promotion, you

know that, Andreas? They're going to love you. A couple of things first. Can you get us to Hagnau by back roads off the lake?"

"North of the shore? Sure. It'll take a little longer. . . . Oh, I see. Go round the roadblocks, you mean? Good. Okay. Can do. But they'll be watching the lake at every little village. Avoiding the road won't do you any good in the long run."

"Nobody's going to be watching the moorings, Andreas. You're going to see to that. You're going to report in, telling the boys at HQ that you've sighted us. Exchanged shots, even. We're out on the lake now headed for Switzerland. Rowing for all we're worth. And you're going to give chase, which will explain your absence once the others arrive at the scene. That way, we'll get all the action down at the east end of the lake, Andreas. And we cross toward the western end. What do you think of that, Andreas?"

"It might work. . . ." he allowed.

"You better pray it does, Andreas," Radok said, tapping the barrel lightly against the side of Volker's head.

Volker reached for the radio.

"Not yet," Radok said. "When's your next call-in expected?"

"Half hour or so."

"Okay. Good. Let's get on toward Hagnau. How long will it take?"

"Thirty minutes. Maybe more. Roads above the lake are bad this time of year."

Radok said, "Make it a half hour."

"That only gives us an hour, hour and a half to cross the lake before sunrise," Frieda said.

"Maybe it'll have to be brunch in Switzerland instead," Radok said.

"Huh?" Volker tried to look around again at what to him was a non sequitur.

"Private joke, Andreas. And keep your eyes on the road. Just drive. We'll wait until we get to Hagnau before radioing. Give ourselves as much time as possible that way. Sound good, Andreas?"

"Great."

The message came through to Friedrichshafen while Hartmann and Krahl were at Gendarme Headquarters. It was 4:30 A.M. and the radio man, a man named Hofer, took the call.

"You sure about that?" he was saying. "Over."

"Fuck the 'over' shit," the other voice crackled across the connection. "I tell you I saw them. A man and a woman fitting the description of the Vienna pair the SD wants. Sorry I didn't have time for introductions, Hofer, but we were on opposite ends of guns from each other. I saw them pushing a dinghy out onto the lake just above Thurnau, and they opened fire when they saw me approaching. I shot back. They're out there now, so over and fucking well out. Get your asses down here fast, cause I'm going after them. There's another boat here. . . ."

"Hold on, Volker. You're to remain there," Hofer said into the microphone. But the crackle of white noise was all that was left from the other end.

"Where's Thurnau?" Krahl said.

"Just the other side of Langenargen, to the east," Hofer said. He was a tiny man and dressed with finicky care. Krahl took a liking to him.

"Crossing distance there?" Krahl said to Hofer, but Hartmann answered for him.

"Too damn wide. They can't row that fast or far. It'll be light before they even reach mid-lake at that point. It makes no damn sense."

"Thirteen kilometers, sir," Hofer said.

"Good." Krahl turned now to the Chief Superintendent, a man of such unprepossessing looks that he could easily have been mistaken for the janitor. His tie was not properly knotted, his hair was mussed, sleep still lodged in the corners of his eyes.

"I want all available men at that crossing point, Chief Superintendent. And I want a motor launch for us at Langenargen, ready to depart in . . . ?" He looked at Hartmann.

"It'll take us ten minutes to get back there," Hartmann said.

"In ten minutes, then," Krahl said. "We'll want a few of your best men aboard. A marksman or two would not go amiss."

The Chief nodded, almost sullenly, Krahl thought. He was, rightly, not yet sure of Krahl's authority inside Germany proper, but was too much of a sycophant to push the point.

"I still don't like it, Lieutenant Colonel," Hartmann said.

"No, Hartmann, I suppose you wouldn't. Shall we be off?"

"He's not stupid enough to try a crossing at Langenargen. He knows he can't make it there. It's the widest part of the lake."

"In fact," Krahl said, "it would be the last place we would expect him, wouldn't it, Lieutenant? Not such a bad place, that. The last place we would look might very well be the first place he would choose."

Nice turn of phrase, that, Krahl thought. And it shut Hartmann up, too. He was learning now to handle Hartmann, how to keep him in line.

The guard posted at Hagnau beach was on his radio. Radok, Frieda, and Andreas Volker watched him from the safety of the police car. The guard nodded his head several times, spoke into the mouthpiece again, then hung up. No last-minute checks for the guard; he just started his motorcycle, put it in gear, and spit gravel as he sped off to the east, toward Langenargen.

Radok clapped Volker on the back.

"Congratulations, Andreas. Looks like they bought it. Fine job."

Volker puffed up for a moment, but then remembered the seriousness of the situation and who was delivering the compliments.

"So you got your boat now," he said. "There's a couple of good-looking dinghies turned over on the beach. The patrols will be heading east. I done my part, right?"

"Right," Radok said. "One complication, however. What are we to do with you now? We leave you behind here and you'll just put them back on our tracks."

"Tie me up." His voice broke.

"I didn't think it out this far, Andreas," Radok said. "You got any other suggestions?"

"You can't kill me," he pleaded. "I helped you."

Silence in the car.

"We're wasting time," Frieda said.

"Take me with you, then. I'll row. I can handle a boat good. You'll see."

Frieda looked at Radok. "It's an idea. I don't much like rowing, how about you?"

"We'd need a big boat," Radok said. "I don't know about the extra weight."

"Look," Volker said. "This is a foot race now, you read me? Your friends, they go to Langenargen. I'm not there, fine. I'm out chasing you guys, like I said. But my car, now that's strange. The car's not there, right? It's here. How long do you think it'll take them to smell this one? You got forty-five minutes. An hour tops. And then all the police in the Reich are going to be out on this lake. You ever speed-row before? Your crossing here is six, maybe seven kilometers. You go all out for an hour, you just might make it. You ever row flat-out for an hour?"

Radok nodded.

"I take your point, Andreas. You speak most eloquently in defense of your continuing to breathe. A reminder, however, Andreas. No bullshitting now. I find you don't know your elbow from an oar, and you'll be doing some long-distance swimming. Understood?"

"So let's get a boat," Volker said.

It took ten minutes to find a dinghy large enough for the three of them, one that was watertight for sure. Radok realized immediately, upon watching Volker choose the boat, that he knew his stuff. It took another five minutes to locate matching oars. They pulled the boat down to the water—guided by the lapping sound of it on the shingle more than by any sight available to them, for it was still pitch-dark—and let the boat sit and float for a moment before Frieda got in, seating herself in the stern. Radok handed her the policeman's Walther and she kept Volker covered as he climbed aboard and Radok pushed them off. A slight wind off the mountains to the north urged them on to Switzerland. The lake was a bit choppy once they were out in it, but Andreas bent to the oars, pulling the dinghy away from land, out into the mist-shrouded waters.

It was four forty-five in the morning.

Chapter Thirty-Seven

Hartmann struck a match and looked at his watch: almost five-fifteen. First light would come in forty or fifty minutes, but it was still black as hell out on the lake. Darkness before dawn.

He still did not like it. The launch bit through the swells, steering a course for Arbon in Switzerland, its searchlights playing across the water, port and starboard. Mist was in Hartmann's face, his clothes were damp from it.

"How long do we look here?" he said to Krahl.

"Until we find them, Lieutenant." Krahl patted Hartmann's hand in the dark. The others on board did not see.

"Don't fret so, Hartmann. We have them now. You said so yourself. They've been sighted. They are out here and we'll take them. Only a matter of minutes now."

"You didn't notice anything strange about this?"

Krahl sighed. "In what way strange?"

"This cop who's supposedly chasing them. Where's his car? Did he drive it into the lake? Maybe he's chasing them in his car."

"Details," Krahl said.

"Think about it. Doesn't add up."

Krahl puffed out his lower lip.

Hartmann went on. "We've got boats all over here and no sighting yet. It's over half an hour. They couldn't row fast enough to get outside our coordinates."

"Shit."

"Leave the rest of them here, Lieutenant Colonel. Let's you and me head for the Hagnau crossing. That's where we'll find them, where the lake's at its narrowest. Radio ahead. Get some men out along the coast there. Maybe a patrol boat out of Konstanz, as well."

"Shit," Krahl repeated.

"Now, Lieutenant Colonel."

Volker was tiring. He'd done a good job in the dark. It was damn difficult keeping the oars in rhythm without being able to see the water, but after a few misses he soon settled into a steady rhythm.

"You'll have to relieve me," he finally said.

It seemed to Radok that they had been out on the lake an awfully long time.

"How far yet to go?" he said.

Volker shrugged, pulled the oars out of the water, and rubbed the blistered palms of one hand with the thumb of the other.

He looked to his right, in the direction of Bregenz. "It's lightening up on the horizon," Volker said. "Be dawn in another half hour. We should be there by then, you bend your back to it. This is not exactly the kind of workout I had in mind for this morning."

A laugh, lewd.

He's getting comfortable with us, Radok thought. Making jokes now. Soon be nudging me in the ribs, at this rate. Radok glanced at Frieda: she was not amused.

"Landschlacht should be about where we come aground in Switzerland," Volker said, still rubbing his palms. They were drifting now, the oars in the locks.

"Better change places, then," Radok said. "You up here in front, me in the center."

Radok got up to move, putting the Luger into the inside pocket of the pressed felt hunting jacket he still had from the von Tratten estate. This was not something he had considered, the awkwardness of seating three in a boat, especially when the man in the middle was the hostile one, despite all his crude jokes. Once he was sitting in the middle, Radok would be blocking the line of fire from Frieda to Volker. How to keep him covered, then? But he answered this quickly enough: so what? Volker's not going anywhere. There's a lake full of water all around. Let him go for a swim now, if he wants, Radok thought. Switzerland was close enough that the man was no longer needed at the oars, anyway.

Radok balanced himself, his feet widespread, and Volker nodded for him to pass.

"We're losing time," Volker said. "Let's get the oars in water again."

Volker was still seated, waiting for Radok to pass by. With the first step, Radok knew he'd made an error of judgment: he felt a hand grip his ankle and the next thing he knew he was tumbling into the icy depths of the lake, his heavy jacket weighing him down like a ball and chain. He managed to surface, heard a scream, and then a hand pushed his head under the water once again. Radok had no other thought now than to try to avoid imminent death. He was going down, down, his lungs aching for oxygen. Not enough air had been taken in, and he tried to fight back the panic that was gripping him at the back of his throat. He had to get rid of the heavy jacket. He fumbled with the buttons; the leather button-hole trim was slippery under his fingers and contracting in the water, making it nearly impossible to slip the buttons through the holes.

He finally got one undone and thought he was going to pass out. He was going beyond pain; beginning to like the pleasant sensation of sinking in the water. Another button undone and the jacket began to slip off his shoulder unaided. He wondered why he was bothering, why he was fighting it—the water was his friend—when the third button popped through the hole, and the heavy jacket jerked off his shoulders. He began to bob up like a float, once unburdened of the wet jacket.

No volition now, only physics at work. His head broke the surface and air rushed into his nostrils. Slowly he came to, heard Frieda's screams from the boat a few strokes away, and saw the man upon her, pawing at her, scratching like a wild animal. Radok was over the side of the boat in an instant, grabbing the first thing that came to hand: one of the oars. Volker looked back over his shoulder just as the oar blade tore into his cranium. Letting out a wild roar, he scrambled for Radok, blood streaming down his face. He was at Radok's legs, biting, tearing, punching wildly, when Radok brought the butt end of the oar down onto the top of his head. It made a sound as of a melon being broken open. Volker hung on to Radok's legs for an instant, then toppled over the side of the boat.

Radok stood panting for a time, knowing he'd killed

the man, then a whimpering from the stern brought him back to another reality. Frieda.

Her blouse was torn open, contusions were on her face, and she was almost hysterical, but Radok soon calmed her, assuring her that everything was okay. They had no time to lose; they must be under way before it was light out. Neither spoke of the death of Andreas Volker. Frieda dried her tears, putting a brave look on her face.

"Man the oars, Inspektor," she said.

He touched her face. "No one will ever hurt you again. I promise."

Radok settled in place, both oars in their locks again. They had drifted during the fight; the line of pearl-gray over the eastern horizon was his compass. Feathering one of the oars lightly he turned the boat back to the south with the other. He kept the horizon to his right as he rowed with his back toward the south, toward Switzerland.

Even with the advent of a bit of light, he still had trouble keeping the oars in the water at first. He missed occasionally, then finally settled into a rhythm and found the right depth for the oars on his forward swing. He felt the pull of it in his back, arms, and thighs. Hard work, but it kept him warm in his wet clothes.

Minutes passed, silently; Frieda breathed rapidly in the stern, but without complaint. No explanations or descriptions, either. Volker must have kicked the pistol out of her hands once he'd dumped Radok overboard. The Walther was now nowhere to be seen. Which left the Luger for defense. At the bottom of the lake in his coat pocket. They were defenseless, but at least the papers were safe with Frieda.

Suddenly there was a new sound besides the lapping of the oars and Frieda's breathing. They both heard it, both tensed. The thrumming of engines on the water. Approaching. Unmistakably the sound was of engines. A boat.

Radok continued to row, faster and faster. He wanted the pounding of blood in his head to blot out the sound of the engines. So close now, so close. *We have to make it.*

The sound grew. A large craft, but he couldn't tell where it was coming from. He rowed them into a pocket of fog and the morning, which had begun to lighten, was again a blackness. Suddenly light refracted through the mist, breaking into millions of glimmering crystals on the moisture-laden air. Then darkness, followed upon closely by the rainbow of light, then darkness once again. Searchlights scanning the water.

Radok pulled the oars out of the water, feathering one to halt the boat.

"We can't outrun them," he whispered. "We'll try and stay in the fog and hide from them."

She said nothing.

"No weapons," he said.

More silence from her. Finally: "It doesn't matter. Nothing matters but that we tried. And we had each other for a time. Give me your hand."

They reached out to each other as the light ripped through the darkness again, spotlighting the boat, their fingers just touching.

The crackle and bluster of a bullhorn sounded: "Small craft there! Prepare for boarding!"

The funny damned accent: the singsong of Swiss-German. Radok almost screamed for joy.

"We are the Swiss border patrol!" the voice said now.

Frieda hugged Radok. "We're in Switzerland! We're safe!"

The police boat, a ten-meter inboard with mounted machine gun in the prow, cabin above decks, and an illuminated red flag with the white cross of Switzerland flying at midships, came into view. Radok could see the personnel aboard her clearly: the searchlights, bouncing off the mist and water, lit the area eerily, like a stage set. The boat glided heavily toward them and a line was thrown out which Radok grabbed, pulling their rowboat alongside the bigger boat. The Swiss captain, bearded and precise-looking, gazed over at them.

"Your business?"

Gruff goddamn voice, Radok thought.

"We're making for Switzerland, Captain."

The Captain was waiting for more, that was obvious, but Radok suddenly realized he did not know what else to say. They were clearly inside Swiss waters on the lake. Perhaps he should merely have lied, saying they were Swiss out for early-morning exercise. Or should he tell nearly all, claiming refugee status? The only thing he did know was that he could not tell these neutrals about the papers they were carrying. Radok was confused.

Frieda took the initiative.

"I'm an American citizen, Captain. And a Jew. The Nazis want me. My friend is helping me to escape. We have money. We wish only safe passage to my consulate in Berne and shall not bother the Swiss."

"A Jew," the Captain repeated.

"An American citizen, Captain," Frieda emphasized.

"Your passport," he demanded, assuming control now.

"We had no time. . . ." She's faltering for the first time now, Radok noticed. "I had to leave quickly and had no time to gather my papers."

"And this money?" the Captain said.

"In Swiss banks. I've visited here before," she said. "On concert tours. I am a pianist. I'm sure if you check with my consulate . . ."

Radok didn't like the way this questioning was going, and now his ears pricked up to another new sound. The high whining noise of an engine revved to its maximum. The Captain heard it too, for he looked in the direction of the sound even as he spoke to Frieda. Nothing to be seen. The mist was still heavy, but there was a silvery, pellucid quality to the water instead of the blackness of night that it had held up to now. The whining engine grew even louder: unmistakably it was the sound of a boat, headed their way.

"No money and no passport," the Captain said. "And you expect us to take you in, to feed and clothe you?"

"I don't expect anything of the sort," Frieda said.

The boat was visible now: two small swastika flags flapping on the front of a lean-hulled cabin cruiser chopping through the waters toward them. Radok did not have to see on board to know who was on that boat. Frieda saw the boat too and grabbed Radok's hand.

"Company," the Swiss Captain said. "They're after you?"

Radok nodded. "Look, send me back, fine. But you can't send her. It's certain death for her in the Reich. They're killing all the Jews."

"Nonsense," the Captain said.

"Yes," Radok replied. "Systematically killing them. In

camps to the east. It's a stated policy. A war aim, for God's sake."

"Don't be absurd, man."

The Captain looked at Radok as if he were well and truly mad; as if he had uttered an obscenity about the Captain's mother. To him the Germans might be belligerent, but not communally insane enough to attempt to kill an entire people. The very proposition was absurd, Radok suddenly realized.

"They'll put you in jail," the Captain blustered on. "For all I know, that's where you belong anyway. Common criminals, as likely as not."

"I'm a police officer," Radok said. "I've spent my adult life keeping the peace, upholding the law."

A stupid damn thing to say; he heard how silly it sounded as it came out.

The German patrol boat stopped several hundred meters away, hovering in the free zone between Switzerland and Germany.

"There's nothing I can do," the Captain said. "You cannot stay here. You must go back. We are a neutral country. We cannot accept half of Europe as refugees."

"Yes," Radok said. "All those new people might gum up your works, is that it? Wouldn't want that. Wouldn't want Swiss clocks running slow. Wouldn't want Swiss hearts to have to feel."

"You're being facile—" the Captain began.

Radok cut him off. "You're sending us back to our deaths and we're the ones being facile? Listen, Captain, if I had a gun I'd blow your head off. You're not human, you don't deserve to live and reproduce other automatons. You're not part of the human race. There's a hole in you where your heart should be."

"Good-bye, then," the Captain said. "Either turn around and row back into German waters, or we sink you."

The young sailor on the mounted machine gun pulled the bolt back on his weapon at this pronouncement.

"Thank you, Captain. May your children die still-born."

"Radok!" Frieda's hand was on his arm.

"Captain," she said reasonably. "Can you at least do us the service of taking these documents with you?" She held out the orange envelope to him. "Merely post it to the American legation in Berne."

"We are a neutral country, Fräulein. . . ."

She continued to hold the envelope out to the Captain. He made no move to take it from her.

"Neutrality owes an obligation to humanity," she said.

"I'm not a spy, Fräulein. You have a ten-count to depart."

He nodded to one of his sailors to cast off the line from their skiff; the other sailor at the machine gun leveled it at them.

"One . . ." the Captain began.

Radok turned to Frieda. The envelope was still in her hands.

"Two . . ."

Radok pondered: die here at the hands of someone who kills only unwillingly, who is not really an enemy, or return to Germany . . .

"Three . . ."

. . . and die at the hands of those who truly were the enemy?

"No choice," she said.

Radok nodded, yet still there was a flicker of optimism in him. Perhaps it was not Krahl and Hartmann waiting in that boat for them.

"Four . . . five . . ."

Frieda seated herself in the stern as Radok took hold of the oars. He set a course at a forty-five-degree angle to the waiting patrol boat. The Swiss border patrol waited just long enough to see that they were headed back to Germany, then moved off, as if not wanting to further dirty their hands, not wanting to see the result of their morning's work.

The patrol boat on the German side began closing on them. Very slowly, very determinedly.

Insane hope, Radok thought. They should have let the Swiss shoot them out of the water. Better to die at the hands of the disinterested. Frieda moved forward from the stern, laying her head in Radok's lap as he oared.

"We tried," she said. "At least we damn well tried. . . ."

Chapter Thirty-Eight

Hartmann watched the two in the skiff as the patrol boat drew nearer to them.

Well, Hartmann, you've finally got her back. Bailed you out again, I have. Any thanks?''

Fuck off.

Why the ire? Hammer said. You should be overjoyed, wanker. Your little plaything is back. Sweet revenge is yours. Plus you get the documents back. You're a hero once again.

Krahl sat in the prow of the boat, rubbing his hands together gleefully. Hartmann hardly thought that Krahl would give him any credit for capturing Frieda and Radok. Hartmann's mind was not on awards or praise, anyway. He was watching the two people in the rowboat. She had laid her head in the man's lap. An extreme act of intimacy, it seemed. There was no show of weapons. The fool had probably lost any gun he had days ago. Anticlimax.

Not a word of thanks, Hammer went on. Not as if I expected one from you. Go ahead and act the snooty independent one. But we both know who's in charge.

What are you talking about?

Obvious, isn't it? Hammer answered. You're ours now. Krahl's and mine. Our little pet. We own you utterly, little Faust. You have sold yourself well and irrevocably. Touching scene, that, with you on your knees, your mouth full of cock. Heroic. Ennobling.

It was you.

Oh no, wanker. That was you. All you. You're the sword-swallower in this duo. And don't kid yourself that it was only in the line of duty. That it disgusted you. I'm inside you, remember that. No lying to me. I was present. I felt the tremble in you when you took his load. You liked it. You fucking thrilled with it. And now you're ours; no

371

*going back. Between Krahl and me, we own every square
centimeter of you.*

Hartmann looked over at Krahl. Hammer, his dark
fellow traveler, was right. Krahl was staring back at him
like some proud owner of a new car. Even as they approached the two in the boat, Krahl's eyes were on him,
Hartmann.

A major stood at the wheel; two gendarme boys, with
Schmeisser machine pistols raised, awaited Krahl's orders. There were no marksmen to be found, but it looked
like they wouldn't be needing them to end this fiasco.
And Krahl's fucking eyes were still on him. Hartmann
wanted to blot out the look; to escape those eyes. He
wouldn't be owned, not by anybody. That was something
he would never allow to happen. He'd always promised
himself that if he felt trapped like that, somebody's pawn,
then he would end it all. Life was not worth living on
those terms.

And now he was owned.

Life was calling his bluff.

Hartmann looked back to the rowboat. Frieda's head
was still in Radok's lap. Hartmann could see the man's
lips moving. Their last minutes alive, and they were still
talking, touching.

He wondered what it felt like, loving another so. Being
so much part of another person that in the last moments
of freedom, of life, all you wanted was to be close to that
other. To touch. No mad scramble in the water for them;
no splitting up in hopes that one might escape. Too
late for that one, anyway, thanks to the Swiss border
patrol.

Hartmann knew now that such love would never be
his; neither would there be any accolades after the war
was over. That had been pure fantasy, just like his dream
of an alpine retreat for himself. All a fucking illusion.
He, Wolf Hartmann, was just a vassal, not a glory boy at
all.

What was it Krahl had said to him after learning of the
death of the border guard? "You just kill for the hell of
it, don't you, Hartmann?" Was that what it had come
down to? Killing just for the thrill of it? Like Hammer.
Like his dark double. No passion, Mad Markl had always
counseled. But Hartmann had to admit to himself that

lately he was liking it; liking the God-quality of life-taking. Killing as if to invest meaning. And he suddenly felt as trapped by that need as he did by Krahl and his perverted needs.

"Give them a warning, Major," Krahl said to the man piloting the boat.

They were close enough now to see them perfectly, to make out the numbers on the starboard prow of their boat: HK2973.

So get used to the idea, Hammer said to Hartmann. *We own you. You are the vassal. There is no way out of this.*

Hartmann thought about that as he watched the big man in the boat rowing for all he was worth, as if trying to outrun their twelve-horsepower Mercedes engine.

"Fire!" the major yelled over the thrumming of his engine.

The two gendarmes let off a blast from their guns that tore into the water just ahead of Frieda and Radok.

She felt safer when she put her head in his lap. Curling so as to snuggle closer into the crutch of his legs, Frieda's hand brushed under the seat where he sat, striking against cold metal. She gripped it: Volker's pistol!

"Radok," she said, trying to restrain her enthusiasm. "Look what I've got here."

He looked down and saw the pistol, showing no emotion on his face.

"The clip in it?" he said, continuing to row.

"Yes."

"Pull it out," he said. "Just depress the button there and pull it out of the grip. Yes. Like that."

She did as he told her and the clip came out in her hand. He looked at it.

"Good. Full. That gives us seven shots," He looked toward the patrol boat. Frieda followed his gaze. Five aboard there, she could see.

Radok bent to the oars again, pulling at them powerfully.

"We can't outrun them," she said.

"I know, love. I just want them to believe that, when I stop rowing, we are defeated. Done in. And to waste some ammo making their point."

She began to sit up.

"No," he said. "Stay down like that. Low. And be ready to hand me the pistol when I tap twice. Like this."

He pounded on the hull of the boat twice with his heel.

"Okay," she said. No fear. Action now. At least there was something they could do. Some way to fight back.

"Will you kill them?" she said.

"As many as I can. The ones with weapons at the ready go first. Make sure the safety's off on the pistol so it's in the shoot position."

He was beginning to breathe hard, Frieda noticed, from the exertion of oaring so quickly. Suddenly gunshots rang out and the water in front of them turned into a froth, as in a feeding frenzy of tropical fish.

"That's what I was waiting for," Radok said, taking the oars out of the water. "We'll just sit here and wait for them, let them come up on our starboard, on my gun arm. Keep the pistol hidden till the very last minute. They'll tell us to put our hands over our heads. Don't. They aren't going to kill us until they get a chance to question us about the papers. I'll give them a line of crap about you being injured."

He touched her face tenderly. "You look the part," he said. "And I'll act as if I'm helping you up. Remember, the signal is two taps. Wait for that. Then hand the gun over and get the fuck down in back of me."

Frieda said nothing, prolonging their touch, not wanting to waste it. The gun, which she had tucked inside her coat, felt heavy in her hand.

"That'll stop them," said Krahl. The Schmeisser machine pistols in the hands of the two cops were still smoking.

"Cheer up, Hartmann," Krahl said to him. "We really do have them now. Sitting dead in the water. The fight's all gone out of them. They finally realize how hopeless their situation is. The Swiss wouldn't let them in even if they did escape from us. That's damned ironic. The Swiss doing our job for us."

The major at the wheel laughed weakly at this. Hartmann said nothing. He was watching the small boat, the two people in it who seemed to be so close to one another. Two lost souls holding on to each other amidst the wreckage of their lives.

"Revenge soon, Hartmann," Krahl went on. "Sweet revenge."

Hartmann nodded, barely hearing him. The sweet, pure scent of water suddenly struck his nostrils after the burn of cordite had been cleared from the air. The distance closed between the two vessels. Hartmann could make out her face, see her one hand gripping Radok's arm, the other hand tucked into her coat.

Hartmann knew his duty; he also knew that he could not allow himself to be owned. Ever.

"Steady on, men," Krahl ordered. "They may be armed, but no shooting unless I order it. We need them alive and in talking shape."

Almost over now, Radok thought. He feathered the left oar, keeping the right one in the water so as to keep their starboard side to the oncoming boat.

"Throw your weapons overboard!" A voice from the approaching patrol boat. "Hands over your heads or we commence shooting at once!"

"Don't do it," Radok reminded her. "Keep still and low. I'll begin lifting you as they approach."

Thirty meters and closing. Daybreak to the east, over the extended antenna of the patrol boat. Orange-pink on the horizon. The two images—the approaching boat and the rising sun—blended for a moment in Radok's mind. Mesmerizing.

"Do you hear?" the voice shouted again. "Weapons overboard, hands over your heads, now!"

Another blast of automatic weapons fire, both in front and in back of their boat this time. Frieda gave a low gasp, gripping onto his arm even more tightly.

"Damn good," Radok drawled. "Use up those rounds on the fish. Get those magazines empty. Get close enough and I'll stick the muzzle of this Walther down your throats."

Saying this made Radok feel strange, as if another person were operating inside of him. As if he were on automatic pilot. He was glad he had a Walther, the only gun he'd ever felt comfortable with. Now, he told himself, let the training take over. Let the drill set in. Take them low and quickly; nothing fancy, no moving. Just stand and fire.

The boat was on them now. Krahl stood in the prow like a conquering hero, a megaphone in his hand. Two gendarmes were holding automatic machine pistols, Radok saw, slung around their necks and aimed square at him and Frieda. The small, dark one, Hartmann, was behind these two. He had no weapon drawn. And a big, burly type at the wheel; he also had no weapon out. The first targets were the guards.

"I love you," he said as he stood, bending over to help her stand.

"I said hands up!" Krahl screamed.

"She's hurt!" Radok shouted, his back to them. "I'm trying to help her!"

She wrapped her arm around him and she held the Walther between them in the other hand.

The boat nudged theirs, almost sending Radok sprawling.

"Take him! He's got a gun!"

This from Hartmann, and Radok tapped his foot twice, receiving the gun, feeling its grip sure in his hand, his finger on the trigger and Frieda slipping down to his feet. He turned slowly, square-legged, screaming for all he was worth. A high, piercing scream that jarred the concentration of the armed men for the instant he needed to swing the Walther up into position two-handed in front of his chest and pull off two quick shots, close enough to aim with his body and not the sights. He caught the gendarme to the left just under his Adam's apple, piercing a clear hole in the man's neck that spouted blood like a geyser as he flew backward. The second one he caught in the chest, throwing him back against Hartmann. The man at the wheel drew out a Luger and Radok took him in the arm, then in the head, tearing off the back of his skull with the shot.

All so clear. Without panic or undue movement. The drill. The training. He sensed movement to his left and began to swing the gun around to where the pig Krahl was, and Frieda screamed. Too late. The explosion of Krahl's gun sent a searing pain into his lower left side, tumbling him over onto his back in the boat, a numbness spreading over him.

A seagull circled overhead and he barely felt the second bullet that ripped into his left arm, but the sound was enormous in his ears. Then someone was over him, crying into his face.

She had no time to think, only to act. Radok's body twitched as Krahl shot again, the bullet ripping into his left arm. The pig was sighting again and Frieda threw her body over Radok's.

"Then die with him, bitch!" Krahl yelled, and fired again. The shot went wide, just above Frieda's head. She felt no fear, only intense anger.

Krahl swore at his miss, and she could see him preparing to swing off the patrol boat into their dinghy to finish things off at close range. She lifted her boot straight-legged just as Krahl jumped, and he landed on her heel, testicles first. A roar of pain, and he crumpled on top of her and Radok, the gun falling to their side.

She had his ear in her mouth, tasting the salt of his blood. Another scream from him as he reached for the weapon. She scratched his face and his right hand left the weapon, lashing out to protect himself. Frieda lunged forward out from under him, took the pistol in her hand, found the trigger, and put the muzzle to Krahl's temple. He lay inert at the feel of the metal, his eyes wide with terror, blood streaming from his ear and the scratches on his face.

"Give me an excuse to pull this trigger," she hissed. "Move a centimeter, you pig. Say a word even and you're dead."

His eyes watered as he looked up at her.

She got to her knees, the gun still pointed directly at Krahl's head. Radok lay under him, moaning, delirious.

"Off of him." She held the gun steadily with both hands as she'd seen Radok do.

Krahl edged off Radok, silent and terrified.

"What now, Frieda?"

Hartmann's voice. She'd forgotten about him. She kept the gun trained on Krahl, and saw Hartmann now out the corner of her eye. He stood by the dead policeman who'd knocked him over when Radok shot. The dead policeman who'd saved Hartmann's life. He was smiling his horrid jack-o'-lantern smile and in his hands were two grenades.

"They're on a one-second fuse," he said. "We all go or we all live."

"He didn't shoot you!" Krahl shouted. His fear was lost for the moment. Frieda could see the pure joy written on his face.

"Then we all die," Frieda said, leveling the gun at Krahl, her finger nudging the trigger.

"No!" Krahl pleaded. "She's crazy, Hartmann! She'll shoot!"

Hartmann nodded appreciatively. "You've learned a lot, Frieda."

"I had the best teachers."

"But it's a bad gamble," Hartmann said. "You could shoot him. Fine. Go ahead. But you won't be able to take me out."

Frieda shook her head. "We'll see."

Krahl raised his hands high, defenselessly. "I tell you, Hammer, she's crazy enough to do it! Don't push her!"

"Shut up, Krahl." Hartmann spat his name out. "Shoot the pig if you like," he said to Frieda. "But if you do, I toss the grenades. No saving your friend Radok in that case."

There was a low moan from Radok and suddenly she had time for fear, for concern. Hartmann's words eroded her resolve. She knew she should have acted immediately; shot and to hell with the consequences.

"Put down the gun," Hartmann said, "and you and your friend have a chance. Shoot and you're finished. We'll all visit hell together."

Radok's eyes were open now, unfocused. His breathing was shallow.

"We'll get a doctor for your friend," Hartmann said.

Frieda looked at Krahl, at Hartmann. A seagull swept by overhead, calling to them. She let the gun slide out of her hand.

Krahl leaped on it.

"Excellent, Hartmann!" He stepped back, cocked the pistol, and aimed at Radok.

"No!" Frieda screamed.

"Put the gun away, Krahl." Hartmann's voice was icy.

"Let's get rid of the bastard once and for all," Krahl said.

"Put the gun away. Get the documents from them."

Krahl hesitated. Frieda watched Hartmann's face closely. A muscle twitched in his cheek.

"Now!" he shouted.

Krahl lowered the gun, replacing it in his holster.

"The documents," Hartmann said to Frieda.

She did not move.

"We will hurt your friend," Hartmann said calmly. "It's no use. Hand them over."

"I should have shot," she said.

"Yes," Hartmann nodded. "You're learning, but terribly slowly."

"The papers," Krahl said as he stepped up to her, slapping her across the mouth forehand and backhand.

The blows stung, but she held back the tears. This was only the beginning, she knew. Only the start of their tortures. She cursed her softness; the humanitarian impulse, the hope that had made her put the gun down.

"So you see, it truly is hopeless now," Hartmann said, the grenades still in his hands. "Just give us the documents and forego needless pain. For you and your friend."

She took the orange envelope containing the documents and photos from her coat, holding it out for Krahl. He reached for it and she tossed the envelope over the side of the boat, into the water.

"You cow!" He was at the edge of the boat, his arm dipping into the water, trying frantically to rescue the papers.

"Gone!" Krahl moaned. "They'll never believe me now in Berlin! Never believe that I actually had the papers!"

He turned to Frieda. "You bitch! You'll die horribly for this! I'll kill you myself!"

He lunged for her, and Hartmann's voice sounded:

"Enough, Krahl!"

Krahl had Frieda by the throat as Hartmann shouted again:

"I said enough!"

Krahl loosened his grip, his face slowly assuming a normal countenance.

"You're right, Hartmann. We can't kill her or Radok just yet. They're our only proof that we retrieved the papers. I'm sure the little lady will corroborate our story given the proper inducement in the cellars of Morzin Platz."

"I'll die first," she said.

"Oh, I think not, my lovely." Krahl surveyed her body. "You don't understand how long it takes to die. How slow, how painfully slow it can be. Nor how much fun for the questioners."

Frieda looked at Hartmann now. "You're as sick as he is, aren't you? You all want to kill the world because you're dead inside yourselves. I pity you, Wolf. Everything you've done has been a lie. Life as betrayal. And for what? For slime like this." She nodded toward Krahl.

"Shut up, you cunt!" Krahl raised his fist to strike her again.

"No!" Hartmann said. "Let her talk. It's amusing."

"Look, Hartmann," Krahl said, "the entertainment's over. We need to get these two back to shore and get a doctor for Radok before he dies and we lose our insurance policy with her. With both alive, one will talk to save the other. . . ."

Frieda looked with disgust from Krahl to Hartmann. "You're lovers, aren't you? That's why he was so crazy when it looked like his precious Hartmann was shot. Lovers! What a joke. You've finally found your true station in life, haven't you, Wolf? You don't know what to do with a real woman, so you turn to half-men for pleasure. Poof Wolf. Poor, lost Wolf."

"Stop her!" Krahl insisted.

Hartmann hefted the grenades in each hand as if weighing them.

"You are progressing, Frieda," he finally said.

"Look," Krahl said, pulling out his weapon again, "get rid of those damned grenades Let's get these two back to shore."

"I trusted you once," Frieda said to Hartmann. "You betrayed us all. Padre, me. Even yourself. You're so small, Wolf. Shriveled. And I once thought you were as large as life itself."

"All right, Fräulein." Krahl grabbed her arm. "Get aboard. You can talk all you want in Vienna."

"Let her go, Krahl."

Krahl looked up at Hartmann. "Are you crazy? The Jew bitch comes with us."

"Let her go. Put down your gun."

Krahl shook his head. "You're not going to let some stupid sentimentality get in our way."

"Now!" Hartmann thrust the grenades out toward him menacingly. "Or I'll blow you into so many pieces they'll have to bury you in shifts."

Krahl dropped Frieda's arm and slowly let his grip on the pistol loosen. It tipped downward, then dropped from his hand.

"I hope you know what the hell you're doing, Hartmann. This is no time for you to be playing Hammer. Forget that role."

Hartmann looked at Krahl closely. "That's exactly what I plan to do. Forget Hammer. He's history. He's a figment of both our imaginations."

"You aren't making any sense, Hartmann. We've *got* them," Krahl whined. "Even if we haven't got the papers, we've got the criminals. Now get rid of those damned grenades. It's all taken care of. No more need for dramatics or bluff."

"Climb aboard, Lieutenant Colonel. And I mean now. Move!" Hartmann was staring at Frieda as he spoke.

Krahl reluctantly climbed aboard the patrol boat once again, leaving Frieda and Radok. Frieda bent down and tried to stop Radok's bleeding.

"There," Hartmann was saying. "Now just sit down, Lieutenant Colonel."

"Put the grenades away, Hartmann. I'll forget this incident. Don't be a fool."

"Shut up, Lieutenant Colonel." Turning to Frieda: "Now you start rowing. Get off to Switzerland. Their border patrol boat will be gone for the next hour. You've got a clean shot for Landschlacht. You'll be able to see the town once the morning mist lifts."

He nodded with his head toward Switzerland. "Go, dammit. Now!"

She looked up at him.

"Why?" she said. Then, "No. Forget the why." The barest laugh from her. "No answers. No questions. Thank you," she said to Hartmann.

Hartmann shook his head. "Don't thank me. It's not what you're thinking. Nothing like it. No sentiment here. No last-minute reversal for me. You two put up a good fight. But you never had a chance. You were fighting for what you take to be the good. The humanitarian cause. Bravo."

Krahl made a gesture as if to stand, but Hartmann shook the grenades at him once, and the Lieutenant Colonel remained huddled as he was by the boat house.

"You see, I knew from the start that we'd have you," Hartmann continued. "Where duty and goodness come to do battle, duty always wins. And yes. Now I am going to help you. I've done my duty, but that extends only to the papers, as I read it. And they're in a place where they'll do no harm to the Reich. So you and your friend, or whatever is left of him, may go. And I don't do this out of any latent goodness. Oh no. Don't confuse my motives. No. I'm letting you go simply because there is something, someone, I hate more than you."

He stopped for a moment, staring down at Krahl, then down to the grenades in his hands.

"I fantasized how I would kill you very slowly when we caught up with you," he went on. "But now . . . No. Just get out of here. Before you drown in your friend's blood."

Krahl spoke up sharply. "You let them go, Hartmann, and you're finished! Your career is gone! You'll find yourself in Russia next week!"

"Good-bye, Wolf," Frieda said, sitting above Radok now, oars in hand. "Maybe you are as big as I once thought you to be."

Hartmann ignored her. "Just keep a level course. You'll be there in twenty minutes."

She looked down and saw Radok still staring up at the sky, to the seagull circling high above them.

"Hold on, Radok," she muttered. "Just hold on. Don't die on me now."

She looked back to the boat, but Hartmann was no longer looking at her. His back was to them and he was speaking softly to Krahl.

Frieda bent to the oars, unfamiliar with them, and the boat moved jerkily. Radok tried to speak, but it came out garbled.

"What?" she said, leaning over him.

"Rhythm," he said. "The oars. In, out. In, out. Rhythm method."

"You bastard." She laughed lightly.

Several minutes passed; she no longer cursed, for she had found the rhythm of the oars. She did not look at the patrol boat, but at Radok lying in front of her, a smile on his face. They glided along quite peacefully and the lake was like a dreamscape, the mist burning off around them, the wildlife waking to the new morning.

Suddenly the peacefulness was shattered by an explosion that echoed in their ears.

"Sweet Jesus," she murmured, looking in the direction of the shattered and burning patrol boat. "Wolf. Poor Wolf."

Their boat bobbed for a time in the wake of the explosion and then Frieda set to rowing once more.

Note to the Reader

Although this has been a work of fiction, there is nothing fictitious about attempts to get the secret of the Final Solution out of the Reich. Many brave Germans, Austrians, and Poles did succeed in bringing documented evidence of the Holocaust out to the Allies, the first of these reaching Switzerland by the summer of 1942.

Despite the evidence, the Allies did not respond to these cries for help. The war against the Jews, as has been said, is the war that Hitler won.

It remains one of the great historical conundrums why nothing was done to stop or even hinder the obscene work of the death camps.